"Gets better with every book."

—*Pioneer Press* (St. Paul)

"A master of plot and suspense."

—*Cincinnati Post*

"Knows what she's doing. . . . This savvy author always comes up with something unexpected."

—*The New York Times Book Review*

More praise for "GRANDMASTER OF MYSTERY WRITING" (*Hartford Courant*) MARY HIGGINS CLARK and her heart-pounding novels

THE SHADOW OF YOUR SMILE

"Clark manages yet again to flawlessly weave a story that will keep you on the edge of your seat until the very last page. . . . Bound to make summertime traveling a lot easier, since you won't notice the time passing while you read it. Just make sure you don't miss your flight."

—SeattlePI

"With unexpected plot twists, interesting characters, and a crisp narrative, Mary Higgins Clark once again spins literary magic."

—*Tucson Citizen*

"A gripping thriller. . . . Clark skillfully mixes spiritual questions with down and dirty deeds."

—*Publishers Weekly*

"As always, she gives her readers more than they expect. Her prose and characters are clearly drawn, which makes for delightful reading. Once again the Queen of Suspense delivers, and I'm hoping we don't have to wait too long for her next heart-pounding bestseller."

—Bookreporter.com

JUST TAKE MY HEART

"A must-read for mystery enthusiasts."

—*Tucson Citizen*

"Intense . . . the action hurtles to a surprising resolution."

—*Publishers Weekly*

"Fans will be as excited as ever coming down the home stretch."

—*Kirkus Reviews*

"Tantalizes readers from the first sentence to the final paragraph. . . . Mary Higgins Clark rarely misses the mark."

—Bookreporter.com

WHERE ARE YOU NOW?

"Clark stays up to date with the latest technologies and detective techniques. Her visual, smooth narrative keeps readers hooked."

—*San Antonio Express-News*

"An imaginative tale of murder and deceit . . . will keep readers guessing to the nail-biting conclusion."

—*Publishers Weekly*

I HEARD THAT SONG BEFORE

"A symphony of suspense."

—*Richmond Times-Dispatch*

"Clark . . . deftly keeps the finger of guilt pointed in many directions until the surprising conclusion."

—*Publishers Weekly*

TWO LITTLE GIRLS IN BLUE

"Riveting. . . . [A] chilling tale of kidnapping, murder, and telepathy."

—*Publishers Weekly*

NO PLACE LIKE HOME

"Credit Clark for her intuitive grasp of the anxieties of everyday life that can spiral into full-blown terror. . . . A cunning variation on the haunted-house theme."

—*The New York Times*

NIGHTTIME IS MY TIME

"Creeping menace that is genuinely scary."

—*The New York Times*

"Clark's multitude of fans will be happy . . . to participate in the guessing game."

—*Publishers Weekly*

These titles are also available from Simon & Schuster Audio and as eBooks

BY MARY HIGGINS CLARK

Just Take My Heart
Where Are You Now?
Ghost Ship (Illustrated by Wendell Minor)
I Heard That Song Before
Two Little Girls in Blue
No Place Like Home
Nighttime Is My Time
The Second Time Around
Kitchen Privileges
Mount Vernon Love Story
Silent Night/All Through the Night
Daddy's Little Girl
On the Street Where You Live
Before I Say Good-bye
We'll Meet Again
All Through the Night
You Belong to Me
Pretend You Don't See Her
My Gal Sunday
Moonlight Becomes You
Silent Night
Let Me Call You Sweetheart
The Lottery Winner
Remember Me
I'll Be Seeing You
All Around the Town

Loves Music, Loves to Dance
The Anastasia Syndrome and Other Stories
While My Pretty One Sleeps
Weep No More, My Lady
Stillwatch
A Cry in the Night
The Cradle Will Fall
A Stranger Is Watching
Where Are the Children?

BY MARY HIGGINS CLARK
AND CAROL HIGGINS CLARK

Dashing Through the Snow
Santa Cruise
The Christmas Thief
He Sees You When You're Sleeping
Deck the Halls

MARY HIGGINS CLARK

The Shadow of Your Smile

POCKET BOOKS
New York London Toronto Sydney

Pocket Books
A Division of Simon & Schuster, Inc.
1230 Avenue of the Americas
New York, NY 10020

This book is a work of fiction. Names, characters, places, and incidents either are products of the author's imagination or are used fictitiously. Any resemblance to actual events or locales or persons, living or dead, is entirely coincidental.

This Pocket Books export edition January 2011

POCKET and colophon are registered trademarks of Simon & Schuster, Inc.

For information about special discounts for bulk purchases, please contact Simon & Schuster Special Sales at 1-866-506-1949 or business@simonandschuster.com.

The Simon & Schuster Speakers Bureau can bring authors to your live event. For more information or to book an event, contact the Simon & Schuster Speakers Bureau at 1-866-248-3049 or visit our website at www.simonspeakers.com.

Manufactured in the United States of America

10 9 8 7 6 5 4 3 2 1

ISBN 978-1-4391-9610-6
ISBN 978-1-4391-9987-9 (ebook)

Acknowledgments

In my last book I wrote about the medical miracle of a heart transplant and that the recipient may have taken on some of the characteristics of the donor.

This story concerns a different miracle, one that medical science cannot explain. Last spring I attended the Beatification Ceremony of a nun who founded seven hospitals for the aged and infirm and is credited, by the power of prayer, with saving the life of a child.

At that beautiful ceremony, I decided I wanted to write about that subject as part of this novel. I have found it to be an insightful journey—one that I hope you will enjoy sharing.

As always I'm indebted to the faithful mentors and friends who make smooth the path as I labor at the computer.

It has been a constant joy that Michael Korda has been my editor for thirty-five years. From page one to *The End*, his guidance, encouragement, and enthusiasm have been an unfailing source of strength.

Senior Editor Amanda Murray has accompanied us every step of the way with her wise suggestions and input.

Thank you always to Associate Director of Copy-editing Gypsy da Silva; my publicist, Lisl Cade; and my readers-in-progress Irene Clark, Agnes Newton and Nadine Petry. What a grand team I have.

Many thanks to Patricia Handal, coordinator of the Cardinal Cooke Guild, for her invaluable and generous assistance in discussing the canonization process.

Many thanks to Detective Marco Conelli for answering my questions about police procedure.

Thanks also to patent attorney Gregg A. Paradise, Esq., who advised me about patent laws, an important element in this story.

It is high time that I give a tip of the hat to marvelous photographer, Bernard Vidal, who for twenty years has journeyed from Paris to take my cover photo and to Karem Alsina, master hair stylist and makeup artist, who allows me year after year to put my best face forward on the back cover of the newest book.

No accomplishment would have any meaning if it were not being shared with my husband, John Conheeney, spouse extraordinaire, and our children and grandchildren. You know how I feel about all of you.

And now my readers and friends, I hope you curl up and enjoy this latest effort. Happy Reading and God bless you one and all.

For my youngest child
Patricia Mary Clark
"Patty"
whose wit, resilience, and charm
has brightened all our lives
With Love

The Shadow of Your Smile

1

On Monday morning, Olivia Morrow sat quietly across the desk from her longtime friend Clay Hadley, absorbing the death sentence he had just pronounced.

For an instant, she looked away from the compassion she saw in his eyes and glanced out the window of his twenty-fourth-floor office on East Seventy-second Street in Manhattan. In the distance she could see a helicopter making its slow journey over the East River on this chilly October morning.

My journey is ending, she thought, then realized that Clay was expecting a response from her.

"Two weeks," she said. It was not a question. She glanced at the antique clock on the bookcase behind Clay's desk. It was ten minutes past nine. The first day of the two weeks—at least it's the start of the day, she thought, glad that she had asked for an early appointment.

He was answering her. "Three at the most. I'm sorry, Olivia. I was hoping . . ."

"Don't be sorry," Olivia interrupted briskly. "I'm eighty-two years old. Even though my generation lives so much longer than the previous ones, my friends have been dropping like flies lately. Our problem is that we worry we'll live too long and end up in a nursing home, or become a terrible burden to everyone. To know I have a very short time left, but will still be able to think clearly and walk around unassisted until the very end is an immeasurable gift." Her voice trailed off.

Clay Hadley's eyes narrowed. He understood the troubled expression that had erased the serenity from Olivia's face. Before she spoke, he knew what she would say. "Clay, only you and I know."

He nodded.

"Do we have the right to continue to hide the truth?" she asked, looking at him intently. "Mother thought she did. She intended to take it to her grave, but at the very end when only you and I were there, she felt compelled to tell us. It became for her a matter of conscience. And with all the enormous good Catherine did in her life as a nun, her reputation has always been compromised by the insinuation that all those years ago, just before she entered the convent, she may have had a consensual liaison with a lover."

Hadley studied Olivia Morrow's face. Even the usual signs of age, the wrinkles around her eyes and mouth, the slight tremor of her neck, the way she leaned forward to catch everything he said, did not detract from her finely chiseled features. His father had been her mother's cardiologist, and he had taken over when his father retired. Now in his early fifties, he could not remember a time when the Morrow family had not been part of his life. As a child he had been in awe of Olivia, recognizing even then that she was always beautifully dressed. Later he realized that at that time she had still been working as a salesgirl at B. Altman's, the famous Fifth Avenue department store, and that her style was achieved by buying her clothes at giveaway end-of-the-season sales. Never married, she had retired as an executive and board member of Altman's years ago.

He had met her older cousin Catherine only a few times, and by then she was already a legend, the nun who had started seven hospitals for handicapped children—research hospitals dedicated to finding ways to cure or alleviate the suffering of their damaged bodies or minds.

"Do you know that many people are calling the healing of a child with brain cancer a miracle and attributing it to Catherine's intercession?" Olivia asked. "She's being considered as a candidate for beatification."

Clay Hadley felt his mouth go dry. "No, I hadn't heard." Not a Catholic, he vaguely understood that that would mean the Church might eventually declare Sister Catherine a saint and worthy of veneration by the faithful.

"Of course that will mean that the subject of her having given birth will be explored, and those vicious rumors will resurface and almost certainly finish her chance of being found worthy," Olivia added, her tone angry.

"Olivia, there *was* a reason neither Sister Catherine nor your mother ever named the father of her child."

"Catherine didn't. But my mother did."

Olivia leaned her hands on the arms of the chair, a signal to Clay that she was about to stand up. He rose and walked around his desk, with quick steps for such a bulky man. He knew that some of his patients referred to him as "Chunky Clay the Cardiologist." His voice humorous, his eyes twinkling, he counseled all of them, "Forget about me and make sure you lose weight. I look at the picture of an ice cream cone and put on five pounds. It's my cross to bear." It was a performance he had perfected. Now he took Olivia's hands in his and kissed her gently.

Involuntarily she drew back from the sensation of his short, graying beard grazing her cheek, then to cover her reaction returned the kiss. "Clay, my own situation remains between us. I will tell the few remaining people who will care very soon." She paused, then, her tone ironic, she added, "In fact I'd obviously better tell them *very* soon. Perhaps fortunately, I don't have a single family member left." Then she stopped, realizing that what she had just said wasn't true.

On her deathbed her mother had told her that after Catherine realized she was pregnant, she had spent a year in Ireland, where she had given birth to a son. He had been adopted by the Farrells, an American couple from Boston who were selected by the Mother Superior of the religious order Catherine entered. They had named him Edward, and he had grown up in Boston.

I've followed their lives ever since, Olivia thought. Edward didn't marry until he was forty-two. His wife has been dead a long time, and he passed away about five years ago. Their daughter, Monica, is thirty-one now, a pediatrician on the staff of Greenwich Village Hospital. Catherine was my first cousin. Her granddaughter is my cousin. She is my only family, and she doesn't know I exist.

Now, as she withdrew her hands from Clay's grasp, she said, "Monica has turned out to be so like her grandmother, devoting her life to taking care of babies and little children. Do you realize what all that money would mean to her?"

"Olivia, don't you believe in redemption? Look at what the father of her child did with the rest of his life. Think of the lives he saved. And what about his brother's family? They're prominent philanthropists. Think what such disclosure will mean to them."

"I am thinking about it, and that's what I have to weigh. Monica Farrell is the rightful heir to the income from those patents. Alexander Gannon was her grandfather, and in his will he left everything he had to his issue if any existed and only then to his brother. I'll call you, Clay."

Dr. Clay Hadley waited until the door of his private office closed, then picked up the phone and dialed a number that was known to very few people. When a familiar voice answered he did not waste time in preliminaries. "It's exactly what I was afraid of. I know Olivia . . . she's going to talk."

"We can't let that happen," the person on the other end of the line said matter-of-factly. "You've got to make sure it doesn't. Why didn't you give her something?

With her medical condition, no one would question her death."

"Believe it or not, it isn't that simple to kill someone. And suppose she manages to leave the proof before I can stop her?"

"In that case we take out double insurance. Sad to say, a fatal attack on an attractive young woman in Manhattan is hardly an extraordinary event these days. I'll take care of it immediately."

2

Dr. Monica Farrell shivered as she posed for a picture with Tony and Rosalie Garcia on the steps of Greenwich Village Hospital. Tony was holding Carlos, their two-year-old son, who had just been declared free of the leukemia that had almost claimed his life.

Monica remembered the day when, as she was about to leave her office, Rosalie phoned in a panic. "Doctor, the baby has spots on his stomach." Carlos was then six weeks old. Even before she saw him, Monica had the terrible hunch that what she was going to find was the onset of juvenile leukemia. Diagnostic tests confirmed that suspicion, and Carlos's chances were calculated to be at best fifty-fifty. Monica had promised his weeping young parents that as far as she was concerned, those were good enough odds and Carlos was already too tough a little guy not to win the fight.

"Now one with you holding Carlos, Dr. Monica," Tony ordered as he took the camera from the passerby who had volunteered to become the acting photographer.

Monica reached for the squirming two-year-old, who had by then decided he'd smiled long enough. This will be some picture, she thought as she waved at the camera, hoping that Carlos could follow her example. Instead he pulled the clip at the nape of her neck and her long dark-blond hair fell loose around her shoulders.

After a flurry of good-byes and "God bless you, Dr. Monica, we wouldn't have made it without you, and we'll see you for his checkup," the Garcias were gone with one final wave from the window of the taxi. As Monica stepped back inside the hospital and walked to the elevator bank, she reached up to gather the strands of her hair and refasten the clip.

"Leave it like that. It looks good." Dr. Ryan Jenner, a neurosurgeon who had been in Georgetown Medical School a few years ahead of Monica, had fallen in step with her. He had recently come on staff at Greenwich Village and had stopped for a moment to chat the few times they had run into each other. Jenner, wearing scrubs and a plastic bonnet, had obviously been in surgery or was on his way to it.

Monica laughed as she pushed the button for an ascending elevator. "Oh, sure. And maybe I should drop into your operating room while it's like this."

The door of a descending elevator was opening.

"Maybe I wouldn't mind," Jenner said as he got into it.

And maybe you would. In fact you'd have a heart attack, Monica thought as she stepped into an already crowded elevator. Ryan Jenner, despite his youthful face and ready smile, was already known to be a perfectionist and intolerant of any lapses in patient care. Being in his operating room with uncovered hair was unthinkable.

When she got off on the pediatric floor, the wail of a screaming baby was the first sound Monica heard. She knew it was her patient, nineteen-month-old Sally Carter, and the lack of visits from her single mother was infuriating. Before she went in to try to comfort the baby, she stopped at the nurses' desk. "Any sign of Mommy dearest?" she asked, then regretted she had been so outspoken.

"Not since yesterday morning," Rita Greenberg, the longtime head nurse on the floor, answered, her tone as annoyed as Monica's. "But she *did* manage to squeeze in a phone call an hour ago to say she was tied up at work and ask if Sally had had a good night. Doctor, I'm telling you, there's something odd about that whole situation. That woman acts no more like a mother than the stuffed animals in the play room do. Are you going to discharge Sally today?"

"Not until I find out who will be taking care of her when the mother is so busy. Sally had asthma and pneumonia when she was brought to the emergency room. I can't imagine what the mother or the babysitter was thinking, waiting so long to get medical attention for her."

Followed by the nurse, Monica went into the small room with the single crib, to which Sally had been moved because her crying was waking up the other babies. Sally was standing, holding on to the railings, her light brown hair curling around her tear-stained face.

"She'll work herself into another asthma attack," Monica said angrily, as she reached in and plucked the baby from the crib. As Sally clung to her, the crying immediately lessened, then evolved into subdued sobs and finally began to ease off.

"My God, how she has bonded to you, Doctor, but then you've got the magic touch," Rita Greenberg said. "There's no one like you with the little ones."

"Sally knows that she and I are pals," Monica said. "Let's give her some warm milk, and I bet she'll settle down."

As she waited for the nurse to return, Monica rocked the baby in her arms. Your mother should be doing this, she thought. I wonder how much attention she gives you at home? Her tiny hands soft on Monica's neck, Sally's eyes began to close.

Monica laid the sleepy baby back in the crib and changed her wet diaper. Then she turned Sally on her side and covered her with a blanket. Greenberg returned with a bottle of warm milk but before she gave it to the baby, Monica reached for a cotton tip and swabbed the inside of Sally's cheek.

In the past week, she had noticed that several times when Sally's mother came to visit, she had stopped at the large courtesy counter in the lounge area and then brought a cup of coffee with her into Sally's room. Invariably she left it half empty on the nightstand by the crib.

It's only a hunch, Monica told herself, and I know I have no right to do it. But I'm going to send word to Ms. Carter that I must meet with her before I will discharge Sally. I'd love to compare the baby's DNA with her DNA from the coffee cup. She swears she's the birth mother, but if she's not why would she bother to lie about it? Then reminding herself once more that she had no right to secretly compare the DNA, she threw the swab into the wastebasket.

After checking her other patients, Monica went to her office on East Fourteenth Street for her afternoon hours. It was six thirty when, trying to conceal her weariness, she said good-bye to her last patient, an eight-year-old boy with an ear infection.

Nan Rhodes, her receptionist-bookkeeper, was closing up at her desk. In her sixties, rotund, and with unfailing patience no matter how hectic the waiting room, Nan asked the question Monica had been hoping to put aside for another day.

"Doctor, what about that inquiry from the Bishop's Office in New Jersey, asking you to be a witness in the beatification process for that nun?"

"Nan, I don't believe in miracles. You know that. I sent them a copy of the initial CAT scan and MRI. They speak for themselves."

"But you did believe that with brain cancer that advanced, Michael O'Keefe would never see his fifth birthday, didn't you?"

"Absolutely."

"You suggested his parents take him to the Knowles Clinic in Cincinnati because it's the best research hospital in brain cancer, but you did it knowing full well they'd confirm your diagnosis out there," Nan persisted.

"Nan, we both know what I said and what I believed," Monica said. "Come on, let's not play twenty questions."

"Doctor, you also told me that when you gave them the diagnosis, Michael's father was so upset, he almost passed out, but that the mother told you that her son was not going to die. She was going to start a crusade of prayer to Sister Catherine, the nun who founded those hospitals for disabled children."

"Nan, how many people refuse to accept that an illness is terminal? We see it every day at the hospital. They want a second and third opinion. They want more tests. They want to sign up for risky procedures. Sometimes the inevitable is prolonged, but in the end the result is the same."

Nan's expression softened as she looked at the slender young woman whose body posture was so clearly showing her fatigue. She knew Monica had been at the hospital during the night, when one of her little patients had a seizure. "Doctor, I know it isn't my place to badger you, but there are going to be witnesses from the medical staff in Cincinnati to testify that Michael O'Keefe should not have survived. Today he's absolutely cancer free. I think you have a sacred obligation to verify that you had that conversation with the mother the very minute you warned her that he could not recover, because that was the moment she turned to Sister Catherine for help."

"Nan, I saw Carlos Garcia this morning. He's cancer free as well."

"It's not the same and you know it. We have the treatment to beat childhood leukemia. We don't have it for advanced and spreading brain cancer."

Monica realized two facts. It was useless to argue with Nan, and in her heart she knew Nan was right. "I'll go," she said, "but it won't do that would-be saint any good. Where am I supposed to testify about this?"

"A Monsignor from the Metuchen diocese in New Jersey is the one you should meet. He suggested next Wednesday afternoon. As it happens, I didn't make any appointments for you after eleven o'clock that day."

"Then so be it," Monica acquiesced. "Call him back and set it up. Are you ready to go? I'll ring for the elevator."

"Right behind you. I love what you just said."

"That I'll ring for the elevator?"

"No, of course not. I mean you just said 'so be it.' "

"So?"

"As far as the Catholic Church is concerned, 'so be it' is the translation for 'amen.' Kind of fitting in this case, don't you think, Doctor?"

3

It was not an assignment he relished. The disappearance of a young woman doctor in New York was stuff for the tabloids and they would be sure to wring it dry. The money was good, but Sammy Barber's instinct was to turn it down. Sammy had been arrested only once, then acquitted at trial because he was a very careful man and never came close enough to his victims to leave DNA evidence.

Sammy's shrewd hazel eyes were the dominant feature in a narrow face that seemed out of place on his short, thick neck. Forty-two years old, with muscles that bulged through the arms of his sports jacket, his official job was as a bouncer at a Greenwich Village night club.

A cup of coffee in front of him, he was seated across the table from his would-be employer's representative in a diner in Queens. Scrupulously aware of small details, Sammy had already sized him up. Well dressed. In his fifties. Classy. Very good-looking. Silver cuff-links with initials D.L. He had been told there was no need for him to know the man's name, that the phone number would be sufficient for contact.

"Sammy, you're hardly in a position to refuse," Douglas Langdon said mildly. "From what I understand, you're not exactly living high on the hog from your lousy job. Furthermore, I have to remind you that if my cousin had not reached several of the jurors, you would be in prison right now."

"They couldn't have proved it anyway," Sammy began.

"You don't know what they could have proved, and you never know what jurors will decide." The mild tone was no longer present in Langdon's voice. He shoved a photograph across the table. "This was taken this afternoon outside the Village hospital. The woman holding the child is Dr. Monica Farrell. Her home and office addresses are printed on the back."

Before he touched anything, Sammy reached for a crumpled paper napkin, then used it to pick up the photograph. He held it under the dingy lamp at the table. "Beautiful broad," he commented as he studied it. He turned the photo over and glanced at the addresses, then without being asked, he handed the photograph back to Langdon.

"Okay. I don't want to have this picture on me if I'm ever stopped by the police. But I'll take care of everything."

"See that you do. And quickly." Langdon shoved the picture back into his jacket pocket. As he and Sammy got up, he reached back into the pocket, took out a billfold, peeled off a twenty-dollar bill, and tossed it on the table. Neither he nor Sammy noticed that the snapshot had caught on the billfold and fluttered to the floor.

"Thanks a lot, mister," Hank Moss, the young waiter, called as Langdon and Sammy exited through the revolving door. As he picked up the coffee cups, he noticed the picture. Setting down the cups, he ran to the door but neither man was in sight.

They probably don't need this, Hank thought, but on the other hand the guy *did* leave a big tip. He turned the picture over and saw the printed addresses, one on East Fourteenth Street, and the other on East Thirty-sixth Street. The one on East Fourteenth had a suite number, the one on East Thirty-sixth, an apartment number. Hank thought of a particular kind of mail that sometimes came to his parents' home in Brooklyn. Listen, he told himself. Just in case this is important to anyone I'll drop it in an envelope and address it to "Occupant." I'll send it to the suite on Fourteenth Street. That's probably the office of the guy who dropped it. Then if it's important, he's got it, at least.

At nine o'clock when his shift was over, Hank went back to the hole-in-the-wall office next to the kitchen. "Okay if I take an envelope and stamp, Lou?" he asked the owner, who was tallying receipts. "Somebody forgot something."

"Sure. Go ahead. I'll take the price of the stamp out of your paycheck." Lou grunted with what passed for a smile. Short-tempered by nature, he genuinely liked Hank. The kid was a good worker and knew how to treat customers. "Here, use one of these." He handed a plain white envelope to Hank, who quickly scribbled the address he had decided to use. Then Hank reached for the stamp Lou was holding out to him.

Ten minutes later he dropped the envelope in a mailbox as he jogged back to his dorm at St. John's University.

4

Olivia was one of the first tenants of Schwab House on the West Side of Manhattan. Now, fifty years later, she still lived there. The apartment complex was built on grounds that had previously been the site of the mansion of a wealthy industrialist. The builder had decided to retain his name, hoping that some of the grandeur surrounding the mansion would be passed on to its sprawling replacement.

Olivia's first apartment had been a studio facing West End Avenue. As she steadily climbed the ladder to the executive branch of B. Altman and Company, she had begun to look for a larger place. She had intended to move to the East Side of Manhattan, but when a two-bedroom with a magnificent view of the Hudson became available in Schwab House, she had happily taken it. Later, when the building became a cooperative, she had been glad to buy her apartment because it made her feel that at last she truly had a home. Before moving to Manhattan, she and her mother, Regina, had lived in a small cottage behind the Long Island home of the Gannon family. Her mother had been their housekeeper.

Over the years Olivia's secondhand furniture had been slowly and carefully replaced. Self-taught, and with innate good taste, she had developed an eye for both art and design. The cream-colored walls throughout the apartment became a setting for the paintings she acquired at estate sales. The antique rugs in the living room, bedroom, and library were the palette from which she chose colorful fabrics for upholstered pieces and window treatments.

The overall effect on a first-time visitor was invariably the same. The apartment was a haven of warmth and comfort and gave off a sense of peace and serenity.

Olivia loved it. In all those competitive years at Altman's, the thought that at the end of the day she would be settled in her roomy club chair, a glass of wine in her hand, watching the sunset, had been an unfailing safety valve.

It had even been her refuge forty years ago at the heartbreaking crisis of her life, when she had finally faced the fact that Alex Gannon, the brilliant doctor and researcher whom she desperately loved, would never allow their relationship to go beyond a close friendship . . . Catherine was the one he'd always wanted.

After her appointment with Clay, Olivia went straight home. The fatigue that was the reason she had consulted Clay two weeks ago completely enveloped her. Almost too weary to take the trouble to change, she had forced herself to undress and replace her outer clothes with a warm robe in a shade of blue that she was vain enough to realize exactly matched the color of her eyes.

A small and unwanted protest at her fate made her decide to lie down on the couch in the living room rather than on her bed. Clay had warned her that overwhelming fatigue was to be expected, "Until one day, you just don't feel able to get up."

But not yet, Olivia thought, as she reached for the afghan that was always on the ottoman at the foot of the club chair. She sat on the couch, placed one of the decorative pillows where it would be directly under her head, lay down, and pulled the afghan over her. She then sighed a relieved sigh.

Two weeks, she thought. Two weeks. Fourteen days. How many hours is that? It doesn't matter, she thought as she drifted off to sleep.

When she awoke, the shadows in the room told her that it was late afternoon. I had only a cup of tea this morning before I saw Clay, she thought. I'm not hungry, but I've got to eat something. As she pushed aside the afghan and slowly got to her feet, the need to review the proof about Catherine again suddenly became overwhelming. In fact, she had the frightening sense that it might somehow have disappeared from the safe in the den.

But it was there, in the manila file her mother had given her only hours before her death. Catherine's letters to Mother, Olivia thought, her lips quivering; the Mother Superior's letter to Catherine; a copy of Edward's birth certificate; the passionate note *he* had given my mother to pass on to Catherine.

"Olivia."

Someone was in the apartment and was coming down

the hallway toward her. Clay. Olivia's fingers trembled as, without putting them back in the file, she thrust the letters and birth certificate into the safe, closed the door, and pushed the button that automatically locked it.

She stepped out of the closet. "I'm here, Clay." She did not attempt to conceal the icy disapproval in her voice.

"Olivia, I was concerned about you. You promised to call this afternoon."

"I don't remember making that promise."

"Well, you did," Clay said heartily.

"You did give me two weeks. I would guess that not more than seven hours have passed. Why didn't you have the doorman announce you?"

"Because I hoped you might be sleeping and if so, I would have left without disturbing you. Or why don't I tell the truth? If I had been announced you might have turned me down and I wanted to see you. I did deliver a bombshell to you this morning."

When Olivia did not answer, Clay Hadley, his tone gentle, added, "Olivia, there is a reason why you gave me a key and permission to come in if I suspected a problem."

Olivia felt her resentment at the intrusion begin to disappear. What Clay had said was absolutely true. If he had called up I would have told him I was resting, she thought. Then she followed Clay's glance.

He was looking at the manila envelope in her hand.

From where he stood he could obviously see the single word her mother had written across it.

CATHERINE.

5

Monica lived on the first floor of a renovated town house on East Thirty-sixth Street. In her mind, being on the tree-lined block was like stepping back in time to the nineteenth century, when all the brownstones had been private residences. Her apartment was to the rear of the building, which meant she had exclusive use of the small patio and garden. When the weather was warm she enjoyed morning coffee in her bathrobe on the patio, or a glass of wine in the evening there.

After the discussion with her receptionist, Nan, about Michael O'Keefe, the child who had had brain cancer, she had decided to walk home, as she frequently did. She had long since realized that walking the one-mile distance from her office was a good way of getting in some exercise, as well as a chance to unwind.

Cooking at the end of the day was relaxing for her. A self-taught chef, Monica had culinary talents that were legendary among her friends. But neither the walk nor the excellent pasta and salad she prepared for herself that evening did anything to settle her uneasy sense that a dark cloud was hanging over her.

It's the baby, she thought. I have to discharge Sally tomorrow, but even if I check the DNA and learn that Ms. Carter *isn't* the birth mother, what does that prove? Dad was an adopted child. I can hardly remember his parents, but he always said that he couldn't imagine being brought up by anyone except them. In fact he used to paraphrase Teddy Roosevelt's daughter Alice. A widower, Roosevelt had remarried when Alice was two years old. When asked about her stepmother, Alice had replied firmly, "She was the only mother I ever knew or wanted to know."

And having quoted that, and fully sharing for his adoptive parents the sentiment of Alice Roosevelt's love for the stepmother who raised her, Dad always wondered and longed to know more about his birth parents, Monica mused. In his last few years, he was pretty much obsessed by it.

Sally was terribly sick when she was brought into the emergency room but there wasn't a hint of any kind of abuse and she was obviously well nourished. And certainly Renée Carter won't be the first person who turns her child over to a babysitter or nanny to raise.

The prospect of testifying about the disappearance of Michael O'Keefe's brain cancer was another reason for concern. I don't believe in miracles, Monica thought vehemently, then admitted to herself that Michael had been terminally ill when she examined him.

As she lingered over demitasse and fresh-cut pineapple, she looked around, as always finding comfort in her surroundings.

Because of the chilly evening, she had turned on the gas fireplace. The small round dining table and the upholstered chair where she was sitting faced the fireplace. Now the flickering flames sent darts of light across the antique Aubusson carpet that had been her mother's pride and joy.

The ringing of the phone was an unwelcome intrusion. She was bone-weary, but knowing it might mean a call from the hospital about one of her patients made her bolt from her chair and dart across the room. As she picked up the receiver she was saying "Dr. Farrell" even before she realized the call was coming through on her private line.

"And Dr. Farrell is well, I trust," a teasing male voice asked.

"I'm very well, Scott," Monica answered, her tone cool, even as she felt a sickening worry at the sound of Scott Alterman's voice.

The teasing note disappeared. "Monica, Joy and I have called it quits. It was always wrong. We both realize it now."

"I'm sorry to hear that," Monica said. "But I think you should understand that has absolutely nothing to do with me."

"It has *everything* to do with you, Monica. I've been quietly seeing an executive search bureau. A top-drawer law firm on Wall Street has offered me a partnership. I've accepted."

"If you have, I hope you realize that there are eight or nine million people in New York City. Make friends with any and all of them, but leave me alone." Monica broke the connection, then, too upset to sit down again, cleared the table, and finished the demitasse standing at the sink.

6

When she left Monica outside the office on Monday evening, Nan Rhodes took the First Avenue bus to meet four of her sisters for their regular monthly dinner at Neary's Pub on Fifty-seventh Street.

Widowed for six years, and with her only son and his family living in California, working for Monica had proven to be a godsend to Nan. She loved Monica and at the dinners she would often talk about her. One of eight children herself, she regularly lamented the fact that Monica had no siblings and that her mother and father, both only children, had been in their early forties when she was born and were now deceased.

Tonight, at their usual corner table at Neary's, over a predinner cocktail, Nan got back on the subject. "While I was waiting for the bus I watched Dr. Monica walking up the block. She'd had such a long day, and I was thinking, poor thing, it's not like she could get a phone call from her mother or dad to talk things over. It's such a damn shame that when her father was born in Ireland only the names of his adoptive parents, Anne and Matthew Farrell, were given on the birth certificate.

The real parents certainly made it their business to be sure he couldn't trace them."

The sisters bobbed their heads in agreement. "Dr. Monica is so classy-looking. Her grandmother probably came from a good family, maybe even an American one," Nan's youngest sister, Peggy, volunteered. "In those days if an unmarried girl got pregnant, she was taken on a trip until the baby was born and then it would be given up for adoption, with no one the wiser. Today when an unmarried girl gets pregnant she brags about it on Twitter or Facebook."

"I know Dr. Monica has lots of friends," Nan sighed as she picked up the menu. "She has a genius for making people like her, but it's not the same, is it? No matter what you say, blood is thicker than water."

Her sisters nodded in solemn unison, although Peggy pointed out that Monica Farrell was a beautiful young woman and it would probably be only a matter of time before she met someone.

That subject exhausted, Nan had a new tidbit to share. "Remember how I told you that that nun Sister Catherine is being considered for beatification because a little boy who was supposed to die of brain cancer was cured after a crusade of prayer to her?"

They all remembered. "He was Dr. Monica's patient, wasn't he?" Rosemary, the oldest sister, said.

"Yes. His name is Michael O'Keefe. I guess the Church feels it has enough evidence to prove that he really is a miracle child. And just this afternoon I was able to persuade Dr. Monica to at least give testimony that when she told the parents he was terminal, the mother never blinked an eye before she said her son wasn't going to die, because she was beginning a crusade of prayer to Sister Catherine."

"If the mother did say that, why wouldn't Dr. Monica be willing to testify?" the middle sister, Ellen, asked.

"Because she's a doctor and a scientist and because she's still trying to find a way to prove that there was a good medical reason for Michael to be cancer free."

Liz, their waitress, who had worked at Neary's for thirty years, was at the table, menus in hand. "Ready to order, girls?" she asked cheerfully.

Nan enjoyed getting to work at seven A.M. She required little sleep, and lived only minutes away from Monica's office, in the apartment complex where she had moved after her husband's death. The early arrival gave her plenty of time to keep up with the mail and work on the endless medical insurance company forms.

Alma Donaldson, the nurse, came in at quarter of nine as Nan was opening the just-delivered mail. A handsome black woman in her late thirties, with a perceptive eye and warm smile, she had worked with Monica from the first day she had opened her practice four years earlier. Together they made an enviable medical team and had become fast friends.

As she took off her outer jacket, Alma was quick to spot the concerned expression on Nan's face. Nan was sitting at her desk, an envelope in one hand, a photograph in the other. Alma skipped her usual hearty greeting. "What's wrong, Nan?" she asked.

"Look at this," Nan said.

Alma walked behind the desk and stood looking down over Nan's shoulder. "Someone took a picture of the doctor with little Carlos Garcia," Alma said. "I think it's sweet."

"It came in a blank envelope," Nan said tersely. "I can't believe his mother or father would have sent it without a note of some kind. And look at this." She turned over the picture. "Someone printed the doctor's home and office addresses. That seems awfully peculiar to me."

"Maybe whoever sent it was trying to decide which address to use," Alma suggested slowly. "Why don't you call the Garcias and see if it came from them?"

"I bet the ranch it didn't," Nan muttered, as she picked up the phone.

Rosalie Garcia answered on the first ring. No, they hadn't sent a picture and couldn't imagine who might have done it. She was planning to frame the one they took of the doctor and Carlos and send it, but she hadn't had time to buy a frame yet. No, she didn't know the doctor's home address.

Monica came in as Nan repeated that conversation to Alma. The nurse and the receptionist exchanged glances and then at Alma's affirmative nod, Nan slipped the picture back into the envelope and dropped it in her desk drawer.

Later Nan confided to Alma, "There's a retired detective from the District Attorney's Office who lives down the hall from me. I'm going to show it to him. Mark my words, Alma, there's something creepy about that picture."

"Do you have the right *not* to show it to the doctor?" Alma asked.

"It's addressed to 'occupant,' not directly to her. I *will* show it to her, but I'd like to get John Hartman's opinion first."

That evening, after phoning her neighbor, Nan walked down the hall to his apartment. Hartman, a seventy-year-old widower with iron gray hair and the weathered complexion of a lifelong golfer, invited her in and listened to her apologetic explanation of why she was bothering him. "Sit down, Nan. You're not bothering me."

He went back to his club chair, where the newspapers he'd obviously been reading were piled on the hassock at his feet, and turned the switch on the standing lamp to full strength. As Nan watched intently she saw a frown that deepened on his face, as holding the picture and the envelope with the tips of his fingers, he studied them both.

"Your Dr. Farrell isn't a juror on some trial, is she?"

"No, she isn't. Why?"

"There's probably an explanation but in my business this is the kind of piece of mail we'd consider a warning. Does Dr. Farrell have any enemies?"

"Not one in the world."

"That's as far as you know, Nan. You've got to show her this picture, and then I'd like to talk to her."

"I hope she doesn't think I'm overstepping my bounds," Nan said anxiously as she got up to go. Then she hesitated. "The only thing that I can think of is that someone from Boston calls her from time to time. His name is Scott Alterman. He's a lawyer. I don't know what happened between them but if he calls the office, she never gets on the phone with him."

"He'd be a good place to start looking," Hartman said. "Scott Alterman. I'll do a little background work on him. I used to be a pretty good detective." Then he hesitated. "Dr. Farrell's a pediatrician, isn't she?"

"Yes."

"Has she lost any patients lately? I mean, did a child die unexpectedly where the parents might blame her?"

"No, on the contrary, she's being asked to testify about one of her patients who was terminal and not only is still living but is cured of brain cancer."

"I didn't think that was possible, but at least we know *that* family isn't going to be responsible for stalking Dr. Farrell." John Hartman bit his tongue. He had not planned to use that word but something in his gut was telling him that someone out there was stalking the young doctor who was Nan's employer.

He reached out his hand. "Nan," he said. "Give that back to me. Did anyone besides you handle the picture?"

"No."

"I've got absolutely nothing important to do tomorrow. I'm going to take it down to headquarters and see if I can pick up any discernible fingerprints. It's probably a waste of time, but then again you never know. You wouldn't mind my taking your fingerprints, would you? Just for comparison purposes. It would only take a minute and I still have a kit in my desk."

"Of course I don't mind." She tried to stifle her rising anxiety.

Less than ten minutes later, Nan was back in her own apartment. John Hartman had promised to return the picture to her by tomorrow evening. "You should show it to Dr. Farrell," he said. "It's up to you whether or not to say you gave it to me."

"I'm not sure what I'll do," she had replied, but now as she locked and bolted her door she found herself thinking of how vulnerable Monica Farrell was in her apartment. That kitchen door to the patio has a big window, Nan thought. Anybody could slice out the glass and reach in and open the lock. I've already warned her she should have a much stronger grille over that window.

Nan did not sleep well that night. Her dreams were haunted by distorted images of Monica standing on the steps of the hospital, Carlos in her arms, with her long blond hair streaming on her shoulders, then coiling like tentacles around her neck.

7

It was late afternoon of the day after his meeting with Sammy Barber before fifty-two-year-old Douglas Langdon realized that the photograph he had snapped of Monica Farrell was missing. He was in his corner office on Park Avenue and Fifty-first Street when the nagging sensation that something was wrong became defined in his mind.

Glancing at the door to be sure it was closed, he stood up and emptied the pockets of his expensively tailored suit. His billfold was always in the right-hand back pocket of his trousers. He took it out and laid it on his desk. Except for a clean white handkerchief the pocket was now empty.

But I wasn't wearing this suit last night, he thought hopefully. I was wearing the dark gray. Then, dismayed, he remembered he had dropped it in the cleaner bag for his housekeeper to give to the in-house valet service. I emptied out the pockets, he thought. I always do. The picture wasn't there or I would have noticed it.

There was only one time he'd had any reason to reach for his billfold and that was when he paid for the coffee in the diner. He had either pulled the picture out then, or less likely, it might have slipped out of the pocket and fallen somewhere between the diner and where he had parked his car.

Suppose someone found it, he wondered. It has two addresses on the back. No name, but two addresses in my handwriting. Most people would just throw it away, but suppose some do-gooder tries to return it?

Every instinct told him the picture could cause trouble. Lou's was the name of that diner in Queens where he'd met Sammy. He reached for the phone, and after a moment was speaking to Lou, the owner.

"We don't have no picture—but wait a minute, a kid who works for me is here, and said something about a customer losing something last night. I'll put him on."

Three long minutes passed, then Hank Moss began with an apology. "I was just bringing out the orders for a table of six. Sorry to have kept you waiting."

The kid sounded smart. Doug Langdon tried to sound casual. "It's not important, but I think I dropped my daughter's picture last night when I was at the diner."

"Is she blond, with long hair and holding a little kid?"

"Yes," Doug said. "I'll send my friend over for it. He lives near the diner."

"I actually don't have the picture." Hank's voice was now nervous. "I could see that one of the addresses on the back seemed to be an office, so I addressed it to 'occupant' and sent it there. I hope that was all right?"

"It was very thoughtful. Thank you." Doug replaced the receiver, not noticing that his palm was moist and his whole body felt clammy. What would Monica Farrell think when she saw that picture? Fortunately both her home and office addresses were listed in the phone book. If her home address on East Thirty-sixth Street were unlisted, it probably would have tipped her off that someone might be stalking her.

There was, of course, a simple and plausible solution. Someone who knew her snapped that picture of her holding the kid, and thought she might like to have it.

"There's no reason for her to be suspicious," Doug said aloud softly, then realized he was trying to reassure himself.

The muted ring of the intercom interrupted his reflections. He pushed a button on the phone. "What is it?" he asked abruptly.

"Dr. Langdon, Mr. Gannon's secretary called to remind you that you are to introduce him tonight at the dinner for Troubled Teens honoring him . . ."

"I don't need to be reminded," Doug interrupted irritably.

Beatrice Tillman, his secretary, ignored the interruption. "And Linda Coleman phoned to say she's caught in traffic and will be late for her four o'clock session with you."

"She wouldn't be late if she had left in enough time to get here."

"I agree, Doctor," Beatrice, long used to coaxing her attractive and long-time divorced boss out of a bad mood, said with a smile in her voice. "As you always tell me, with patients like Linda Coleman, you need to see a psychiatrist yourself."

Douglas Langdon turned off the intercom without responding. A chilling thought had come to him. His fingerprints were on that picture he had taken of Monica Farrell. When something happened to her, if that picture was still around, the police might test it for prints.

There was no question of calling Sammy off. How do I work this out? Doug asked himself.

He had no answer when three hours later, at the Pierre Hotel on Fifth Avenue, seated at the table of honor at the black-tie dinner honoring Greg Gannon, he was asked quietly, "The meeting yesterday evening was satisfactory?"

Doug nodded affirmatively, then, as his name was announced, he arose and strode to the microphone to deliver his speech praising Gregory Gannon, president of the Gannon Investment Firm and as Chairman of the Board of the Gannon Foundation, one of New York City's most generous philanthropists.

8

On Tuesday morning, Olivia woke early, but did not get up for nearly an hour. Then, slipping on a robe, she went into the kitchen. She always made a fresh pot of tea to start the day. When it was ready, she set the pot and a cup on a tray and carried it into the bedroom. She set the tray on the night table and, propped on pillows, sipped the tea as she gazed down at the Hudson River.

Her thoughts were scattered. She knew there were boats still anchored to buoys in the yacht basin on Seventy-ninth Street. In a few weeks most of them will be gone, she thought, and so will I. I've often wondered what it would be like to go sailing. I had thought that someday I'd get around to it.

And also to taking lessons in ballroom dancing, she added, smiling at the thought. And what about all the college courses I meant to sign up for? Of course, none of that matters now. I should start counting my blessings. I had a successful career working at a job I loved. Since I retired, I've traveled a lot, and have enjoyed deep friendships . . .

As she savored the last of the tea, Olivia turned her

mind back to the pressing problem of what to do about the evidence in her safe. Clay absolutely wants me to let it go, she thought, but when the chips are down it's none of his business, even if he is on the board of the Gannon Foundation. Catherine was *my* cousin. And Clay had no right to walk in here Monday evening, no matter how concerned he may be about me.

Of course when Mother died I agreed with him that it was better to leave things as they were, she reminded herself, but that was before the miracle of Catherine's saving the little boy's life, and before the beatification process began.

What would *she* want me to do? For an instant Catherine's face was crystal clear in Olivia's mind. Catherine at seventeen, with that long blond hair, and those eyes the blue green of the sea on a spring morning. Even when I was only five years old I was smart enough to know how truly beautiful she was.

A thought crossed her mind: Clay saw that file folder in my hand with Catherine's name on it. He's the executor of my estate, such as it is. When I'm gone, if I haven't resolved this one way or the other myself, I wouldn't be surprised if when he opens the safe he gets rid of the file. He would think he was doing the right thing. But is it the right thing?

Olivia got up, showered, and dressed in her favorite casual outfit: slacks, a tailored blouse, and a warm cardigan sweater. Over toast and a third cup of tea, she tried to decide what to do. She was still unsure as she tidied up the kitchen and made the bed.

Then the answer came to her suddenly. She would visit Catherine's grave in Rhinebeck, where she was buried on the grounds of the motherhouse of her order, the Community of St. Francis. Maybe I'll get a sense of what she would want me to do there, Olivia thought. It's a pretty good drive, at least two hours, but once I'm out of the city, the country is so pretty. I'll enjoy it.

In these last few years she had given up driving long distances herself and instead called on a service to send a driver, who would take her where she wanted to go in her own car.

An hour later the intercom buzzed to let her know that her driver was in the lobby. "I'll be right down," she said.

As she was putting on her coat, she hesitated, then went to the safe and took out Catherine's file. She slipped it into a tote bag, and feeling relieved to have it with her, left the apartment.

The driver turned out to be a pleasant-faced man in his mid-twenties, who introduced himself as Tony Garcia. To Olivia, there was something reassuring about the way he offered to carry the tote bag, then put a guiding hand under her elbow at the step in the garage. With approval she noticed that once in the car he immediately checked the gauge and told her there was plenty of gas for the round trip. After reminding her to fasten her seatbelt, he concentrated on the driving. The Henry Hudson Parkway North was crowded. As usual, Olivia noted wryly. She had tucked a book in her tote bag, along with the Catherine file. An open book, she had learned, was the best way to discourage a loquacious driver.

But in the next two hours Garcia did not say a word until they drove through the gates of the St. Francis property. "Just turn left and go up that hill," she told him. "Beyond it you'll see the cemetery. That's where I'm going."

A picket fence encircled the private cemetery, where four generations of Franciscan nuns were buried. The wide entrance was framed by a trestle that Olivia remembered as being ablaze with roses in the summer. Now it was covered with green vines that already were tinged with brown. Garcia stopped the car at the flagstone walk and opened the door for Olivia to get out.

"I'll only be ten or fifteen minutes," she told him.

"I'll be right here, ma'am."

Low stone markers were on the individual graves. Occasional benches offered a place for visitors to rest. Catherine's grave was opposite one of them. With an unconscious sigh, Olivia sat down on the bench. Even such a short walk makes me so tired, she thought, but I guess I should expect that now. She looked down at the lettering on Catherine's marker: SR. CATHERINE MARY KURNER: SEPTEMBER 6, 1917–JUNE 3, 1977. R.I.P.

"Rest in peace," Olivia whispered. "Rest in peace. Oh, Catherine, you were my cousin, my sister, my mentor."

She reflected on the tragedy that had entwined their lives. Their mothers had been sisters. Catherine's parents Jane and David Kurner and my father had all been killed in a car accident, when a drunken driver crashed into their car on the highway. That was a month before I was born, Olivia thought. Catherine was only a child herself, just turning twelve. She had come to live with us, and, from what I know, she became my mother's right hand, the strong one. Mother told me that she could barely handle the grief and that Catherine was the one who got her through it.

Olivia felt the familiar hurt as her thoughts turned to Alex Gannon. "Oh, God, Catherine, no matter how strong your vocation, how could you not have loved him?" she whispered into the silence.

Alex's parents, the Gannons. Olivia wished she could better remember the faces of the people who had been so kind to her mother. They had insisted she stay on as their housekeeper and live in the cottage on their estate in Southhampton after her father, who had been their chauffeur for many years, had died.

I was only five, but I remember Alex and his brother sitting on our porch talking to you, Catherine, Olivia reflected. Even then I thought Alex was like a young god. He was in medical school in New York, and I can remember Mother telling you that you were crazy to think of the convent when it was clear that he adored you. Long before it happened, I remember her saying, *"Catherine, you're making a mistake. Alex wants you. He wants to marry you. In a thousand years there'll never be another one like him. Seventeen is not too young to get married. And why don't you admit it? You are in love with him. I see it in your eyes. I see it when you look at him."*

And you said, "*And seventeen is not too young to know that I am called to a different path. It is not supposed to be. That's all there is to it.*"

Olivia felt the unwanted tears come to her eyes. Six months after Catherine left for the convent, Mother remarried and we moved into the city, she thought. But when old Mrs. Gannon died, I went to her funeral with Mother and met Alex again. That has been over forty years ago.

Olivia bit her lip to keep it from trembling and clasped her hands. "Oh, Catherine," she whispered, "how could you have given him up, and what shall I do now? I have the letter Alex asked my mother to give you, the letter begging your forgiveness. Shall I destroy it, and the record of your son's birth? Shall I give it to your granddaughter? What do you want me to do?"

The faint rustling of the leaves falling from the trees that were scattered around the cemetery made Olivia aware that she was suddenly chilled. It's almost four, she thought. I'd better get started for home. What did I expect? Another miracle? Catherine to materialize and counsel me? Her knees stiff, she got up slowly and, with a final glance at Catherine's grave, walked through the cemetery back to the car. She realized that Tony Garcia must have watched for her approaching, because he was standing beside the car with the door already open.

She got into the backseat, grateful for the warmth, but without any sense of resolution. On the way back the traffic was much heavier and she was impressed by Garcia's steady and skillful driving. When they were nearing her exit off the Henry Hudson Parkway, she commented on that and asked, "Tony, do you work full-time for the service? If you do, I'd like to request you if I have any more trips to make."

I should add, any trips that I make in the next few weeks, she thought sadly, realizing that for an instant she had forgotten how very little time she had left.

"No, ma'am, I'm a waiter at the Waldorf. Depending on my hours there, I let the service know when I'm available to drive."

"You're ambitious," Olivia said, remembering how when she began at Altman's all those years ago, she had always tried to work overtime.

Garcia looked into the rearview mirror and she could see his smile. "Not really, ma'am. I've got a lot of medical bills. My little guy was diagnosed with leukemia two years ago. You can imagine how my wife and I felt when we heard that. Our doctor told us he had a fifty-fifty chance, and those odds were good enough for her and for him. Two days ago we got the final word. He's cancer free."

Garcia fished into his jacket pocket, pulled out a photograph, and handed it back to Olivia. "That's Carlos with the doctor who took care of him," he explained.

Olivia stared at the picture, not believing what she was seeing. "That's Dr. Monica Farrell," she said.

"Do you know her?" Garcia asked eagerly.

"No, I don't," and then before she could stop herself, she added, "I knew her grandmother."

When they were down the block from the garage, she

reached for the tote bag and said, "Tony, please stop at the curb for a moment. I'd like you to put this bag in the trunk. There's a blanket quite far to the back. Slip it under the blanket, please."

"Of course." Without showing that he was surprised at the request, Garcia followed instructions, then drove Olivia the rest of the way home.

9

Greg Gannon brought the latest proof of his generosity to his private office in the Time Warner Center at Columbus Circle. "Where'll we put it, Esther?" he asked his longtime assistant, as he stopped at her desk and took it out of the box.

The tribute was a Tiffany engraved glass prism about ten inches high.

"Looks like an ice cube," he commented, laughing. "Shall I save it for when I have a martini?"

Esther Chambers smiled politely. "It will go in the case with the rest of them, Mr. Gannon."

"Es, can you just imagine how it will be when I kick the bucket? Who'd want them?"

It was a rhetorical question that Esther did not attempt to answer as Gannon walked into his private office. Your wife certainly won't and your sons would throw them in the garbage, she thought as she picked up the prism. And I'll bet she wasn't with you last night at that dinner. Then, with an unconscious sigh, she placed the prism on her desk. I'll put it in the trophy case later, she thought as she read the inscription. FOR GREGORY ALEXANDER GANNON IN RECOGNITION OF HIS

CONTINUING KINDNESS TO THOSE WHO NEED IT MOST.

Alexander Gannon, Esther thought. Instinctively, she glanced through the open door that led to the Foundation reception area, where a magnificent portrait of Greg's uncle dominated the room. He had been a medical scientist whose genius for inventing replacement parts for knees and hips and ankles was the basis of the family fortune.

He died thirty years ago, before he realized how much good his inventions would do, Esther thought. I remember meeting him when I started working here. He was so handsome, even when he was seventy years old. He walked so straight, and he had silver hair and those unforgettable blue eyes. He never lived to see how successful his patents would become. The patents have all expired, but the Gannons got hundreds of millions of dollars for years from them. At least the family put some of the money in the Gannon Foundation. But I doubt Dr. Gannon would have approved of the lifestyle of his brother's family.

Well, it's none of my business, she reminded herself, as she settled at her desk. Still, you can't help thinking . . . Sixtyish, with an angular figure and an unbending disposition to match, Esther was given to meditation whenever Greg brought in yet another trophy proving his oft proclaimed benevolence.

Thirty-five years ago she had begun working for Greg Gannon's father's small investment firm. Their office at that time was in lower Manhattan, and the business had been struggling until the medical devices invented by Alexander Gannon had released a tsunami of money and recognition. The investment firm had flourished and the income from the patents had changed the life of the Gannon family.

Greg was only eighteen then, Esther thought. At least after his father passed, he took over the investment firm and the foundation. His brother, Peter, never did much except pour money into Broadway musicals that closed on opening night. Some producer he is. If anyone knew how comparatively little those two give away, they'd stop kissing their feet in a moment.

Funny about those boys. Boys, she admonished herself sarcastically. They're middle-aged men. But it is funny how Peter got all the looks in the family. He could still be a movie star with that handsome face and big brown eyes and charm to spare. No wonder the girls were always throwing themselves at him. Still are, I bet.

On the other hand, Greg never did outgrow his pudgy teenaged shape and, let's face it, he's as plain as Peter is gorgeous. Now Greg's starting to go bald and he's always been sensitive about his height. Kind of unfair, I guess. But neither one of them, in my opinion, has lived up to his father and certainly not to Dr. Gannon.

Oh well, better remind myself that I get well paid, I have a nice office, I have a fat retirement package when I choose to take it, and a lot of people would love to be in my situation.

Esther began to go through the batch of mail that had been placed on her desk. It was she who examined the hundreds of requests for grants and steered the appropriate ones to the board, which consisted of Greg and Peter Gannon, Dr. Clay Hadley, Dr. Douglas Langdon, and for the past eight years, Greg's second wife, Pamela.

Sometimes she was able to pass along "grassroot pleas," as she called them, from smaller hospitals or churches or missions in desperate need of money. For the most part the requests that went through had been the kind that would put the Gannon name on hospitals and art centers where the family name would be displayed large, and their largesse could not be missed. In the past couple of years, there had been fewer and fewer of those grants.

I wonder how much money they really *do* have left? she asked herself.

10

Monday night after Scott Alterman's call, Monica had barely slept. Tuesday night was the same. Her first thought on waking at six A.M. on Wednesday had again been of him. He's not serious, she thought, as she had tried to convince herself all the previous day. He's got to be bluffing. He wouldn't give up his practice in Boston to move here.

Or would he? He's a brilliant lawyer. He's only forty years old and he's successfully defended high-ranking politicians all over the country and has a national reputation. That's just it. With that reputation he can go anywhere. Why not New York?

But even if he does relocate, except for occasional phone calls and sending flowers to the apartment once or twice, he hasn't really bothered me much in the four years I've been here, she reassured herself. She tried to take comfort in that thought as she showered, dressed in a maroon sweater and matching slacks, and clipped on small pearl earrings. I shouldn't even wear these, she thought. The babies always grab at them. Over coffee and cereal, she began to worry about Sally Carter again. Yesterday, I didn't discharge her and that was a stretch.

Today, unless she developed a fever during the night, I *have* to let her go.

At eight fifteen she was at the hospital to make her early rounds. She stopped at the nurses' desk to speak to Rita Greenberg. "Sally's temperature has stayed normal and she's been eating pretty well. Do you want to sign her discharge papers, Doctor?" Rita asked.

"Before I do I want to talk to the mother myself," Monica said. "I've got a heavy schedule at the office. Please call Ms. Carter and tell her I have to meet with her before I discharge Sally. I'll be back here at noon."

"I left a message yesterday to say that as a precaution you were keeping Sally for another twenty-four hours. I guess she got the message, because Mommy dearest never came to visit Sally. I checked with the evening shift. That lady is some piece of work."

Dismayed, Monica walked into the cubicle containing Sally's crib. The baby was sleeping on her side, her hands tucked under her cheek. Her light brown ringlets framed her forehead and curled around her ears. She did not stir when Monica's trained hands felt her back, listening for a sign of a rattle or a wheeze, but there was none.

Monica realized she was yearning to pick up Sally and have her wake up in her arms. Instead, she turned abruptly, left the cubicle, and began to make the rest of her rounds. All her little patients were progressing well. Not like Carlos Garcia, who was touch and go for so long, she thought. Not like Michael O'Keefe, who should have died three years ago.

In the corridor to the elevator she ran into Ryan Jenner, who was approaching from the opposite direction. This morning he was wearing a white jacket. "No surgery today, Doctor?" she asked as she passed him.

She had expected a casual "Not today" kind of answer tossed over his shoulder, but Jenner stopped. "And no windswept blond tresses," he replied. "Monica, some of my friends from Georgetown are coming up for the weekend. We're having cocktails at my place and going out to a Thai restaurant on Friday night. A couple of them, Genine Westervelt and Natalie Kramer, told me they hoped you'd be there. How about it?"

Startled at the suddenness of the unexpected invitation, Monica's response was hesitant. "Well . . ."

Then, realizing she was being asked to meet with former fellow students and not for a personal date, she said, "I'd love to see Genine and Natalie again."

"Good. I'll e-mail you." Jenner moved briskly down the corridor away from her. As Monica again began to walk to the elevator, she impulsively turned her head to look at his retreating back and was embarrassed to meet his glance.

Sheepishly, they nodded to each other as they simultaneously quickened their pace in opposite directions.

Promptly at noon Monica was back in the hospital waiting for Renée Carter, who arrived at twelve thirty, seemingly oblivious to the fact that she had kept Monica waiting. She was wearing an obviously expensive olive green suit with a short belted jacket. A black high-neck sweater, black stockings, and impossibly high black heels gave her the look of a fashion model about to embark on the runway. Her short auburn hair was tucked behind her ears, creating a frame for a very pretty face that had been further enhanced by expertly applied makeup. *She's not going home to take care of Sally,* Monica thought. *She's probably got a lunch date. I wonder how much time she spends with that poor baby?*

A week ago it had been the elderly babysitter who brought Sally to the emergency room. Renée Carter had arrived an hour later, wearing an evening gown and defensively explaining that the baby had been fine when she left her earlier that evening, and that she hadn't realized her cell phone was turned off.

Now Monica realized that even with the makeup, Carter looked older than she had appeared that night. At least thirty-five, she thought.

Today, Carter was accompanied by a young woman of about twenty, who nervously volunteered that she was Kristina Johnson, Sally's new nanny.

Carter made no attempt at apologizing for being late. Nor, Monica noticed with dismay, did she make any attempt to pick up Sally. "I fired the other babysitter," she explained in a voice that bordered on being nasal. "She didn't tell me that Sally had been coughing all day. But I know Kristina won't make that kind of mistake. She's been highly recommended."

She turned to Kristina. "Why don't you dress Sally while I talk to the doctor?"

Sally began wailing when Monica, followed by Renée Carter, left the cubicle. Monica did not turn back to look at her. Instead, heavyhearted at the thought that Sally was being taken away by this seemingly indifferent mother, she firmly warned Carter to pay close attention to Sally's allergies. "Do you have any pets, Ms. Carter?" she asked.

After a moment's hesitation, Renée Carter said reassuringly, "No, I don't have time for them, Doctor." Then, with visible impatience, she listened as Monica explained the importance of watching for signs of asthma in Sally.

"I certainly understand, Doctor, and I want you to take over as Sally's pediatrician," she said hurriedly, when Monica asked her if she had any questions. Then she called into the cubicle, "Kristina, you about ready? I'm running late."

She turned back to Monica. "I've got a car waiting outside, Doctor," she explained. "I'll drop Sally and Kristina at my apartment." Then, seeing something in Monica's face, she added, "Of course, I'll make sure Sally is settled before I leave her."

"I'm sure you will. I'll call you this evening to see how Sally is doing. You will be home, won't you?" Monica asked, not caring that the tone of her voice was icy and disapproving. She looked at the chart. "This is your correct number, isn't it?"

Renée Carter nodded her head impatiently as Monica read off the number, then turned and hurried back into the cubicle. "For Pete's sake, Kristina," she snapped, "hurry up! I haven't got all day."

11

He's on the warpath, Esther Chambers thought as Greg Gannon strode through her office after lunch on Wednesday without acknowledging her presence. What's happened since this morning? She watched as he went into his private office and picked up the file she had prepared for him. A moment later he was standing at her desk. "I haven't had time to go through this stuff," he snapped. "You're sure everything is in order?"

She wanted to snap back, *Tell me one time in thirty-five years it hasn't been in order.* Instead she bit her lip and said quietly, "I double-checked, sir."

With mounting resentment, she watched as he stalked toward the double glass doors and turned down the corridor that led to the conference room of the Gannon Foundation.

He's worried, Esther thought. What's he got to worry about? His funds are all showing an excellent return, but half the time he's in a rotten mood. I'm sick of it, she thought wearily, he's getting worse and worse. With a flash of anger she remembered how Greg's father was barely in his grave twenty-five years ago when Greg announced he was moving the offices of both the investment firm and the foundation to lavish suites on Park Avenue. That was also when he told her that for appearances' sake, it would be better if she always addressed him as "Mr. Gannon," not "Greg."

Now they were in even more lavish suites in the Time Warner Center on Columbus Circle. "Dad was the little man's hero, but no more of the butcher, the baker, and the candlestick maker clients for me," he had said derisively.

Not that it didn't turn out he was right to go after big clients, Esther thought, but he didn't have to be so dismissive of his father. Maybe he's a big success now but it sure doesn't look to me as though he bought himself any happiness with all those mansions of his and his trophy wife. I swear the first words that woman ever uttered were "I WANT." His sons don't even talk to him after the way he treated their mother, and he and his brother are probably fighting at the board meeting right now.

"I'm sick of both of them." Esther did not realize she had spoken aloud. She looked around quickly but of course there was no one in her office. Even so she felt her cheeks redden. One of these days I will say what I think, and that would *not* be smart, she warned herself. Why am I hanging around here? I can afford to retire, and when I sell the apartment, I'll buy a house in Vermont instead of just renting there for a couple of weeks in the summer. The boys love to ski and snowboard. Manchester is a beautiful town and has great skiing nearby . . .

Her lips relaxed into an unconscious smile as she

thought of her sister's teenaged grandchildren whom she loved as if they were her own. No time like the present, she thought as she swiveled her chair to face her computer desk. Her smile widening, she opened a new file, labeled it "Bye-bye Gannons," and started to type: "Dear Mr. Gannon, after thirty-five years I feel it is time. . . ."

The final paragraph read, "If you wish I will be glad to screen possible replacements for my position for one month, unless of course you prefer I leave sooner."

Esther signed the letter, and feeling as if she had lifted a weight from her shoulders, put it in an envelope and at five o'clock placed it on Greg Gannon's desk. She knew that he might stop to check his messages after the board meeting and she wanted him to have a chance to digest the fact of her resignation overnight. He doesn't like change unless he's the one who makes it, she thought, and I don't want him to persuade or bully me into staying longer than a month.

The receptionist was on the phone. Esther waved good-bye to her and went down in the elevator to the lobby floor, trying to decide if she should take time to shop in the gourmet supermarket on the lower level. I don't need anything for tonight, she decided. I'll go straight home.

She walked up Broadway to her apartment building opposite Lincoln Center, quietly enjoying the brisk temperature and the gusts of wind. Living in Vermont in the winter may be too much for some people, but I enjoy cold weather, she thought. I will miss the activity of the city, but that's the way it is.

In her apartment building she stopped at the desk to get her mail. "There are two gentlemen waiting for you, Ms. Chambers," the concierge told her.

Puzzled, Esther looked over at the seating area in the lobby. A dark-haired man, neatly dressed, was walking toward her. Speaking quietly so that the concierge could not hear him, he said, "Ms. Chambers, I'm Thomas Desmond from the Securities and Exchange Commission. My associate and I would like to have a word with you." As he handed her his card, he said, "If possible we would prefer to talk in your apartment, where there's no chance that we might be overheard."

12

Sammy Barber had not become a successful hit man by behaving impulsively.

In the most unobtrusive way possible Sammy began to methodically study the daily pattern of Monica Farrell's comings and goings. Within a few days he was able to establish that she never arrived at the hospital later than 8:30 A.M. and two days out of three returned there at five P.M. Twice she took the Fourteenth Street bus across town from the hospital to her office. The other day she walked in both directions.

She was a fast walker, he noticed, taking long, graceful strides in her low-heeled boots. He doubted that trying to push her in front of an oncoming bus would work. She never stood perched on the edge of the curb, or tried to beat a light as it was turning red.

On Friday morning, at eight o'clock, he was sitting in his car on the opposite side of the street from the converted brownstone where she lived. He had already canvassed the neighborhood and knew that there was a wall about four feet high and a narrow alleyway separating the backyard of her residence from the backyard of the identical brownstone directly behind it. He decided it might be possible to get into her building that way.

When Monica left her apartment at 8:10 Sammy waited until she was safely in a cab, then got out of his car and walked across the street. He was dressed in a hooded ski jacket and wearing dark glasses. Across his chest was a heavy canvas sack with empty boxes protruding from it. He knew that anyone seeing him would think he was a private service messenger.

Averting his face to avoid the security camera, Sammy opened the door into the outer vestibule of Monica's residence. In an instant he learned what he had come to find out. There were eight buzzers with name cards next to each of them. Two apartments to a floor, he thought. Monica Farrell was in 1B. That's got to be the back apartment on this floor. His hands in gloves, he rang the bell of the tenant on the fourth floor, claimed a delivery, and gained entry into the inner hallway. Then, wedging the inner door open with his bag, he immediately called that woman back and claimed he had rung the wrong bell and the delivery was for the tenant in 3B, whose name he read from the card next to that bell.

"Next time be more careful," an annoyed voice told him.

There won't be a next time, Sammy thought as the door closed behind him. Wanting to know the layout of Monica's apartment, he walked noiselessly down the long, narrow hall to 1B. He was about to try his string of master keys to unlock the door when he heard the whine of a vacuum coming from her apartment. Her cleaning woman must be in there, he thought.

Turning swiftly, he retreated down the hallway. The elevator was descending. He did not want to run into a tenant who might remember him. Moving rapidly now, he left the building. He had learned what he needed to know. Monica Farrell lived on the ground floor in the rear. That meant her apartment was the one with the patio, which meant she has a back door. There's no lock I can't open, Sammy thought, and if she has a back window, too, so much the better.

It's the best way to handle it, he thought dispassionately. A burglary attempt gone wrong. Intruder apparently got nervous when Dr. Farrell woke up and saw him. It happens every day.

But as he got back in his car and tossed the delivery bag on the backseat, Sammy's expression became morose. A dedicated Internet researcher, he had printed out all the information he could find on Monica Farrell. It wasn't as if she was a celebrity, but that didn't mean she was just any doctor. She'd written some articles about kids and gotten some awards.

Who'd want to kill her and why? Sammy wondered. Am I doing it too cheap? That was a question that nagged him as he drove to his apartment on the Lower East Side, his eyes burning for sleep. He had worked at his regular job as bouncer from nine P.M. until four A.M., then gone directly to Monica's street on the chance that she might have a middle-of-the-night emergency call.

He'd been prepared for that, with a dark jacket, tie, and limo service ID, figuring that if she did come running out, she might very well take a gypsy limo instead of trying to find a taxi.

I'm covering a lot of bases, Sammy thought. He pulled off his sweatshirt and jeans and threw himself into bed, too tired to undress fully.

13

Cardiologist Dr. Clay Hadley and psychiatrist Dr. Douglas Langdon had gone to medical school together and over the years had kept in close touch. Both in their early fifties, both divorced, and both members of the board of the Gannon Foundation, they had a mutual and very good reason that the foundation should stay in the hands of Greg and Peter Gannon.

As a young doctor, Clay had been introduced to the Gannons by Olivia Morrow's mother, Regina, and had quickly grasped the potential value of developing a strong friendship with Greg and Peter. It was not long before he had ingratiated himself onto the foundation board. Later, it was he who had introduced the Gannons to Langdon and suggested that he would make an ideal replacement when one of old Mr. Gannon's friends retired from the board.

On Friday evening, he and Langdon met for a cocktail in the Hotel Elysée on East Fifty-fourth and chose a quiet corner table where they felt they could talk privately. Visibly nervous, and aware that his habit of running his fingers through his hair often gave him a disheveled appearance, Clay deliberately clasped his hands on the table. He waited impatiently for the waitress to serve their martinis and get out of earshot, then, his voice low but strained, said, "I found out where Olivia went the other day."

His voice equally low, but calm, Langdon asked, "How did you manage that?"

"One of the maintenance staff in her building tipped me off that she'd met a driver in the lobby and was gone most of Tuesday afternoon. He buys the story that I'm very worried about her health, so he was anxious to help me keep tabs on her, but he didn't know where she was going. Then yesterday, I remembered that she always uses one car service and called them. Her driver that day, Tony Garcia, was off until this afternoon and they wouldn't give me his phone number. Today he called me back."

Langdon waited. Impeccably dressed in a charcoal gray suit with faint blue stripes, his dark hair framing his strikingly handsome face, he exuded confidence and an air of calmness and strength. His thinking process was anything but calm, however. Clay may have been the one to tip me off about the granddaughter, but he's not much good at helping to get rid of the old lady, he thought. "And what did the driver tell you?" he asked.

"He said that he had taken Olivia up to Rhinebeck."

Langdon's eyes widened. "Did she go to the motherhouse? Are you telling me she gave the Catherine file to the nuns?"

"No. That's the one good part of it. She only went to

the cemetery where Catherine is buried. That says to me that she's still trying to decide what to do."

"That would have been a very unfortunate development if Olivia Morrow had given the proof to the nuns. Monica Farrell's death, coming on the heels of that discovery, would have seemed too coincidental to any decent investigator. Are you assuming that the file is still in Olivia's safe?" Langdon's voice was now icy.

"She was putting it there when I was in the apartment the other night. Her two best friends died in the past year, so it's not as though there's anyone she would trust with it. My guess is that it's still in the safe."

Langdon was silent for a long minute, then pressed, "You still can't find a way to give Olivia something that would cause her to die at home in your presence?"

"Not yet. Think about the risk. If she has passed on the Catherine file or shown it to anyone, even at her age and state of health the cops might decide to request an autopsy if Monica Farrell is suddenly dead as well. What about that guy you hired?"

"I received a phone call, too. Sammy Barber's price has gone up. It's now one hundred thousand dollars, in cash, up front. As he artlessly expressed it, 'You know I have a reputation as a man who never goes back on his word. But, given the target, I believe that my original fee was, regrettably, much too low.' "

14

Monica had no idea of what kind of living accommodations Ryan Jenner might have. She knew that if he was still paying off college and medical school loans, as most of his peers were, he might be in a small apartment even though he had a good income now. She found herself looking forward to the gathering of friends from Georgetown. Ryan had e-mailed her the details: cocktails seven to eight, then dinner at his local Thai restaurant.

On Friday evening, thanks to several last-minute patients, she did not get home until quarter of seven. Painfully aware that she would be almost an hour late for the party, she took a quick shower, dressed in black silk pants and a fitted white cashmere sweater. Not too dressy, not too casual, she thought. Mascara and lip gloss were her only makeup. She had planned on twisting her hair into a chignon, but after a glance at the clock decided to let it hang loose. If I don't show up by eight, they may think I'm not coming and then leave to go to the restaurant, she thought. I don't even have Ryan's cell number to let them know I'll be late.

That possibility speeding her even more, she stuffed

her mother's black pearls and earrings into her handbag and remembered to check the back door to see that it was bolted. Grabbing a coat, she darted out of her apartment, ran down the hallway, and rushed out of the town house.

"Monica."

At the sound of the familiar voice she whirled around.

It was Scott Alterman.

He was standing on the sidewalk clearly waiting for her. "It's cold," he said. "Let me help you put your coat on. You're beautiful, Monica. Even more beautiful than I remembered."

Monica pulled her coat away as he tried to take it from her. "Scott, you've got to understand something," she said, her voice unsteady from the combination of shock and dismay she felt at his presence. "We're not only finished. We never began. You drove me out of Boston. You are not going to drive me out of New York."

A cab with the available light glowing on its roof was passing. She raised her hand in a futile gesture to stop it.

"I'll drive you, Monica. My car is here."

"Scott, leave me alone!" Monica turned and ran down the street, wishing she had not at the last minute chosen to wear high heels. When she reached First Avenue, she glanced back over her shoulder. Scott had not tried to follow her. He was standing there, his hands in the pockets of the all-weather coat she was sure had been custom-made, his tall, straight body illuminated by the streetlight.

It was five minutes before she could find an empty

cab and it was twenty past eight before she was on her way up in the elevator to Ryan's apartment on West End Avenue. Reassured by the doorman that Dr. Jenner and his friends had not left yet, Monica tried to calm herself down, but could not overcome her dread at what might be coming her way now that Scott had reappeared.

Scott's wife, Joy, had been her best friend from their first day in kindergarten together. They had been like sisters, and as an only child, being so often included in Joy's family activities had given Monica a sense of extended family that had become even more important after her mother's death when she was only ten years old.

Joy had been the one who constantly visited Monica's father at the nursing home in Boston. She and Scott were with him when he died while I was taking final exams, Monica thought. She and Scott helped me make funeral arrangements. Because he's a lawyer, Scott took on settling Dad's affairs. But why in the name of God did he become obsessed with me? Joy blames me, but I know I never for one second encouraged him.

It's like that old joke, "My wife ran off with my best friend and I miss him." Scott destroyed my friendship with Joy and I miss her terribly. Now if he's moved to New York to be near me, what can I do? A restraining order, if it comes to that?

She realized that the slow, creaking elevator had stopped on the ninth floor and the door was open. She managed to step out before the door closed again. I'm lucky I'm not on the way back down to the lobby, she thought. Resolutely she tried to put Scott out of her mind as she scanned the apartment numbers. Ryan had told her that he was in 9E. This way, she decided, and turned left.

The door of the apartment opened the instant she put her finger on the bell. Ryan Jenner's welcoming smile immediately lifted her spirits. He interrupted her apology. "Listen, I've been kicking myself for not getting your cell phone number. Don't worry. I called the restaurant and we pushed the reservation back an hour."

Anything else he might have said was drowned out by the enthusiastic welcoming cries of her Georgetown colleagues. Seeing them again, Monica realized how much she still missed the companionship she had enjoyed in Georgetown. It was eight years of my life, she thought as she hugged her friends. We worked hard those years, but there sure were a lot of good times.

She knew two of the eight visitors, Natalie Kramer and Genine Westervelt, very well. Genine had just opened her private practice as a plastic surgeon in D.C. Natalie was an emergency room doctor. I know them better than I know Ryan, Monica thought, as she settled down in a chair with a glass of wine. He was three years ahead of me, and I never had a class with him, and from a distance he always seemed so reserved. Even now, except when he's wearing scrubs or a white jacket, anytime I run into him he's got a suit and tie on. Tonight, in a corduroy shirt and jeans sitting cross-legged on the floor, a beer in his hand, he looked totally relaxed and was obviously enjoying himself.

She looked at him thoughtfully. His specialty is brain

injury. I wonder what his opinion would be if he saw Michael O'Keefe's CAT scans. Should I ask him to take a look at them before I meet with the priest about that supposed miracle? Maybe I will, she decided.

She glanced around instinctively, hoping to get some overall sense of Ryan Jenner from his surroundings. The room was surprisingly formal, with matching couches in a patterned blue fabric, an antique armoire, side tables with elaborate crystal lamps, occasional chairs in blue and cream, and an antique blue and maroon carpet.

"Ryan, this is a lovely apartment," Genine was saying. "You could put my whole place in this living room. And that's the way it's going to be until I'm off the hook with school loans. By then I'll need to be performing do-it-yourself plastic surgery on my own face."

"Or replacing my own knee," Ira Easton chipped in. "Between Lynn and me, our school loans are matched only by our annual malpractice insurance premiums."

I don't have school loans, Monica thought, but I don't have much else. Dad was sick for so long that I'm lucky to be okay financially.

"First of all," Ryan Jenner was saying. "This is *not* my apartment. It's my aunt's, and everything in it except my toothbrush is hers. She never leaves Florida, and sooner or later she's going to put it on the market. However, in the meantime she invited me to live in it if I keep up with the maintenance expenses, so here we are. I am paying off school loans, too."

"Now we all feel better," Seth Green told him. "Let's go. I'm hungry."

An hour later in the restaurant, the talk turned from the cost of malpractice insurance to the difficulty their various hospitals were having in expanding because of the problems with fund-raising. Ryan had arranged the seating so that he was next to Monica. “I don't know whether you heard,” he said quietly, “but the money Greenwich has been promised for the pediatric wing may not come through. The Gannon Foundation is claiming reduced income and intends to renege on their pledge.”

“Ryan, we *need* that wing,” Monica protested.

“I heard today there's talk of having some people meet with the Gannons and try to get them to change their minds,” Ryan said. “No one's been more persuasive about the pediatric needs at Greenwich than you. You should be there.”

“I'll make sure I am,” Monica said hotly. “That guy Greg Gannon always has his face in the Sunday *Times* as a major-league philanthropist. My dad was a research consultant at a Gannon lab in Boston for a few years before he died. It was the patents on the orthopedic parts that gave the Gannons their money. He said they collected zillions of dollars over the life of the patents. They pledged fifteen million to the hospital. Now let them pay up.”

15

Wrapped in a bathrobe, Rosalie Garcia woke her sleeping husband up at six A.M. on Monday. "Tony, the baby has a fever. He's caught my cold."

Tony struggled to open his eyes. The night before, he had driven a couple to a wedding in Connecticut, and then waited to drive them home, which meant he'd had three hours' sleep. But as what Rosalie was saying sank in, he was instantly awake. Tossing back the covers, he rushed into the tiny second bedroom of their walk-up apartment on East Fourth Street. A sleepy Carlos, his face flushed, ignoring his bottle, was fretfully moving around the crib. With a gentle hand, Tony touched his son's forehead and confirmed that it was unnaturally warm.

He straightened up and turned to his wife, understanding the panic he saw in her eyes. "Look, Rosie," he said soothingly. "He doesn't have leukemia anymore. Remember that. We'll get some aspirin into him and at eight o'clock we'll call Dr. Monica. If she wants to see him, I'll take him right over. With that cold you can't go out."

"Tony, I want her to see him. Maybe it's just a cold but . . ."

"Honey, she told us that we should remember to treat him as a kid who bumps his head or gets a cold or has an earache, because he is a normal, healthy kid now. His immune system is perfect." But even as he was speaking, Tony knew that neither he nor Rosalie would have any peace of mind until Dr. Monica Farrell had seen Carlos.

At seven o'clock he phoned and reached Nan as she was walking into the office. She told him to bring Carlos over at eleven, because that was when the doctor would be back from the hospital.

At ten thirty Tony bundled a sleepy Carlos into a warm jacket and cap and put him in his stroller. He tucked blankets around him, then snapped in the protective plastic shield that kept out the wind. With long strides he began to walk the ten blocks to Monica's office. He had vetoed the suggestion that he take a cab there. "Rosie," he had said, "I can get there faster walking, and round-trip in the traffic it could cost up to thirty dollars. Besides, Carlos likes the feel of being pushed in the stroller. He'll end up taking a nap."

When he reached Monica's office twenty minutes later, she was just taking off her coat. She took one look at the fear in Tony's eyes, then quickly unsnapped the plastic shield and, as Tony had done earlier, felt the small forehead of Carlos Garcia. "Tony, he has a fever, but not much of a fever," she said reassuringly. "Before we even get his hat off, let me assure you of that. Alma will get Carlos set up for me to look at him, but my diagnosis as of this moment is that all he needs is an antibiotic." She smiled. "So stop looking like that and don't have a heart attack on me. I'm a pediatrician, not a cardiologist."

Tony Garcia smiled back as he tried to blink away the sudden moisture in his eyes. "It's just, Doctor . . . You know."

Monica looked at him and suddenly felt infinitely older than the young father. He's not more than twenty-four, she thought. He looks like such a kid himself and so does Rosalie and they've gone through such hell these two years. She touched his shoulder. "I know," she said gently.

Thirty minutes later, Carlos, again dressed in his outerwear, was back in the stroller. Tony had samples of an antibiotic and a prescription for a three-day dosage of it in his pocket. "Now remember," Monica cautioned, as she walked with him to the outer door, "I can just about promise you he'll be running you ragged again in a couple of days, but if his fever *does* go up I want you to call me on my cell phone day or night."

"I will, Dr. Monica, and thanks again. I can't tell . . ."

"Then don't. I can't hear you anyhow." Monica nodded her head to the waiting room, which now had four little patients, among them a pair of screaming twins.

Tony, his hand on the outer door, stopped. "Oh, just quick, Dr. Monica. I drove a very nice elderly woman last week. I showed her Carlos's picture and told her how you had taken care of him and she told me she knew your grandmother."

"She knew my grandmother!" Monica looked at him astonished. "Did she say anything about her?"

"No. Just that she knew her." Tony pulled open the outer door. "I'm holding you up. Thanks again."

He was gone. Monica was tempted to run after him but then stopped herself. I can call him later, she thought. Could this person possibly have known my paternal grandmother? Dad didn't have a clue who his birth mother was. He was adopted by people in their midforties. They've been gone for years and so are Mom's parents. Dad and Mom would both be in their midseventies now. If their parents were still alive they'd be over 100 years old. If this lady knew my adoptive grandparents she must be really old herself. She must be mistaken.

But all through the rest of her busy day, Monica had a nagging sense that she ought to call Tony and ask for the name of the woman who had claimed to know her grandmother.

16

Sammy Barber had used the weekend to do some serious thinking. The guy he was dealing with was big-time. When he'd arranged the meeting in the diner, he had not given his name, only his cell phone number, and of course that was one of those prepaid untraceable ones. But it was obvious he wasn't used to making this kind of deal. The stupid guy drove to the diner in his own car and thought he was being smart by parking it down the block!

Sammy had followed him and used the camera on his cell phone to photograph Douglas Langdon's license plate, then, through one of his contacts, traced down his name.

He had not told Langdon that he knew who he was when he had called to raise the price for the hit on Dr. Farrell because he had wanted to decide his next step first. When he had called Langdon, Sammy had phoned the cell number he had been given. But over the weekend, Langdon had ignored his demand, so Sammy knew exactly what he would do next.

Langdon was a shrink, but better than that he was on the board of the Gannon Foundation and that was worth millions and millions of dollars. If he was desperate enough to order a hit on that doctor, he must be in big trouble, Sammy reasoned. He ought to be able to dip into that foundation and get a million-dollar grant approved for Sammy Barber's favorite charity. Meaning myself. Of course, it wouldn't be put that way. Langdon could skim a million off a legit grant. It must happen all the time.

Sammy bitterly regretted that he had not taped his meeting with Langdon, but he was sure he could make Langdon think he had. And of course at their next face-to-face meeting he would be sure that a tape was running.

On Monday morning at eleven o'clock, Sammy showed up in the lobby of the Park Avenue building where Douglas Langdon's office was located. When the security desk phoned to confirm his appointment, Langdon's secretary, Beatrice Tillman, emphatically said, "I have no record of an appointment with Mr. Barber."

When the person at the desk passed the word to Sammy, it was the response he was expecting. "She doesn't know that the doctor talked to me over the weekend and told me to come in. I'll wait till he's available." He saw the mistrust in the security officer's eyes. Even though he'd worn his new jacket and slacks and his one tie, he was fully aware that he didn't have the look of someone who had thousands of bucks to throw away on a shrink.

The guard gave that message to Tillman, waited, then

put the phone down and reached for a pass. He scribbled Langdon's name and suite number and handed it to Sammy. "The doctor isn't expected for another fifteen minutes, but you can go upstairs and wait for him."

"Thanks." Sammy took the pass and sauntered over to the elevator bank, where another guard allowed him to go through the turnstile. Mickey Mouse security here, he decided disdainfully.

Nice offices, though, he thought when he entered suite 1202. Not big, but nice. It was clear that the shrink's secretary still wasn't sure if she bought his story but she asked him to sit down in the reception area near her desk. Sammy took care to settle himself so that Langdon would not see him when he opened the door.

Ten minutes later Langdon came in. Sammy watched as he started to greet the secretary, who interrupted him and, her voice too low for Sammy to hear, said something to him. Langdon turned and Sammy chortled to himself at the look of sheer panic that crossed his face.

He stood up. "Good morning, Doctor. It's really nice of you to see me on such short notice and I do appreciate it. You know how sometimes my head gets all messed up."

"Come in, Sammy," Langdon said abruptly.

With a cheerful wave at Beatrice Tillman, whose face was a study in curiosity, Sammy followed the doctor down the hall into what he guessed was his private office. It was carpeted in deep crimson. The walls were lined with mahogany bookshelves. A handsome leather-topped desk dominated the room. A wide leather swivel chair was behind it. Two matching chairs finished in a red and cream fabric faced the desk.

"No couch?" Sammy asked, his tone bewildered.

Langdon was closing the door. "You don't need a couch, Sammy," he snapped. "What are you doing here?"

Without being invited, Sammy walked around the desk to the swivel chair and sat down on it. "Doug, I made you an offer and you didn't get back to me. I don't like to be disrespected."

"You agreed to a twenty-five-thousand-dollar price and raised it to one hundred thousand," a shaken Langdon reminded him.

"Twenty-five thousand for murdering Dr. Monica Farrell isn't very much, I figure," Sammy commented. "She's not like some intern nobody ever heard of. She's what would you say . . . distinguished?"

"You agreed to that price," Langdon said, and now Sammy could hear the panic he'd expected in Langdon's tone.

"But you didn't get back to me," Sammy reminded him. "So that's why the price has gone up again. It's now one million, payable in advance."

"You've got to be crazy," Langdon whispered.

"I'm not," Sammy assured him. "I taped you the other night in the diner and I'm taping you now." He opened his jacket and exposed the wire he had attached to his cell phone. With a slow, deliberate movement he buttoned his jacket and got up. "What you or someone you know has on me wouldn't mean much if it came to a trial. The cops would drop that charge in a minute in exchange for this tape and the other one. Now listen real carefully. I want one million dollars, then I do the job. I've figured out how to make it look like a burglary gone sour. So get the money, and you can sleep at night. You have to be smart enough to know that when the job is done, I won't be sending any tapes to the cops."

He got up, brushed past Langdon, and put his hand on the doorknob. "Have it by Friday," he said, "or I go to the police myself." He opened the door. "Thank you, Doctor," he said, in a voice loud enough that he hoped the secretary could hear. "You've been a big help. Like you say, I can't blame all my problems on my old lady. She did her best for me."

17

Esther Chambers had had a dismal weekend. Her visit from Thomas Desmond of the Securities and Exchange Commission and his partner had thoroughly unsettled her. When she had found them waiting for her in her lobby on Wednesday evening, she had allowed them to come up to her apartment as Desmond had requested.

There, in the privacy of her home, he had told her that her boss had been watched for some time by the SEC and that criminal charges against him for insider trading might be forthcoming.

He had also told her that she had been thoroughly checked and that her finances had shown that in no way was she living beyond her income, so they felt confident that she was not engaged in any illegal activities. They told her that they wanted her to work with them and provide them with information about Greg's business dealings. They stressed that confidentiality was of the utmost importance and that she would almost certainly be called to testify before a Grand Jury.

"I simply cannot believe that Greg Gannon would be guilty of insider trading," she had told Desmond. "Why should he? The investment firm has always been very successful, and for years he's received a big salary as chairman of the board of the Gannon Foundation."

"It's not a case of how much he has, but how much he *wants*," Desmond told her. "We've had multimillionaires who couldn't spend all their legitimate money in a lifetime, and still they cheat. Some of them do it because it gives them a sense of power. But in the end, before they get caught, most of them are running scared."

Running scared. Those words convinced Esther that it wasn't all some kind of mistake. Greg Gannon *is* running scared, she thought.

Desmond had not been happy to learn that she had just submitted her resignation. He'd asked her if she could rescind it, then corrected himself. "No, I don't think that's a good idea. My bet is that right now he's afraid to trust anybody. He might see a sudden change of heart as a tip that we've approached you. You say you offered to stay for one month?"

"Yes."

"Then my guess is that he'll take you up on it. He's in deep trouble now. One of his big tips about a merger didn't go through at the last minute. He lost a quarter of a billion for one of his hedge funds. He won't want to worry about breaking in someone new right now."

And that's the way it's turning out, Esther thought on Monday morning. When Greg had seen her note on Thursday morning, he had come out to her desk. "Esther, I'm not surprised that you're ready to retire. Thirty-five years is a heck of a long time to keep working in one place. But I do want you to stay for at least one month and do the interviewing for your replacement, then when you find someone, break her in." He paused. "Or him," he added.

"I know we're not gender-conscious. I'll find someone good to replace me, I promise," Esther said.

For a moment, watching the troubled face of Greg Gannon, Esther's heart had softened, seeing in it the ambitious young man who had joined his father's business a week after his graduation from college. But then any pity she felt evaporated. With all that he had, if he really was cheating, he was doing it for himself, and gambling with other people's hard-earned money, she thought scornfully.

Thomas Desmond had asked her to copy him on Greg's appointments. "We need to know who he's wining and dining," Desmond had said. "I doubt they're all in his official appointment book. We know some of his calls go through your office phones, but not all of them. We've wiretapped the people we suspect of tipping him off to mergers and acquisitions but all those calls that Gannon made to our other targets were on prepaid phones. Fortunately some of the guys who are passing on tips aren't smart enough to use the phones we can't trace."

"Many of Greg's calls don't come through me," Esther had agreed. "Obviously he has a cell phone, but I pay the bills for it and it's all routine stuff. But there are plenty of times when I try to pass on a business call to him in his private office and he doesn't pick up. I'm supposed to assume that he's on with the family or personal friends, but it happens so often he couldn't just be on his regular cell phone."

Acutely aware that she had promised Thomas Desmond that she would provide evidence regarding Greg Gannon's business activities, including his lunches with clients, Esther said, "Mr. Gannon, I've got you down for lunch with Arthur Saling. Shall I make a reservation for you?"

"No, Saling wanted me to meet him at his club. He's a potential new client and a big one. Keep your fingers crossed." Gannon turned to go back into his own office. "Hold all calls until I let you know, Esther."

"Of course, Mr. Gannon."

For the rest of the morning it was business as usual. Then Esther received a call from Greenwich Village Hospital. It was from the executive director of development. This time she heard and understood the lack of cordiality that had previously been present in his voice. "Esther, this is Justin Banks from Greenwich Village Hospital. As you certainly must understand we are planning to break ground for the new Gannon Pediatric Wing. The pledge the foundation made has been overdue for six months and quite frankly it is absolutely necessary that it be fulfilled now."

Dear God, Esther thought, Greg made that pledge almost two years ago. Why hasn't it been paid? Carefully she chose her words. "Let me look into it," she said, her voice professionally calm.

"Esther, that isn't good enough." His voice was rising. "The word is getting around that the Gannon Foundation is announcing grants that it has no intention of fulfilling, or at least not fulfilling until they have been so watered down that the purpose for receiving them is defeated. I and several of my associates insist on having a meeting with Mr. Gannon and with anyone and everyone on the foundation board. We want to tell them they simply can't do this to the children we serve and hope to serve in the future."

18

Monday afternoon, after his first day at his prestigious new law firm, Scott Alterman went for a run in Central Park. Over the weekend, he had been constantly berating himself. It had been a stupid and serious mistake to show up at the brownstone where Monica lived. He had startled her, maybe even frightened her, and that was not the way he intended to pursue her.

He knew that four years ago he had come on much too strongly to her and should have had the brains to realize that Monica would never even *think* of dating her best friend's husband.

But now Joy and I are totally split, he thought, as he jogged through Central Park, enjoying the crisp autumn breezes. It was an amicable divorce and Joy even admits that getting married six months after we met was crazy. We didn't really know each other. She came to work for the firm fresh out of law school and before it made sense I had bought her a ring and we'd made a down payment on a co-op facing the Common.

It's one of the reasons we put off having a family, he reflected, as he began to build his case to present to Monica. Joy realizes now that it was hurt pride that made her so adamant about trying to save our marriage. It didn't do any good, of course. Three long years of being in counseling and trying to make it work were a waste. But I knew I'd never have any chance with Monica until Joy agreed that the marriage was hopeless. Now Joy admits that she never really believed Monica had been seeing me on the side. In the year we've been split both of us have been much happier . . .

I wonder if I could get Joy to call Monica and explain that to her? Joy even said that I was more than generous in the settlement, turning over the condo and all the furniture to her. The paintings, too. They're worth a lot more than when I bought them. I have an eye for good art. I'll start a new collection.

Joy has the condo, a healthy bank account, a good job. Before I told my partners I was leaving I asked them to consider making her a partner and I think they may do it. She's grateful to me for that, but she's also a darn good lawyer and deserves it. I know she's happy that I've left the firm. She doesn't want to run into me every day. I've heard that she's been dating different people, which is all to the good. God bless my successor.

Scott had started his run on the West Ninety-sixth Street entrance to Central Park. He'd gone south to Fifty-ninth Street, then up the east side of the park to 110th Street, then down on the west side back to Ninety-sixth Street. With a glow of satisfaction at how easily he had handled the run, he returned to his rented apartment, showered, changed, then, sipping a scotch, settled in a chair that overlooked the park.

Even without Monica in the equation I was happy to make the move, he thought. There's more visibility for a trial lawyer in Manhattan than in Boston.

Monica. As always, when he allowed himself to think about her, her face in every detail filled his mind. Especially, he thought, those incredible blue-green eyes that had looked so warm and loving when she told Joy and him how much their kindness to her father in the nursing home meant to her, and how she hoped that someday she would meet someone exactly like Scott. But those eyes had withered him with scorn when he had been fool enough to ask her to have dinner with him alone.

Scott did not like to remember how dumb he had been to keep calling her, thinking she would change her mind. But she did have some feelings for me, he told himself. I *know* she did, he thought defensively.

When did I fall in love with Monica? When did I stop seeing her as Joy's best friend and start looking at her as a desirable woman, the woman I wanted to spend the rest of my life with?

Why didn't I tell her to listen to her father's suspicions about his parentage? She saw the photos her father had compared and immediately dismissed them. "Dad always tried to find his birth parents, Scott," she had said. "He always used to point to a photo in the newspaper of someone whom he resembled, and wonder whether it was his own father. It was a sad, running joke. His need to know was so great, and of course never satisfied."

Scott felt his sense of well-being begin to slip away.

There has to be a way to trace Edward Farrell's birth parents. The resemblance between him and Alexander Gannon is absolutely startling. Gannon never married, but in 1935, he wrote a will which never mentioned a wife, but significantly left his estate first to his issue if any existed, and only then to his brother. There's a good chance her father was right about his suspicions. Maybe telling that to Monica is the way to get her to see me. I want to marry Monica, but if that doesn't happen, he thought ruefully, second best would be to represent her in court. As her lawyer, I'd receive a healthy percentage of any money she received.

Scott cast a disdainful eye on the serviceable but ordinary furniture in his rented co-op. I've got to get busy finding a place I want to buy, he thought, a place where Monica might want to live someday.

It isn't just about the money in the Gannon Foundation that may be hers. I want her and I want everything for her.

19

On Monday evening, retired detective John Hartman phoned his neighbor Nan Rhodes. By now he knew that she sometimes met her sisters on Monday evenings, but he wasn't sure whether it was a weekly commitment.

A childless widower who had been the only child of two only children, Hartman, despite his wide circle of friends, often regretted that he had not been born into a large family. Tonight for some reason, he felt particularly down and was immeasurably cheered when at seven thirty Nan answered her phone on the first ring.

At his suggestion that he half expected her to be at dinner with her siblings, Nan laughed. "We meet once a month," she told him. "Weekly, and we'd probably be resuming old battles like 'Remember when you wore my new sweater before I even had a chance to wear it myself?' It's better this way."

"I've kept the picture of Dr. Farrell longer than I intended," he said. "The fingerprints on it don't match any known felon. Shall I slip it under your door?" Why did I make that suggestion? he asked himself. Why didn't I ask if I could drop it off?

He was delighted to hear Nan's response. "I just

made a pot of tea and sinful as it's now considered, I bought a chocolate layer cake at the bakery. Why don't you just come in and sit down for a few minutes and share it with me?"

Not realizing that Nan was at once shocked at her invitation to him and pleased that he had accepted it, Hartman hastily grabbed a freshly cleaned cardigan from his closet and buttoned it over his casual shirt. Five minutes later he was sitting opposite Nan at her dinette table.

As she poured tea and sliced a generous piece of cake for him, he decided that he would not hand over the picture immediately. He found himself savoring the warmth that emanated from Nan Rhodes. He knew she had a son. Always ask about the offspring, he told himself. "Nan, how is your son doing?"

Her eyes lit up. "I just got a new picture of him with his wife, Sharon, and the baby." Nan rushed to get the picture, and when she returned and he had made the appropriate comments, they began to talk about her family. Then the normally reserved John Hartman found himself telling her about his experience of growing up as an only child and how as a kid he already knew that someday he would be a detective.

It was only after the second cup of tea and a small second slice of chocolate cake that he pulled the envelope with the photograph of Monica holding the Garcia baby from his pocket. "Nan," he said soberly. "I'm a pretty good detective, and when I was working I would get a hunch about a case and many times I was on target. As I told you when I phoned, whoever was holding that picture has no known past history of crime. But that doesn't mean that there isn't something very wrong about the fact this picture exists and that Dr. Farrell's two addresses are on it."

"As I told you last week, that was my hunch, too, John," Nan said. She reached for the envelope, took the picture out, studied it, then turned it over to read again the block printing with Monica's addresses. "I have to show it to her," she said reluctantly. "She might be annoyed that I didn't give it to her last week, but that's a chance I have to take."

"I walked over to the hospital the other day," John said. "I took some pictures from across the street to try to get the same angle of the steps and hospital that we see in this one. I think whoever took that picture was sitting in a car."

"Do you mean someone might have been waiting for Dr. Monica to come out?" Now Nan's voice was incredulous.

"It's possible. Do you remember if anyone phoned last Monday to ask about her schedule?"

Nan frowned as she tried to sort out the myriad of calls that came into the office. "I'm not sure," she said slowly. "But it isn't unusual for someone like a pharmacist to phone and ask when the doctor is expected in. I wouldn't even have noticed that as being unusual."

"What would you have said if you had been called about her schedule last Monday?"

"I would have said that she'd be in around noon.

There are often staff meetings at the hospital on Monday mornings and I don't schedule anything at the office for her until one o'clock."

"What time did she step out of the hospital with the Garcias to take that picture?"

"I don't know."

"When you give it to the doctor, please ask her what time it was."

"All right." Nan realized her throat was dry. "You really think that someone is stalking her, don't you?"

"Maybe stalking is too strong a word. I checked on Scott Alterman, the ex-boyfriend, or whatever he was to the doctor. He's a well-known, well-respected lawyer in Boston, recently divorced, and moved to Manhattan only last week to join a big-shot law firm on Wall Street. But he wasn't the one who took the picture. Last Monday his firm had a farewell luncheon for him at the Ritz-Carlton in Boston and he was there."

"Could he have had someone else take the picture for him?"

"He could have. But I doubt it. That doesn't have the ring of truth to me." Hartman pushed back his chair. "Nan, thanks for the hospitality. The cake was delicious and every time I have tea brewed in a teapot, I promise myself I'll never use a tea bag again."

Nan stood up with him. "I'll be very aware of anyone phoning to try to get the doctor's schedule," she said, then brightened. "Oh, I have to tell you something interesting. The Garcia baby, the one who recovered from leukemia, was in today. Just a cold, but you can understand the concern of the parents. Tony Garcia, the father, works part-time as a driver. He told Dr. Monica that an elderly lady he drove last week claimed to know the doctor's grandmother. Dr. Monica told me she thought it had to be a mistake, because she never knew her grandparents, but I couldn't resist following up. I called Tony and he gave me the lady's name. It's Olivia Morrow, and she lives on Riverside Drive. I gave it to Dr. Monica and urged her to give the lady a call. As I told her, 'What have you got to lose?' "

20

In his office near Shubert Alley, in the theatre district of Manhattan, Peter Gannon stood up from his desk and pushed aside the sheets of paper that were littered over it. He walked across the room to the wall of bookshelves and reached for his copy of *Webster's Encyclopedic Unabridged Dictionary*. He wanted to look up the exact definition of the word "carnage."

"carnage (kar'nij)," he read, "n. 1 the slaughter of a great number of men as in battle; butchery; massacre; 2 archaic, dead bodies as of men slain in battle."

"That about defines it," he said aloud, although he was alone in the room. Slaughter and butchery by the critics. Massacre by the audience. And dead bodies of all the actors, musicians, and crew who worked their hearts out to have a big hit.

He replaced the heavy dictionary, sat at his desk again, and put his head in his hands. I was so sure that this one would work, he thought. I was so sure of it I even promised to personally guarantee half the investment some of the big-bucks guys put in it. How am I supposed to do that now? The patent income has been finished for years, and the foundation is too heavily committed. I told Greg that I thought Clay and Doug were pushing too hard for those mental health and cardiac research grants, but he told me to mind my own business, that I was getting plenty for my theatre projects. How do I tell them that I need more now? A *lot* more!

Too restless to stay seated, he stood up again. The musical extravaganza had opened and closed last Monday night. A week later, he was still adding up the cost of the debacle. One critic had written, "Producer Peter Gannon has effectively presented small dramas, suitable for off-Broadway, but his third attempt at a musical is once again a resounding failure. Give it up, Peter."

Give it up, Peter, he thought, as he opened the small refrigerator behind his desk and took out a bottle of vodka. Not too much, he cautioned himself, as he unscrewed the bottle and reached for a stem glass from the tray on top of the refrigerator. I know I've been drinking too much, I know it.

After he had poured a moderate amount of vodka into the glass and added ice cubes, he replaced the bottle, closed the refrigerator, and sat down again. Then he leaned back in his chair. Or maybe I *should* turn into a drunk, he thought. Blotto. Out of it. Not able to string two sentences together. Not able to think, but able to sleep, even if it's a drunken sleep that ends in a blinding headache.

He took a long sip of the vodka and with his free hand reached for the phone. Susan, his ex-wife, had left a message telling him how sorry she was that the play had closed. Any other ex would have been thrilled that it flopped, he thought, but Sue meant it.

Sue. One more constant regret. Forget about calling her. It's too painful.

As he was withdrawing his hand, the phone rang. When the caller's number came up, he was tempted to pretend he wasn't in his office. Knowing that would solve nothing, he picked up the receiver and mumbled a greeting.

"I expected to hear from you before this," a querulous voice told him.

"I meant to call you. It's been pretty hectic."

"I don't mean a phone call. I mean my payment. You're overdue."

"I . . . just . . . don't . . . have . . . that . . . much now," Peter whispered, his voice strangled.

"Then . . . get . . . it . . . or . . . else."

The phone slammed in his ear.

21

When she woke up on Tuesday morning, Olivia Morrow felt as if a quantity of her small stockpile of remaining energy had disappeared while she was sleeping. For some odd reason, a scene from *Little Women*, a book she had loved as a young teenager, became fresh in her mind. Beth, the nineteen-year-old who is dying of tuberculosis, tells her older sister that she knows she will not get well, that the tide is going out.

The tide is going out for me, too, Olivia thought. If Clay is right, and my body is telling me he is right, I have less than a week to live.

What shall I do?

Pulling on her reserve of strength, she got up slowly, put on a robe, and made her way to the kitchen. As she walked the short distance she was too exhausted to reach for the kettle and sat on a chair in the dining alcove until her breath became stronger. Catherine, she begged, give me direction. Let me know what you want me to do.

After a few minutes she was able to get up, make the tea, and plan her day. I want to go back to Southhampton, she thought. I wonder if the Gannon House is still there, and the cottage where Catherine and Mother and I lived . . .

The cemetery in Southhampton was where generations of Gannons were entombed in an imposing mausoleum. Where Alex was entombed. Not that I have the feeling that he'll be waiting for me on the other side, she thought sadly. Catherine was his love, but when she died she certainly wasn't looking to be reunited with him.

Or was she?

A childhood memory that had been coming to the surface of her mind over and over in these past few days once again filled her mind. Am I making this up, or did I witness it? she wondered. Is my mind playing tricks or am I remembering seeing Catherine in her habit shortly after she entered the convent? I thought the novices were not allowed to see their families for a while. It was on a dock, and there was another nun with her. Catherine and Mother were crying. That must have been when she sailed to Ireland . . .

Why does that suddenly seem so important to know? she asked herself. Or is it that I am trying to reject death by dragging up scenes from my childhood, as if I could begin to relive my life?

She would call the car service and go out to Southhampton today. Even in a few days it may be too late, she thought. I wonder if I can get that nice young man who drove me last week? What was his name? Yes, I remember. It was Tony Garcia.

She finished sipping the tea and debated about forcing herself to have a slice of toast, then decided against it. I'm not hungry, she thought, and at this point what is the difference if I eat or don't eat?

She got up slowly and carried the cup to the sink, rinsed it out, and put it in the dishwasher, suddenly acutely aware that this kind of mundane activity would soon be over forever.

In the bedroom she called the car service and was disappointed to learn that Tony Garcia was not coming in today.

"He's supposed to be available," an aggravated voice told her. "But he phoned to say that his wife and kid are sick and he has to stay home."

"Oh, I am sorry," Olivia said quickly. "It's not serious, is it? He told me about his little boy having had leukemia."

"Nah. It's just a bad cold. I swear if that kid gets sniffles, Tony makes a big deal about it."

"In his case, I would, too," Olivia responded, an edge in her voice.

"Yeah, of course, Ms. Morrow. I'll send a good driver for you."

At noon the driver, a heavyset man with a windburned face, appeared in the lobby. This time she was already there waiting for him. Unlike Tony Garcia, he did not offer her his arm on the way to the garage. But he did tell her that he knew she was a good customer and that everyone said what a nice lady she was and if she wanted anything like to stop on the way to Southhampton if she needed a restroom, just say the word.

She had fully intended to ask him to take the tote bag with the Catherine file from under the blanket in the trunk, but decided against it.

I know by heart those letters Catherine wrote to Mother, she thought. I can read them in my mind. And I don't want this man to get them out, then put them back in the trunk later. He's obviously already discussed me with other people.

And why am I hiding the file? What is the point?

She had no answer, only an instinct to leave it in the trunk for the present.

It was one of those unexpectedly warm October days with the sun high and bright, and puffs of clouds drifting through a tranquil sky. But even though she had worn a warm cape over her suit, Olivia felt chilled. When they were on the way across town she asked the driver to slide back the cover of the overhead glass panel so that the filtered sun could warm the backseat of the car.

What was that prayer or psalm her mother kept at her bedside in her last year? It began "When in death my limbs are failing . . ." Maybe I'd better look it up and start reciting it, she thought. I know it gave Mother comfort.

With the heavy traffic it took nearly half an hour to get to the Midtown Tunnel. Olivia found herself looking with new eyes at storefronts and restaurants, remembering the times she had either shopped or eaten in one or the other of them.

But after they had gone through the tunnel and were on the Long Island Expressway the drive seemed to go quickly. As they passed the various towns Olivia found herself reminiscing over friends long gone. Lillian lived in Syosset . . . Beverly had that beautiful house in Manhasset . . .

"I don't have the street address in Southhampton," the driver said as they approached the town.

Olivia recited it to him and just doing so brought back the scent of the salt water that had wafted into her room in the cottage. Even the cottage faced the ocean, she thought. And the Gannon House was so beautiful, with the wraparound porch. The Gannons always dressed for dinner.

Another memory. Catherine walking on the beach, barefoot, her long hair swirling behind her. I know I'm right. I was standing there. It must have been shortly before she left for the convent. Then Alex came up behind her and put his arms around her . . .

Olivia closed her eyes. So much is coming back to me, she thought. Does this happen to everyone who is dying?

She wasn't sure if she had dozed, because it seemed only a moment later that the driver was opening the door for her. "We're here, Ms. Morrow."

"Oh, I'm not getting out. I just wanted to see the house again. When I was a young child I lived here." She looked beyond him and saw immediately that the property had been subdivided and the cottage was gone, replaced by an imposing mansion. But the Gannon home was just as she remembered it. Now it was painted a soft yellow that enhanced its century-old beauty. Olivia could visualize Alex's mother and father on the porch, greeting people who came to one of their frequent gatherings.

The name GANNON was on the mailbox. So they still own it, she thought. It must have been left to Alex as the older son. That means the rightful owner is Alex's granddaughter, Monica Farrell.

"You lived in this house, Ms. Morrow?" the driver asked, his tone alive with curiosity.

"No, I lived in a cottage that is no longer here. I have one more stop to make." I went to Catherine's grave looking for an answer, she thought, and didn't get one. Maybe I'll be able to come to a decision if I stop at the cemetery and visit the Gannon mausoleum. Alex is there.

But when the driver parked in front of the mausoleum she was too tired to leave the car, let alone wrestle with her conscience. The only emotion she felt was her sense of profound loss that Alex had never loved her. We began to have dinner after we met at his father's funeral. We saw each other regularly for six months. She remembered again his shock and astonishment when she had asked him to marry her. He had said, "Olivia, you will always be my dear friend. But there will never be anything more between us."

That was the last time I saw him, she thought. It hurt too much to be around him. That was more than forty years ago! I didn't even attend his funeral Mass. Alex chose a lifetime alone rather than share any part of it with another woman, even one who loved him as passionately as I did.

She stared at the Gannon name over the door of the mausoleum. Someday in the distant future, here is the rightful resting place for Monica Farrell, she thought. Her grandparents and her great-grandparents are lying here.

But that doesn't mean I have the right to break Mother's promise to Catherine, she reminded herself. I would never have learned the truth if Mother had not revealed it when she was heavily medicated.

She had come out here looking for guidance and there was none. All the journey had done was to dredge up painful memories. "I guess it's time to get started," she told the driver. I'm sure this visit will be talked about where he works, she thought. Well, in another week or so, they'll understand to some extent why I'm here. My farewell pilgrimage.

When she arrived home Olivia undressed and went straight to bed. Too weary to even think about preparing food, her only thought was that she still had no resolution to the decision she needed to make immediately.

Her eyes began to close. The ringing of the phone was an unwelcome distraction. She was tempted to ignore it, but then realized it might be Clay Hadley. Her failure to pick up at this time would almost surely mean that he would call the concierge, verify that she was home, then come running over.

Sighing, Olivia fumbled for the receiver and picked it up.

"Ms. Morrow?"

It was an unfamiliar voice. A woman's voice.

"Ms. Morrow, I'm probably wasting your time. My name is Monica Farrell. I'm a pediatrician. You had a driver last week whose little boy is my patient. The driver, Tony Garcia, happened to mention that you said you knew my grandmother. Was he mistaken?"

Catherine's granddaughter is calling me, Olivia thought. It was just after I left Catherine's grave that I told Tony Garcia I knew Monica's grandmother and he told her. Catherine *has* sent me a sign.

Her voice trembling, she answered. "Yes. I knew her very well and I want to tell you about her. It is very important that you know everything before it is too late. Can you come and visit me tomorrow?"

"Not until late afternoon. I have office hours in the morning, then I have an appointment in New Jersey I cannot break. I'm sure I could be at your apartment by five o'clock at the latest."

"That will be fine. Oh, Monica, I'm so glad you called. Did Tony give you my address?"

"Yes, I have it. Ms. Morrow, one question. Are we talking about the woman who was my father's adoptive mother, or about my maternal grandmother?"

"I'm talking about your father's birth parents, your flesh-and-blood grandparents. Monica, I am very tired. I have been out all day. Tomorrow I will be sure to rest. I look forward so much to seeing you."

Olivia broke the connection. She knew how close she was to tears and she didn't want Monica to hear them in her voice.

She closed her eyes and fell asleep immediately. She

was dreaming of the moment when she would meet the young woman who was the grandchild of Catherine and Alex when the phone rang again.

This time it was Clay Hadley.

Still half asleep, Olivia said, "Oh, Clay, I'm so happy. Monica Farrell called me. Can you believe it? She called me! It's a sign. I'm going to tell her everything. It's such a relief to be sure, isn't it? Now I'm content to die."

22

Stunned at what Olivia Morrow had told her, Monica put down the phone and sat at the desk in her small private office, her mind jumping.

Does she mean what she told me, that she knew Daddy's *birth* parents? She sounds old, and even feeble. Maybe she's confused? But if she *did* know them and could tell me who they were, it would be so wonderful. Dad spent his life longing to discover the truth about his background. He said he wouldn't care if his blood relatives had been drunks or cheats, just to learn who they were would be enough.

Maybe tomorrow by this time I'll know, she thought. I wonder if I have any cousins or extended family? I'd love that . . .

Monica pushed back her desk chair and stood up. I wish I didn't have to go and testify at that beatification hearing tomorrow. Dad was a devout Catholic and I know my mother was, too. I remember the three of us in church every Sunday, as regular as clockwork. I'm of the generation that drifted away from it, although I do go to Mass sometimes. Dad said they had made it too easy for all of us. "You guys have the idea that if you want to go out on a rowboat and pray on Sunday mornings, that will be just fine," he told me. "Well, it's not fine."

Ryan Jenner had promised to stop by and look at the Michael O'Keefe file at seven o'clock. It was seven now. That thought made Monica hurry into the small staff bathroom and look in the mirror. Other than a touch of lip gloss and a dab of powder, she never wore makeup during the day. But now she found herself opening the cabinet and reaching for foundation and mascara.

It's been another long day, she thought. It's time to give my face a little pickup. After she applied the foundation, she decided she might as well go for it, and added a light eye shadow. Then remembering Ryan's remark about liking to see her hair loose, she pulled out the pins holding it up.

This is ridiculous, she told herself. He's coming to look at Michael O'Keefe's medical history and MRIs and CAT scans, and I'm letting myself get all done up for him. But he *is* nice.

Over the weekend she had savored the memory of the evening at Ryan's apartment. She acknowledged to herself that she had always admired him in his role as surgeon, but she had never imagined how warm and charming he could be on a personal level. I barely knew him in Georgetown, she thought. He was in his last year when I was just starting med school. He always looked so serious.

At twenty after seven the doorbell rang. "I'm so sorry," Ryan began when she opened the office door.

"That was my line at your apartment on Friday,"

Monica interrupted. "Come on in. I have everything I want to show you ready. I know you said that you're on the way to the theatre."

She had placed the Michael O'Keefe files on a table in her waiting room. The children's books that were normally there were stacked in the corner. Jenner glanced at them. "When I was a kid, Dr. Seuss was my favorite author," he said. "How about you?"

"High on the list," Monica agreed. "How could he not be?" As Jenner sat down and reached for the file, she pulled up a chair across the table from him and watched as he reached in his pocket for his glasses.

She studied his face as he began to read the MRIs and CAT scans. The grave expression that came over it as he held up one after another of them was exactly what she expected to see. Finally he laid them down and looked at her. "Monica, this child had incurable brain cancer that ought to have resulted in his death within twelve months. Are you telling me he is still alive?"

"Those MRIs and scans were taken four years ago. I had just opened my practice here, so as you can imagine I was pretty nervous. Michael was four years old then. He had started having seizures and the parents thought they were looking at epilepsy. But you can see what I found. Now look at the other file. It has diagnostic tests that have been taken of Michael in the past three years. Incidentally he's a great kid, a top student, and the captain of his Little League team."

His eyebrows raised, Jenner opened the second file, studied its contents, went through them one by one again, and finally laid them down. He looked at Monica for a long moment before speaking.

"Do you see any possibility of spontaneous remission?" Monica asked.

"None. Absolutely impossible," Jenner said firmly.

Monica nodded. "Be careful. You might end up on a witness list for this beatification process."

Ryan Jenner stood up. "If they want another opinion I'll be glad to give it to them. From everything I have learned and seen as a doctor and a surgeon, if these records are truly those of Michael O'Keefe, that child should not be alive. Now I'd better get going. A certain young lady is going to get very unhappy if I'm not at the theatre by curtain time."

On Wednesday morning, after a considerable debate with herself, Monica told Nan that she had called Olivia Morrow and was going to visit her when she returned from testifying at the Bishop's Office in Metuchen, New Jersey.

"Does she know your grandmother?" Nan asked breathlessly.

Monica hesitated, then carefully chose her words. "She claims she does but I will say from the sound of Ms. Morrow's voice, I get the impression that she's quite old. I'm reserving judgment until I meet her."

Why didn't I tell Nan that Olivia Morrow claims she knew both my birth grandparents? she asked herself later that afternoon as she got into her six-year-old car for the drive to New Jersey. It's because I'm sure that would be too good to be true. And if she did know them and can tell me about them, I will start to believe in miracles, she thought as she inched through the traffic on Fourteenth Street heading for the Lincoln Tunnel.

One hour later she was parking her car in front of the building that was the office of the Bishop of Metuchen. Wishing she was a thousand miles away, she stopped at the reception desk in the spacious lobby. She introduced herself and said, "I have an appointment with Monsignor Joseph Kelly."

The receptionist smiled. "Monsignor is expecting you, Doctor. He's on the second floor, room 1024."

As she turned, Monica could see there was a chapel to the left. Is that where the formal beatification ceremony takes place? she wondered. Over the weekend she had read up on the process. It seems almost medieval, she thought. If what I read is correct, Monsignor Kelly is the Episcopal Delegate, who actually runs the investigation. Two other people will be with him when I'm questioned. One is the Promotor of Justice, whose job it is to make sure there are no phony miracles. They used to call him the Devil's Advocate. The other person will be the Notary in the Inquiry. I guess her job is to record my testimony. And I gather I have to start by taking an oath to tell the truth.

Ignoring the elevator, she walked up the carpeted stairs. The door of Monsignor Kelly's office was open. He caught her eye and waved her in with a genial smile. "Dr. Farrell, come in. Thank you so much for joining us." As he spoke he sprang up and hurried around his desk to shake her hand.

Monica found herself immediately drawn to him. He was a man in his late sixties with dark hair only moderately sprinkled with gray, a rangy build, and intense blue eyes.

As she had expected, there were two other people in the sitting area of the large office. One, a younger priest, was introduced as Monsignor David Fell. He was a slight man in his early forties with a boyish face. The other, perhaps ten years older than Monsignor Fell, was a tall woman with short, curly hair. She was introduced as Laura Shearing. Monica was sure she was the Notary.

Monsignor Kelly invited Monica to sit down. He thanked her again for coming, then asked, "Do you know anything about Sister Catherine?"

"Certainly not personally. I was aware of the fact that she was the foundress of seven children's hospitals, so as a pediatrician I have great respect for her," Monica said, suddenly more comfortable that this was not going to be an inquisition about her belief or lack of belief in miracles. "I'm aware that she was a Franciscan nun and her hospitals individually had a target of treating patients with a specific disability, much the way St. Jude Hospital was founded by Danny Thomas to treat children with cancer."

"That is exactly right," Kelly agreed. "And after her death thirty-three years ago there were many people who believed she had been a saint living among us. We are specifically investigating the healing of the O'Keefe child, but countless parents wrote or called this diocese to say that she seemed to have special healing powers in the sense that many gravely ill children turned the corner after being in her presence." Monsignor Kelly looked at Monsignor Fell. "Why don't you take over, David?"

David Fell's quick smile brightened his solemn demeanor. "Dr. Farrell, let me give you a brief background of someone whose cause is presently being studied in Rome. Terence Cooke was the Cardinal-Archbishop of New York. He died about twenty-five years ago. Have you ever heard of him?"

"Yes I have. My father loved New York," Monica said. "After my mother died, when I was ten years old, he and I would come down to Manhattan and spend weekends going to the theatre and visiting museums. We never missed the Cardinal's Masses at St. Patrick's on Sunday morning. I remember seeing Cardinal O'Connor there. I know that was after Cardinal Cooke died."

Fell nodded. "He was a man who was loved by countless people. To know him was to feel blessed to be in his presence. After Cardinal Cooke's passing thousands of people wrote letters about him to the archdiocese, about his goodness, his kindness, and how he had affected their lives. One of those letters you might be interested to know came from President and Nancy Reagan."

"They weren't Catholic," Monica said.

"Many of the letters were from people who are not Catholic, and they were people from all walks of life. It is not generally known that when he was shot, President

Reagan was much closer to death than had been released to the public. Michael Deaver, President Reagan's chief of staff, asked him if he would like to speak to a spiritual advisor. The president wanted Cardinal Cooke flown to Washington and he spent two and a half hours at Reagan's bedside."

Fell continued. "The investigation into the cause of Cardinal Cooke has been an ongoing process for many years. Over twenty-two thousand documents, meaning letters as well as verbal testimony and his own writings, have been examined. Like Sister Catherine, he is credited with the miracle of saving the life of a dying child."

"You have to understand where I am coming from," Monica said, carefully choosing her words. "It is not that I don't believe in the possibility of divine intervention, but as a doctor I continue to look for other reasons why this child, Michael O'Keefe, had spontaneous remission. I'll give you an example. A person with dissociative identity disorder, multiple personality as it used to be called, may be able to sing like a lark in one personality, and be tone deaf in another. We have examples of some of those people who require eyeglasses in one identity and have twenty-twenty vision in another identity. As a scientist I am still looking for an explanation for the remission or cure of Michael O'Keefe's cancerous brain tumor."

"When you were contacted by us, you did readily acknowledge Michael's mother's response when you told her and his father that he was terminally ill?"

"After urging Mr. and Mrs. O'Keefe to seek other

opinions from qualified specialists, I begged them not to subject Michael to fake promises of a cure. I said I was sure the doctors in Cincinnati would verify my diagnosis, and after that they should take Michael home and enjoy him for the year that he would live."

"And how did the parents respond?"

"Michael's father almost collapsed. His mother looked at me and said, 'My son is not going to die. I am going to begin a crusade of prayer to Sister Catherine and he will get well.' "

Monsignors Fell and Kelly exchanged glances. "Dr. Farrell, we need to take your testimony under oath and then we can let you go," Monsignor Kelly said. "What you have said is crucially important to this proceeding."

"I'll be happy to testify under oath," Monica said quietly. Isn't it funny, she reflected. The Hippocratic oath is the only one I've ever taken. Words from Hippocrates' *Precepts* ran through her mind . . . "for some patients, though conscious that their condition is perilous, recover their health simply through their contentment with the goodness of the physician."

I wonder if, after all, Michael O'Keefe recovered not because of the goodness of the physician, meaning me, but because of the intervention of a deceased Franciscan nun, Sister Catherine, who spent her life caring for disabled children? Michael's mother had absolute confidence that Sister Catherine would not suffer her to lose her only child.

It was a thought that stayed with Monica as she repeated her testimony under sacred oath.

23

Gregory Gannon's duplex apartment was in one of the Museum Mile buildings, so called because of their proximity on Fifth Avenue to the Metropolitan Museum of Art as well as the Guggenheim and others. It had terraces that allowed him to look over Manhattan in all four directions, with a dazzling view of the most famous island in the world.

Before his second marriage eight years ago, Greg had lived in the corner building next door, in a comfortable twelve-room cooperative apartment that was still occupied by his first wife, Caroline. His two sons had grown up there. Aidan was now a lawyer working as a public defender in the Manhattan Legal Aid Society office. The other, William, was a teacher, who after receiving his master's degree in sociology had volunteered to serve at an inner-city school. After the divorce neither one of them had chosen to have any further dealings with Greg. "You announced in the media that you were divorcing Mom to marry Pamela when Mom didn't even have a clue you were running around," Aidan had told him. "Well, good for you. You've got Pamela. You were also quoted as saying 'for the first time in my life I know what real happiness is.' So forget about us. You don't need us and we don't want you."

The boys were in their late twenties now. Occasionally, if Greg decided to walk to or from the office, he would run into one of the boys who was going to visit his mother. Greg did not like to admit to himself that he always chose to walk past Caroline's building in the hope of a chance meeting with his sons. But when it did happen neither son responded to his greeting.

Once in a while, at a benefit, he'd see Caroline across the room. He'd heard that she was getting serious about Guy Weatherill, the CEO of an international engineering firm that specialized in building roads and bridges. Weatherill was a widower, and from all Greg had heard, a very solid citizen. He hoped so for Caroline's sake. She deserved a good guy. And she got plenty from me in the divorce, Greg always reminded himself defensively.

All this was running through Greg's mind as he sat in the library at home sipping a vodka and looking out through a terrace window to the brooding early evening sky.

How much would this apartment bring? he asked himself. Eight years ago when Pamela and I were married, I paid eighteen million for it. But then Pam tore it apart and I put another eight million into renovating it. I don't think I'd get twenty-six million in this market. And how can I face Pam and tell her that I've got to cover my losses or else?

I've been pretty lucky with the tips I've been given. I haven't made any trades that would look suspicious until these last few years when I got too greedy. The lunch today went great. This guy always lived well, but his trust fund had him on a tight leash. Now that his mother is dead he wants to invest his inheritance and have it make real money for him. He's heard such good things about me, and a lot of his friends are my clients. If he puts me in charge of his portfolio, I may be able to stay liquid until I make a few killings again.

The foundation. Everybody knew that the returns on investments were way down. The patents have expired and money isn't pouring in anymore. It hasn't been for years. But we've hit the principal too aggressively, he reflected. I've helped myself to money from so-called charities that couldn't stand the light of day. Peter's theatre grants would at best be questionable, under close scrutiny. At least Clay as a cardiologist and Doug, the king of mental health research, make us look good with the charities they put us in.

I need to take money, lots of money, from the foundation. But it isn't there to take anymore.

"Greg?"

As always the seductive voice that had thrilled him the first time he'd met her did its usual magic on Greg Gannon. "In here," he called.

"You hide in that big leather chair," his wife said, her tone teasing. "You're not trying to hide from *me*, are you?"

Greg Gannon felt arms slide around the back of his chair and wrap themselves around his neck. The exquisite, breathtakingly expensive perfume that Pamela always wore wafted softly through his nostrils. Without seeing her, he could visualize her startling beauty. Not infrequently people mistook her for Catherine Zeta-Jones.

With a tremendous surge of willpower, he pushed aside the demons that were warning him he could not solve his financial problems and that like so many others, he would end up facing a long prison term. He reached up and closed his hands over Pamela's arms. "Hide from you? Never. Pam, you do love me, don't you?"

"Silly, silly question."

"No matter what, you'd never leave me, would you?"

Pamela Gannon laughed, a low, amused laugh. "Why would I ever leave the most generous man in the whole wide world?"

24

At six o'clock on Wednesday evening, Kristina Johnson phoned her mother.

"Mom, I don't know what to do. Ms. Carter didn't come home last night and she doesn't answer her cell phone. I'm still here alone with the baby."

"For heaven's sake, that's crazy. Today is your day off. Who does that woman think she is?"

"She stayed out one night last week, but she was home in the morning. She's never been out of contact this long. And I'm worried about Sally. She's wheezing a little." Kristina looked down at Sally, who sat quietly on the carpet with a doll in her lap.

"Aren't you keeping her away from that dog?"

"I try to but Sally loves the dog and he loves her. But Labs shed, and the doctor warned her mother that Sally is allergic to animals."

"Renée Carter shouldn't have a pet when she knows it will make her child sick. She's some kind of mother, let me tell you."

A tired Kristina could visualize her mother warming up to tell her that being a nanny was hard, hard work, and that she should have gone on to get a degree in nursing. Then she wouldn't be at the mercy of one of these spoiled rich women who only have a child so that they can take it to Central Park occasionally and have the photographer from Page Six of the *New York Post* snap their picture together.

Kristina stopped the flow before it began. "Mom, I'm really just calling to say I'm obviously not coming home tonight. The one thing you have to admit is that Ms. Carter is paying me double my salary because I've been here all week. I'm sure she'll be back soon."

"Have you tried to reach any of her friends?"

Kristina hesitated. "I called two of them I know she sees all the time."

"What did they say?"

"One of them laughed and said, 'That's Renée. She must have some new guy on the hook.' The other one just said that she had no idea where she was."

"Well there's nothing you can do except wait it out, I guess. When she left last night do you know who she was meeting?"

"No, but she was in a great mood."

"All right, but I want you to think about giving up that job. And something else, keep a close watch on that baby. If she's wheezing, get the vaporizer on. And if she gets bad, don't take any chances. Call the doctor. Do you have the doctor's number?"

"Yes. Dr. Farrell called a couple of times checking on Sally. Every time she does, she gives me her cell phone number again."

"All right. I guess you can't do anything more for

now. But if that woman doesn't come back tomorrow maybe you'll have to call the police."

"I'm sure she'll be back. I'll talk to you, Mom."

With a sigh, Kristina replaced the phone on the cradle. She had called from Sally's bedroom, the one place where she had managed to keep the dog from entering. It was large and furnished in white wicker. The carpet was a pink and white design. The walls were fancifully painted with nursery figures. The windows were framed in pink and white eyelet draperies. A row of shelves opposite the crib was filled with toys and children's books. When Kristina saw the room for the first time she had complimented Renée Carter on it. Her response had been, "It should be nice. The decorator charged me a fortune."

Sally had barely eaten any dinner. She had begun to play with her dolls but now, to Kristina's concern, she wandered over to her crib, pulled her security blanket from it, and lay down on the floor.

She is getting sick again, Kristina thought. I'll turn on the vaporizer and I'll sleep on the sofa bed in here with her. If she isn't better in the morning, whether or not her mother is back, I'm going to call Dr. Farrell. I'm sure Ms. Carter will be furious. I'll have to admit to the doctor that she isn't here but I don't care.

Kristina walked across the room, bent down, and picked up the sleepy baby. "You poor kid," she said. "You certainly got one bum break when you were born to that miserable woman."

25

Monica had hoped to go home and freshen up before her meeting with Olivia Morrow. It would be cutting it too tight, she decided, as she drove back through the Lincoln Tunnel. I'd rather be in her neighborhood early than run the risk of keeping her waiting. She's obviously not well.

She claims she knew my grandparents, Dad's birth mother and father. How did that happen? Dad's birth mother did everything she could to conceal her identity. The names listed in the birth records in the hospital in Ireland had the Farrells as the natural parents. What did Olivia Morrow mean when she said she wanted to tell me about them before it's too late? Too late for what? Is she sick enough to be actually dying? If it weren't for that chance remark to Tony Garcia when he drove her, I would never have contacted her. Would she ever have contacted me?

At twenty minutes of five, after parking the car in a nearby garage, Monica entered the lobby of Schwab House. At the desk she gave her name. "I have an appointment at five o'clock with Ms. Morrow," she explained. "I'm a little early, so I'll just wait before you call her."

"Certainly, ma'am."

The twenty minutes seemed like hours before Monica went back to the desk. "Will you call her now, please? Tell her Dr. Farrell is here."

Her anticipation rising to a fever pitch, Monica watched as the desk clerk dialed a number. She saw the expression come over his face that clearly suggested a problem. Then he broke the connection, dialed the number again, and waited for several long minutes before he disconnected.

"She's not answering," he said flatly. "There may be a problem. I know for sure that Ms. Morrow has not gone out today. She's not at all well, and when she came back yesterday, she looked too tired to walk to the elevator. I have her doctor's number. I'm going to call him. The night clerk told me he was here last evening to see her."

"I'm a doctor," Monica said quickly. "If you think there is a medical problem, time may be of the essence."

"I'll call Dr. Hadley and then if it's okay with him, I'll go upstairs with you now."

In an agony of impatience, Monica waited while the clerk made the call to Hadley. He was not in his office, but he answered on his cell phone. From what she could hear the clerk saying, he was concise in explaining the situation. Finally he hung up. "Dr. Hadley will be here as fast as he can make it, but he said for me to bring you to Ms. Morrow's apartment immediately, and if she has the bolt on to break in."

When the clerk turned the superintendent's key in the lock they heard a click, and when he turned the handle the door opened. The bolt of the apartment where Olivia Morrow had lived for more than half her life was not on. "I'm sure she hasn't gone out," the clerk said again. "Dr. Hadley was here last night. If she was in bed, she probably didn't bother to get up and slide the bolt closed after he left."

There were no lights on, but there was still sufficient natural light coming in from the west for Monica to glance at an orderly living room, a dining area, the open door to a kitchen, and then hurry behind the clerk down the hall. "Her bedroom is at the end," he said, "the next door from the den."

He took a moment to knock on the closed bedroom door, then hesitantly opened it and entered the bedroom. From the doorway Monica could see the small figure, her head resting on a raised pillow, the rest of her body under the covers.

"Ms. Morrow," the clerk said, "it's Henry. We're just checking up on you. The doctor is worried that you may need him."

"Turn on the light," Monica ordered.

"Oh, sure, Doctor, sure," Henry stammered.

The overhead fixture flooded the room with light. Monica walked swiftly to the side of the bed and looked down on the waxy face, the teeth clamped on a corner of her bottom lip, her eyes partially open. She's been dead for hours, she thought. Rigor mortis has set in. Oh God, if only I had called her earlier! Will I ever know about my birth family now?

"Call the police, Henry," she ordered. "It is necessary

to report a death when someone dies alone. I'll wait here until her own physician comes. He's the appropriate person to sign the death certificate."

"Yes, ma'am. Yes. Thank you. I'll call from downstairs." Henry clearly was eager to be out of the presence of the body.

There was a chair in the corner of the room. Monica pulled it over and sat by the remains of the woman whom she had wanted so much to meet. Obviously Olivia Morrow had been very ill. She looked almost emaciated. Had she really known about me, Monica wondered, or was it all a mistake? Now I'll probably never know.

Fifteen minutes later, Dr. Clay Hadley came rushing in. He reached under the covers and lifted Olivia Morrow's hand then gently laid it back down and pulled the covers over it again. "I was here last night," he told Monica, his voice husky. "I begged Olivia to let me admit her to a hospital or to a hospice so she wouldn't die alone. She was adamant that she wanted to be in her own bed when the end came. Have you known her for long, Doctor?"

"I never met her. I was supposed to see her this evening." Her voice was soft. "My father was an adopted child and Ms. Morrow claimed she had known my birth grandparents and wanted to tell me about them. Did she ever mention me to you?"

Hadley shook his head.

"Dr. Farrell, please don't put any stock in anything Olivia said. These past few weeks since I had to tell her how very sick she was she had begun to hallucinate. The poor woman had no family and she began to think that anyone she ever met or heard of was in some way related to her."

"I see. Frankly, I wondered if that wasn't the case. I guess I had better stay until the police come because I was with the clerk when we found the body. They'll probably want a statement from me."

"Why don't we wait in the living room?" Hadley suggested.

With a final glance at the bed where Olivia Morrow was lying, Monica left the room. But as she walked down the hall she had the nagging sensation that something was out of order, something was wrong.

Maybe I'm the one who's going crazy, she thought. I guess I didn't realize how very much I was counting on Olivia Morrow really being able to tell me about my background. I'm so desperately disappointed.

Sitting in the living room that was a tribute to the discerning good taste of Olivia Morrow, Monica continued to be troubled by the sense that somehow she had missed something important, something that was wrong about the death of a woman she had never met in her life.

But what?

26

On Thursday morning Doug Langdon phoned Sammy Barber. Acutely conscious that what he was about to say was possibly being recorded, he spoke briefly and tried to disguise his voice. "I agree to the terms of your settlement offer."

"Oh, Dougie, relax," Sammy told him. "I'm not taping you anymore. I've got all I need in case the terms aren't satisfactory. You got the cash in old bills, right?"

"Yes." Langdon spat out the word.

"Here's the way I figure we do it. We each have a big black suitcase, the kind that we can pull down the block. We meet in the parking lot of our favorite diner in Queens. We park near each other and switch bags in the lot. No bothering to stop for a cup of coffee, even though their coffee, as I remember it, wasn't bad. Sound like a plan?"

"When do you want to meet?"

"Dougie, you don't sound happy. I want you to be happy. The sooner the better. How about this afternoon, maybe around three? It's quiet then and the boss at the nightclub wants me to come in early this evening. We've got some red-hot celebrities who've booked tables, and I'm his man when the jerks try to bother them."

"I'm sure you are. This afternoon at three o'clock in the parking lot of the diner." Douglas Langdon no longer tried to disguise his voice. If Sammy Barber took the money and did not fulfill the contract there was absolutely nothing he could do about it. Except, he told himself grimly, find someone to take care of Sammy, but if that came to pass, he would make very sure there would be no way to trace Sammy's demise back to him.

And yet I think that when he has the money he'll go through with it, Langdon thought, as he sat in his office waiting for Roberta Waters, his first patient, another one who was chronically late. Not that he cared. He always stopped her at precisely the time her hour was up, even if she had only been on the couch for fifteen minutes. At her protest, he had said, "I cannot delay my next patient. That would not be fair. Think about it. One of the reasons for your strained relationship with your husband is that he gets frantic because you are never on time for anything, and in consequence you make him embarrassingly late for your joint engagements."

God, was he sick of that woman!

Face it, he was sick of them all. *But be careful,* he warned himself. *You've been getting pretty snappy with Beatrice, who is after all a good secretary, and no question, she was oozing curiosity when Sammy showed up here.*

The phone rang. A moment later Beatrice announced, "Dr. Hadley calling, sir."

"Thank you, Beatrice." Doug forced warmth into his voice. His tone changed when he heard her click off. "I tried to get you last night. Why didn't you answer your phone?"

"Because I was a wreck," Clay Hadley replied, his voice quivering. "I'm a doctor. I save lives. It's one thing to talk about killing someone. It's another to hold a pillow over the head of a woman who was my patient."

Disbelieving, Doug Langdon heard the unmistakable sound of sobbing on the other end of the line. If Beatrice hadn't disconnected immediately she would have heard the outburst, he thought frantically. He wanted to shout at Hadley to shut up, but then he swallowed over the tightness in his throat and said calmly, "Clay, get hold of yourself. At the most Olivia Morrow had only a few days to live. By eliminating those few days you saved yourself from spending the rest of your life in prison. You did tell me she was going to tell Monica Farrell about Alex and the Gannon fortune?"

"Doug, Monica Farrell was in Olivia's apartment when I went back yesterday evening. She was in the bedroom, sitting by Olivia's bed. She's a doctor. She may have noticed something."

"Like what?"

Langdon waited. Hadley had stopped sobbing, but there was a hesitation in his voice when he said, "I don't know. I guess I'm just nervous. I'm sorry. I'll be all right."

"Clay," Langdon began, trying to keep his voice reassuring, "you have to be all right, for your sake *and* for mine. Think about all the money you have in that Swiss bank account and the life you can lead with it. And think about what will happen to you and to me if you don't stay calm."

"I hear you. I hear you. I'll be all right. I promise."

Langdon heard the click in his ear as the other phone rang. With his handkerchief he dried the perspiration from his forehead and his hands.

The intercom came on. "Doctor, Mrs. Waters is here," Beatrice announced. "And she's so happy. She wants me to point out to you immediately that today she's only four minutes late. She said she knew that would make your day."

27

Andrew and Sarah Winkler had lived all their married lives in a comfortable apartment on York Avenue and Seventy-ninth Street in Manhattan, a block from the East River. Childless, they had never been tempted to move to the suburbs. "God forbid," Andrew would say. "When I see a pile of leaves, I want them to belong to someone else." Andrew, a retired accountant, and Sarah, a retired librarian, were perfectly content with their lifestyle. Several evenings a week they were at Lincoln Center or a lecture at the 92nd Street Y. Once a month they treated themselves to a Broadway show.

A fixture in their daily routine was their after-breakfast walk. They never broke that personal commitment unless the weather was extreme. "Mist is okay, but not a downpour," Sarah would explain to her friends. "Cold okay, but not below twenty degrees; warm okay, but not if the thermometer hits ninety. We don't want to turn into couch potatoes, but neither do we want to die of frostbite or heatstroke."

Sometimes they would stroll in Central Park. Other days they would choose the pedestrian path along the East River. This Thursday morning they had opted for the river walk, and set out for it in their matching all-weather jackets.

It had rained unexpectedly during the night, and Sarah remarked to Andrew that the weatherman never gets anything right and that it made you wonder how much they got paid to stand up in front of the camera and point to the map, waving their arms to show wind currents. "Half the time when they say rain is a possibility, if they opened the window they'd be drenched," she commented, as they approached the area of Gracie Mansion, the official residence of the mayor of New York. "But at least it cleared up nicely this morning."

She broke off her commentary on the exasperating unpredictability of meteorologists by suddenly clutching her husband's arm. "Andrew, look! Look!" They were passing a bench along the path. Partially wedged under it was an oversized garbage bag, the kind used on construction sites. Protruding from the bag was a foot with a woman's high-heeled shoe dangling from it.

"Oh my God, my God . . . ," Sarah moaned.

Andrew reached in the pocket of his jacket for his cell phone and dialed 911.

28

On Thursday morning, Monica went straight to the hospital, after her nearly sleepless night. Sometime around three A.M. she had tried to assuage her crushing disappointment at the death of Olivia Morrow by promising herself that she would hire a detective if necessary to investigate any possible connection Morrow might have had with her birth grandparents.

But even so, the sense of missed opportunity haunted her, and it didn't make matters easier when Ryan Jenner stopped at the pediatric floor looking for her. "Monica, how did that interview at the Bishop's Office go?" he asked.

"Pretty much as I expected. I talked about the possibility of spontaneous remission and they talked about miracles." As she spoke, Monica unwillingly realized how good it felt to be so close to Jenner, to relive for the moment the sensation of sitting next to him in the restaurant on Friday night, their shoulders touching at the crowded table.

"I'll be honest, Monica, I can't get the Michael O'Keefe file out of my head. It does include everything from the first CAT scan you ordered to the MRIs and CAT scans a year later showing the total disappearance of the cancerous tumor, doesn't it?"

"Absolutely. The whole works."

"Would you lend the file to me for a few days? I really want to study it. I still find it hard to believe what I saw."

"That was my reaction, too. After the doctors in Cincinnati confirmed my diagnosis, the O'Keefes took Michael home. I phoned from time to time and all they said was that he was holding his own. In the beginning he continued to have seizures, but then they moved to Mamaroneck and stopped coming to my office. Mrs. O'Keefe did not want more medical procedures, even MRIs, because they frightened Michael. But when she finally *did* bring him in, I knew I was looking at a healthy little boy, and the tests confirmed it."

"Then is it okay if I borrow the file? I can stop by late this afternoon at your office for it. And I *will* be on time."

"That's fine. I'll be there until about six." As Ryan turned to go she asked, "How was the theatre?"

He stopped and turned back. "Great. It was the revival of *Our Town*. That's always been one of my favorite plays."

"I played Emily when I was in high school." Why am I telling Ryan that? Monica asked herself. Is it because I want to prolong this conversation?

Ryan smiled. "Well, I'm glad you were acting. I still get a lump in my throat at the end, when George throws himself on Emily's grave." As he turned again to leave, he gave her the quick smile that she knew would instantly be replaced by his usual serious expression.

She had been standing by the nurses' desk. She turned back to it. Rita Greenberg was sitting there, her eyes on Ryan's retreating figure.

"He sure is cute, isn't he, Doctor?" Rita sighed. "He has so much authority, and yet he seems a little shy."

"Um-hum," Monica answered noncommittally.

"I think he likes you. This is the second time he came down looking for you this morning."

Good Lord, Monica thought. That's all I need, to have the nurses talking about an office romance. "Dr. Jenner wants to look at the file of one of my patients," she said crisply.

It was clear that Rita had gotten the implied rebuke. "Of course, Doctor," she said, her voice equally crisp.

"I'm off. You know where to get me," Monica said as she felt the stirring of her cell phone in the pocket of her jacket.

It was Kristina Johnson. "Doctor," she said, her voice frightened, "I'm in a cab on the way to the hospital. Sally is really, really sick."

"How long has she been sick?" Monica asked, the question rushing from her lips.

"Kind of since yesterday. She was wheezing, but then she slept pretty well. But this morning it kept getting worse, and I got really scared. She was gasping for breath."

In the background Monica could hear the combined

coughing and sobbing o
from the hospital are you?” she s
“We’re on the West Side Highwa
there in fifteen minutes.”

It suddenly occurred to Monica that Renée C
Sally’s mother, should have been the one calling her. “Is Ms. Carter with you?” she asked sharply.

“No. She hasn’t been home in two days, and I haven’t heard from her.”

“I’ll meet you in the emergency room, Kristina,” Monica said. She turned off her cell phone and dropped it in her pocket.

Rita Greenberg had been listening. “Sally’s had another asthma attack.” It was not a question.

“Yes. I’m going to admit her, and before I release her again I’m going to have Family Services look into that situation. I only wish I had done it last week.”

“I’ll have a crib all set up,” Rita promised.

“Put her in the alcove again. The last thing she needs is to pick up a bug.”

Fifteen minutes later Monica was standing at the entrance to the emergency room when the cab pulled up. She ran over to it, opened the door, and reached inside. “Give her to me.” Not waiting for Kristina to pay the driver she raced back into the hospital. Sally was wheezing and gasping. Her lips were blue and her eyes were rolling back in her head.

She can’t breathe, Monica thought as she carried her to a cubicle and laid her on a stretcher. Two nurses were waiting for her. One of them swiftly undressed Sally and the labored gasps of breath were com- her lips not her chest. It's gone into pneumo- nia, Monica thought as she reached for the oxygen mask the nurse was holding out to her.

An hour later she was settling Sally in the intensive care unit on the pediatric floor. The oxygen mask was still in place. Intravenous fluids and medicine were dripping into Sally's arm. Her hands had been tied to keep her from pulling the needle out. Her frightened wails had given way to sleepy moans.

Kristina Johnson, her eyes welling with tears, had followed them and was waiting for Monica to leave the side of the crib. Monica looked at the young girl's tired, worried face and the admonition she had intended to give died on her lips.

"Sally is a very, very sick baby," she said. "Kristina, am I right that you said her mother has not been home in the last day or two?"

"She left night before last. Yesterday was supposed to be my day off. But when I woke up I could see that her bed wasn't slept in. I haven't heard from her at all."

Kristina began to cry. "If anything happens to Sally it's my fault, but Doctor, I was afraid if I brought Sally in yesterday, Ms. Carter would be furious. And Sally didn't really seem that sick until she was going to bed last night. So I put on the vaporizer and I slept on the couch in her room and I was sure her mother would come home and look in, then maybe we'd bring Sally to the hospital if she started wheezing any harder and . . ."

Monica stopped the flow of words. "Kristina, this is

tions without expecting an answer. "It is my job to make sure that miracles are really miracles, and that only people of extraordinary virtue, not extraordinary beauty may someday be listed on the Calendar of Saints," he said.

Monsignor Kelly nodded and did not choose to mention that ever since yesterday's meeting with Dr. Monica Farrell his memories of Sister Catherine kept playing through his mind. *Maybe it's because I saw the pain in that lovely young doctor's face when she talked about breaking the news to the O'Keefes that Michael was terminal.*

She had that same look that I remember seeing on Sister Catherine when she shared the heartbreak of parents whose children were dangerously ill.

31

On the way back to Renée Carter's apartment on Central Park West, Kristina Johnson called her best friend, Kerianne Kennan, with whom she shared a tiny apartment in Greenwich Village. Kerianne, a student at the Fashion Institute of Technology, answered her cell phone on the first ring.

"Keri, this is Kris."

"I can tell by your voice that something's wrong. What's the matter?" Keri demanded.

"Everything," Kristina wailed. "The baby I'm minding is in intensive care and the mother isn't around. You wouldn't believe what's been going on." Twenty minutes later, when the taxi stopped on the corner of Ninety-sixth Street and Central Park West, Kristina had the comforting assurance that Kerianne was rushing to be with her and would stay for the rest of the day.

"I just know Renée Carter will start screaming at me that I didn't take good care of Sally," Kristina had explained tearfully. "Maybe if you're there she won't go too crazy. And if she doesn't come back by this evening, I'm going to leave a note for her, and take off. I can't work for that miserable woman anymore."

Kristina got out of the cab, went into the lobby, and took the elevator to the apartment. As she opened the door, the dog's frenzied barking reminded her that it had not been out for a walk since last night. Oh God, she thought as she ran to get its leash. She did not take the time to look through the apartment, but it was obvious that everything was exactly as she had left it, and Ms. Carter had not come home.

Downstairs again, as the Lab strained to pull her along, she called to the desk clerk, "Jimmy, when my friend Kerianne gets here, tell her I'll be right back, okay?"

Fifteen minutes later, when she returned to the building, she was relieved to see Keri waiting for her in the lobby. But before they went to the elevator she stopped again at the desk. "Jimmy, did Ms. Carter come in while I was walking the dog?"

"No, Kristina," the young clerk answered. "Haven't seen her all morning."

"Or all day yesterday," Kristina murmured to Keri as they went up in the elevator. "The first thing I want to do is make a pot of coffee. Otherwise I'll fall asleep standing up."

Inside the apartment she headed straight for the kitchen. "Take a look around," she told Kerianne. "Because once she gets here, we're on our way."

A few minutes later, Kerianne joined her in the kitchen. "This is a gorgeous apartment," she commented. "My grandfather was in the antique business and trust me, there are some pretty nice pieces of furniture here. Ms. Carter must have money and lots of it."

"She's an event planner," Kristina said. "She must have some really big event going on now, if she doesn't show up here, or answer her cell phone. Think about it. She has a baby who was in the hospital a week ago and is back in now. I'm definitely going to quit this job, but I worry what will happen to Sally." She sighed heavily as she took out two coffee cups and set them on the counter.

"What about Sally's father?"

"Who knows? I've been here for a solid week and I haven't seen any sign of *him*. I guess he's another winner as a parent. The coffee's ready. Let's have it at the bar."

The elaborate built-in bar was in the den. They had just begun to settle on the chairs at the counter when the intercom sounded. Kristina jumped up. "That must be Jimmy tipping me off that Ms. Carter is on the way up."

But when she answered, the desk clerk had a different message. "There are two detectives here inquiring about your boss. They asked me who was in the apartment. I told them you and your friend and they said they wanted to talk to you."

"Detectives?" Kristina exclaimed. "Jimmy, is Ms. Carter in trouble?"

"How would I know?"

Kristina locked the dog in the den, and when the bell rang, she opened the door to find the men standing in the vestibule. They held up their badges for her to see.

"I am Detective Tucker," the shorter man introduced himself. "And, this is Detective Flynn. May we come in?"

"Of course," Kristina said nervously. "Did something happen to Ms. Carter? Was she in an accident?"

"Why do you ask?" Tucker inquired as he stepped into the apartment.

"Because she hasn't come home since night before last, and she doesn't answer her cell phone, and Sally, her baby, is so sick I had to take her to the hospital this morning."

"Is there a picture of Ms. Carter around?"

"Oh, yes, I'll get one." As a shocked Kerianne stood, coffee cup in hand, Kristina went down the hall to Renée Carter's bedroom. A table by the window had framed pictures of Renée at a variety of black-tie events. Kristina grabbed several of them and rushed back to the living room.

When she handed them to Tucker, she saw the grim look he gave his partner. "She's dead, isn't she?" Kristina gasped, "and I've been saying such mean things about her."

"Why don't we sit down and you tell me all about her," Tucker suggested. "We understand she has a baby. You say the baby is in the hospital?"

"Yes. I brought her there this morning. She's really sick. That's why I was so mad at Ms. Carter. I didn't know what to do, so I waited too long to bring Sally to the emergency room." Her eyes brimmed with tears.

"What about the baby's father? Did you try to contact him?"

"I don't know who he is. When Ms. Carter left she was all dressed up, so I figured she was going to one of her parties. But looking back, I think she may have been meeting him. When she waved good-bye to Sally, she yelled something like, 'Keep your fingers crossed, baby. Your old man is finally coughing up the money.' "

32

Now that she was aware that Greg Gannon was under investigation by the Securities and Exchange Commission, Esther Chambers was keenly attuned to the tension building in him. It seemed to her that every day, Greg's expression became increasingly more troubled except, of course, when a client dropped into the office.

If his door was partially open, she could hear him on the phone, and the tone of his voice was either warm and jovial with a client, or abrupt and curt when he was speaking to one of his fellow three foundation board members, Dr. Hadley, or Dr. Langdon, or his brother, Peter. The gist of what she could gather he was telling them was to forget any new grants they wanted to suggest, that there was already too damn much money being spent supporting Hadley's heart research and Langdon's mental health clinics, and that there wouldn't be another dime for Peter's theatre projects.

On Thursday morning he came into the office scowling, his shoulders bunched together, and dropped a list on her desk.

"Call them," he said abruptly. "When one of them is available to talk, give me the name fast."

"Of course, Mr. Gannon." Esther had only to take one look at the list to know they were all potential clients, and that he was going to try to rope them in.

The first three were not able to take his call. Others stayed on the line for only a few minutes. Esther guessed that whatever bond or stock issue Greg was hawking had been turned down. But at twenty past eleven Arthur Saling accepted the call. Saling, a prospective client, had lunched with Greg last week. A timid-looking man in his early sixties, he had come back to the office with Greg, and had been duly impressed with the lavish setup. He had confided to Esther that he was considering investing with a number of money managers, and had heard glowing reports about Greg. "I want to be very sure of whom I select," he had said quietly. "You can't be too careful these days."

Out of curiosity Esther had googled him. After the recent death of his mother, Saling had come into the principal of a family trust, close to one hundred million dollars.

The door was closed, but she could hear Greg's booming jovial tones even though the words were muffled. Then for a long time she could not hear a sound from his office. Which means, she decided, that now he's oozing charm and giving Saling his confidential pitch. She knew it by heart: "I've been following this stock for four years and its time has come. The company is about to be bought out, and you can imagine what that means. It's the best opportunity in the market since Google went public."

Poor Arthur Saling, she thought. If Greg is frantic to cover his losses, a lot of these paper profits he's been posting probably don't even exist, and this is one more victim in the making. I wish I could tip him off.

When the call to Saling ended, Greg got back on the intercom. "That turned out to be a good morning's work, Esther," he said, his voice warm and relieved now. "I think we'll hold the other calls until this afternoon. My wife is joining me for lunch and I should be on my way."

"Of course." I wish I was out of here, Esther thought, as the clock on her desk registered the noon hour. Not just for lunch, but out of here altogether. It makes me feel slimy to be reporting on Greg to the SEC, even though he might have just convinced someone else to trust him with his money.

Greg was still at his desk when Pamela Gannon swept in at quarter past twelve. "Is anyone with him?" she asked Esther.

"No, Mrs. Gannon," Esther said, trying to force a friendly note into her voice. I've got to admit that woman is beautiful, she conceded, as Pamela strode past her desk, stunning in a fur-trimmed red suit and suede boots. But her kind marries people like Greg Gannon for one reason only, a five-letter word spelled m-o-n-e-y.

She watched as Pamela, without knocking, turned the handle of Greg's door and flung it open. "Surprise, I'm here, Papa Bear," she called. "I know I'm early but I couldn't wait till one o'clock to meet you at Le Cirque. I'm sorry I wasn't awake before you left this morning.

I wanted to wish you a happy tenth anniversary of the wonderful day we met."

Papa Bear! God spare me, Esther thought, shuddering at Greg's delighted response.

"I've been thinking about it every minute," Greg was saying, "and I've had such a good morning that I planned to stop at Van Cleef and Arpels before I met you for lunch. But now you can go with me and help me pick out something really special."

How about a tiara? Esther asked herself as they passed her desk, ignoring her. They're going out to buy pricey jewelry on the poor guy who's probably just committed a fortune for Greg to handle.

It's not going to happen, she told herself. On her way to have lunch, Esther stopped at a CVS pharmacy and bought plain paper and a plain envelope. In block letters she wrote, "THIS IS A WARNING. DO NOT INVEST WITH GREG GANNON. YOU WILL LOSE YOUR MONEY." She signed it, "A friend," then put a stamp on the envelope, addressed it, and took a cab to the main post office, where she dropped it in a mailbox.

33

For hours Monica did not leave the side of Sally's crib after she managed to resuscitate her. The baby's lungs kept filling with fluid and she continued to burn with fever. Finally Monica lowered the side of the crib and, leaning in, cradled Sally in her arms. "Come on, little girl," she whispered. "You've got to make it." The thought of what the Monsignor had told her about Sister Catherine praying over sick children ran through her head.

Sister Catherine, she thought, I don't believe in miracles, but I know so many believe you saved lives, not only terminal kids like Michael O'Keefe, but other kids who were at death's door. Sally has had such a rotten break. A mother who neglects her, and no father around. She's wrapped herself around my heart. If she lives, I promise I'll take care of her.

It was a long afternoon but at seven o'clock she felt that it was safe to go. Sally's fever had gone down and even though she still had an oxygen mask clamped around her face, her breathing had eased. "Call me if there's any change," Monica told the nurse.

"I will, Doctor. I didn't think we were going to be able to save her."

"Neither did I." With an attempt at a smile, Monica left the pediatrics floor and the hospital. The temperature had dropped but as she buttoned her coat she decided to walk to the office. I'll check on my messages, she thought, and see how much Nan has been able to rearrange my appointments. I'll walk over. It will feel good to clear my head.

Her shoulder bag in place, she put both hands in her pockets and at her usual rapid pace began to walk east across Fourteenth Street. Now that she felt reasonably secure about Sally, her thoughts reverted to the crushing disappointment of finding Olivia Morrow dead. In her mind she could see every detail of Morrow's face, the gaunt thinness of her features, the gray pallor of her skin, the wrinkles around her eyes, her teeth clamped on the corner of her lower lip.

She must have been an exquisitely neat person, Monica thought. Everything was in perfect order. The apartment was furnished in such good taste. Either she died right after she went to bed, or else she certainly couldn't have been a restless sleeper. The top sheet and comforter weren't wrinkled at all. Even the pillow her head was resting on looked brand new.

The pillow. It was pink and the sheets and the other pillows were peach. That's what I noticed, Monica thought. But what difference does it make? None. The only hope I have now is to ask Dr. Hadley if he can give me a list of her friends. Maybe she talked to one of them about me.

She was at the busy corner of Union Square and

Broadway by a crowded bus stop. The light was changing from yellow to red and she watched in disapproval as a number of people darted across the street as the oncoming traffic rushed at them. A bus was approaching the bus stop when she suddenly felt a violent push and tumbled over the curb onto the street. As onlookers shouted and screamed, Monica managed to roll out of the way of the bus, but not before it had run over and crushed the shoulder bag that had been thrown from her arm.

34

Peter Gannon looked across the table at his former wife, Susan. He had asked her to have dinner with him at Il Tinello, which had always been one of their favorite restaurants during their twenty-year marriage. They had not spoken or met in the four years since their divorce until he received the phone call from her saying how sorry she was that his new play had closed.

Now, desperate for help, he looked across the table at her: Forty-six years old, her wavy hair streaked with silver, her face dominated by her wide hazel eyes. He wondered how he had ever let her go. I was never smart enough to realize how much I loved her, he thought, and how good she was to me.

Mario, the owner, had greeted them by saying, “Welcome home.” Now, after the bottle of wine he had ordered was served, Peter said, “I know it sounds corny, but being here with you at this table *feels* like being home, Sue.”

Her smile was wry. “That depends on how you interpret the word ‘home.’ ”

Peter flinched. “I’ve forgotten how direct you are.”

“Try to remember.” Her light tone took the sting out

of the rebuke. "We haven't talked in ages, Peter. How is your love life? I assume robust, to put it mildly."

"It is not robust, and has not been in a very long time. Why did you call me, Sue?"

Her quizzical expression disappeared. "Because when I saw that picture of you after those dreadful reviews I knew I was looking at the face of a man in despair. How bad a bath did you take on the play?"

"I'm going to have to declare bankruptcy, which means a lot of very good people who had faith in me are going to lose a great deal of money."

"You have considerable assets."

"I *had* considerable assets. I don't anymore."

Susan sipped the wine before answering, then said, "Peter, in this financial climate a lot of people who over-extended themselves are in the same boat you are. It's embarrassing. It's humiliating. But it does happen."

"Sue, a company emerges from bankruptcy. A failed theatrical producer doesn't, at least not for a long time. Who do you think would ever put a nickel in one of my plays again?"

"I seem to remember that I warned you to stick with drama and avoid musical comedy."

"Well, you should be pleased, then. You always wanted the last word!" Peter Gannon said, with a spark of anger.

Susan looked quickly around. The diners at the nearby tables of the intimate restaurant had apparently not noticed Peter's raised voice.

"I'm sorry, Sue," he said hastily. "That was a stupid

thing to say. What I should have said is that you were right and I knew you were right, but I've been on an ego trip."

"I agree," Susan said, her voice amiable.

Peter Gannon picked up his glass and gulped the wine. As he put it down he said, "Sue, I gave you five million dollars in the divorce settlement."

Susan's eyebrows raised. "I'm quite aware of that."

"Sue, I beg you. I need one million dollars. If I don't get it, Greg and I could end up in jail."

"What are you talking about?"

"Sue, I know how conservatively you invest. I'm being blackmailed. When I was drunk I told a person too much about the money we were taking from the foundation and about my brother's investment firm. I told that person that I was sure Greg was doing some inside trading."

"You *what*?"

"Sue, I was drunk. I know he is trying to dig himself out of a hole. If this person goes to the press, Greg could end up in prison."

"Who is this person? A woman, I assume. God knows you had your share of them."

"Sue, will you lend me a million dollars? I swear I'll pay you back."

Susan pushed back her chair and stood up. "I don't know whether to be insulted or amused. Or maybe both. Good-bye, Peter."

With despairing eyes, Peter Gannon watched the trim figure of his former wife as she abruptly left the restaurant.

35

At six o'clock, Dr. Ryan Jenner rang the bell of Monica's office and waited expectantly. Maybe she's in one of the back rooms, he thought, and rang the bell again. But after the third try, when he'd pressed the bell for an extended time, he decided that Monica had completely forgotten her promise to turn over the file of the O'Keefe boy to him.

He realized that he had been looking forward to spending the evening studying all of the diagnostic tests to see if there was any explanation for the advanced brain cancer to simply disappear.

Shrugging off his disappointment, he walked from the sidewalk to the curb and hailed a cab. On the way home, he wondered if he would find Alice Halloway waiting for him there. He had not been able to refuse his aunt's request when she told him that Alice, "one of her favorite people in the whole world," was coming up to Manhattan on a business trip and had asked to stay in the apartment. And did Ryan mind?

"It's your apartment so how can I mind?" Ryan had asked. "She even has her choice of your two guest bedrooms." In his mind he had expected that

Alice Halloway would be a contemporary of his aunt, somewhere between seventy and seventy-five. Instead when Alice arrived last week, she had turned out to be a very pretty woman in her early thirties who was going to be attending a convention of beauty editors in Manhattan.

The convention had lasted two days but Alice stayed on. A few nights earlier she had invited Ryan to join her at the theatre. She had told him she managed to get two house seats for the sold-out revival of *Our Town*. They had gone to get a quick bite after the show, and it had been too late for Ryan's taste when they finally got back to the apartment. He was operating at seven the next morning.

It was only when Alice tried to insist they have an after-dinner drink by the fire that Ryan had caught on to the fact that his aunt was trying to set him up with "one of her favorite people in the whole world," and that Alice was more than willing to go along with it.

Now, in the cab on the way uptown, Ryan pondered what to do about the situation. Alice kept delaying her departure. She was always in the apartment when he got there, with cheese and crackers and chilled wine waiting for him.

If she's not gone soon, I'm going to a hotel until she clears out, he decided.

Usually at the end of the day he was relieved and pleased to turn the key in the door of the large, comfortable apartment. Tonight, he grimaced as he pushed the door open. Then the enticing scent of something baking in the kitchen teased his nostrils and he realized he was hungry.

Alice was curled up on the couch in the living room watching a quiz show on cable. She was wearing a casual sweater and slacks. A small plate of cheese and crackers, two glasses, and a bottle of wine in a cooler were on the round table in front of her. "Hi, Ryan," she called as he stopped in the vestibule.

"Hello, Alice," Ryan said, trying to sound cordial. He watched as she unfolded herself from the couch and walked across the room to greet him. Planting a butterfly-light kiss on his cheek, she said, "You look done in. How many lives have you saved today?"

"None," Ryan said briefly. "Look, Alice—"

She interrupted him. "Why don't you shed that jacket and tie and put on something comfortable? Virginia ham, macaroni and cheese, biscuits, and a salad is the dinner I'm famous for."

It had been Ryan's intention to say that he had dinner plans, but the words died on his lips. Instead he asked, "Alice, I do have to know. How long are you planning to stay?"

Her eyes widened. "Didn't I tell you? I'm leaving Saturday morning so you'll only have to put up with me for two more days, a day and a half, actually."

"I'm embarrassed. This is not my apartment, but . . ."

"But you don't want the doorman smirking at you. Don't worry. I already told him you were my step-brother."

"Your step-brother!"

"Sure. Now how about that Virginia ham dinner? It's your last chance. *I* have plans for tomorrow night."

She's leaving Saturday, and she's out tomorrow night, Ryan thought with relief. I can at least be civil now. With a genuine smile he said, "I'm delighted to take you up on dinner, but I won't be much company. I'm operating at seven tomorrow morning again, so I'll be turning in early."

"That's fine. You don't even have to help clear the table."

"I'll be right back."

Ryan went down the corridor to his room and walked over to the closet to hang up his jacket. The phone rang but Alice picked it up on the first ring. He opened the door in case she called him but she did not. Must be for her, he thought.

In the kitchen Alice lowered her voice. A woman who introduced herself as Dr. Farrell had asked for Dr. Jenner. "He's just getting changed," Alice said. "May I take a message?"

"Please tell him that Dr. Farrell phoned to apologize for not being in her office to give him the O'Keefe file," Monica said, trying to keep her voice steady. "I'll make sure he has it in the morning."

36

Now that positive identification had been made on the body of Renée Carter, the elaborate process of finding and apprehending her killer was set in motion. While her friend Kerianne sat protectively by her side, Kristina told the detectives the little she knew about her late employer.

Renée Carter had been an event planner who slept late, then was gone for most of the day, and was always out till very late at night. She spent little or no time with her child. "She showed a lot more affection to Ranger, the Lab, than she did to Sally," Kristina recalled. In the short time Kristina had been there, Renée had had no company. She did not have a land line, so any calls that came while she was in the apartment rang on her cell phone.

"I just don't know very much about her," Kristina said apologetically. "I was hired through the agency."

Barry Tucker gave her his card. "If you think of anyone we might contact, get back to me. You handled it very well by taking the baby to the hospital, so you go home and get some rest. We'll be talking to you again."

"What's going to happen to Sally?" Kristina asked.

"We don't know yet," Tucker told her. "We'll start looking for relatives."

"If you do find out who her father is, I don't think he'll want her. Unless she was joking, the way Ms. Carter said that he was ready to finally cough up some money doesn't sound as if he was supporting her."

"No, it doesn't."

"And what about Ranger?" Sally asked. "We can't just leave him alone. Can I take him with me for now? Kerianne and I have a really small apartment, but my mother loves dogs. She'd look after him. I know she would."

"I think that's a pretty good temporary solution," Tucker agreed. "All right. I'll walk you girls down and put you in a cab. I want to talk to the people at the desk. They must have a contact for someone to call if there was a problem in this apartment and they couldn't reach Ms. Carter."

Ten minutes later, after dispatching the young women and the Labrador, Barry Tucker had introduced himself to Ralph Torre, the manager of the building, and after explaining that Ms. Carter had been the victim of a homicide, began to question him.

Eager to be cooperative, Torre told him that Renée Carter had been in the apartment for a year. Before she was allowed to sign a lease she had submitted financial information which showed she had made one hundred thousand dollars at her last job as the assistant manager of a restaurant in Las Vegas and had assets of "give or take a million bucks." She had listed a Flora White as the person to contact in case of emergency. Torre wrote down White's cell phone and business number. "Will Ms. Carter's family be giving up the apartment?" he asked hopefully. "We have a waiting list for the park view."

"I wouldn't know," Barry said curtly, and went back up to the apartment to phone Flora White. He tried her cell phone first.

She picked up on the first ring. The somewhat breathy tone of her voice changed when Tucker told her he was calling about Renée Carter.

"I really don't give a damn about Renée Carter," White snapped. "She was in charge of one of our big events last night, and she never showed up. You can tell her for me she's fired."

Tucker made the decision to hold off telling White that Renée was dead. "I am Detective Barry Tucker," he said. "When did you last see Renée Carter?"

"Detective? Is she in trouble? Did anything happen to her?" To Tucker's trained ear, the shock in Flora White's voice sounded genuine.

"She didn't come home night before last," Tucker said. "The babysitter had to take her child to the hospital."

"She must have met someone really good," White scoffed. "It wouldn't be the first time she got on a private plane to nowhere with someone she just met. From what I hear that kid is sick a lot."

"When was the last time you saw Renée Carter?" Tucker repeated.

"Night before last. We did the red carpet routine for the premiere of some lousy movie, and ran the party after it. But Renée took off at ten o'clock. She was meeting someone. I don't know who."

"Did she ever speak about the father of her child or about her own family?"

"If you can believe her, which is doubtful, she ran away from home when she was sixteen, got some bit parts in movies in Hollywood, then was out in Vegas for a while. I met her here about three years ago. We were hostesses at the same club in SoHo. Then she found out she was pregnant. She must have gotten some big payoff from her boyfriend to get out of town because suddenly she's not around anymore. I heard nothing from her for a year. Then one day she called me up. She'd gone back to Vegas but now was bored. She missed New York. I'd started the event planning business, and asked her if she was interested in working at it."

Tucker had been making notes as Flora White talked. "She was interested, I suppose?"

"You bet she was. Where better to connect with another guy with money?"

"She never talked about her baby's father?"

"If you mean did she tell me his name, the answer is no. But my guess is that she got plenty to make sure that baby wasn't born, but then decided she'd be better off having a hold on the guy."

Flora White is a fountain of information, Barry Tucker thought, the kind of person any detective would love to find in an investigation, but her casually brutal assessment of Renée Carter left him acutely sorry for the child who was now in a hospital and might easily end up unwanted by anyone.

"Let me know when you hear from Renée," Flora White was saying. "I didn't mean it about firing her. I mean, of course, I could kill her for not showing up last night, but on the other hand she's really good at what she does. When she wants to turn on the charm, she puts people at ease and makes them laugh, and they come back to us when their next lousy movie is being screened for their friends."

"Ms. White, you've been very helpful," Barry said. "You tell me that Renée left the party early night before last. Do you know if a driver picked her up or if she took a cab?"

"A cab? Renée? Are you kidding? She has a driving service and boy oh boy, the chauffeur had better have a uniform and cap on, and the car better be a Mercedes 500 and looking like it just came off the lot. She always wanted to give the impression that she was loaded."

"Do you know the name of the service?"

"Sure. I use them, too. But I don't drive them crazy the way Renée does. They're Ultra-Lux. I'll give you the phone number. It's . . ." She paused. "Wait a minute, I never get numbers straight. I have it here."

It was time to tell Flora White that Renée Carter would not be available for future screenings.

After he had heard her cries of dismay and managed to calm her down, Tucker requested that she meet him at the District Attorney's Office in the morning to sign a statement verifying the facts she had just given him.

A few minutes later, as Detective Dennis Flynn went through Renée's desk looking for any information on next of kin, Barry Tucker talked to the dispatcher of the Ultra-Lux driving service, who told him that Renée Carter had been dropped off at a bar on East End Avenue in the vicinity of Gracie Mansion, and she had told the driver that he didn't have to wait for her.

"We were short that night," the man explained, "and when Ms. Carter's driver checked in to say he was free, I wanted to make real sure he had it straight. I didn't need her calling me screaming if the driver wasn't there. My guy was insistent. He said that Ms. Carter told him her date would drop her off home because he lived not far from her on Central Park West. Then he told me something else. It's kind of gossip, if you know what I mean, but it may help you. When Renée was in a good mood she was really friendly. Anyhow, the other night she laughed and told our guy that her date thought she was broke, so she didn't want to have a fancy car waiting for her when she came out."

37

Shaken, and with blood dripping from her badly scraped hand and leg, Monica nevertheless refused the suggestion of several bystanders to call an ambulance. The bus driver who thought he had run her over was trembling so badly that for twenty minutes he was unable to continue his route.

A police car summoned by a frantic 911 call from a woman who also thought Monica had gone under the wheels of the bus arrived on the scene, which now became the center of attention at Union Square.

"I can't really say how it happened," Monica heard herself saying. "I absolutely wasn't trying to cross the street, because the light was turning red. I guess the person behind me was rushing and I was in his way."

"It wasn't an accident. A man pushed you deliberately," an elderly woman at the front of the crowd insisted, her voice rising above the comments of the other spectators.

Startled, Monica turned to look at her. "Oh, that's impossible," she protested.

"I know what I'm talking about!" Her head wrapped in a scarf, her coat collar up, her face half covered with round-framed glasses, her lips a tight line, the witness tapped the police officer on his sleeve. “He *pushed* her,” she insisted. “I was standing right behind him. He elbowed me to one side, then his arms went back and he gave her a shove that sent her flying.”

“What did he look like?” the cop asked quickly.

“A big guy. Not fat, but big. He had on a jacket with a hood, and the hood was up. He was wearing dark glasses. Who needs dark glasses when it’s dark out? I could tell he wasn’t a kid. Past forty anyhow, I’d say. And he was wearing thick gloves. Do you see anyone else around here wearing gloves? And did he do what the rest of us did when we thought this poor girl might be dead? Did he holler or scream or try to help? No. He turned and shoved his way out of the crowd and took off.”

The policeman looked at Monica. “Do you feel as if you might have been pushed?”

“Yes. Yes, I do, but it couldn’t have been deliberate.”

“We don’t know that,” the policeman said, soberly. “There are mentally ill people who shove people in front of trains or buses. You may have just come in contact with one of them.”

“Then I guess I’m very lucky to be here.” I want to get home, Monica thought. But it was another fifteen minutes, after telling the cop she was a doctor and could take care of her scrapes, then giving her name, address, and phone number for the police records, before she was able to get into a waiting cab and escape. Her crushed shoulder bag beside her, she leaned her head back and closed her eyes.

In an instant, she was reliving the sharp pain in her arm and leg as she slammed onto the pavement, then the acrid smell of the bus as it bore down on her. She tried to calm herself but the cabdriver had seen the commotion and wanted to talk. Trying to keep from trembling, she answered in monosyllables to his sympathetic diatribe that there ought to be a way to make sure crazies took their meds regularly and didn't end up going off half-cocked and hurting innocent people.

It was when she was finally in her apartment, with the door closed and locked, that the full impact of having come so close to death hit her. Maybe I should have gone to the hospital, she thought. I don't have a single thing in the medicine chest to calm me down. It was then, with the blood now crusted on her hand and leg, that she realized she had forgotten that Ryan Jenner was coming for the Michael O'Keefe file.

I have his home phone, she thought. He gave it to me the other night. I'll call and apologize. Will I tell him what happened? Yes, I will. If he offers to come over I'll take him up on it. I could use some company.

I could use Ryan's company, she told herself.

Okay, admit it, she thought.

You're attracted to him, big-time.

His apartment and cell phone numbers were now in the small address book she always carried in her shoulder bag. Wincing at the sight of her crushed compact and sunglasses, she fumbled for the book. Still sitting at the table with her coat not yet off, she dialed Jenner's apartment number, the first one she had listed. But when a woman answered and said that Ryan was changing his clothes, Monica left the message that she would send the file to him in the morning.

She had just replaced the receiver when the phone rang. It was Scott Alterman. "Monica, I was listening to the radio and heard that you were almost run over by a bus, that someone pushed you?" She was surprised that reporters had released her name, and wondered how many friends and colleagues had also heard the report.

Scott's voice was shocked and concerned, and Monica found it comforting. It brought back the memory of how kind Scott had been to her father when he was in the nursing home, and that he had been the one to phone her with the news that her father had passed away.

"I just can't believe that it's true," she said, her voice tremulous. "I mean that I was pushed, that it wasn't an accident."

"Monica, you sound pretty shaken up. Are you alone now?"

"Yes."

"I could be there in ten minutes. Will you let me come?"

Suddenly feeling her throat tighten and tears welling in her eyes, Monica said, "That would be nice. I could really use some company right now."

38

Everything had been going so well. Sammy Barber had collected the money from Dougie-the-Dope Langdon, driven to the storage building in Long Island City, and stashed all those beautiful hundred-dollar bills in his safe in the space he rented there. Then, feeling on top of the world, at five thirty he had called Monica Farrell's office, giving his name as Dr. Curtain in honor of a guy who had been his jail cell mate while he was awaiting trial. The secretary had told him that Dr. Farrell had canceled all her appointments because of an emergency at the hospital.

He had the money. He was set for life. He was feeling good about life, in fact. Sammy was convinced that it was his lucky day and he wanted to get the job done. That was why he had rushed over to the hospital and found a parking spot across from the main entrance, the one the doctor had used the couple of times he'd tracked her before. He had changed his mind and decided he would try to push her in front of a bus.

He waited for about an hour and a half until he spotted Farrell coming down the steps. There were two cabs passing, but she ignored them and turned right toward Fourteenth Street.

Ten to one she's gonna walk back to her office, Sammy thought as he reached on the passenger seat for his gloves and dark glasses. He slipped them on, got out of the car, and began to follow her from a distance of about a quarter of a block. She wasn't walking fast, at least not as fast as she had last week when he had trailed her. There were a lot of people on the street tonight, and that was good, too.

At Union Square he saw his chance. The light was turning red but people were still scurrying across the street trying to beat the oncoming traffic. A bus was charging across Fourteenth Street heading for the bus stop. Farrell was at the edge of the curb.

In an instant Sammy was behind her and, with the bus only a few feet away, gave her a shove then watched in disbelief as she somehow managed to roll out from under the tires as, brakes screeching, the bus skidded in a useless attempt to stop. He knew the old lady standing next to him had seen him push Farrell and, trying not to panic, Sammy ducked his head as he hurried past her and headed downtown.

At the end of three blocks, he turned right and took off his gloves and dark glasses and pushed back the hood of his sweat jacket. Trying to look casual, he walked at a normal pace back toward his car. But when he got to where he could see it, he stared unbelieving at the sight of it, wheels clamped, being hoisted onto a police department carrier.

The meter. In his rush to follow Monica Farrell, he had forgotten to feed the meter. His impulse was to go and argue with the driver of the tow truck, but instead he forced himself to turn away and start walking home. I know they bring the cars to some dump near the West Side Highway, he thought, trying to stay focused. If that old lady talks to the cops about Farrell being pushed and describes me, I can't show up in these clothes to claim the car . . .

He felt his forehead breaking into a sweat. If the old lady *did* talk to the cops and they took her seriously they might figure that someone was staking out the doctor, then follow up on my car being towed across the street from the hospital. Then if they look me up, they'll find out that I've got a record. They might want to know what I was doing parked at the hospital and where I was when the meter ran out right around the time the doctor was pushed . . .

Stay calm. Stay calm. Sammy walked downtown to his Lower East Side apartment, and changed into a shirt, tie, sports jacket, slacks, and polished shoes. From his prepaid cell phone he called information and, after being savagely irritated by the computer voice droning, "I'll pass you on to an operator," obtained the number he needed.

A bored voice told him to be sure to have his license, insurance card, and registration and to bring cash in order to claim his automobile. Sammy gave his license number. "Is it there yet?"

"Yeah. It just came in."

After twenty frustrating minutes in a cab crawling along the narrow streets of downtown Manhattan to

West Thirty-eighth Street, Sammy was presenting his license to the clerk at the pound. "The insurance and registration are in the glove compartment," he said, trying to sound friendly. "I was visiting a friend in the hospital and forgot about the meter."

Should he have said that? Was the clerk looking at him as if he knew he was lying? Sammy was pretty sure the young cop was giving him a steely-eyed once-over. But maybe I'm just nervous, he thought, trying to comfort himself as he walked to his car to get the insurance card and registration. Finally he completed the paperwork, paid the fine, and was able to go.

He had driven barely a block before his cell phone rang. It was Doug Langdon. "Well, you botched that one," Langdon said, his voice trembling with fury. "The whole city knows that an attractive young doctor was pushed in front of a bus and nearly lost her life. The description of you is pretty accurate, too. A bulky middle-aged guy in a dark sweat jacket. Did you give her your business card as well, by any chance?"

For some reason the panic in Langdon's voice forced Sammy to calm himself down. He didn't want Langdon to go off the deep end. "How many bulky middle-aged men are walking the streets of Manhattan in a dark sweat jacket?" he demanded. "I'll tell you right now what the cops will think. If they do believe that old crow, they'll think it's one of those guys who didn't take his medicine. How many of them go loopy and push people off the train tracks? So quit worrying. Your doctor used up her one good-luck charm tonight. The next one is mine."

39

Barry Tucker left his partner, Dennis Flynn, in Renée Carter's apartment to wait for a police technician to padlock the door. "That lady sure was careless with her jewelry," Flynn observed. "There's a lot of stuff that looks valuable scattered around in that tray on her dresser, and more in boxes in her closet."

"You keep looking for anything that indicates next of kin," Tucker told him. "And make a list of all the people you find in her daily appointment book. Then start with the men and check their addresses in the Manhattan phone book. See if one of them lives around here. I'm heading for that bar where Carter was supposed to meet the guy who may be the baby's father."

As he spoke he took a picture of Renée from its frame. "With any luck we may solve this one pretty fast."

"You always hope that," Flynn observed dryly.

"Dennis, this one has a kid involved, who's going to end up in a foster home if we can't find a relative willing to take her," Barry Tucker reminded him.

"After what we heard from the babysitter, my guess is that the kid will be better off in a foster home than she was with the mother," Flynn said quietly.

That remark stayed in Barry Tucker's mind as he drove across town to the restaurant near Gracie Mansion where Renée Carter had been dropped off to meet the mystery man. He tried to imagine either one of his children alone in a hospital, with no relative or close friend to care for them. Not in a million years, he thought. If anything happened to Trish and me, both grandmothers, to say nothing of all three of Trish's sisters, would be fighting for custody of the kids.

The restaurant turned out to be an English-style pub. The bar was directly inside the entrance, and Barry could see that the dining room beyond it held no more than a dozen tables. A neighborhood kind of place, he thought. I bet they get a lot of repeat customers. Let's hope Carter was one of them. From what he could see, all the tables seemed to be taken, and most of the stools at the bar were occupied.

He walked to the end of the bar, waited until the bartender came to take his order, then slid his gold badge and a picture of Renée across the counter.

"Do you recognize this lady?" he asked.

The bartender's eyes widened. "Yes, sure I do. That's Renée Carter."

"When was the last time she was here?"

"Night before last, Tuesday, around ten thirty, give or take ten minutes."

"Was she alone?"

"She came in alone, but some guy was waiting for her. He pulled out a stool for her to sit here at the bar, but she said they should get a table."

"What was her attitude toward the man she met?"

"Snippy."

"Do you know who he is?"

"No. I don't think he's ever been here before."

"What did he look like?"

"Late forties, early fifties. Dark hair. Really good-looking guy, and his clothes didn't come off a pipe rack, I can tell you that."

"What was his attitude toward Renée Carter?"

"Not happy. I could tell he was nervous. He polished off two scotches before she even got here."

"So then they went to a table?"

"Yeah. Most of the tables were empty by then. We close the kitchen at ten. While they were still standing at the bar, he ordered two scotches and said something to her like, 'I assume you still have a taste for single malt?' "

"What did she say?"

"She said something like, 'I can't afford single malt scotch anymore, but it's clear *you* can.' I mean, it sounded stupid coming from someone who was all dolled up like Renée Carter was."

"All right. So they went to the table. How long did they stay there?"

"Not long enough to finish their drinks. I mean, I kept my eye on them, because by then it was slow and I had nothing better to do. I saw him hand her the big shopping bag he'd been carrying—you know, one of those gift bags. She grabbed it from him, got up so fast she almost knocked over the chair, and hightailed it out of here with an expression on her face that would have stopped an eight-day clock. He threw fifty bucks on the table and rushed out behind her."

"Would you recognize that man if you saw him again?"

"Oh, sure. I never forget a face. Detective, did something happen to Renée?"

"Yes. She was the victim of a homicide after she left this restaurant. She never got home that night."

The bartender's face blanched. "Oh, God, that's a shame. Did she get mugged?"

"We don't know. How often did Renée Carter come here?"

"Maybe once or twice a month. Mainly for a nightcap, and she was never alone. Always with a guy."

"Do you know the names of any of the men she was with?"

"Sure, some of them anyhow. I'll make a list."

The bartender reached for a pad and picked up a pen. "Let's see," he murmured to himself. "There's Les . . ." Aware that other people at the bar were looking at him, he clamped his lips firmly shut, then straightened up and hurried down the length of the bar to where a man was sitting alone sipping a beer.

Sensing the bartender might have remembered something about Renée Carter, Barry Tucker followed him down past the row of barstools. He got there in time to hear him say, "Rudy, you were here Tuesday night and you noticed Renée Carter leaving in a hurry. I just remembered, you said something about being surprised that the guy with her had the price of a drink. Do you know his name?"

Rudy, a florid-cheeked man, began to laugh. "Sure I do. Peter Gannon. He's the guy they call 'the loser-producer.' You must have read about him. He's laid more eggs on Broadway than Perdue has chickens."

40

On Friday morning Monica awoke at quarter of six and for long minutes lay in bed, quietly searching out the aching parts of her body. Her left arm and leg were badly scraped. Besides that the impact of the fall had made her lower back feel bruised and sore. She promised herself that for the next week or so she would take the time each morning to soak in the Jacuzzi instead of taking a quick shower.

That decided, she turned her attention to the events of the previous evening. After Scott Alterman had called, realizing that some of her friends might have heard the same broadcast, the first thing she did was to change the message on her telephone. "Hi, this is Monica. I know you may have heard the report about my accident. I'm really fine, but am going to take it easy, so I won't be returning messages this evening. But thanks anyway for calling."

Then she had turned off the ringer of the phone. Feeling relieved at having thought to avoid the concerned calls she knew she would be receiving, she had gone into the bathroom. There she had stripped off her damaged clothes, sponged the dried blood from her arm and leg, coated the injured areas with an antibiotic salve, and still shivering from the aftermath of her nearly fatal encounter, changed into pajamas and a woolly robe.

When Scott arrived, his concern for her had been so obviously genuine that for the present it took away the hurtful realization that Ryan Jenner had a close relationship with another woman. Scott had taken her hand and insisted she lie down on the couch. "Monica, you're pale as a ghost and your hands are freezing," he told her. He piled pillows behind her head, covered her with an afghan, and fixed a hot toddy for her. Then, realizing she had not had any dinner, he looked into the refrigerator, selected tomato and cheese, and grilled a delicious sandwich for her. "My specialty," he said cheerfully.

It was good to see him, Monica acknowledged now, as she decided to give herself another ten minutes before getting up. She hadn't intended to tell him about Olivia Morrow, but found herself explaining to him the events of the past few days and her disappointment that Morrow had died before Monica could talk with her about her grandmother.

Scott, however, had been quick to say, "Monica, I will bet you the ranch that Olivia Morrow has a connection to the Gannons. Trust me. I'm going to find out. Your father believed that Alexander Gannon might have been his father. There were plenty of articles about Alexander Gannon, and a number of them had biographical information in them. Seeing the pictures your dad had collected, and comparing photos of him and Gannon at the same age throughout their lives was startling." He spoke quickly, obviously excited that Monica might allow him to help her.

Before he left, Scott had said, "Monica, I'm going to say this once and then never refer to it again. I am desperately sorry I was stupid enough to ask you out while I was still married to Joy. If you'll allow me to see you now, it will be as a friend. On my word of honor, I will not in any way make you uncomfortable. Let's do it this way. I'm going to follow up on Olivia Morrow, and in two weeks I'll call you for dinner. And I'm going to ask Joy to phone you. Would that be okay?"

I told him it would be fine, Monica thought. And it *will* be, if he's sincere about simply wanting to resume our friendship and nothing more. Scott was a good friend to Dad when he was so sick, and I'll never forget how helpful he was when Dad passed away.

Having settled that in her mind, Monica sat up. Wincing at the pain that shot through her arm and leg, she got out of bed slowly, went into the bathroom, and turned on the taps in the Jacuzzi.

The very warm swirling water did help the stiffness and by the time she was dressed, she was feeling better. She put on a small pot of coffee and as it perked, she went into the bedroom. I look like a ghost, she thought, as she dabbed on some blush, then twisted her hair and fastened it up with a clip.

Leave it like that. It looks good.

The memory of Ryan saying that to her less than two weeks ago, when little Carlos pulled that same clip out, caused a sudden lump in her throat, and she felt her eyes stinging with tears she had no intention of shedding. I'll phone Nan and ask her to bring the O'Keefe file over to Ryan's office, she decided. I don't want to run into him, and from now on there's no real reason I should. It's a big hospital.

Her final decision, as she sipped the coffee, was to downgrade the possibility that she had been deliberately pushed. As I told Scott, if that man was just trying to shove me aside so he could make the light, he was probably horrified that I might have been run over. No wonder he ran away. Most people would in that situation.

In a cab on the way to the hospital, Monica made the call to Nan, then phoned ahead to inquire about Sally Carter. She was relieved to learn that Sally had had a good night, but outraged that there had still been no visit from her mother. I'll notify Family Services this morning, she vowed.

Her first stop at the hospital was to visit Sally. She was sleeping quietly, and Monica decided not to risk waking her up. The nurse on duty reported that Sally's temperature had gone down to only a degree above normal, and that the asthma attack had passed. "Doctor, last night, after you left, when she woke up, I thought she was crying for Mommy, but actually she was saying, 'Monny.' I think it's possible that when she was here last week she heard other kids calling you Dr. Monica."

"I wouldn't be surprised," a familiar voice said. "I've heard that's the effect you have on your patients."

Monica turned swiftly. It was Ryan Jenner. "I doubt

Sally knows my name," she said, then catching the look the nurse was giving her and Ryan, she added, "Dr. Jenner, may I speak with you in private?"

"Of course," he said, his tone immediately as formal as hers. She walked with him to the corridor. "I've sent the file on Michael O'Keefe to your office," she told him.

"It just came. Your secretary told me you'd probably be here checking on Sally. Monica, I just heard about what happened last night. Is it possible that you were pushed? My God, I can't imagine how frightening it must have been."

"I'm all right. Ryan, I have to ask you not to visit me on this floor, unless of course it involves a patient. I get a feeling that there's some gossip about us."

He looked at her. "And you don't like that?"

"No, I don't. And I should think that you certainly wouldn't, either."

Without waiting for him to reply, she went back inside the Pediatrics Ward and began to make her rounds of the other small patients in her care.

41

After his initial panic attack at the realization that he had murdered Olivia Morrow, Dr. Clayton Hadley composed himself by reviewing over and over again every detail of his final visit to Olivia.

Tuesday evening he had told the clerk at the desk that Ms. Morrow was feeling very ill, and he had asked Olivia to be sure to leave the bolt of her front door unlocked so that she would not have to get out of bed to let him in. If the bolt had been on, the risk would have been much greater—she would have had to physically let him in herself. But the bolt was not on, so he had been able to slip into the apartment noiselessly.

She had been asleep when he tiptoed into her bedroom, but woke instantly when he stood over her. Olivia had a night-light near the bathroom door and he could see that as soon as she recognized him, her expression of surprise turned into one of fear.

She slept on two pillows on her queen-sized bed, and two other pillows were next to her. Long ago when he had visited her at home, after she had suffered a mild heart attack, she explained that she sometimes brought a cup of tea and the newspaper back to bed in the morning and piled those extra pillows behind her back.

As he reached for one of those spare pillows, the thought that ran through his head was, *She knows I'm going to kill her.* He remembered saying, "I'm sorry, Olivia," as he held the pillow over her face.

Frail as she was, he was shocked at how fiercely she tried to push it away. It couldn't have been more than a minute, but to him it seemed an eternity before her emaciated hands finally relaxed and fell limp on the coverlet.

When he removed the pillow, he saw that while she was struggling Olivia had bitten her lip. A single drop of blood was on the pillow he had used to suffocate her. Nervously he had considered switching it with the one under her head, but he realized that the sight of the blood there might raise questions. Instead he went to the linen closet. Neatly stacked on the middle shelf he found two other complete sets of sheets and pillowcases. Each set consisted of two sheets and four pillowcases. One set was cream-colored, the other pale pink. The set on the bed was a shade of peach.

Hadley decided he had to take the chance to replace the soiled pillowcase with one of the pink ones. It's not much different, he had consoled himself, and if anyone notices, they'll probably think the other peach pillowcase was lost at the laundry. He knew Olivia sent her sheets out to the laundry weekly because she had joked to him that one of her luxuries was fine cotton sheets, which she had professionally washed and ironed. When he changed the pillowcase, he was horrified to realize that the blood had also gone through to the pillow itself. Panicked, he knew it would be noticed if he tried to take it with him. He decided that the best he could do was to have the new pillowcase on it and hope it would never be noticed.

He had folded the stained pillowcase and tucked it in the pocket of his topcoat, then had begun to search the apartment for the Catherine file. Olivia had made him executor of her estate and given him the combination to her safe, so that when the time came the will would be probated without delay. It was a very simple document. There were a few small bequests to longtime service people in the building and her cleaning woman. The contents of her apartment, her car, and her jewelry were to be sold. The money from them together with her small portfolio of stocks and bonds were to be left to various Catholic charities. In the will she noted that she had already made and paid for arrangements with The Frank E. Campbell Funeral Chapel. She didn't wish to have a viewing, but after a funeral Mass at St. Vincent Ferrer, to be cremated. Her ashes were to be buried in her mother's grave in Calvary Cemetery.

The will was in the safe, as well as her few pieces of jewelry—pearls and a small diamond ring and earrings—certainly not worth more than a few thousand dollars.

But to his dismay, the Catherine file was not there. Acutely aware that the concierge might be noticing how long he was staying, Clay Hadley had searched every inch of Olivia's apartment without success. The Catherine file was missing.

What had she done with it? Clay had asked himself, desperately. Was there any chance she had destroyed it then changed her mind about revealing the truth when she heard from Monica Farrell? It was the only reasonable explanation he could imagine. On the way out of the building, the clerk at the desk had stopped him. "How is Ms. Morrow, Doctor?" he asked solicitously.

Weighing his words carefully, Clay had said, "Ms. Morrow is a very, very sick woman." Then in a husky voice added, "She's not going to be with us for more than a few days or a week."

The next evening, after he received the call that Olivia had been found dead, he had sat with Monica Farrell in Olivia's living room. When the Emergency Medical Services group arrived Monica had not stayed long. She had nothing to tell them except that she had come because she had an appointment with Olivia Morrow. In retrospect, Clay prided himself on how well he had handled the medics, explaining that he was Olivia's longtime doctor, that she was terminally ill, that only last night he had begged her to go to a hospice . . . Then, when the mortician from Campbell's arrived, the medics toe-tagged her body, and he signed the death certificate.

After a sleepless night and frantic phone call to Doug, Clay had kept himself busy blotting out any trace of suspicion of his connection to Olivia's death for the rest of Thursday. He called in the obituary notice to the *Times*, called the small list of people in her address book, arranged for the funeral Mass, and called a liquidator he had met socially and arranged to meet him at the apartment and inventory the contents. Then, having felt he had done everything he could to present the picture of a solicitous friend and executor, he took a sleeping pill and went to bed.

At nine o'clock on Friday morning, the first phone call he received when he reached his office was from a man he did not know, Scott Alterman. "He's inquiring about Olivia Morrow," his secretary informed him.

Who is this guy? Hadley wondered, his stomach in knots. "Put him on," he said.

Scott introduced himself. "I am a friend of Dr. Monica Farrell. I believe you met her in Olivia Morrow's apartment Wednesday evening."

"Yes, I did." Where is this going? Hadley wondered.

"Only the night before her death, Ms. Morrow had told Dr. Farrell that she knew her grandmother. By that it was clear that she meant her birth grandmother. From what you told Dr. Farrell at that time, you have been a longtime friend of Ms. Morrow's, as well as her physician and the executor of her estate. As such, you must have some knowledge of Ms. Morrow's family history?"

Hadley tried to keep his voice steady. "That's entirely true. I became her mother's cardiologist, then Olivia's. Olivia was an only child. Her mother died many years ago. I never met anyone else at all who was a relation."

"And Ms. Morrow never spoke about her background to you?"

Be close to the truth, but no specifics, Hadley warned himself. "I know that Olivia told me her father died before she was born and her mother remarried. By the time I met them, her mother had been widowed a second time."

Then came the question that made Hadley's mouth go dry. Scott Alterman asked, "Dr. Hadley, haven't you been on the board of the Gannon Foundation for many years?"

"Yes, that's true. Why do you ask?"

"I don't know yet," Alterman said. "But I'm sure there's an answer to be found and I warn you, I will find it. Good-bye, Dr. Hadley."

42

Peter Gannon woke up on Friday morning with a hangover that put any previous hangover he had ever experienced to shame. His head was bursting, he was nauseous, and he had the crashing feeling that his world was about to disappear from under him.

He knew he would have to declare bankruptcy. There was no way he could pay off the backers of his play. Why was I so sure that this one was going to be a hit? he asked himself. Guaranteeing them half of what they invested was stupid, but it was the only way they'd put up any money. I'll be a pariah to them now.

For long minutes he stood in a hot shower, then, wincing, turned on the cold water. As he shivered under the needlelike impact of the freezing spray against his skin, he forced himself to deal with the fact that he would have to admit to Greg that he had once told Renée Carter he was sure Greg was involved in an insider trading fraud. Not only that, but I told her that except for the charities we support because of Clay in cardiology research and Doug in psychiatric research, a lot of our donations from the foundation are small and strictly for show. If she hadn't decided to blackmail me about the baby, no doubt she would've threatened to expose the fraud. God, if they were ever investigated! Peter did not finish the thought.

Greg will simply have to give me a million dollars to pay off Renée, and he'll have to do it now. I saw her Tuesday night. For all I know she's already thought about how much she'd collect for being a snitch. I gave her two million dollars when she left town almost two and a half years ago to keep her mouth shut, and that was supposed to be it. She said she would give up the baby for adoption.

Renée. Unsteadily, Peter got out of the shower and reached for a bath towel. I was drinking all Tuesday afternoon, he thought. I was afraid to tell her that all I could scrape up was one hundred thousand dollars, not a million. Then, when I was waiting for her in the bar, I had those two scotches. I should have told her that the hundred thousand was all I could give her for now. I should have strung her along . . .

What happened then? he asked himself. She got mad when I gave her the bag with the hundred thousand, and that was all she'd ever get. Final payment. No more money. I'd have her charged with extortion. Then, when she ran out and started down the street, I ran after her and grabbed her hand. She dropped the bag, slapped me, and her fingernail nicked my face.

What happened then?

I don't remember, Peter thought miserably. I just don't remember. Oh, God, he thought, as he slipped into a bathrobe, *where did I go?* What did I *do*? I don't know. I just don't know. I woke up on the couch in the office on Wednesday afternoon. That was fifteen hours later. Then I started thinking that Sue might lend me the money and I met her at Il Tinello. After Sue turned me down, I got drunk again. Renée hasn't called me back yet, or has she? I've been having blackouts. Maybe I didn't hear the phone . . .

Peter looked into the mirror over the bathroom sink. Some mess, he observed. Eyes bloodshot. I never did shave yesterday. Wonder what Sue thought when I met her?

Sue. Renée was the straw that broke the camel's back in our marriage. I had sworn to Sue I'd quit womanizing, then she read in the gossip column that I'd been seen with Renée. The mistake of my life, four years ago. Sue wouldn't believe I was sick of Renée and breaking up with her. Crazy, the way the ball bounces. Sue had three miscarriages in the twenty years we were married and Renée managed to get pregnant just when she knew I was about to break off with her. Of course she did it on purpose, he thought angrily, but at least Sue never knew about the baby. That would have been hell for her . . . And now, divorced or not, he hoped Sue never finds out.

Why didn't Renée give up the baby for adoption? When I paid her off, she said she would. She sure wasn't into kids. She did it because she wanted to have a hold over me. A hold called Sally, whom I've never met, nor ever *want* to meet. Why did Renée come back to New York? Guess she'd not gotten her claws into another rich boyfriend in Vegas and needs me to feather her nest again.

If only I could prove the kid isn't mine, but Renée was smart enough to have saved DNA from me and had it matched with the baby's. She's mine, like it or not.

Peter Gannon reached for his shaving soap and razor. As he started to shave, he winced when the blade hit the spot where Renée's nail had caught him. What happened after she slapped me? he asked himself again.

A half hour later, dressed in a casual shirt, sweater, and khakis, a cup of coffee in his hand, Peter forced himself to pick up the phone to dial his brother, Greg.

Before he could complete the connection, the concierge called on the intercom. "Mr. Gannon, Detective Tucker and Detective Flynn are here to see you. May I send them up?"

43

On Friday morning, after she spoke to Ryan Jenner in the hospital, Monica tried to phone Renée Carter and when there was again no answer went down to see Sandra Weiss, the director of Family Services in the hospital. "I have to talk about my patient Sally Carter," she began.

"I was about to call you," Weiss told her somberly. "We have just heard from the police. The body of a woman found on the pedestrian walkway near the East River yesterday has been identified as Renée Carter, Sally's mother."

Monica stared at her. "Renée Carter is dead?" she asked numbly.

"Yes. The police are trying to locate the next of kin. Until then we'll take custody of Sally. When you're ready to discharge her, if no relatives have been found, we'll place her in foster care, for the present."

Renée Carter dead! Shocked, Monica could only visualize the petulant woman who had had so little interest in her baby. Who would the next of kin turn out to be? she wondered. What's going to happen to Sally?

Even though she needed to get to the office where

she knew patients were already waiting, she stopped to see Sally again before she left the hospital. The little girl was still sleeping, and not wanting to wake her up, Monica stood at the crib wistfully for a long minute, then hurried away.

When she reached the office, the waiting room was beginning to fill up. Nan followed her into her private office and cornered her. "I heard the report on the radio last evening, Dr. Monica," she said, breathlessly. "I almost died. I tried to call you right away. Thank God you put that message on the phone to say you were all right. But the first thing I did was to tell John Hartman, the retired detective who lives down the hall from me, about it. He says he's going to call one of his detective friends and tell him to have the security cameras around the hospital checked. Maybe that guy who pushed you was following you? Maybe it had something to do with that picture of you standing in front of the hospital that I showed you. You didn't think that it meant anything."

Monica raised her hand to stop the torrent of words. "Nan, you know how much I appreciate your concern, but I just don't think anyone deliberately shoved me. I think that guy was so anxious to cross the street that he tried to get me out of his way. So if any of my friends call here asking how I am, please reassure them I'm fine, and I absolutely believe it was an unfortunate accident. Now please tell Alma I'm ready to get started. God help the poor parents who came in yesterday and then had to drag the kids in again today."

Nan took a few steps toward the door, then hesitated. "Doctor, one more question. How is Sally Carter?"

It felt surreal to Monica to say that Sally's mother was not only dead, but the victim of a homicide. "I don't know anything more than that," she said hurriedly, as she buttoned her white jacket and headed for the examining room.

For the next seven hours, she only gave herself a five-minute break for a cup of tea and two bites of a sandwich before the last little patient was gone at six o'clock. Alma left, saying, "Please take it easy over the weekend, Doctor."

"I intend to. Thanks, Alma." Monica went to her small private office and took off her white coat. That was when Nan followed her in and asked the question that had been bothering her all day. "Dr. Monica, what happened when you met Olivia Morrow Wednesday? Did she really know your grandmother?"

Monica turned away as she felt her eyes begin to glisten. The crushing disappointment that Olivia Morrow was dead, her near-fatal accident, the near certainty that Sally might be headed for foster care, and finally the deepening knowledge that she cared far more for Ryan Jenner than she had realized were all sinking in.

She took a minute to swallow hard before she began to speak. Even though her voice was steady, she was forced to turn from the sympathy in Nan's face as she told her about going to the Morrow apartment and finding that Olivia had passed away during the night. "So, I guess that if there was any substance to the story, I'll never know it," she concluded.

"What are the funeral arrangements?" Nan asked.

"When I spoke to Dr. Hadley, while we were waiting for the EMS squad, he said he would be taking care of them."

"I have a copy of the *Times*," Nan said. "Maybe there's something in the obituary section." She ran out to her desk and returned with the newspaper opened to that page. "Doctor, there is a notice here about Ms. Morrow. There is a funeral Mass being offered for her tomorrow morning at St. Vincent Ferrer, at ten o'clock. If I were you I'd go to it. It says right here that she didn't have any next of kin, but she must have had some friends. I'd like to go with you. Between us we might be able to talk to some of the people who attend the Mass and find out if she ever talked about you. Who knows what you may find out? You've got nothing to lose."

"That's not a bad idea," Monica said slowly. "You said ten o'clock tomorrow, at St. Vincent Ferrer?"

"Yes. That's at Sixty-sixth and Lexington."

"I'll meet you there at quarter of ten." Monica reached into the closet for her coat. "Sufficient unto the day is the evil thereof," she quoted, wearily.

As they passed Nan's desk on the way to the outside door, the phone rang. Nan ran to see who was calling. "It's Dr. Jenner," she said, her voice pleased.

"Let it ring," Monica said, emphatically. "Let's go."

44

On Friday morning Scott Alterman took an early run in Central Park, got back to his rented apartment, showered, shaved, and dressed casually. Then at eight o'clock, feeling guilty, he called and left a message for his secretary to say that he had some pressing private business and would be in later in the day.

He made coffee and toast and scrambled eggs as he tried to replace his sense of guilt with a sense of purpose. He knew it was not wise to take time away from his new office on Wall Street. He had accepted a considerable amount of money to become a partner. However, the chance to comfort Monica after her accident reinforced his feeling that more than anything in the world he wanted to prove himself to her.

She knew how much her father wanted to find his roots, Scott thought, and I think that, far more than she realizes, she shares that need. She was heartsick last night when she told me that Olivia Morrow, the woman who might have known her grandparents, had died. Learning everything I can about that woman might be the only way to follow the trail to Monica's father's parentage, and it's a trail that could go cold very quickly. If it turned out that Olivia Morrow had any connection to the Gannons, then we'd really have something to go on.

Scott knew that he was consumed with his need to follow his instinct that Monica's father might have been the "issue" Alexander Gannon referenced in his will, and that she might be the legitimate heir to the money generated by Alexander Gannon's genius.

How often, he mused, did adopted children share the same talents of their birth family? Monica's father, Edward Farrell, had been a medical researcher who helped discover why some patients rejected implants, particularly the hip, knee, and ankle replacements that were the cash cows of companies like Gannon Medical Supplies.

The main headquarters of the company was in Manhattan, but the research laboratory was in Cambridge. When he was in his sixties, Edward Farrell had been invited to join the staff there. By then, Alex Gannon was dead, but Edward Farrell's startling resemblance to him was a subject that came up from his co-workers over and over again until his retirement. It would be an irony of fate, Scott thought, if Monica's father had indeed worked for the company founded by his birth father.

The constant reference to his similarity in appearance had been sufficient to make Edward Farrell begin a hobby of finding articles about Alexander Gannon and comparing their pictures at different ages.

Monica really doesn't understand how fixated her father was on that subject, Scott thought, as he opened a lined pad and, over a second cup of coffee, began to list the starting points of his investigation. How much had Olivia known about Monica's grandparents? Was there anyone who might still know about a family connection to the Gannons?

Monica had told him that Olivia Morrow's physician of many years had rushed to the apartment after Monica and the clerk had found her dead. Clayton Hadley was the doctor's name, Scott remembered. He wrote it on the pad.

Morrow's apartment at Schwab House. Monica had the impression that Morrow had been a longtime resident there. I'll talk to the staff, Scott thought. They'd probably be familiar with any regular visitors.

Almost certainly Morrow had a cleaning woman or cleaning service. Follow that up, he told himself.

Who was the executor of her will and what were the contents of it? He'd put his secretary on that one.

Scott finished his coffee, put the cup in the sink, and tidied up the kitchen. Funny, he thought. That was just one more thing that didn't work between Joy and me. I don't think I'm a Felix Unger, but I do feel better when a place is orderly. When she walked in the door, Joy dropped everything she was carrying on the nearest chair or table. I used to wonder if her coat ever saw the inside of the closet.

There wasn't a thing out of place in Monica's apartment, he recalled.

He went into the small den that he used as an at-home office, turned on his computer, and began a search for Dr. Clayton Hadley. Then as he read the lengthy references he came to one that made him emit a soundless whistle. Hadley was on the board of the Gannon Foundation!

Monica had said that from what Dr. Hadley told her it must have been shortly after her phone call to Olivia Morrow that Hadley had gone to the apartment and checked on Olivia. A coincidence? Probably, Scott thought. Monica *did* tell me that Morrow sounded very feeble. Nevertheless, something that was not yet actual suspicion made Scott decide to call Dr. Hadley immediately. If he was Olivia Morrow's longtime physician then he had to know a fair amount about her background, he thought, as he reached for the phone.

When he was put through to Hadley, as an experienced trial lawyer, it was obvious to him that the doctor was evading his questions and that his claim of knowing virtually nothing about Olivia Morrow's background was patently a lie.

But I didn't have to put him on guard by warning him that I'd find a connection between Olivia Morrow and the Gannon Foundation, Scott told himself, as he hung up the phone. Maybe someday I'll learn to sit back and bide my time. That call was the same kind of impulsive stupidity I engaged in when I went rushing down to Monica's building and startled the wits out of her when she came out . . .

Cool it, he thought. Cool it.

Thoroughly dissatisfied with himself, he decided to walk to Schwab House and speak to some of the staff members, particularly those who had worked in the building for a long time.

When he arrived there, Scott waited until there was a lull in activity of people entering and leaving, then spoke to the doorman. The man readily told him the little he knew. Ms. Morrow was a lovely, quiet lady, always very gracious, always a thank-you when he held the door for her, always generous at Christmas. He'd miss her.

"Did she go out much?" Scott asked.

"For the last six months anyhow, when I put her in a cab, it was always to the doctor, the hairdresser, or to church on Sunday. We joked about it."

Not very helpful, Scott thought, as he went inside and stopped at the concierge's desk. He explained that he was an attorney, sure that the concierge would get the impression that he had been Morrow's attorney. "I know she's been here for many years and want to be sure that anyone who is close to her is notified of her passing," he explained.

"She wasn't one to have much company," the concierge explained. "There was one lady on the eighteenth floor who used to go out to the theatre with her, but she passed away a few years ago. It's been obvious to all of us that Ms. Morrow has been in very poor health and she didn't go out much at all."

As Scott was about to turn away, he thought to ask, "Did Ms. Morrow keep a car in the garage here?"

"Yes, she did. From what I understand she just about gave up driving herself. When she didn't take a cab to go someplace local, she used a service where the driver would take her in her own car. In fact she went out for a few hours on Tuesday."

"This *past* Tuesday! You mean the day before she died?" Scott exclaimed. "Was she out long?"

"Most of the afternoon."

"Do you know where she went?"

"No, but I have the number of the service here. Quite a few of our residents use it." The concierge reached into a drawer, pulled out some cards, and went through them. "Here it is," he said, handing one over. "You can have this if you want it. I've got a few of them."

The address of the driving service was only a few blocks away. Scott decided to walk over to it. He had long since learned that it was much better to try to get information in person rather than over the phone.

The clouds that had started to gather on his walk over to Schwab House had become thicker and darker. He moved quickly, not wanting to get caught in a downpour. What would make a very sick woman leave her home for hours? he wondered. A week earlier, Olivia Morrow had told the driver whose child was Monica's patient that she had known Monica's grandmother. Why did she wait until Monica's phone call to disclose that to Monica, and even say she knew the identity of both her grandparents? Knowing that she was dying, why didn't she do it sooner? That last day of her life, did Olivia Morrow visit someone else who also knew the truth?

As these questions rushed through his mind, nothing in Scott's psyche warned him that by his call to Clayton Hadley, he had signed his own death warrant and that the process of eliminating him had already begun.

45

His throat dry, Peter Gannon invited Detectives Barry Tucker and Dennis Flynn into the living room of his apartment. Why are they here? he wondered. Did I do something crazy when I blacked out? I don't think I took the car out. God, I hope I didn't run someone over!

Even deciding where to sit was nerve-wracking. Not the couch, he thought. It was lower than the chairs. He would feel even more intimidated. He chose the high-back wing chair, which forced the detectives to sit side by side on the couch.

The somber expression on both their faces telegraphed to Peter that whatever their purpose in coming, it was a serious matter. They seemed to be waiting for him to speak first. He had not intended to offer them coffee but he realized he was still carrying the cup that he had been sipping when the concierge phoned. Now he heard himself saying, "I just made a fresh pot of coffee. May I offer you . . . ?"

Before he had finished the sentence they both shook their heads. Then Detective Tucker spoke. "Mr. Gannon, did you meet Renée Carter last Tuesday evening?"

Renée, Peter thought, dismayed. She *did* go to the cops and tell them that Greg is an insider trader! Be careful, he warned himself. You don't know that yet. Be cooperative. "Yes, I met her on Tuesday evening," he said, trying to keep his voice calm.

"Where did you meet her?" Tucker asked.

"At a bar-and-grill type place, near Gracie Mansion." I can't even remember the name of the place, he thought. I've got to keep my head straight.

"Why did you meet her there?"

"It was at her suggestion."

"Did you quarrel with her?"

They know that already, Peter thought. There were people at the bar who were probably watching us. Some of them would have heard her raise her voice and then would have seen her storm out. "We had a disagreement," he said. "Look, what is this all about?"

"What it's all about, Mr. Gannon, is that Renée Carter never reached home Tuesday night. Yesterday her body was found stuffed in a garbage bag on the East River walkway, near Gracie Mansion."

Stunned, Peter stared at the two detectives. "Renée is dead? That can't be," he protested.

"Are you the father of her child?" Barry Tucker shot the question at him.

Renée is dead. They know we quarreled. They may think I killed her. Peter moistened his lips. "Yes, I am the father of Renée Carter's child," he said.

"Have you been supporting the child?" Detective Flynn asked, quietly.

"Supporting? The answer to that is yes and no." I sound like a fool, Peter told himself. "Let me explain what I mean by that," he added hastily. "I met Renée over four years ago at the opening-night party of a play I was producing. My former wife is an attorney and skipped that kind of late-evening event. I ended up escorting Renée home and getting involved with her. It lasted less than two years."

"You mean you haven't been involved with her for two years?" Tucker asked.

"Renee knew I was sick of her and regretted the relationship had ever begun. That was when she managed to get pregnant. She told me that she wanted two million dollars from me to take care of her while she had the baby, then she planned to give it up for adoption."

"Did you agree to that?" Flynn asked.

"Yes. That was before several of my spectacular flops on Broadway. I thought it was worth it to have Renée out of my life. She told me she knew some very nice, substantial people who would give anything to have a baby and that they would be overjoyed to adopt it."

"You had no interest in your own child?" Flynn asked.

"I'm not proud of that fact, but frankly no, I didn't. Renée cost me my marriage. My wife had found out about the affair and divorced me. When I got back some sense in my head, I realized I had thrown away something terribly precious and would regret it for the rest of my life. The last thing I wanted was to hurt her even more by having her find out that Renée was pregnant with my child. Renée was bored with New York. She told me she was moving to Vegas for good and that the two million dollars would be the last I'd ever see or hear from her."

"Were you sure that the child was yours, Mr. Gannon?"

"I absolutely believed it when I paid her the money. I knew the way Renée's mind worked. It was worth getting pregnant to get that money out of me. Then, nineteen months ago, when the baby was born, she sent me a congratulations card and enclosed with it was a copy of the DNA report of her, me, and the baby. She had been smart enough to collect some DNA from me before she left, just in case I had lingering doubts. I had it checked. I'm the baby's father."

"When did you hear from Renée Carter again?"

"About three months ago. She told me that she was back in New York, that she had decided to keep the baby, and that she would need help raising it."

"You mean child support?" Tucker queried.

"She demanded an additional one million dollars. I told her I simply didn't have that kind of money anymore. I reminded her that our agreement when I gave her the two million was that it was the end of any obligation I had for her and the baby."

"Have you ever seen your child, Mr. Gannon?" Flynn asked.

"No."

"Then you don't know that she is in the hospital and has been gravely ill with pneumonia?"

Peter felt his face redden at the scorn in Tucker's voice. "No, I didn't know that. You said she was gravely ill. How sick is she now?"

"Sick enough. By the way, her name is Sally," Flynn told him. "Do you know that?"

"Yes, I do," Peter snapped.

"When you told Ms. Carter that you couldn't raise that kind of money, how did she react?" Flynn asked.

"She demanded that I find a way to get it. I was panicked and told her that she had to give me time. I've been stalling her, frankly. When I met her on Tuesday night I had one hundred thousand dollars cash for her and told her that would be it."

"Even if you had one million dollars, how could you be sure she still wouldn't go to court and demand child support?" Tucker leaned forward as he asked the question, his eyes boring into Peter's face.

Be careful, Peter warned himself again. You can't let them know she was blackmailing you. It would bring Greg down. "On Tuesday evening, I warned Renée that we had made a deal and that if she got nasty I would go to the police and charge her with extortion. I think she believed me."

"All right," Tucker told him. "You met her. You tried to scare her off. You handed her one hundred thousand dollars, not a check for a million. What was her reaction?"

"She was furious. I guess I'd given her the impression I was going to have the full million. She grabbed the shopping bag with the money out of my hand and took off."

"Do you think anyone saw her take the bag from you?"

"I wouldn't be surprised. Almost every barstool was taken, and there were a few people still lingering over dinner. Renée raised her voice."

"When you followed her out of the restaurant, what happened?"

"I caught up with her on the street. I took her arm and said something like, 'Renée, be reasonable. You've read the papers. I just lost a fortune in the musical. I haven't got it.' "

"What happened then?"

"She hauled off and whacked me across the face. She dropped the bag." Let them know how much you were drinking, Peter told himself. Get that in now.

"Who picked up the bag?" Tucker asked.

"She must have picked it up. You don't think Renée Carter would leave one hundred thousand dollars on the street, do you? Frankly, I'd been so down in the dumps about the play closing and the bills I couldn't pay piling up and then having to meet Renée that I'd been drinking all day in my office. I got to that bar first, and had two double scotches while I was waiting for her. By the time I ran after her I was close to passing out. My memory is that I said something pretty nasty to her, then walked away. That's all I know until I woke up in my office yesterday afternoon."

"You just left her standing on the street?"

"Thinking about it, I'm sure of that. She was leaning down to pick up the bag. I thought I was going to get sick and hurried away."

"Oh, now you definitely remember that she bent down to pick up the bag. That's helpful, Mr. Gannon," Tucker said sarcastically. "I notice you have a nick on your face. How did you get it?"

"Renée's nail scratched me when she slapped me."

"And you remember that?"

"Yes."

Tucker stood up. "Would you be willing to give a sample of your DNA? It only involves a swab with a cotton tip on the inside of your mouth. We have a kit with us. We can't force you to take the test now, but if you refuse we will get a court order, and you will have to comply with it."

They think I killed her, Peter thought. Panic-stricken, he tried to keep his voice steady. "I am perfectly willing to take that test now. I have no reason to refuse. I had an argument with Renée. I absolutely did not kill her."

Tucker looked unimpressed. "Mr. Gannon, where are the clothes you were wearing Tuesday evening?"

"In a private bathroom in my office suite. I always keep a change of clothes there. When I woke up on the couch there yesterday, I showered and changed. The dark blue jacket and tan slacks are in the closet. My underwear and socks are in the bin in the bathroom. I wore the dark brown loafers home."

"You're referring to your office on West Forty-seventh Street."

"Yes. That is my only office."

"Very well, Mr. Gannon, you are required to leave this apartment at once. A police officer will be stationed at the door until we have obtained a search warrant for these premises, as well as your office. Do you have a car?"

"Yes. A black BMW. It's in the garage in this building."

"When did you last use it?"

"I think last Monday."

"You *think* last Monday?"

"I simply don't know if I used it after I left Renée. Frankly, I thought I might have driven it and you were here to follow up on a fender bender."

"We'll obtain a search warrant for your car as well," Tucker told him, crisply. "Would you be willing to come down to headquarters and give a formal statement of everything you have just told us? That does not mean you are under arrest. However, we consider you to be a person of interest in the death of Renée Carter."

Peter Gannon realized he was in the fight of his life. Everything that had happened before, all the money problems and Broadway failures, did not compare with what was happening to him now. I was wild at her, he thought. I was furious and frustrated. *Did* I kill her? Dear God, did I kill her?

He looked straight into Tucker's eyes. "You may take the DNA sample. However, I will not cooperate with you any further. I will not answer any more questions nor sign any statements until I have consulted an attorney."

"Very well. As I told you, you are not under arrest at this time. You will be hearing from us shortly."

"What hospital is my daughter in?"

"She is in Greenwich Village Hospital, but you will not be allowed to visit her, so please don't try."

Ten minutes later, after allowing the DNA sample, Peter Gannon walked out of his apartment building. The weather was threatening rain. His head was splitting and he was close to despair. Help me, dear God, help me, please, he prayed, I just don't know what to do.

He began to walk aimlessly down the block, thoroughly traumatized. "Where do I go?" he agonized. "What do I do?"

46

Ryan Jenner did not like to admit to himself how bitterly disappointed he was at Monica's obvious annoyance that they had been gossiped about in the hospital. The fact that her secretary had dropped off the Michael O'Keefe file at his office without any kind of personal note from Monica had also been a clear message that she wanted no direct contact with him.

I know now that she wasn't in her office to give me the O'Keefe file last evening because she stayed so late in intensive care with the Carter baby, he thought on Friday afternoon, after his last surgery, as he stopped in the hospital cafeteria for a cup of tea. And then Monica was nearly run over by a bus on the way home . . .

The possibility that Monica might have died sent a cold shudder through him. One of the operating room nurses had told him that she heard on the radio the old woman who was a witness to the near tragedy. "She swears that Dr. Farrell was pushed," the nurse told him. "It would raise the hair on the back of your neck to hear that lady describe how she thought the wheels of the bus had gone over Dr. Farrell."

It *does* raise the hair on the back of my neck, Ryan

thought. Monica must have been so frightened. How would it feel to be on the ground with a bus bearing down on you?

The nurse also told him that Monica had passed the word this morning that she was sure it was an accident. Meaning, let it go, Ryan thought, but then I asked her about it, and made a personal remark about how wonderful she is with children in front of the nurse. I was overstepping myself. Maybe if I wrote her a note and apologized she'd understand?

Understand *what*? he asked himself. I *am* interested in her. Last week, when she came to the apartment, she looked lovely. I swear when her hair is loose on her shoulders, she could pass for twenty-one. And she was so apologetic about being late. That's why it's funny that when she sent the O'Keefe file this morning, knowing we had made an appointment for six o'clock last evening, she didn't just scrawl a few lines to say that she'd been delayed at the hospital. It's just not like her, he decided.

As if it were happening now, he could feel again the sensation of their arms touching as they sat next to each other at the crowded table in the Thai restaurant. She was enjoying herself, too, Ryan told himself. There's no *way* that was an act.

Is there some guy important in her life? Maybe she was just being kind to warn me off? I'm not going to give up that easily. I'm going to call her. Last night, if she had been there, I intended to ask her to have dinner. Earlier this week, when I looked at the O'Keefe file in her office, I would have asked her to go out for dinner, but Alice had already roped me into going to that play.

Ryan finished his tea and got up. The cafeteria had thinned out. The daytime people were all in the process of leaving, and it was too early for the evening shift to have a dinner break. I'd like to go home, he thought, but Alice is probably still hanging around. She said she was busy tonight, but what does that mean? I don't feel like sitting over a glass of wine with her until she goes out. I don't know what time her plane is tomorrow, but as soon as I get up I'm leaving the apartment. I don't know what excuse I'll make, but I'm not sitting across the breakfast table with her while she's still in her fancy bathrobe. I feel as if she's trying to play house with me.

Now if it was Monica across the table, it would be different . . .

Impatient and out of sorts, Ryan Jenner walked out of the cafeteria and went back to his in-hospital office. Everyone had left, and the cleaning woman was emptying wastebaskets. Her vacuum was in the middle of the reception area.

This is ridiculous, he thought. I can't go home because I'm a nonpaying guest in my aunt's apartment and I'm annoyed that she is allowing someone else to share it. I think that an impartial observer would call that colossal nerve on my part. I know now what I'm going to do tomorrow: I'm going to start hunting to find my own place.

The decision cheered him. I'll stay here and go back through the O'Keefe file, he thought. Maybe I missed something when I looked at it the first time. Brain cancer doesn't simply disappear. Could there have been a misdiagnosis? The general public hasn't a clue how many times some seriously ill patients are given an all clear, and others are treated for conditions that don't exist. If we were more open about it, the average person's trust in the medical community would be shaken to the core. That's why smart people get second and third opinions before they submit to radical treatment, or if after they're told there's nothing wrong, they listen to their own bodies telling them they have a problem.

The cleaning woman spoke. "I can vacuum later, Doctor," she said.

"That would be great," Ryan said. "I promise I won't be too long."

With a feeling of relief, he went into his private office and closed the door. He settled at his desk and reached into the drawer for the Michael O'Keefe file, then realized that his mind was churning with a question: is there any possibility that some nut is stalking Monica?

Ryan leaned back in his chair. It's not impossible, he decided. There are all kinds of people in and out of this hospital around the clock. One of them, maybe a visitor to some patient, might have seen Monica and become fixated on her. I remember my mother telling the story that years ago, when she was a nurse in a hospital in New Jersey, a young nurse was murdered. A guy with a history of assault had spotted her when he was visiting someone, followed her home, and killed her. It does happen.

Monica is the last person to want any kind of sensational publicity, but is she making a mistake not taking that witness seriously? I'm going to call her, Ryan decided. I simply have to talk to her. It's just six o'clock. She might still be in her office.

He dialed, hoping against hope that she would either pick up the phone herself, or that her receptionist would still be there and pass it on to her. Then, when the message machine took over, he quietly replaced the receiver. I have her cell phone number, he thought, but suppose she's out with some guy? I'll wait and call her Monday, when I can catch her in her office. Intensely disappointed at not hearing her voice, he opened the O'Keefe file.

Two hours later he was still there, going back and forth between Monica's reports on the early symptoms of dizziness and nausea that Michael had experienced when he was only four years old, the tests she had conducted, the MRIs from the Cincinnati hospital that clearly confirmed Monica's diagnosis that Michael had advanced brain cancer. Michael's mother had stopped bringing him in for treatment to relieve the symptoms, then months later when she did set up an appointment with Monica, the next MRI showed an absolutely normal brain. It was astonishing. A miracle?

There is no medical explanation for this, Ryan confirmed to himself. Michael O'Keefe should be dead. Instead, according to these notes, he's now a healthy kid on a Little League team.

He knew what he was going to do. On Monday morning, he was going to phone the Bishop's Office in

Metuchen, New Jersey, and volunteer to testify that he believed Michael's recovery was not explicable by any medical standards.

After making the decision he leaned back in his chair, his thoughts on the day when he had been fifteen years old and at the bedside of his little sister, who died of brain cancer. That was the day I knew I wanted to spend my life trying to cure people with injured brains, he thought. But there will always be some people who are beyond our human skills to help. Michael O'Keefe was apparently one of them.

The very least I can do is to testify that I believe a miracle was performed. I only wish to God we had known about Sister Catherine then. Maybe she would have heard our prayers, too. Maybe Liza would still be with us. She'd be twenty-three years old now . . .

The wrenching memory of four-year-old Liza's small flower-covered white casket filled Ryan Jenner's mind as he left his office, went down to the lobby, and left the hospital. He walked to the corner and waited, as a Fourteenth Street bus thundered past him. The thought of Monica lying in the street in the path of that bus sent sickening fear rushing through his body.

And then, as if she were standing there, he remembered the moment when Monica told him she once played Emily in *Our Town.* I told her that I still get choked up at that last scene, when George, Emily's husband, throws himself on her grave.

Why do I think about Monica as Emily? Ryan asked himself. Why do I have this awful premonition about her? Why am I filled with dread that Monica is going to relive the role she performed in that high school play?

It's exactly the way I felt when I was kneeling beside Liza's bed, knowing her time was running out and I was helpless to stop it . . .

47

On Saturday morning, Nan picked Monica up in a cab at nine fifteen and they drove uptown to St. Vincent Ferrer Church on Lexington Avenue. The funeral Mass for Olivia Morrow was scheduled for ten A.M. On the way up, Nan phoned the rectory and asked to speak to the priest who would be celebrating the Mass. His name, she learned, was Father Joseph Dunlap. When he got on the phone she explained to him why she and Monica would be present.

"We're hoping you can help Dr. Farrell find someone who may have been a confidant of Ms. Morrow," Nan told the priest. "Dr. Farrell had an appointment to meet her on Wednesday morning because on Tuesday Ms. Morrow had revealed that she knew the identity of the doctor's birth grandparents. Dr. Farrell's father was adopted, so she's never known anything about her ancestry. Unfortunately Ms. Morrow passed away during the night. Dr. Farrell is hoping that someone attending the funeral Mass may have the information Ms. Morrow planned to give her."

"If anyone can understand the need to trace family roots, I can," Father Dunlap responded. "Over the years I have encountered that situation regularly in my pastoral duties. I intend to eulogize Olivia following the gospel. Why don't I tell Dr. Farrell's story when I conclude my remarks, and say that she will be waiting in the vestibule to speak with anyone who might be helpful?"

Nan thanked him and hung up. When they arrived at St. Vincent's, Monica and Nan deliberately sat near the back so that they could observe the people who attended the funeral Mass. At five minutes of ten the rich sound of the organ began to fill the church. By then there were not more than twenty people in the pews.

"Be not afraid, I go before you . . ." As Monica listened to the lovely soprano voice of the soloist, she thought, Be not afraid, but I *am* afraid. I am afraid that I may have lost my only link to my father's ancestry.

At precisely ten o'clock, the door opened and Father Dunlap walked down the aisle to receive the casket. To Monica's astonishment, the only person following it was Dr. Clay Hadley.

As the casket was escorted to the foot of the altar, Monica did not miss the startled look Hadley gave her when their eyes met. She watched as he took a place in the first pew. No one joined him there.

"Maybe that man is a relation who could be helpful," Nan whispered to Monica.

"That's her doctor. I met him Wednesday evening. He's not going to be any help," Monica whispered back.

"Then I don't think we're going to get very far," Nan said, keeping her naturally resonant voice low. "There are so few people here and that man is the only one in the area that's usually reserved for family."

Monica thought of her father's funeral in Boston five years earlier. The church had been crowded with friends and colleagues. The people sitting with her in the first row had been Joy and Scott Alterman. Just after that Scott became obsessed with her. Monica stared at the casket. As far as family goes, that's the way it's going to be for me, she thought. Olivia Morrow apparently doesn't have a single relative to mourn her and neither would I if that bus had hit me. Pray God that will change someday.

Unwanted, Ryan Jenner's face came into her mind. He seemed so surprised when I told him I didn't want any gossip about us. In a way that's as disappointing as the fact that he's involved with someone else. Is he so casual about his relationships that he could have a serious girlfriend at home and allow himself to be linked with me in the hospital?

The same question had made her lie awake during the night.

The Mass had begun. She realized she had been making the responses to the opening prayers by rote.

The Epistle was read by Clay Hadley: "If God is for us, who shall be against us . . ." His voice was strong and reverential as he read the letter of St. Paul to the Romans.

Father Dunlap offered the intercessions. "We pray for the repose of the soul of Olivia Morrow. May the angels attend her to a place of refreshment, light, and peace."

"Lord, hear our prayer," the congregation murmured.

The Gospel was from St. John and the same one Monica had chosen to be read at her father's funeral. "Come all of you who are heavily burdened . . ."

When the Gospel ended and they sat down again, Nan settled back in the pew. "He's going to talk about her now," she whispered.

"Olivia Morrow was a parishioner here for the past fifty years," the priest began. As Monica listened, he spoke of a caring and generous person, who after her retirement and until her health failed had been a Eucharistic minister who regularly had brought Holy Communion to patients in hospitals. "Olivia never wanted recognition," Father Dunlap said. "Even though she had worked her way to a position of authority in a renowned department store, in private she was modest and unassuming. An only child, she had no relatives to be with us today. This was not to be, but she is now in the presence of the God she served so faithfully. There is a reason to wish she had been with us for one more day. Let me share with you what Olivia told a young woman only hours before her death . . ."

Let someone have something to tell me that will be helpful, Monica prayed. *I'm finally understanding Dad's need to know. I need to know. Let someone here be able to help me.*

The final prayers were said. Father Dunlap blessed the casket and the attendants from the funeral home came forward and lifted it to their shoulders. As the soloist sang, "Be not afraid, I go before you," the mortal remains of Olivia Morrow were moved from the church to the hearse. In the vestibule, Monica and Nan watched as Clay Hadley got into a car behind the hearse.

"That was her doctor and he didn't even take a minute to talk to you," Nan said, her tone critical. "Didn't you tell me that you sat and talked with him while you waited for the medics to come?"

"Yes, I did," Monica replied. "But the other day he did specifically say that he knew nothing about whatever it was Olivia Morrow was going to tell me."

As the congregation began to leave, a few people stopped to say that they were employees at Schwab House but didn't know anything about any personal information Ms. Morrow intended to share. Several others explained they had sometimes spoken to her after Mass, but she had never referred to anything of a personal nature.

The last to leave was a woman who obviously had been crying. With graying blond hair, wide cheekbones, and a broad frame, she looked to be in her mid-sixties. She stopped to speak with them. "I am Sophie Rutkowski. I was Ms. Morrow's cleaning woman for thirty years," she said, her voice quivering. "I don't know anything about what she wanted to tell you, but I wish you had met her. She was such a good person."

Thirty years, Monica thought. She might know more about Olivia Morrow's background than she realizes.

It was obvious Nan had the same thought. "Ms. Rutkowski, Dr. Farrell and I are going to have a cup of coffee. Won't you join us?"

The woman looked hesitant. "Oh, I don't think—"

"Sophie," Nan said briskly. "I'm Nan Rhodes, the doctor's receptionist. This is a sad time for you. Talking about Ms. Morrow with us over a cup of coffee will make you feel better, I promise."

A block away they found a coffee shop and settled in at a table. Monica watched in admiration as Nan made the other woman comfortable telling her that she could so understand how sad Sophie must be. "I've been working for Dr. Farrell for almost four years," she said, "and when I heard that she was almost killed in an accident, I can't tell you how upset I was."

"I knew that the end was coming," Sophie said. "Ms. Morrow has been failing for this last year. Her heart was bad, but she said she didn't want any more surgery. She had the aortic valve replaced twice. She said . . ."

Sophie Rutkowski's eyes filled with tears. "She said that there is a time to die and that she knew her time was coming soon."

"Didn't she have any family at all whom you met?" Nan asked.

"Just her mother, and she died ten years ago. She was very old, in her early nineties."

"Did she live with Ms. Morrow?"

"No. She always had her own apartment in Queens but they saw a lot of each other. They were very close."

"Did Ms. Morrow have much company as far as you know?" Monica asked.

"I honestly couldn't be sure. I was only there on Tuesday afternoons for a couple of hours. That was all she needed. No one ever lived who was neater than Ms. Morrow."

Tuesday, Monica thought. She died sometime between Tuesday night and Wednesday morning. "How did she seem to you when you saw her this past Tuesday?"

"I'm sorry to say I didn't see her. She had gone out." Sophie shook her head. "I was surprised she wasn't home. She's been getting so weak. I vacuumed and dusted and changed the sheets on her bed. I did the little wash there was. I don't mean I washed the sheets. She sent them out. They were very fine cotton and she liked them to be done at a special laundry. I used to tell her I'd be happy to iron them but she wanted them done just so. This past Tuesday, I was only there for an hour. She was so generous. She always paid me for three hours, even though I told her I couldn't find another thing to clean or polish."

Olivia Morrow liked everything done just so. That was obvious, Monica thought. Why is it I keep thinking about that pillowcase that didn't match the others: "Sophie, I noticed that there were lovely peach sheets on the bed but that one of the pillowcases didn't match the other three. It was a pale pink shade."

"No, Doctor, you must be wrong," Sophie said flatly. "I'd never make that mistake. This past Tuesday, I put on the peach sheets. She had other sets, of course, but she preferred the pastels. One week the peach set went on. The next week the pink set."

"What I'm getting at, Sophie," Monica said, "is that when I saw Ms. Morrow's body on Wednesday evening, I could see that she had bitten her lip. I thought it might have bled on the pillowcase and she decided to change it."

"If she bit her lip and bled onto the pillowcase, she would have put that pillow aside and used one of the two spares on the bed," Sophie said emphatically. "You must have noticed how full those pillows are. She wouldn't have had the strength, or even tried, to change the pillowcases. No way." She sipped her coffee. "No way," she repeated for emphasis. Then she paused. "I work for a number of people at Schwab House. One of the handymen told me that Dr. Hadley had been to see Ms. Morrow Tuesday night. Maybe if there was blood on the pillowcase, she asked him to change it. That she would do."

"Yes, of course that's possible," Monica conceded. "Sophie, I'm going to run ahead to visit a patient at the hospital. Thank you for joining us, and if anything comes to you about anyone who might have any knowledge of what Ms. Morrow wanted to tell me, please call. Nan will give you the phone numbers where both of us can be reached."

Twenty-five minutes later she was stepping off the elevator to the Pediatric floor of the hospital. When she stopped at the nurses' desk, a slender woman with salt-and-pepper hair was talking to Rita Greenberg. Monica noticed that Rita looked relieved to see her.

"You'd better speak to Sally's doctor," she told the woman. "Dr. Farrell, this is Susan Gannon."

Susan turned to face Monica. "Doctor, my former husband, Peter Gannon, is the father of Sally Carter. I know he is barred from visiting her, but I am not. Will you take me to her, please?"

48

On Saturday morning at ten o'clock Detective Carl Forrest was seated in his car, parked directly opposite Greenwich Village Hospital. He had worked with John Hartman before his retirement. It was Forrest who had checked for fingerprints on the picture that Hartman had brought in, the one that had been sent anonymously to Monica Farrell's office.

After Monica's narrow escape from death, it was Forrest, again at Hartman's urging, who had studied the security tapes of Greenwich Village Hospital, the ones that covered the time that Monica left the hospital on Thursday evening, minutes before her encounter with the bus.

Accompanying him was his partner, Jim Whelan. They were studying the pictures they had just taken of a young policewoman standing on the steps of the hospital. They had asked her to stand in the same spot where Monica had been photographed so that they could analyze the location from which the shot had been taken.

Forrest had his computer on his lap and printed out the pictures, then with a grunt of satisfaction, he handed them to Whelan. "Compare them, Jim," he said, as he held up the snapshot that had been mailed to Monica's office. "Whoever took the picture of the doctor with the kid in her arms was probably sitting in a car parked right here. The angle is exactly right. I thought at first that John Hartman was wasting our time, but I don't think that anymore. Let's review it."

"Thursday evening the hospital security cameras show the doctor coming down the steps. Next frame we see someone getting out of his car, parked in this spot, following her down the street. This guy is wearing a hooded sweatshirt, gloves, and dark glasses, the exact description the old lady gave us. The break of the century is that fifteen minutes later the security camera shows his car being towed because the meter ran out! Now we know it was reclaimed by Sammy Barber, a two-bit thug who was acquitted of being a hitman."

"Acquitted because he or one of his slimy friends either threatened or paid off jurors," Whelan remembered. "They don't come any guiltier than he was. I did a lot of work on that case. I'd love to find a way to nail him now."

The policewoman who had posed for the picture came over. A traffic officer, she had agreed to give up a few minutes of her break to help them out. "Did you get what you wanted?"

"You bet," Forrest told her. "Thanks."

"Anytime. I never thought of myself as being a model. Neither did anyone else." With a brief wave, she was on her way.

After she left, Forrest turned on the ignition. "Even if

we bring Sammy in for a lineup and the old lady identifies him, you know what will happen. If it got to trial, which is doubtful, a lawyer would shoot holes in her identification. It was dark. He was wearing sunglasses. His hood was pulled up. On top of that, there was a crowd on the corner. The bus was coming and people were lining up for it. She was the only one who thinks the doctor was shoved. The doctor herself claims it was an accident. Case dismissed."

"But if Barber was stalking her, it was because someone is paying him to do it. Does she have any idea of who that could be?" Whelan asked.

John Hartman mentioned Scott Alterman. "I checked him out. He's a successful lawyer. Just moved to New York, but apparently about five years ago he was stalking Dr. Farrell in Boston. He's the only one John heard about as someone who might have a reason to take that picture of the doctor."

"Or have someone like Sammy take the picture for him?" Whelan suggested.

"Possibly. But where are we going with that?" Forrest asked. "If it is Alterman, he won't be the first rejected guy to order a hit on the woman who turned him down. We'll keep an eye on him and see if there's anything illegal Sammy has done at that bar where he's a bouncer that we can make stick and get him off the street."

49

On Saturday morning Scott Alterman followed the route Olivia Morrow had taken on the day of her death. After he left the Schwab House on Friday, he had called the driver service Olivia used and asked to speak to the chauffeur who had driven her on Tuesday.

He was told that the man's name was Rob Garrigan and he was on a job now but would call him later. Scott had gone to his office and late in the afternoon Garrigan had phoned back. "Like they probably told you in the office, it was a four-hour round trip to Southampton," he said. "She didn't visit nobody. She just had me drive on the ocean block, and then to a cemetery."

Scott had been dismayed. "She didn't visit anybody?"

"Nope. She did have me stop in front of some pretty ritzy house. Well, they're all ritzy on that block. She told me she lived there when she was a kid, not in that house, but in a cottage that was on the property. Then she had me drive to the cemetery and stop in front of a mausoleum. Is that the way you say it? Funny word, isn't it? And she just sat there and looked at it, and I could tell she felt real bad."

"If you went back could you point out the house and the mausoleum?"

"Sure. I've got eyes in my head."

"Did she say anything else besides the fact that she lived in that cottage when she was young? I mean about her family?"

"Hardly a word. It seemed like it was an effort for her to talk. I mean, some people don't want to talk, and I always respect that. Other people like to gab and that's okay with me, too. My wife says I never shut up and I do her a favor if I get the talk bug out of my system on the job."

Now on the way out to Southampton, Scott was realizing that Rob Garrigan, who had probably given him as much information as he knew, would be hard to silence for the rest of the drive.

"You know what Long Island Expressway stands for?" Garrigan asked.

"I guess not," Scott said.

"Think of the initials. L. I. E. Spells 'lie.' That's the Long Island Expressway. It's not an expressway. It's one long parking lot, especially in the summer. A seventy-mile parking lot. I could tell you wouldn't know. You're from Boston, aren't you? I mean like the people who take 'a waaak in the paaak.' "

"I didn't realize I talked like that. Do you think I should learn to say, 'Noo Yawk'?" Scott asked.

"That's the way people from New Jersey say it, not New Yorkers."

Scott did not know whether to be angry or amused.

Eight generations of Altermans had lived in Bernardsville, New Jersey. I'd have been brought up there if Dad hadn't taken the job in Boston after he graduated from Harvard, he thought. Then he met Mom and that was that. When I was a kid I loved coming down to the big house to visit my grandparents.

After they passed away, the family property had been sold and a country club with a golf course had been built on it.

Grandparents! Mine were such an important part of my life, Scott reflected.

Olivia Morrow had specifically told Monica that she had known both her birth grandparents. I bet anything that there is a link somehow to the Gannons, Scott thought. If I could only find it for Monica.

"Is it okay if I turn on the radio real low?" Garrigan asked.

"That would be absolutely fine," Scott told him gratefully.

Nearly an hour later they were driving into Southampton. "The house she had me stop at was on the ocean," Garrigan said. "Maybe I told you that. Not far now." He drove for a few more minutes then Scott felt the car slowing down and stopping.

"Here we are," Garrigan announced. "It's one of the really big ones."

Scott was not looking at the house. His eyes were riveted on the mailbox with the name GANNON in handsome raised letters. I knew it! I *knew* it, he thought. She was going to tell Monica something about the Gannons.

There was a Ferrari sports car parked in the circular driveway.

"Someone's home. Are you going in there?" Garrigan asked.

"I'm going to stop in later but first I'd like to have you show me the mausoleum that you say Ms. Morrow visited."

"Sure thing. Did you ever hear the biggest benefit of living next to a cemetery?"

"I don't think so."

"You have quiet neighbors."

Too quiet, Scott thought minutes later, as he got out of the car and stood in front of the handsome mausoleum with the name GANNON carved in stone over the archway. I wish Alexander Gannon could talk to me now.

Olivia Morrow had lived as a young child on the Gannon estate, he mused. She was eighty-two, when she died last Wednesday. Alexander Gannon would be over one hundred years old now. Monica's father was in his seventies when he died. If he was Alexander's son, he was born when Alexander was in his mid-twenties. Olivia was a child at that time, so she certainly couldn't have been the mother.

But what about Olivia's mother? Scott asked himself. How old was *she* when they lived here? She could easily have been in her twenties. Was she involved with Alex and became pregnant, and gave up the baby for adoption? If so, did the Gannons buy her off? Why did Alex have that provision in his will, leaving his estate to a child if he had had one? Maybe he never knew, but simply suspected that someone who had worked for the family became pregnant with his child. Maybe his parents ended the relationship and made the girl swear to keep the secret? In those days, if something like that happened, the girl was usually sent away to have the baby and paid off to keep quiet about it.

With one last look at the mausoleum, Scott got back in the car.

“Where to?” Garrigan asked, cheerfully.

“Back to the house where we just were. Let’s see if the owner of that fancy sports car lives there, and if so, would be willing to chat with an unexpected visitor.”

50

On Friday afternoon, after he was forced by the police to leave his apartment, Peter Gannon found himself on the corner of Fifth Avenue and Seventieth Street, at the door of the apartment building where he had lived with Susan for twenty years. He had given her the co-op in the divorce settlement four years ago, and he couldn't miss the uncomfortable expression on the face of the doorman, even though his greeting was cordial.

"Mr. Gannon, how nice to see you."

"Nice to see you as well, Ramon." Peter understood the reason for the man's unease. He could not allow him to enter the building without Susan's permission. "Will you call and see if my wife is in?" he asked, then wanted to bite his tongue. "I mean will you see if Ms. Gannon is in?"

"Of course, sir." As he dialed the number of Susan's apartment, Peter waited nervously. She's probably at work, he thought. She wouldn't be home at this time on a Friday. What's the matter with me? Or better yet, what *else* is the matter with me? I can't think straight. What was Ramon saying?

"Ms. Gannon said to go right up, sir."

Peter could see the curiosity in the man's eyes. I know I look like hell, he thought. He went into the lobby and walked across the familiar carpet to the elevator. The door was open. The operator, another longtime employee, welcomed him warmly and, without being asked, pressed the button for the sixteenth floor.

As he rode up, Peter realized he didn't know what to expect from Susan. When he had passed a newsstand he had seen Renée's picture and the headlines about her death on the front page of both the *Post* and the *News*. Susan must have seen the morning newspapers, too. She would immediately remember Renée and guess that she was the reason why he had begged her to lend him a million dollars.

The elevator stopped. Peter saw the operator's questioning glance as he hesitated before getting out. Then, when the door closed behind him, he stood for a full minute. Their apartment was the corner duplex. Feeling icy cold, his hands in the pockets of his leather jacket, he turned to walk toward it.

The door was ajar and before he could knock, Susan was standing in the doorway. For a long minute they looked at each other without speaking. Peter could see that she was shocked at his appearance. I guess showering and shaving didn't hide the effects of a drunk blackout, he thought.

She was wearing a belted gray wool dress that accentuated her small waist. A colorful scarf was knotted around her throat. Her only jewelry was silver earrings that complemented the salt-and-pepper hair that had been artfully contoured to frame her face. She looks just like what she is, Peter thought, a wonderfully attractive, classy, intelligent woman, and in twenty years I was never smart enough to realize how lucky I was to have her.

"Come in, Peter," Susan told him. She stood aside as he passed. He was certain that she wanted to avoid any attempt on his part to kiss her. Don't worry, Susan, he thought. I wouldn't have the nerve to try.

Without speaking, he walked from the foyer to the living room. The windows looked down on Central Park. He walked over to them. "The view doesn't change," he commented, then turned to her. "Sue, I'm in a lot of trouble. I have no right to be bothering you, but I don't know who else to turn to for advice."

"Sit down, Peter. You look as if you're going to cave in. I read the papers this morning. Renée Carter, the woman you were, or are, involved with, is the same Renée Carter who was murdered, isn't she?"

Peter sat down heavily on the couch, feeling as if his legs no longer had the strength to hold him. "Yes, she is, Sue. I swear to God, I hadn't seen nor heard from her for two years. That was when she moved back to Vegas. I was sick of her. I knew what a horrible mistake I had made. I've regretted it and will regret it every day of my life."

"Peter, according to the papers, Renée Carter has a nineteen-month-old child. Is she yours?"

It was the question Peter Gannon had hoped never to have to answer. "Yes," he whispered. "Yes. I never wanted you to know about the baby. I knew how much the miscarriages tore you apart."

"How considerate of you. Can you be sure it's yours?"

Bleakly, Peter looked into the scornful eyes of his former wife. "Yes, I'm sure it's mine. Renée cleverly produced the DNA reports as proof for me. I've never seen the child. I never want to see her."

"Then shame on you." Susan spat out the words. "She is your flesh and blood. According to the papers she's been in critical condition in the hospital with pneumonia, and you're not the least concerned about her? What kind of monster are you?"

"Sue, I'm not a monster," Peter pleaded. "Renée told me she had friends who were desperate for a baby, that they were substantial and fine people. I thought that was the best way to go. Two years ago, I gave Renée two million dollars so that she could have the baby and then get out of my life. But she called me three months ago, and demanded a million more. That's why I asked you for a loan. I couldn't get it anyplace else."

He saw the expression on Susan's face change from scorn to alarm. "Peter, when did you last see Renée Carter?"

"Tuesday night." Get it out, he thought. Don't try to make it sound like anything except what it is. "Sue, I didn't have a million dollars. I couldn't raise it. I brought a bag with one hundred thousand in cash to give her. I met Renée in a bar and told her that. She took the bag and rushed out of the bar. I followed her. I grabbed her arm and said something like, 'I can't get any more.' She slapped me and dropped the bag. As she picked it up I knew I was going to be sick. I'd been drinking scotches all day. I left her on the street."

"What did you do then?"

"I blacked out. I don't know another thing until I woke up on the couch in my office the next afternoon."

"Your *office*? Didn't someone wake you up in the morning?"

"No one else came in. I let everyone go. I couldn't pay anyone's salary. Sue, the cops came to my apartment today. I let them take a DNA swab. They're getting a search warrant for the apartment and the office. They made me leave my apartment."

"Peter, are you telling me that you left Renée Carter on York Avenue after you had quarreled and she slapped you and was picking up the bag with one hundred thousand dollars in cash that she said wasn't enough money? And now you say that you don't remember anything until you woke up in your office and that her body was found not far from where you left her? My God, do you realize how much trouble you're in? You're not only a person of interest. You're the prime suspect."

"Susan, I swear to you I don't know what happened to her."

"Peter, what you're saying is that *you* don't know what happened. Period. Did you tell the police that Renée Carter was blackmailing you because of the foundation money and what you think Greg is up to in the market?"

"No. No. Of course not. I've got to keep Greg out of

this. I told them that she was after me for more money after what I gave her two years ago." Peter knew he was close to tears. Not wanting to break down in front of Susan, he got to his feet. "Sorry to inflict you with all of this, Sue," he said, struggling to steady his voice. "I just needed someone to talk to. You came up first on the list." He attempted to smile. "In fact, you *are* the list."

"That doesn't say much for you. Peter, you're not going anywhere until you've had coffee and a sandwich. When did you last eat?"

"I don't know. When I woke up in the office Wednesday I went home and went to bed. I stayed home all day yesterday until I met you. Then after you blew me off, I got drunk again."

"Peter, on Tuesday evening, you had already told Renée Carter you couldn't give her any more money. Why did you try to borrow from me Wednesday night?"

"Because I knew she wasn't finished with me, and that if she set the cops on Greg he'd be in big trouble."

"Peter, you said the police were getting a search warrant. Are they going to find anything at all in your office or apartment that might incriminate you?"

"Susan, absolutely not."

"Do you remember if you struggled with her? Did you hit her back when she slapped you?"

"I swear, I never would have hurt her. I just wanted to get away from her."

"Peter, you've already told the police that Renée Carter was trying to extort more money from you. Listen to me. You're going to need an attorney. I'm in corporate law, not criminal defense, but a first-year law student could shoot holes in your convenient blackout. Fortunately, they can't subpoena me as a witness because I'm an attorney, and I will tell them you spoke to me only to seek legal advice. But don't say a single word about this to anyone else or answer any more questions from the police. The police should be finished with searching the apartment by now so after I fix you something to eat, I want you to go home and get some rest. You're going to need it. Stay there until you hear from me. I'm going to make some calls and hire the best criminal defense attorney I can find."

An hour later when he left Susan's apartment, Peter Gannon took a backward glance at the exquisitely furnished living room with its deep, comfortable matching sofas, antique carpet, and the grand piano he had bought Sue for one of their anniversaries. He thought of lying on the couch and listening to her play. She was a fine pianist, far more than "a pretty good amateur," as she labeled herself.

And I gave all this up for Renée Carter! he thought. *And now Renée may cost me the rest of my life. Even that wouldn't be enough for her*, he thought bitterly.

When he got back to his apartment, he found it in total disarray. Every drawer had been pulled out and the contents dumped on the carpet. The contents of the refrigerator were on the countertops. Cushions from the chairs and couch had been tossed on the floor. Furniture was pushed to the center of the living room. Paintings had been removed from the walls and stacked on top of each other. A copy of the search warrant had been left on the dining room table.

Like an automaton, Peter began to clean up. The physical effort helped to limber his back, cramped from inactivity. Susan thinks I might be arrested, he thought. The prospect seemed impossible to him. I feel as if I'm in a bad movie. I've never lifted a finger to hurt anyone. I never even had a fight with another kid when I was growing up. Even after I knew Renée wasn't going to settle for one hundred thousand dollars, I still was trying to borrow money from Susan to pay her off.

I wouldn't have done that if I had already killed her. I wouldn't have killed her. Why can't I remember what I did after I left Renée on York Avenue?

As he put back the contents of the drawers, straightened the furniture, and rehung the pictures, his mind kept swirling with unanswered questions. Where did I go after I left Renée? Did I talk to anyone or am I imagining it? Did I see someone who looked familiar across the street? I don't know. I just don't know.

It was shortly after midnight when the concierge phoned him. "Mr. Gannon, Detectives Tucker and Flynn are here to see you."

"Send them up." Virtually paralyzed with fear, Peter waited by the door until the bell rang. He opened it and the two detectives, unsmiling and businesslike, entered the apartment.

"Mr. Gannon," Barry Tucker said, "you are under arrest for the murder of Renée Carter. Turn around, Mr. Gannon." As he handcuffed him behind his back,

Tucker began the Miranda ritual. "You have the right to remain silent. Anything you say can and will be used against you . . ."

Every word was a physical blow.

"You have the right to an attorney . . ."

Trying to blink back tears, Peter's mind flashed back to the moment when, at that party after the opening of his play, Renée Carter had linked her arm in his and asked him if he was lonely.

51

On Saturday morning, Ryan put his plan into motion. He got up at seven and showered and shaved, grateful that somewhere along the way the large apartment had been renovated so that a bathroom was directly off the master bedroom and he did not have to risk bumping into Alice in the hall before he was fully dressed. Maybe she's still asleep, he hoped.

But when he went out to the kitchen, she was already there, wrapped in a satin robe, wearing light makeup, every hair in place. A very pretty woman, he thought, as he forced a smile, but she's just not for me.

"You don't give yourself a break on Saturdays and stay in bed for an extra hour or so?" she asked, her tone teasing, as she poured coffee for him. He saw that fresh orange juice and a bowl of cut-up fruit were already on the breakfast table.

"No. I have a lot of errands, so I want to get an early start, Alice."

"Well, surely as a doctor you know that a good breakfast is the best way to start the day? I've seen the way you rush out during the week. How about poached eggs on toast?"

Ryan had intended to decline, but the offer sounded good to him and he knew he could not refuse to have something to eat without being rude. "Sounds great," he said, uncomfortably. He sat at the table, sipped the orange juice, and thought, I just want out of here. If Monica walked in right now, or if I saw her in the same situation, I know what I'd think.

"I hope I didn't wake you up when I came home last night," Alice said, as she broke eggs into a pan of boiling water.

"I didn't hear you come in. I went to bed around eleven," Ryan answered, as he thought about how he had spent the previous evening. I went to a lousy movie because I didn't want to be here with you. Turns out I could have come straight home the way I wanted to, since you weren't here anyway. *Home*, he thought. We both used the word "home" just now. Isn't that cute?

"You haven't asked, but I'm going to tell you anyhow what I was doing and why it's so important," Alice said, as she put bread in the toaster.

"I'm asking now." Ryan tried to sound interested.

"Well, I was at a dinner given by the publisher of *Everyone* magazine. It was for the retiring editor of the celebrity-beauty section. He offered me her job. That means I get to pick the celebrities I want to feature and analyze what they're wearing, their hairstyles, and makeup. It's the kind of job I've been hoping for ever since I got into the beauty and fashion business."

"I'm really delighted for you, Alice," Ryan said sincerely. "I have friends in the publishing world and it's a tough field to crack. Little as I know about *Everyone* magazine, I do know it's one of the most successful ones. I see it everywhere."

"As you know, I'm going back to Atlanta today," Alice continued. "I'm going to have to scramble to get an agent to rent my apartment there, and put my furniture into storage, and get my clothes packed, and all the rest that goes with moving. They want me to start in two weeks. Would you mind very much if your stepsister comes back here until I can find my own place? It's a big apartment and I promise I won't be in your way."

Stepsister? Oh, she told the doorman I was her stepbrother, Ryan remembered. "Alice, people share apartments all the time in New York, and in every big city I guess, but I'm long overdue to have a place of my own. That's what I'm going to be looking for today. So I'm sure I'll be gone when you get back."

I *will* be gone, too, he thought, even if it's to a residential hotel.

"Well, I hope that doesn't mean you won't come for a cocktail or dinner sometime? I pride myself on being a good hostess, and I have some really interesting friends in New York." Alice put the plate of poached eggs in front of him and refilled his coffee cup.

Ryan made the only response possible. "Of course I'll come, if I'm invited." Alice is very nice, very attractive, and I'm sure very smart, he thought. If it weren't for Monica it might be different, but it's not going to be different. Giving Monica back the file on Monday will be an excuse to talk to her and apologize for making her feel uncomfortable in front of the nurses. When she was here that Friday, she enjoyed herself. I know she did.

"Well, how are my eggs?" Alice asked. "I mean they're done to perfection, don't you agree?"

"Absolutely," Ryan agreed hastily. "Many thanks, Alice. And now I'm off. I have to stop at the hospital." I do have to stop in my office there, he thought. I want to see the Michael O'Keefe file. The O'Keefes' address and phone number are in it. I am going to do some apartment hunting today, but I'm also going to call and ask if I can visit Michael. I want to see him for myself before I ask to testify in Sister Catherine's beatification process as an expert witness.

With a final good-bye to Alice, and her unwanted kiss on his lips, Ryan went down in the elevator. As it descended, he remembered a fragment of the dream he had had during the night. Monica had been in it somehow. No reason she wouldn't be, he thought. Ever since she was almost hit by that bus, I've been sick with worry about her.

But it was not just that she was *in* it. He remembered that she had been speaking to a nun.

Good Lord, he thought. Now I'm dreaming about Sister Catherine, too.

52

At three o'clock Dr. Douglas Langdon and Dr. Clayton Hadley met for a late lunch at the St. Regis Hotel. They decided to select from the light menu served in the King Cole Bar, and chose a table out of any possible earshot of the few other diners.

"Physician, heal thyself," Langdon said dryly. "For God's sake, Clay, things are bad enough without you falling apart. You look awful."

"Easy for you to say," Hadley shot back. "You weren't at the funeral with Monica Farrell staring at you. You didn't pick up the urn at the crematorium and escort it to the cemetery."

"It was a nice show of respect," Langdon told him. "That's important now."

"I told you we should have given Peter the money he needed to pay off Carter," Hadley complained.

"You know perfectly well the foundation couldn't produce that much, and anyway she'd have been back for more in another month. When all is said and done, Peter did us a favor by killing her."

"Have you talked to Greg today?" Hadley asked. "I've been afraid to call him."

"Of course I've spoken to him. We wrote a statement together for the press, the usual party line. 'We firmly stand behind Peter Gannon, who is innocent of these outrageous charges. We are confident that he will be fully vindicated.' "

"Fully vindicated! They found the hundred thousand dollars he claimed to have given that Carter woman hidden in his office. That was in the newspaper."

"Clay, what did you expect us to say in the press release? That we knew how desperate Peter was when he tried to get us to release foundation money to him? It was Greg who tried to convince him that if it came out that Renée Carter had his child, so what? What's the big deal? That kind of stuff is in the papers every day. Unfortunately, Peter didn't see it that way, and he snapped. It happens."

Both men fell silent as the waiter approached them. "Another round?" he suggested.

"Yes," Hadley said, as he drained the last of his vodka on the rocks.

"Just coffee for me," Langdon said. "And we'd better order now. What are you having, Clay?"

"Sliders."

"And I'll have a tuna salad." When the waiter left, Langdon remarked, "Clay, you're putting on more weight. May I point out that the sliders, those three small hamburgers with cheese, don't look like much, but they have a lot of calories. As a psychiatrist, I warn you that you are compensating for stress by overeating."

Hadley stared at him. "Doug, sometimes I don't believe you. Everything could fall apart and we could both end up in prison, and you're lecturing me about calories?"

"Well I actually *do* have more serious concerns. As we both know, we handled the first problem, Olivia Morrow, before she could hurt us. Monica Farrell, our second problem, will not be with us much longer. Soon we will announce that due to some unwise investments the Gannon Foundation will be closing down. Greg can handle the paperwork for that. Then I intend to retire and enjoy the rest of my life in places like the south of France, with great gratitude to the largess of the Gannon Foundation. I suggest you start thinking in the same vein."

Feeling the vibration of his cell phone, Langdon reached into his pocket. He glanced at the phone number that appeared on the screen and quickly answered. "Hello, I'm having lunch with Clay."

As Langdon listened to the caller, Hadley watched his expression darken.

"You're right. It's a problem. I'll get back to you." Langdon snapped the cell phone shut. He looked at Hadley. "Maybe you're right to worry. We're not out of the woods yet. That guy Alterman, who was nosing around the Schwab House yesterday, was in Southampton today. He's already made the connection between Morrow and the Gannons. If he keeps digging, it's all over."

Another person will have to die. Clay Hadley thought

of the frightened look on the face of Olivia Morrow just before he held the pillow over her head. "What are we going to do?" he asked.

"We don't have to do anything," Langdon replied, coldly. "It's already being taken care of."

53

After sharing coffee with Monica and Nan following Olivia Morrow's funeral Mass, Sophie Rutkowski went home to her nearby apartment, the memory of her many years with Olivia paramount in her mind.

I wish I had been there when she died, Sophie thought, as she changed from her good slacks and jacket into the sweatshirt and cotton pants that were her work clothes. It's such a shame she was alone. When I go, I know my children will be around me to say good-bye. If they get any warning that I am dying, nothing on earth would keep them away . . .

Dr. Farrell, what a lovely-looking girl she is. Hard to believe that she's a doctor and very highly respected, according to what they wrote in the paper after that bus almost killed her. Ms. Morrow didn't have a single family member at the funeral. The priest even mentioned that in his sermon. He spoke so nicely about Ms. Morrow. Dr. Farrell was so disappointed when I couldn't tell her what Ms. Morrow meant when she said she knew the doctor's grandparents. Dr. Farrell has no family, either. Ah, dear God, people have so many problems and it's hard to face them alone . . .

On that somber note Sophie picked up her knitting needles. She was making a sweater for her newest grandchild and had a spare half hour until it was time to go to the one job she didn't like. It was at Schwab House on Saturday afternoons, starting at one o'clock, in an apartment three floors down from the one where Olivia Morrow had lived.

The couple who owned it were both writers who worked at home. The reason they liked to have their apartment cleaned on Saturday afternoon was because by noon they were on their way to their country home in Washington, Connecticut.

Sophie continued at the job for only one reason; they paid her double to give up her Saturdays, and with fifteen grandchildren that money made it possible for her to do all the little extras for them their parents couldn't afford.

Even so, it gets harder and harder to work here, Sophie thought, as at one o'clock promptly, she put her key in the door of the apartment. Those two are nothing like Ms. Morrow, she told herself, not for the first time. A few minutes later she started to empty overflowing wastebaskets, pick heaps of damp towels off the bathroom floor, and clear the refrigerator of half-empty cartons of Chinese food. There's a word for them, she sighed: slobs.

At six o'clock, when she left, the apartment was spotless. The dishwasher had been emptied, the laundry folded in the linen closet, the shades drawn exactly halfway down in all five rooms. They tell me how nice it is to come home on Monday and find it like this, Sophie thought. Why don't they try *keeping* it like this?

Ms. Morrow's apartment, she sighed. People would be going through it. It's such a nice one, a lot of people will want to buy it. Ms. Morrow had told her that Dr. Hadley would take care of everything.

As Sophie pressed the button for the elevator, a thought occurred to her. If Ms. Morrow had bled on the pillow when she bit her lip, the soiled pillowcase would be in the laundry bag. And what about the bed? When they took away poor Ms. Morrow's body, I bet nobody bothered to make the bed. I don't want strangers to go into her home and see it with an unmade bed and a soiled pillowcase in the laundry bag, she thought.

The elevator came. She pushed the button to go up to the fourteenth floor. I have a key to her apartment, she thought. I'm going to do the last thing I can ever do for the poor soul—change her sheets. Take that soiled pillowcase home, launder it, make her bed and put the spread on, so that whoever goes into her apartment can appreciate what it looked like when she lived in it.

Comforted at the thought that she could offer one final service to a lady who had been very kind to her, Sophie got off on the fourteenth floor, took out her key, and opened the door of Olivia Morrow's apartment.

54

With mixed emotions, but believing that she was genuinely concerned, Monica took Susan Gannon to Sally's crib. Sally's eyes were open, and she was holding a nearly full bottle of water. The oxygen mask had been replaced by tubes in her nostrils. At the sight of Monica she struggled to her feet and raised her arms. "Monny, Monny." But when Monica picked her up, she began to punch at her with her small fists.

"Oh, come on, Sally," Monica said, soothingly. "I know you're mad at me, but I couldn't help hurting you with those needles. I had to make you get better."

The intensive care nurse held the chart for her. "As I told you when you phoned, Doctor, Sally had a pretty good night. She hates the IV of course, and fought it until she fell asleep. She did drink her bottle this morning and ate a little fruit."

Susan had been standing a few feet away. "Does she still have pneumonia?" she asked quietly.

"There's still some fluid in her lungs," Monica said. "But thank God, she's off the critical list. When the babysitter brought her in on Thursday morning, I was afraid we were going to lose this little girl. We couldn't let that happen, could we, Sally?"

Sally's fists stopped flailing and she laid her head on Monica's shoulder.

"She's the image of her father," Susan said softly. "How long will she be in the hospital?"

"For another week at least," Monica said.

"Then what?" Susan asked.

"Unless some relative comes to claim her, she'll be put into a foster home, at least temporarily."

"I see. Thank you, Doctor." Abruptly Susan Gannon turned and walked quickly down the corridor. It was clear to Monica that she was becoming very emotional and was eager to get away.

After Monica examined Sally and put her back in the crib, wailing in protest, she reconnected the IV, and then checked her two other young patients. One of them was a six-year-old boy who had a bad strep throat. He was surrounded by his parents, big brothers, and grandmother. Books and games were piled on the windowsill. "I think I should keep you here for a couple of more days, Bobby, so you can read all those books," she told him, as she signed his discharge papers.

At his alarmed look, she said, "Just kidding. You're out of here."

Four-year-old Rachel, who had been admitted with bronchitis, was her other patient. She, too, was recovered enough to go home. "And you two had both better get some rest," Monica told the weary-looking parents. She knew that neither one of them had left Rachel's side since she'd been brought to the hospital four days ago. Bobby and Rachel were never really in danger, she thought. Hospitalizing them was only a precaution. But Sally almost didn't make it. The other kids have families who haven't left them alone for one single minute. Sally's only visitors have been her babysitter, who knew her for only a week, and the ex-wife of her father, who is now suspected of murdering Sally's mother.

In the hospital lobby, Monica bought the *Post* and the *News*, and on the way home in the cab, she read the stories behind the headlines about Peter Gannon. The large gift bag Gannon claimed he had given Renée Carter had been found crumpled in his wastebasket. One hundred thousand dollars in one-hundred-dollar bills, the money that had been in the gift bag, was hidden in the false bottom in his desk drawer.

He's guilty as sin, Monica thought. No one in that family will ever want Renée Carter's baby. According to these stories, Peter Gannon has never even laid eyes on her. Oh, God, with all the people who yearn for a child, why did Sally have to be born to these people?

But Sally would not be Sally if she were not the offspring of Peter Gannon and Renée Carter. No matter what kind of people they are, or were, she is a beautiful, sweet little girl.

"We're here, Miss," the cabby said.

Monica looked up, startled. "Oh, of course." She paid the fare, tipped generously, and went up the steps, key in hand. She opened the outer door, used the key for the inner door to the vestibule, and walked down the hallway to her apartment. It was only when she was inside, and had dropped her shoulder bag and the newspapers on the chair, that the events of the past few days flooded through her mind.

She stared at the worn shoulder bag she had been using in place of the new one that had been crushed by the bus. She felt the panic of that awful moment again when the bus was rushing at her. Then she thought of her intense disappointment that Olivia Morrow had died only hours before they were to meet, of her futile attempt to find a possible confidante of Morrow's at the funeral Mass, and finally of the emotional pain of learning that Ryan was involved with another woman. A feeling of intense sadness enveloped her.

Close to tears, she went into the kitchen, put on the kettle, and looked in the refrigerator for salad makings. I'm more banged up than I realized, she thought. My back and shoulders are sore and aching.

There's something else, she told herself. What is it? It has to do with Sally. Something I said this morning. What was it?

Let it go, she thought. If it's important, it will come back.

There's something I *do* know is important, she mused, as she opened a can of crabmeat. The meeting at the Gannon Foundation has been set for Tuesday. I wonder if they'll try to cancel it, with all this going on. We need the fifteen million dollars they promised us for the addition to the hospital. We need that new pediatric wing that's going to be part of it. Isn't it incredible that one of the Gannons is Sally's father?

The salad and two cups of tea made Monica feel a bit better. She knew that her land phone was backed up with calls from her friends who had heard about the bus incident. With a pad in hand, she listened to the messages. They all ran in a similar vein, how concerned and shocked they were at her narrow escape from the bus, and was there any truth to that old lady's story that she had been pushed? Three of her callers wanted her to stay at their apartments, in case she was being stalked.

Monica began to return the calls. She reached six of her friends and left messages for the others, and she declined several invitations to join them for dinner, even though she had no plans for the evening. When she was finished, she went into the bathroom, undressed, and got into the Jacuzzi. For forty-five minutes she relaxed in the soothing warm water and began to feel the strain ease from her bruised body.

She had planned to put on comfortable slacks and a sweater and take a long walk, but the almost sleepless night was taking its toll on her. Instead, she lay down on the bed, pulled the comforter over her, and closed her eyes.

When she opened them again the slanting shadows told her it was late afternoon. For a few minutes she stayed wrapped in the comforter, feeling more in focus. I'm glad I don't have plans, she thought. I haven't seen a good movie in ages—I'll find one, go to an early show by myself, and grab something to eat on the way back. I really don't feel like taking a walk anymore. But I do want to get some fresh air . . .

She pushed her feet into chenille slippers, walked from the bedroom to the kitchen, opened the back door to the small patio, and stepped outside. It was chilly, and the robe that had felt so comfortable was no match for the outside temperature.

A couple of deep breaths, she thought, and that's it. Then as she glanced around, her eyes focused on the decorative water can that stood to the left of the door.

It had been moved.

She was sure of it.

She always left it placed on the one patio stone that was badly cracked. It was heavy enough so that even a strong wind wouldn't move it. Now it was halfway onto the next stone.

But it hadn't been like that yesterday.

Before I left for the funeral Mass, I came out on the patio, she thought. I'd slept so badly I felt groggy and wanted fresh air. I'm sure I remember looking at the can and thinking that I should get around to replacing the broken stone. Or, maybe Lucy moved it, if she swept the patio when she was here yesterday?

Suddenly shivering, Monica went back into the kitchen, pulled the door closed behind her, and slid the bolt into the lock position.

I always mean to leave the bolt fastened, she thought, nervously, but it hadn't been fastened just now. Sometimes, like yesterday, when I go outside for a few minutes I forget to slide the bolt. I must have done that yesterday. After I finally fell asleep last night, I woke up so suddenly. Was it because I heard a sound that startled me awake? If I had been in a sound sleep and hadn't turned on the light, would someone have tried to come in? Had someone been out there?

The incongruous thought ran through her mind that the reason she hadn't slept well had a name.

It was Ryan Jenner.

55

Sammy Barber worked as a bouncer at the Ruff-Stuff Bar from nine P.M. till closing. The so-called nightclub was basically a strip joint, and Sammy's job was to make sure none of the drunks got out of hand. He also had to protect the D-list celebrities and their hangers-on from being bothered by jerks who tried to get too close to their tables and slobber over them.

It was a job that had lousy pay, but it kept his profile low. It also meant that he could sleep late, unless he had been hired to do a hit job and had to tail someone until he got his chance to make that target disappear.

On Saturday evening Sammy was in a foul mood. The first bungled attempt to kill Farrell had left him unsure of himself for the first time in years. And the fact that the old crow had seen him push Farrell and could describe him was scary. In the last couple of years, he had bumped two people onto train tracks without anyone suspecting they hadn't fallen accidentally. Then, yesterday afternoon, from the alleyway behind her house, using a long-distance lens, he had taken a picture of Farrell's back door. When he developed it, he could see that the top half of the door consisted of squares of glass covered by a metal grille. The grille was a laugh. He could see that it would be easy to cut out the pane nearest the lock and reach his hand in to turn the knob. If there was a security bolt he'd just have to cut another pane to get to it. Simple stuff.

At three o'clock in the morning, he had gone through the alleyway, hoisted himself over Farrell's joke of a fence, and had taken out his glass cutter. One minute more and he'd have been inside her apartment, but in the dark he hadn't seen whatever it was that had caused him to stumble. It was heavy and he didn't knock it over, but it almost made him lose his balance. His foot hit it hard and gave it a push, and it made a scraping sound on the patio. It was probably one of those stupid lawn statues.

Farrell had good ears if she had heard it, Sammy thought, and I guess she did, because the next thing I knew, a light went on inside the apartment. That was it for *that* plan.

Restlessly, Sammy began to consider alternate ways to get at Farrell, but then his eyes narrowed. The place was starting to fill up with the usual losers, but two guys in business suits were being led to a table. They're cops, Sammy thought. They might as well be wearing their badges.

It was obvious that the waiter who seated them knew that, too. He looked across the room at Sammy, who nodded, meaning he'd spotted them.

Some jerk who'd been pretty loaded when he came in was staggering to his feet. Sammy knew he was heading for the D-list rapper, who was sitting with his groupies in the celebrity section. The drunk had been trying to get that guy's attention for the last half hour. In an instant, Sammy was on his feet, and with quick steps, surprising for his bulk, was at the drunk's side. "Sir, please stay right here." As he spoke he squeezed the guy's arm hard enough to make him get the point.

"But I just wanna pay my reshpechs . . ." He looked up into Sammy's face and his vacant expression changed to a frightened stare. "Okay, okay, pal. Don't wanna make problums." He slumped back into his seat.

As Sammy turned to go back to his table, one of the two men he'd spotted as cops signaled to him.

Here it comes, Sammy thought, as he made his way across the room.

"Pull up a chair, Sammy," Detective Forrest invited, as he and Detective Whelan passed their badges across the table to him.

Sammy glanced at them, then looked quickly at Whelan, remembering that he had been the lead detective on his case and a witness at his trial. He could still remember the disgusted look on Whelan's face when he was acquitted. "Nice to see you again," he told him.

"Glad you remember me, Sammy," Whelan said. "But you always did have a way with threats, I mean words."

"This joint is clean. Don't waste your time looking for trouble," Sammy snapped.

"Sammy, we know this dump could serve as a day care center," Forrest told him. "We're only interested in you. Why did you bother to change from your sweat suit to your version of dress-up clothes when you picked up your car at the pound? You remember, Thursday, you were in such a hurry to follow Dr. Farrell when she left the hospital that you didn't even take time to feed the meter?"

Sammy had been questioned enough in the past by cops that he had trained himself never to appear to be nervous. But he had a sick feeling in the pit of his stomach this time. "I don't know what you're talking about," he mumbled.

"We all know what I'm talking about, Sammy," Forrest told him. "We hope nothing happens to Monica Farrell, because if it does, Sammy, you'll think you were caught in a tsunami. On the other hand, we'd be very interested to know who hired you."

"Sammy," Whelan asked, "why were you parked in front of the hospital? Just in case you forgot, as Carl just told you, the security cameras show your car being hauled away."

"Not feeding the meter cost me big bucks, but no one ever mentioned that it was a crime. And when you look at it, it helps the city. All those extra bucks, you know what I mean?" Sammy was beginning to feel confident. They're trying to rattle me, he thought, scornfully. They're trying to get me to say something stupid. They wouldn't talk to me like this if they could prove anything.

"By any chance do you know Dr. Monica Farrell?" Detective Forrest asked.

"Doctor who?"

"She's the young woman who fell, or was pushed, in front of a bus the other night. It was in all the papers."

"Don't get much chance to read the papers," Sammy said.

"You should. They keep you abreast of current events." Forrest and Whelan stood up together. "Always interesting to chat with you, Sammy."

Sammy watched as the two detectives worked their way through the now crowded tables to the exit. I can't be the one to take Farrell out, he thought. I've got to hand off the job, and I know just the right guy to take my place. I'll offer Larry one hundred grand. He'll snap at it. But I'll make sure it happens while I'm at work so I have a rock-solid alibi. Then those cops will be off my back. And I still come out ahead. I got paid one million to do it, and I subcontract the job for one-tenth of that!

Smiling at the thought, but with a sense of failure, Sammy admitted to himself that for the first time in his long career as a hit man, he had bungled two attempts to carry out his contract to eliminate an unwanted problem. Maybe it *is* time to quit, he thought. But not before I see this one through.

Like I told Dougie, I always keep my word.

56

Tony, Rosalie, and little Carlos Garcia went for a drive on Saturday afternoon. They were on their way to visit Rosalie's sister Marie and her husband, Ted Simmons, at their home in Bay Shore, Long Island.

Tony had been working nonstop for almost two weeks between the chauffeuring jobs and events at the Waldorf, where he was a waiter. As he explained to Rosalie, the minute October came all the big charities had their black-tie dinners. "Sometimes I hear the people I'm driving talk about how many of these affairs they've gone to in a week," Tony told Rosalie. "And don't think they're cheap."

But this Saturday he was off, and it was a nice day to drive to Bay Shore. Tony liked his in-laws. Marie and Ted had three kids a little older than Carlos, and Ted's mother and brother would be there as well. Ted had opened a hardware store in Bay Shore and was doing great. Their house was a big colonial, and they had a fenced-in yard where Carlos and his cousins could run around with no one worrying about the traffic.

"It's going to be so much fun today, Tony," Rosalie said happily, as they emerged from the gloom of the

Midtown Tunnel onto the expressway. "I was so scared when the baby got that terrible cold this week, but he hasn't even sneezed in four days." She looked back over her shoulder. "Have you, love?" she asked Carlos, who was securely ensconced in his car seat.

"No, no, no," Carlos responded in a singsong voice.

"Boy, is that ever his new word," Rosalie laughed.

"It's his only word these days," Tony answered, then thought of something he'd been meaning to tell his wife: "Rosie, I told you about that nice old woman I drove two weeks ago to that cemetery in Rhinebeck? She's the one who said she knew Dr. Monica's grandmother. I saw in the paper yesterday that she had died. She's being buried today."

"That's too bad, Tony."

"I really liked her. Oh, God!" Tony slammed his foot on the accelerator. In the midst of the heavy traffic, the car had stopped dead. Frantically, he turned the key in the ignition as the screeching of brakes from the truck behind him warned him that they were going to be hit. "No!" he shouted.

Rosalie turned to look at Carlos. "Oh, my God!" she wailed.

As Rosalie screamed, they felt a bump that shook them back and forth, but the driver of the truck had managed to brake and slow down before he hit them.

Shaking with relief, they turned to look at their two-year-old son. Totally unruffled, Carlos was trying to climb out of his car seat.

"He thinks we're there," Tony said, his voice quivering, his hands still clutching the wheel. A moment later, still shaking, he opened the door of the car to greet the man whose quick reaction had saved their lives.

Three hours later they were in Ted and Marie's house in Bay Shore, at the dining room table. It had taken forty minutes for the tow truck to arrive. They had caused a massive traffic delay on the expressway. Ted had driven over to pick them up at the service station where they were stranded.

The awareness that if the driver behind them had been tailgating, or if he'd been unable to stop, they might be dead, filled all the adults at the table, Rosalie and Tony, Marie and Ted, Ted's mother and brother, with a profound sense of gratitude. "It could have been so different," Rosalie said, as she glanced out the windows. One of his big cousins was pushing a delighted Carlos on the swing.

"It could still be so different if you don't get rid of that old car of yours, Tony," Ted, a heavyset man with a decisive manner, said bluntly. "You've been nursing that rattletrap much too long. I know you've been putting off buying a new car, and I know why—all those medical bills for Carlos have been burying you. But he didn't beat leukemia so that all of you could be killed in an accident. Look around for a decent car, okay? I'll lend you the money."

Tony looked gratefully at his brother-in-law. He knew that Ted might say that he'd lend the money, but he also knew he would never let him pay it back. "I know you're right, Ted," he agreed. "I'm not putting my family in that old heap again. Even before it broke down, I was thinking about a car that would be perfect for us and it can't be too expensive. It's a ten-year-old Cadillac. I drove the old lady who owned it, a couple of weeks ago. It was a pretty long trip. You know I know cars. This one is in perfect condition. It's probably heavier on the gas than the new ones, but I bet I could get it at book value, which can't be much."

"Tony, you mean the lady we were talking about on the way out?" Rosalie asked. "The lady whose funeral was today?"

"Yes, Ms. Morrow. It's her car that's probably going to be for sale."

"Look into it, Tony," Ted said. "Don't waste time. There isn't much of a market for a ten-year-old Caddy. You'll probably get it."

"I'll go to her apartment building. Someone there can probably tell me who to call about it," Tony promised. "I really liked Ms. Morrow and I have the feeling that she liked me."

And I have the crazy hunch that she'd want me to have her car, he thought.

57

Peter Gannon went through the shocking ritual of being fingerprinted, having his mug shot taken, being strip-searched, and finally led to a cell in the Tombs, the crowded and noisy jail where prisoners awaiting trial in Manhattan were incarcerated.

With every inch of his being he wanted to protest his innocence, to shout to everyone within earshot that he could never hurt Renée, no matter how much he hated her. On Saturday morning, he read in his cellmate's newspaper that the shopping bag and money had been found in his office. Too numb for coherent thought, he sat in the cell until late Saturday afternoon, when the lawyer Susan had found for him came to see him.

He introduced himself as he handed Peter his card. "I'm Harvey Roth," he said, his tone of voice low but resonant.

Peter looked at him, still feeling as if he was experiencing a nightmare. Roth was a compact man with iron-gray hair, and rimless glasses framing a thin face. He was dressed in a dark blue suit with a blue shirt and tie.

"Are you expensive?" Peter asked. "I have to tell you straight up that I'm broke."

"I am expensive," Roth answered, mildly. "Your ex-wife, Susan, has paid the retainer for my services, and guaranteed all the costs of defending you."

Susan did that, Peter thought. It was one more whiplash reminder of the kind of person she was, and that he had traded her for Renée Carter.

"Mr. Gannon, I assume you know that the money you claimed was in Renée Carter's possession was hidden in the false bottom of your desk drawer?" Roth asked.

"I didn't even know that any drawer in my desk had a false bottom," Peter said, his voice a monotone. At the incredulous look on Harvey Roth's face, Peter felt as if he were caught in quicksand and sinking into it ever deeper. "Four years ago, when the Gannon Foundation and my brother Greg's investment firm moved to the Time Warner Center, a decorator was hired to re-do the offices from scratch. I asked that whoever was hired also take care of my new theatre production office. At that time I was doing well, and I had a suite on West Fifty-first Street. Two years ago, when I downsized, I got rid of a lot of the furniture, but kept the desk. No one ever told me about the false bottom in it."

"Who was the decorator?" Roth asked.

"I don't know her name."

"You didn't have meetings with her? She didn't show you any sketches or samples?"

"I'm not a detail man," Peter said wearily. "I liked what she was doing at the offices in Time Warner."

"Didn't you talk to her about how much the project would cost?" Roth asked.

"The foundation paid for it, because it was sponsoring my theatre projects. What I mean is, the foundation voted a grant that included the expenses of my office."

"I see, Mr. Gannon. Then you claim you never knew there was a false bottom in your desk?"

"I swear, I swear I didn't know that." Peter buried his face in his hands, hoping to shut himself away from the persistent questions Harvey Roth was asking him.

"And you don't know the name of the decorator who bought the desk for your office?"

"No, I don't," Peter said, wearily. "Let me say it again. I don't know her name. I asked Greg's secretary to have her take care of my new production office. I don't think I even *met* the woman. She did the job while I was away with Renée."

Where did we go that time? he wondered. Oh, I remember. Paradise Island. He managed to choke back a desperate fit of laughter.

"How can I learn who the decorator is?" Roth persisted.

"The secretary at my brother's office would know. She handles that kind of thing."

"What is her name?"

"Esther Chambers."

"I'll talk to her."

Peter looked at Roth. He thinks I'm lying. He thinks I killed Renée. Peter knew he had to ask the questions that had been swirling through his mind during the sleepless night in the cell. "If I told someone that I thought—let's say it straight, that I *knew*—my brother was doing insider trading, would that person have an obligation to report it to the SEC?"

"Read the facts about the master financial crook, Bernie Madoff, Mr. Gannon," Roth said matter-of-factly. "When his sons learned what he was doing, they knew they had to report it immediately. Of course, they were employees of his firm so that changes the picture. It depends on the person to whom you disclosed that information."

I can't drag her into it, Peter thought.

"Mr. Gannon, why did you say you're sure your brother was involved in insider trading?"

"A couple of years ago, at a cocktail party for the Wall Street types, I overheard a guy from Ankofski Oil and Gas thank Greg for the money. He told Greg he had been able to take the kids to Europe for their spring break. That was about a month after Ankofski was taken over by Elmo Oil and Gas, and the stock tripled."

"What was your brother's response?" Roth asked.

"He went wild. He said something like, 'Shut up, you fool, and get out of here.' "

"Did your brother know you had overheard that conversation?"

"No, he didn't. I was standing behind him. I didn't want him to know that I heard it. But I *do* know that Greg's hedge fund made a fortune on that takeover. It's not that everything isn't bad enough already, but could criminal charges be filed against me if Greg is ever caught and it came out that I knew what he was up to?"

He saw the contempt in Harvey Roth's eyes. "Mr.

Gannon, I would suggest that you concentrate on assisting me in preparing a defense for you on the charge of murder. I will do everything in my power to give you the best defense I can, but it would be most helpful if you can try to recall what happened in those fifteen hours between the time you blacked out and the time you woke up on your couch. Let's talk about the shopping bag that contained the money. One that fits the exact description of the one you told the police that you gave Ms. Carter was found in the wastebasket under your desk."

"Why would I hide the money and leave the shopping bag where anyone could find it?" Peter asked, with a spark of anger.

Roth nodded. "That has occurred to me. On the other hand, by your own admission you were drunk. Let me tell you how we are going to proceed. Our investigative staff will go to the bar where you met Ms. Carter and question any patrons we can learn were there. They will also go to other bars in the area. We hope we may find someone who saw you alone after you left Ms. Carter."

"*If* I left Ms. Carter, you mean," Peter said. "That is really what you're saying, isn't it?"

Without answering, Roth got up to leave. "We are trying to get your bail reduced from five million to two million dollars."

"I think my brother will put it up for me," Peter said.

"I hope so. If not, there is another source who will guarantee it."

"Susan?" Peter asked.

"Yes. Against all odds, she believes firmly in your innocence. You are a very fortunate man, Mr. Gannon, to have a champion like Susan in your corner."

Peter watched Roth as he walked away from him, then felt a tap on his shoulder.

"Let's go," the guard ordered brusquely.

58

On Saturday night, before she went to bed, Monica had double-locked and bolted the door to the patio, then wedged a chair under the knob on the kitchen side. She had talked to some of her friends and asked about their alarm systems, and afterward she left an urgent message for one company asking for the immediate installation of a state-of-the-art system, including security cameras on the patio.

That done, she hoped to feel somewhat more secure, but her dreams had been filled with memories of her father. Fragmented as they were, she remembered that in one of them she had been with him in St. Patrick's Cathedral. She woke with the sensation of his hand in hers.

Did I ever really appreciate him? she asked herself, as she got up and began to make coffee. Looking back I can begin to understand how much he loved Mom. He never looked at another woman after she died, and he was such a handsome man.

That year that she was so sick, I was ten years old. I never wanted to go anywhere or do anything. I just wanted to come straight from school to be with her.

After she was gone, Dad made me join school activities, and that first year he brought me to New York on so many weekends. We went to plays and concerts and museums and did the fun, touristy stuff. But we were both so sad about Mom . . .

He was a great storyteller, Monica remembered with a smile, as she decided to boil an egg and have a slice of whole wheat toast instead of an English muffin. When we went to Rockefeller Center at Christmastime, he told me all about the first tree that was ever put up there. It was a little one the workmen had put up because it was during the Depression and they were so grateful just to have jobs. He knew the history behind every place we visited . . .

He loved history, but he didn't have any concept of his background, his own history. Knowing that I was so close to learning about it has finally made me understand how important that was to him. I used to joke with him about it. "Dad, you may be the illegitimate son of the Duke of Windsor. What would Queen Elizabeth think about that?" I thought I was being funny.

If only Olivia Morrow had lived *one* more day! If only she had lived one more day . . .

While the egg boiled, Monica called the hospital. Sally had slept through the night. Her temperature was only slightly elevated. She hadn't coughed much. "Every day, she's so much better, Doctor," the nurse reported, happily. "But you should know that some reporters were trying to get up here to take her picture. The security desk got rid of them."

"I would hope so," Monica said, fervently. "You have my cell phone. Call if there's any change with Sally, and if any reporters manage to sneak upstairs, don't let them anywhere near Sally."

Shaking her head, she scooped the egg into a cup and put it on a plate with the toast. The thoughts of her father would not leave her mind. It's Sunday morning. Dad and I always went to St. Patrick's for the ten fifteen Mass there, when we came to New York for the weekend, she remembered. And after that we'd have brunch, and it was his surprise to me where we were going for the afternoon. Being away from home and doing different things like that helped both of us.

Maybe I'll go to the ten fifteen at the cathedral, she mused. It would make me feel closer to Dad. I need that feeling right now.

I wonder what Ryan and his girlfriend are planning to do today?

Stop it, Monica warned herself. Make some plans for your own afternoon. Going to that movie last night was one miserable letdown. It was terrible. What do the critics see in something that makes absolutely no sense? Maybe I'll call a few people and, if they're free, have them in for dinner. I haven't cooked for company in the last three weeks. I always love doing that, but these past few weeks have been so crazy . . .

But somehow the idea was not appealing.

But I *will* go to St. Pat's this morning, she decided fifteen minutes later, as she finished a second cup of coffee, enjoying the luxury of lingering over it as she read the newspapers that had been delivered to the door.

At ten fifteen, she was in the cathedral, kneeling in a pew toward the front left side of the main altar, the area that her father had always chosen. Yesterday at this time, I was in St. Vincent's listening to Father Dunlap eulogize Olivia Morrow, then talk about me. No one could help, and I guess no one ever will. I know what I was trying to remember that had to do with Sally, she suddenly recalled: it's that I told Susan Gannon Sally almost didn't make it.

It wasn't by a miracle or the power of prayer that Sally survived. The reason is that the kid who was her babysitter was smart enough to bring her to the hospital in time, and that we had the medicine to save her.

The choir was singing, "I have heard you calling in the night." I guess I've answered enough calls in the night, Monica thought wryly. I went to that beatification hearing, and testified that there had to be some medical reason why Michael O'Keefe is still alive. When Ryan saw the file, he said that there was absolutely no way Michael's brain tumor wasn't terminal. Ryan's a neurosurgeon. I'm not, but I am a good pediatrician. I know perfectly well there are no medical facts that justify Michael's recovery. Sister Catherine spent her life taking care of disabled children. She opened seven hospitals for them. I'm proud of myself that I was there for Sally, and that I helped Carlos to beat the leukemia.

I took an oath that I was testifying about the case to the best of my ability and knowledge. Am I being stubbornly blind? I need to see Michael. It's been three years. I want to see him again.

Monica tried to focus on the Mass, but her thoughts kept drifting. The O'Keefes had moved to Mamaroneck from their Manhattan apartment shortly after Michael was diagnosed with brain cancer. It was only when Michael seemed to be fully recovered that they had triumphantly brought him back to her office . . .

"Go in peace, the Mass is ended," the Archbishop pronounced.

As Monica left the cathedral, the choir was singing "Joyful, joyful, we adore thee." She fumbled for her cell phone and dialed information. The O'Keefes' phone number was listed. She dialed it and the call was picked up on the first ring. "This is Dr. Monica Farrell," she said, "is this Mrs. O'Keefe?"

"Yes, it is," a warm voice responded. "It's nice to hear from you, Doctor."

"Thank you, Mrs. O'Keefe. I'm calling because I am very anxious to see Michael again. Would you mind if I came up to visit you? I promise I won't stay long."

"That's absolutely fine. We're home all day. Do you want to come this afternoon?"

"I'd very much like to come this afternoon."

"Has it anything to do with Sister Catherine's beatification?"

"It has everything to do with it," Monica said quietly.

"Then come right up. Will you be driving yourself?"

"Yes."

"We look forward to seeing you, Dr. Monica. Isn't

it funny that a neurosurgeon, Dr. Ryan Jenner, was here only yesterday afternoon? He also wanted to meet Michael before he speaks to the beatification committee. What a wonderful person he is. I'm sure you must know him?"

Monica felt a stab of pain. "Yes, I do," she said quietly. "I know him quite well."

Two hours later, Monica was in Mamaroneck having a sandwich and coffee with Richard and Emily O'Keefe. Michael, their energetic eight-year-old son, had politely visited with Monica and had answered her questions with only a tinge of restlessness. He told her that his favorite sport was baseball, but that in the winter he liked to go skiing with his father. He never, ever felt dizzy, the way he used to when he was real sick.

"His last MRI was only three months ago," Emily told Monica. "It was absolutely clear. They've all been perfect after that first year." She smiled at her son, who was now fidgeting. "I know. You want to go to Kyle's. It's okay, but Dad will walk you over there, and he'll pick you up later."

Michael broke into a grin, revealing two missing front teeth. "Thanks, Mom. It's nice to see you again, Dr. Farrell," he said. "Mom told me that you really helped me to get better." He turned and scampered out of the dining room.

Richard O'Keefe got to his feet. "Wait up, Mike," he called.

After they were gone, Monica protested, "Mrs. O'Keefe, I didn't help Michael get better."

"You certainly did. You recognized what it was. You told us straight out to get other consultations, but that he was terminal. That was when I knew I needed to beg for a miracle."

"Why did you choose to pray to Sister Catherine in particular?"

"My great-aunt was a nurse in one of her hospitals. I remember her telling me when I was a little girl that she had worked with a nun who was like an angel. She told me that you would think every child she held in her arms was her own. She would comfort them and pray over them. My great-aunt was convinced that Sister Catherine had been gifted from God with a special power of healing, that she had an aura about her that words couldn't describe, and that everyone who was in her presence felt it, too. When you told us that Michael was going to die, my first thought was of Sister Catherine."

"I remember," Monica said quietly. "I felt such pity for you because I knew there was just no hope for Michael."

Emily O'Keefe smiled. "And you still don't believe in miracles, do you, Monica? In fact, didn't you come here believing that no matter how well he seems, and no matter how clean his tests, that the tumor could come back someday?"

'Yes, I did," Monica said, reluctantly.

"Why can't you believe in miracles, Monica? What makes you so certain that they don't happen?"

"It's not that I don't want to believe, but as I testified

to the beatification committee, I know from my medical training that throughout history events have occurred that seem to be miracles, but in reality they have a scientific explanation that just wasn't understood at the time."

"Have any of those events ever included a little boy whose massive and malignant brain tumor completely disappeared?"

"Not that I'm aware of."

"Monica, Dr. Jenner is one of several respected neurosurgeons who are testifying that there is no medical or scientific explanation for Michael's recovery. I don't know whether you realize it, but it will be a long time before the Church itself concludes that this was a miracle. They will follow Michael's medical status for many years." Then Emily O'Keefe smiled. "We had pretty much this same conversation yesterday with Dr. Jenner. He told us he believed that in twenty years or fifty years there will still be no scientific explanation for Michael's cure."

She reached for Monica's hand and held it, gently. "Monica, I hope that you don't think I'm overreaching, but I do very much sense that you are conflicted. And also that you are ready to accept the possibility that Sister Catherine intervened, and that because of her, our only child is with us now."

59

Esther Chambers devoured the newspapers over the weekend with a combination of shock and disbelief. The fact that Peter Gannon had been arrested for the murder of his former girlfriend seemed to her absolutely incredible. Greg is the one who has a nasty temper, she thought. I'd believe it of him, but never of Peter. And the fact that Peter was the father of a baby girl who was in the hospital, a baby Peter had never seen, sickened her.

Poor little tyke, she thought. Her mother's dead, her father's in jail, and if these articles can be believed, none of her mother's relatives are looking to claim her.

Greg's public relations firm had issued the statement to the press saying that the family was standing behind Peter and believed he would be vindicated. I hope so, too, Esther thought. Peter spends the foundation money like water, but he's basically a decent human being. In my wildest dreams I cannot imagine him strangling that woman and stuffing her into a garbage bag.

She deliberately went to work early on Monday to avoid having to face the other employees and hear the gossip that she knew would be sweeping the office. But when she settled at her desk, Esther realized that her hands were trembling. She knew that by now Arthur Saling must have read the warning she had mailed to him. Would Greg suspect her of having written it? If Saling decided not to invest, she was sure Greg's whole house of cards would collapse within weeks.

Did I have the right to do that? she asked herself. The people from the Securities and Exchange Commission would probably be furious if they found out. But Greg was drawing in Mr. Saling, and I felt so sorry for him and his family. If Saling *does* invest, his money will be wiped out when the SEC closes in on Greg. Bad enough for the dozens of people who are going to lose everything—I just couldn't let one more person get hurt, not when I could prevent it, she told herself.

Through the glass doors that opened into the area where the rest of the office staff worked, she saw Greg Gannon approaching. Help me, Lord, she prayed. I don't know what he would do if Saling shows him that letter, and he thinks I wrote it.

With a hard push that sent the door flying open, Greg came into the suite and walked straight to Esther's desk. "I assume you've read the newspapers and seen the television stories," he said abruptly.

"Of course. I'm so very sorry. And I know it's all a terrible mistake." Esther was glad that she was able to keep her voice quiet and convincing.

"There'll be plenty of phone calls from the media. Refer them to Jason at the PR firm. Let him earn his money for a change."

"Yes, sir. I'll take care of it immediately."

"I'm not available for calls. I don't care if it's the Pope on the line."

He surely wouldn't be calling *you*, Esther thought.

Greg Gannon started toward his private office, then stopped. "But if Arthur Saling phones, put him right through. I expect to be meeting with him later today."

Esther swallowed hard. "Of course, Mr. Gannon."

"All right." Greg took a few steps away from Esther's desk, then stopped again. "Wait a minute," he snapped. "Haven't we got a foundation meeting with the Greenwich Hospital group scheduled for tomorrow morning?"

"Yes, at eleven o'clock."

"Cancel it."

"Mr. Gannon, if you'd allow me to offer a suggestion, that's not a good idea. They're very upset that the grant the foundation promised them hasn't come through. I think it's really necessary for you to meet with them and give them some reassurance. Otherwise, if they get the press involved, it could be ugly. You don't need more pressure right now."

Greg Gannon hesitated, then said, "You're right as usual, Esther. Remind Hadley and Langdon to be here. It's obvious my brother won't be available."

"Will you tell Mrs. Gannon yourself or shall I remind her, sir?"

Astonished, Esther watched Greg Gannon's face darken with rage. "Mrs. Gannon is very busy these days," he snapped. "I doubt she'll be available."

Oh boy, Esther thought, as she watched Greg stride into his office. Maybe there's something to that rumor that Pamela has a boyfriend, and now Greg has heard about it. I wonder who the guy is?

If it really *is* true, Pamela won't be making any more trips to Cartier.

She'll be doing her jewelry shopping in a bargain store basement.

60

After he had lunch with Doug Langdon at the St. Regis, Dr. Clayton Hadley spent the rest of the weekend in a state of near panic. The memory of holding the pillow over Olivia Morrow's face haunted his every waking moment. How did I let myself get into this? he wondered, frantically. I had a good practice. I was being paid well for my job at the foundation. I actually did steer money from the foundation into cardiac research. That, at least, would stand up, if anyone ever investigates where the foundation money really has gone . . .

When the money from Alex Gannon's patents was still flowing in, it was easy for me to set up phony research centers that were little more than rented rooms with a so-called lab technician, Clay thought. Doug got me started on that. Now I have a fortune in my Swiss bank account.

A lot of good that will do me if I'm indicted for murder.

How about Doug? For the last ten years, since we've been on the foundation board, he's been funneling small grants into worthwhile mental health projects, as well as pots of money into storefront clinics with one part-time attendant. The money flowed out the back door of those places, and straight into Doug's pockets.

The Gannons were oblivious, Clay thought. They gave the okay to anything Doug or I proposed. They were too busy scooping out the foundation money themselves to maintain their own extravagances. They rubber-stamped us, and we rubber-stamped them.

Then, when Doug introduced Pamela to Greg eight years ago, Greg fell for her like a ton of bricks, divorced his wife, married her, and made her a member of the foundation board. For eight years, Pamela's been playing Lady Bountiful all over Manhattan. If Greg wasn't available to take the bows at any of those dreary dinners honoring the foundation for its legitimate grants, she was there doing it for him.

Greg's spending has been out of control ever since he married Pamela, Clay thought nervously. And these past four years, Peter's been boasting about his grants for his off-Broadway projects, while he's been pouring foundation money into his own musical fiascos.

All these thoughts were torturing Clay as he sat trying to read the papers in his comfortable Gramercy Park apartment. Like Doug, he had been divorced for years, but as a welcome guest in the social world, he never lacked for female company. His solicitous manner, as well as his ability to make small talk, made him an excellent extra man, the kind hostesses were always trying to find. Unlike Doug, who escorted any number of different and very attractive women, Clay found his current status absolutely satisfactory. It's taken me more than fifty years to realize that I'm a loner, he thought.

Olivia Morrow. I actually have the nerve to miss her. Olivia and I were friends. She trusted me. How many times over the years did we go out for dinner or to the theatre together? I knew her for such a long time. Her mother, Regina, was my patient. I'm sorry that her mother told us about Alex's granddaughter, and gave Olivia that file. If only Olivia had buried it with her mother . . . If only! But what good does that do?

But *did* Olivia destroy it at the end? I'm almost sure she did. It wasn't anywhere in the apartment, and her safety deposit box hasn't been opened for years. If she hadn't received that call from Monica Farrell Tuesday night, she'd have died and it would all be over. But instead Olivia saw that phone call from Catherine's granddaughter as a sign from Catherine, of all things.

Now with Peter all over the newspapers, will it put the foundation in the spotlight? If they ever start digging into the finances, it's all over. Doug seems to think that Greg can doctor up the paperwork to show that because of the present economic climate and some unwise investments, it's necessary to close the foundation. Doug doesn't believe that too many questions will be asked. But I'm not so sure it would be like that at all. I think I'm going to self-diagnose a heart condition, close down my practice, and get out of the country.

That decision made, Clayton Hadley felt somewhat better. At seven o'clock, he sent down for dinner from the in-house restaurant in his upscale condominium. As usual, he ate heartily, then managed to abolish Olivia Morrow's face from his consciousness and fall into a deep sleep.

On Monday morning, he arrived at his office at nine thirty, as usual. His secretary reported that a Ms. Sophie Rutkowski had phoned and would call back in fifteen minutes.

Sophie Rutkowski, Clay thought. Who's she? Oh, I know who she is—Olivia's cleaning woman. Olivia left her five thousand dollars in her will. She probably knows about it and is waiting to get her hands on it.

But when Sophie phoned back, it was not about the money. "Dr. Hadley," she began, her voice respectful. "Did you take the pillowcase with the blood on it from Ms. Morrow's apartment? You see, if you did, I'd like to get it from you and wash it so that the complete set is in the linen closet just the way Ms. Morrow would like it to be. Would that be all right with you, Doctor?"

61

The offices of the prestigious corporate law firm where Susan Gannon worked were on the tenth floor of the former Pam Am Building, on Park Avenue. On the twelfth floor was the equally prestigious criminal defense firm that Harvey Roth headed. Casual friends, they sometimes joked that they still thought of the building by its original name rather than by its present one, the MetLife Building.

Before she hired Roth to defend Peter, Susan had carefully researched who would be the best possible lawyer for the job. Four of the five attorneys whose opinions she had sought recommended Harvey Roth. The other one had suggested himself.

On Monday, at noon, Susan and Harvey met in his office. After ordering sandwiches from a local delicatessen, they went into his conference room and sat down at the table. "Harvey, how did Peter appear to you when you saw him Saturday?" Susan began.

"Numb. In shock. Bewildered. I could go on, but you get the picture," Harvey answered. "He claims he absolutely didn't know there was a false bottom in his desk drawer. I called his brother's secretary to ask her about it an hour ago."

"Esther Chambers. What did she say?"

"She never knew about it, either. She had nothing to do with the decorating, except to okay the bills. She said that the prices were, and now I'm quoting, 'ludicrously expensive.' "

"Did she give you the name of the decorator?"

"Chambers didn't have it at her fingertips, but said she knows that the woman has retired and spends most of her time in France. She's going to follow up and get in touch with her. She told me she'd do anything to help Peter."

"I believe that," Susan said. "Harvey, tell me the truth. If Peter's trial were starting now, what would happen?"

"Susan, you know as well as I do that he'd be found guilty. But the trial isn't starting now. Let's take a look at whatever positive facts we can find. Peter was out on the street with Renée Carter. He says he left her and the bag of money. But even if he *didn't* leave her, what happened next? That bag must have been fairly heavy. He certainly didn't carry it and drag Renée Carter down York Avenue at the same time. Even if the street wasn't crowded, he would almost certainly have been noticed."

Susan nodded. "If I were the cops, I'd want to see if there is a record of Peter getting into a cab."

"I'm sure that the cops are doing that," Harvey agreed. "Of course, there are plenty of those unlicensed limo drivers cruising around. He might have hailed one of them, with or without her, or Renée might have gotten into one of them alone. There's another possibility that we're looking into. The restaurant where Peter met Renée had at least eight or ten people hanging out at the bar. Last night we got the names of the regulars and we're following up on them. If anyone suspected that there was money in that bag, he might have followed Renée out. Maybe some guy had a car parked nearby and offered her a ride. Peter's car is clean, by the way. They have no physical evidence that Renée was ever in it, dead or alive."

Harvey Roth looked across the conference table at the slender woman, whose hazel eyes suddenly blazed with hope. "Susan," he said hurriedly. "Don't forget. Someone may surface who remembers seeing Renée walking east, and Peter following her."

"Why would she walk east?" Susan demanded. "She lived on the West Side. She certainly wasn't going to stroll along the river alone carrying a bag full of money at that hour of the night."

Harvey Roth shrugged. "Susan, we're looking for answers," he said flatly. "We won't leave a stone unturned. As I told Peter when I saw him Saturday, our investigators will visit every bar in that area to see if he staggered into one of them, hopefully alone. Let's keep our fingers crossed that he did. Now I've got to get back to work."

He stood up and tucked the plastic plate that had held his sandwich into the paper bag that had contained it. "Gourmet dining," he said, with a quick smile.

Susan put her sandwich, with only a few bites nibbled

from it, into the paper bag in front of her. She dropped it and her empty coffee container into the wastebasket, then picked up her purse and a Barnes & Noble bookstore shopping bag.

Answering Harvey's unspoken question, she smiled, wryly. "I'm going to the hospital to see Peter's baby," she said. "I'm not good at this sort of thing, but in the children's section, the clerk assured me that the books she helped me select were perfect for a nineteen-month-old. I'll let you know if she was right."

62

When Ryan returned from visiting the O'Keefes on Saturday afternoon, he entered the apartment half afraid that Alice would have found some reason to stay over. But she was gone. A note from her on the coffee table in the living room urged him to give himself enough time to find the right place to rent or buy, that there was no reason for him to rush out and do it just because they'd be sharing this apartment for a little while longer.

Alice ended the note by writing, "I'll miss you. It's been fun." She signed it, "Love, A."

With an exasperated sigh, Ryan glanced around the room. During the week, Alice had moved some of the furniture so that two club chairs were now facing each other on either side of the couch. She had tied back the heavy draperies with knotted cords that picked up one of the colors in the fabric, giving the room a much brighter appearance. The bookshelves around the fireplace had been rearranged so that the books were in neat rows rather than stacked haphazardly. The room felt as if it had Alice's imprint on it and it made him uncomfortable.

Then he went into his room, and found to his dismay

that there were new reading lamps on the night tables, and a handsome comforter in a brown and beige pattern with coordinating pillows covering the bed. There was a note on the top of the dresser. "How did you ever manage to read with those lamps? My grandmother had one of those heavy old quilts. I took the liberty of packing them all away where I hope they'll never be found." The note was unsigned but a caricature of Alice was drawn on it.

So she's an artist, too, Ryan thought. Get me out of here.

After the long morning, which he spent apartment hunting, and then the trip to Mamaroneck, he did not feel like going out again. I'll settle for cheese and whatever else I find, he decided. He went into the kitchen and opened the refrigerator. A casserole of lasagna had instructions taped on it, "Heat at 350 degrees for about forty minutes." Next to it, a smaller dish contained an endive salad. The note indicated there was a freshly made garlic dressing that went with it.

I wonder if Alice comes on with such a heavy hand to other guys she's met? Ryan thought. Someone should warn her to tone it down a bit.

But I'm not looking a gift horse in the mouth, he thought. I'm hungry and Alice is a good cook. He followed the instructions on heating the lasagna, then, when it was ready, he collected some newspapers and read them as he ate.

In the car on the way from Mamaroneck he had heard on the radio that the first frost of the season would occur during the night. When he carried his second cup of coffee into the living room, he could tell by the chill in the high-ceilinged room that the temperature was dropping outside.

One of the few modern touches in the old apartment was a gas fireplace. Ryan pressed the switch and watched as the flames leaped up behind the glass shield. His thoughts turned to his visit with the O'Keefes.

Monica did everything right, he decided. According to Emily O'Keefe, she diagnosed Michael immediately and didn't give them any false hope. I can't explain those MRIs. No one can. His first tests show how advanced the cancer was. Michael was so frightened by the MRIs that the O'Keefes decided to not have any more tests since he was terminal. At least, Michael's father decided that. His mother says that he didn't need MRIs because he was in the care of Sister Catherine.

A year later, when they took Michael to Monica to show her how well he was doing, Monica was astonished at how good he had looked. They allowed her to order another MRI and the tumor was gone. Michael's brain was normal. Monica was as shocked as I would have been. Michael's father was disbelieving at first, then absolutely overjoyed. Michael's mother offered a prayer of thanks to Sister Catherine.

I told the O'Keefes that I was going to ask to be allowed to testify at the beatification hearing, and I told them that I don't care how many years from now they keep testing Michael, he will die of old age before he dies of that cancerous brain tumor. It's gone. I'll make that call Monday.

That resolved, Ryan opened his computer. The available apartments he had seen so far were nothing like what he had in mind. But there are plenty more to see, he thought, philosophically. The problem is that I want to find something that's available immediately.

On Sunday morning he began to visit the ones he considered the most likely possibilities. At four o'clock Sunday afternoon, just after he'd decided to give it up until next weekend, he found exactly what he wanted: a spacious, tastefully decorated, four-room condominium in SoHo, overlooking the Hudson River. The owner, a photographer who would be overseas on an assignment, was offering a six-month lease. "No animals, no kids," he told Ryan.

Amused by the order of descending importance, Ryan had said, "I have neither, but someday hope to have both. However, that won't happen in the next six months, I guarantee you."

Satisfied that he would soon be in his own space, he slept well on Sunday night, and was at the hospital at seven o'clock on Monday morning. His schedule in the operating room was turned upside down by an emergency case, a young jogger hit by a car whose driver didn't see him because he was texting. It was quarter past six before he found time to call Monica's office.

"Oh, you don't have to worry about returning the O'Keefe file," Nan reassured him. "Dr. Farrell had me run over and pick it up from your office."

"Why did she do that?" Ryan asked, astonished. "I

certainly intended to bring it back myself. May I please speak with her?"

By the uncomfortable pause, he knew that Monica's secretary had been told to say she was unavailable to him.

"I'm afraid she's already gone, Doctor," Nan said.

In the background, Ryan could clearly hear Monica saying good-bye to a patient. "Then tell Dr. Farrell, for me, to keep her voice down when she's asking you to lie for her," he said sharply, and with a decisive click, hung up the phone.

63

On Monday morning Monica made an exceptionally early visit to the hospital because she knew her office schedule was packed. When she arrived, Nan and Alma were already there, gearing up for a busy day. Nan's first question was about Sally.

"She's really good," Monica answered, gratefully. "Almost too good, in fact. I won't have much justification for keeping her in the hospital longer than a few more days."

"No relatives showed up over the weekend?" Alma asked.

"No. From what I read in the newspapers, even if Peter Gannon gets out on bail, he's forbidden to go near her. No one seems to know anything about Renée Carter's background, although, putting it bluntly, if her relatives are anything like her, Sally is better off never meeting them."

At ten o'clock, as she was about to go on to the next patient, Nan called her on the intercom. "Doctor, would you please step into your consulting room?"

It had to be important. Nan would never have interrupted her for a casual visitor. Alarmed, Monica darted down the corridor to her private office. Two men were standing there waiting for her.

"We can see how busy you are, Doctor, so we'll make this brief," the taller man said, reaching behind her to shut the office door. "I'm Detective Carl Forrest. This is my partner, Detective Jim Whelan. We have come to the definite conclusion that last Thursday evening you were deliberately pushed in front of that bus. Security tapes at the hospital show a man whom we know to be mob-connected followed you when you left the hospital. We're certain he was the one who pushed you."

"Who is he?" Monica asked, bewildered. "And why on earth would he want to kill *me*?"

"His name is Sammy Barber. Do you know him, Doctor?"

"No, I don't."

"I'm not surprised," Forrest said. "He's a hit man for hire. Do you have any idea why someone would want to hurt or kill you? Think about it. Have you had any problems about a missed diagnosis, say, where you lost a child?"

"Absolutely not!"

"Dr. Farrell, do you owe anyone money, or does anyone owe you money?"

"No. No one."

"How about a rejected boyfriend? Is there anyone like that in your life?"

Forrest caught the hesitation in Monica's face. "There *is* someone, Dr. Farrell, isn't there?"

"But it was in the past," Monica protested.

"Who was he?"

"I can tell you, you're going nowhere asking about him and I certainly don't want you to put his new job in jeopardy by giving anyone the impression that he's a stalker."

"Dr. Farrell, why would you suggest that this person is a stalker?" Forrest asked sharply.

Calm down. Get your bearings, Monica told herself. "The man I'm talking about was married to a close friend. He was also my father's attorney. He developed a crush on me just before I left Boston. I hadn't seen him in four years. He is now divorced and recently moved to Manhattan. He is very interested in trying to help me trace my father's background. My father was adopted. I consider him a friend, nothing more, nothing less."

"What is his name?"

"Scott Alterman."

"When was the last time you saw him?"

"Last Thursday evening. He heard on the radio about the bus almost hitting me and called. I guess he could tell by my voice that I was pretty shaken up. He came to my apartment and stayed for about an hour."

"He came immediately after the accident?"

"Yes, but you must get something straight. In one hundred million years Scott Alterman would never harm me. I'm *sure* of that."

"Have you spoken to him since Thursday?"

"No, I have not."

"Where does he live?"

"In Manhattan, on the West Side. I don't have his address."

"We'll find it. Do you know where he works?"

"As I told you, Scott is an attorney. He just started at a New York law firm. It's one of those with three or four names. One of them is Armstrong. Look, I really have to get back to my patients," Monica said, her voice tinged with exasperation. "But what about this Sammy Barber? Where is he?"

"He lives on the Lower East Side. We've already confronted him about being on the security tape. He denies having anything to do with you, but we are keeping a twenty-four-hour tail on him."

Forrest reached in his pocket and took out the mug shot of Barber. "Here is his picture, so you know what he looks like. He knows we're watching him, so I don't think he'll try again. But, Doctor, *please* be careful."

"I will. Thank you." Monica turned and hurried back down to the examining room, where a six-month-old was now screaming. When they started talking about Scott, I never even thought to mention that the watering can had been moved the other night, she thought. But before I tell anybody, I'm going to ask Lucy if she pushed it aside when she swept the patio.

Scott would never, ever want to harm me, she thought. Then the uncomfortable memory of how he had suddenly appeared on the street when she was hailing a cab to go to Ryan's apartment came back to her.

Is it possible, she asked herself, is it even remotely possible that Scott is still obsessed with me and would hire someone to kill me?

64

At two o'clock on Monday afternoon, Arthur Saling phoned Greg Gannon and twenty minutes later arrived at Gannon's office. Esther tried to keep from looking at the sheet of paper he was holding in his hand. She knew it was the letter she had sent him.

"Mr. Saling, it's so nice to see you," she began. "I'll tell Mr. Gannon that you are here."

It was not necessary to announce him. The door of Greg's office had opened, and Greg was hurrying to meet Saling with a welcoming smile and extended hand. "Arthur, I can't tell you how sorry I am that you got one of those poison-pen letters a former employee is sending out. Thank you so much for bringing it to me. A number of our clients have received them. They're being turned over to the FBI. The man who has been sending them is demented. They're about to arrest him."

"I don't want any part of having to testify at a trial," Arthur Saling said anxiously.

"Absolutely not," Greg agreed, as he put a friendly arm around Saling's shoulders. "We've got plenty of evidence and this nutcase will be forced to plead guilty. He's married and has a family. What the FBI agent told me is that he'll probably end up getting probation and being ordered to undergo psychiatric treatment. That will be easier for both the poor guy and his family."

"How kind of you," Arthur Saling said. "I'm not so sure I'd be that benevolent if somebody was trying to ruin my good name."

With a sigh that was partly relief, partly compassion for Arthur Saling, Esther watched the men disappear into Greg Gannon's private office. As the door closed behind them, she was sure that Saling was about to put Greg in control of his portfolio. I did my best to warn him, she thought. There are none so blind as those who will not see.

Her nerves frayed, Esther realized that she could barely wait until the month was up and she could retire. Of course, it's possible that the SEC will swoop down on Greg even before then, she thought. I don't want to be around for that. What would everybody think of Greg being led out of here in handcuffs? God spare me *that* scene, she thought.

Esther got down to the task she had been undertaking, the effort to track down Diana Blauvelt, the decorator who had designed these offices four years ago. It was nearly an hour later when she finally managed to find her phone number in Paris and make the call. There was no answer, only a request in both English and French to leave a message. Carefully choosing her words, Esther requested Diana Blauvelt to try to remember if she had ever told Peter Gannon that there was a false bottom in the desk she had ordered for his office, and to please return her call as soon as possible.

Esther had barely replaced the receiver on the cradle when Greg Gannon and Arthur Saling came out of Greg's office. Both men were smiling broadly. "Esther, please welcome our new and very important client to the firm," Greg said, his voice genial.

Esther forced a smile as she looked up into the face of Arthur Saling. You poor devil, she thought, as she stood and shook the hand he offered her.

At that moment, the phone on her desk rang. Esther picked it up. "Is my husband there? He's not answering his cell phone." Pamela Gannon's voice was tight and high pitched.

"Yes, he is," Esther replied and looked at Greg. "It's Mrs. Gannon, sir."

Greg was standing behind Arthur Saling. His voice still friendly, but his expression turning explosively angry, he said, "Ask my wife to hold. I'll be right with her."

"Never keep the ladies waiting," Arthur Saling joked, as Greg walked with him to the elevators.

"Mrs. Gannon, he'll be right with you," Esther began, but was interrupted.

"I don't give a damn whether he's *with* me or not. Where is my jewelry? There's absolutely nothing in the safe in the apartment. What is he trying to pull?"

Think, Esther warned herself. "Is it possible that he pledged the jewelry to post bail for Peter?" she asked.

"The jewelry is mine. He has plenty of other assets." By now, Pamela Gannon was shrieking.

"Mrs. Gannon, please, it's not for me to say." Esther realized that she sounded as though she were pleading.

"Of course it isn't for you to say, Esther," Pamela Gannon snapped. "Put him on."

"He'll be right with you."

Greg Gannon came hurrying back into the office. He grabbed the phone out of Esther's hand. "I took the jewelry," he said, his voice cold and furious. "You've seen the last of it unless you can give me a satisfactory explanation of why you were with some guy in Southampton on Saturday afternoon. But there *is* no explanation, is there, Pam? Just for the record, I'm not as stupid as you think I am."

He slammed down the phone and stared at Esther. "You know I trust my hunches," he said. "You sent that letter. I want you out of here. But as a final gesture of loyalty, tell me the truth, Esther. Is the SEC coming after me?"

Esther stood up. "I wonder why it would ever occur to you to ask that question, Mr. Gannon. I'm delighted to be out of here. But may I offer one final comment?" She looked him in the eye. "It's too damn bad that neither you nor your brother ever came close to being the kind of upstanding, splendid men your father and uncle were. They'd be ashamed of both of you. Thanks for the last thirty-five years. I have to say, they haven't been dull."

65

At five thirty on Monday evening, Peter Gannon was taken from the Tombs, an electronic bracelet clasped around his wrist, and released on the bail that Susan had guaranteed. With Harvey Roth at his side, the terms of his temporary freedom had been spelled out. He was not to leave Manhattan without the permission of the judge, and he was not to visit his daughter in the hospital.

At last, he and Roth were outside. Peter inhaled deeply of the crisp late-October air. "I have a car," Roth told him. "I'll drop you off at home if that's what you want. I would suggest you get some rest. I'm sure the last two nights in the Tombs have not been conducive to sleep."

"I'll take up that offer," Peter said, quietly. "I have a feeling it's the best one I'll get for a while."

Roth's driver pulled up to the curb and the two men got in the car. Peter waited until they were on the West Side Highway before he said, "I'm not sure if you're the right lawyer for me. I need to have someone who believes that I am *not* a murderer, and I get the feeling that you think I am. I want a lawyer who does more than look for legal loopholes. I want somebody who is going to fight hard to prove my innocence."

"I prefer not to consider myself an attorney who deals in legal loopholes," Harvey Roth said mildly.

"You know what I mean. I've started to be able to think a little more clearly. What have you found out about the clothes I was wearing when I met Renée? Are there any bloodstains on them? Or is there any of her DNA on them?"

"The detective heading the case told me there are no apparent bloodstains, but the DNA evidence will take time to evaluate. On the other hand, you claim you were afraid of becoming nauseous when you left her. I understand there is absolutely no hint on your clothes that you became ill that night."

Peter smiled grimly. "What you're saying is that I'm a tidy drunk. Let's consider this. The bar where I met her was in the eighties, on York Avenue. My office is nearly two miles away. Maybe I went directly there and passed out? Is that so improbable?"

"Mr. Gannon, it is very unfortunate that your office building does not have security cameras to back up that scenario," Roth said. "Apparently they have been out of commission for quite a while."

"The building that my present office is in is a dump," Peter agreed.

"Nevertheless," Roth said, "to get into it, a key to the outer door is required, as well as a key to your own office. Are you suggesting that you went directly there and that someone came in while you were passed out and hid that money in your desk? Isn't that what you are telling me? Isn't that a little far-fetched?"

"Mr. Roth, the couch where I was asleep is in the reception area of the suite. My office is in the next room. There's a separate entrance for it, in case I want to go in without having to walk through the waiting room."

"Peter, we might as well get on a first-name basis. We're going to be spending a lot of time together. Let's not waste any of it grasping at straws. Who else would have keys to your office building, your suite, and your private office?"

"As Susan can verify, I'm not very organized. I'm one of those people who is always losing keys."

"Peter, a lot of people are careless with keys. But most of them aren't carrying a shopping bag containing one hundred thousand dollars and leaving it in your office, to say nothing of putting the money in a hidden panel in your desk."

Then, even in the semidarkness, Roth could see the expression on Peter's face suddenly change. "Peter," he asked sharply. "Can you think of anyone who had access to spare keys, and who might also have known about that one hundred thousand dollars?"

Peter did not answer. He looked out the window of the sedan as it moved slowly forward in the evening traffic. "Let me think about that," he answered. He knew he could not yet bring himself to speak the name of the person who he was almost certain had been the one to put that money in his office.

I'm starting to remember, he thought. That car that

was parked across the street when Renée slapped me. It looked familiar. She would have accepted a ride from him. If he suspected that she knew, he might have told her that he'd pay her off to keep quiet about his insider trading.

My brother, Greg.

66

Dr. Monica, one more thing," Nan Rhodes said. "Sophie Rutkowski called this morning. She wouldn't say what it was about, but she sounds upset. I promised that you'd call her back when your office hours were over."

"I'll do that. You run ahead. It's been a busy day," Monica replied. Nan had just relayed Ryan's message to her: "The next time you lie for Dr. Farrell . . ." She felt stressed out and humiliated, but she wasn't sure she wanted to confide to Nan why she was avoiding Ryan Jenner's calls.

Nan wanted to protest but, seeing the expression on Monica's face, decided it would be better to leave her alone. She probably needs some time to herself, Nan thought. In the morning, after the two detectives came to the office, she had immediately called John Hartman to see if he knew why they were there. She had not seen Hartman over the weekend because he'd been in Philadelphia, visiting an old friend who was also a retired detective.

Hartman told Nan that he had suggested to his former partner, Detective Carl Forrest, that they check the security cameras at the hospital and that had led to seeing Sammy Barber get out of his car and follow Monica. He had then tried to calm her by saying that they hoped they had scared him off from attacking her again.

"John, you're telling me that thanks to you they traced this Barber guy?"

"Nan, they probably would have thought of it themselves," Hartman answered. "But, be that as it may, you see Dr. Farrell at least eight hours a day, five days a week, and some Saturdays. You're in the position to be on the watch for anyone who might be a danger to her."

Hartman then suggested that they have dinner together, "if it isn't one of your nights at Jimmy Neary's with your sisters."

It was an invitation that Nan had both been hoping for, and expected would come. Now, reluctant as she was to leave Monica, she was also eager to go home and freshen up before John came for her.

"Well then, I'll see you in the morning, Dr. Monica," she said. She was about to add, "Be sure to double-lock the door behind me," but pressed her lips together. *I'm sure she's had enough advice from those detectives,* she decided.

Alone in the suddenly quiet office, with the phones no longer ringing and no small patients scampering through the reception room, Monica went into her private office, put her elbows on the desk, and rested her chin on her hands.

The import of what the detectives had told her, that a hit man had tried to kill her, was beginning to sink in. Scott *has* to be behind this, she thought. Who else would have any interest in wanting to hurt me? He did call out of the blue only a few minutes after I got home Thursday night. I was so foolish to let him come over to the apartment. Maybe I was lucky that he didn't try to hurt me then. God knows, he was obsessed with me after Dad died. He phoned twenty times a day, and even followed me around in the street . . .

He's the reason I didn't take the job at the hospital in Boston. I had to get away from him. He obviously needs psychiatric help. But I do know one thing. He's not going to drive me out of New York. I love the hospital. I have a good practice. I have plenty of friends.

Inevitably, that thought led to the situation with Ryan Jenner. Why would I be so stupidly unprofessional as to ask Nan to lie for me to Ryan? she asked herself. I'm acting like a spurned girlfriend, when in fact I've never even had a single date with him. I'm sure he understands that I didn't want any gossip about us in the hospital. I'm certain that when he really thinks about it, he doesn't want it, either.

I have both his home and cell numbers. I'll call tomorrow and apologize. I'll simply say that I was concerned about the gossip but that I had no right to be rude to him. I'm sure he'll be more gracious than I've been, and that will be that . . .

Monica sighed as she fished into her pocket for the slip of paper Nan had handed her with Sophie Rutkowski's number on it. Nan had said that Sophie sounded nervous and upset. Monica found the paper, laid it on her desk, and began to dial. Do I dare hope that she's remembered something about Olivia Morrow that would help me to learn about my grandparents? But I know that's not going to happen.

Sophie answered her phone on the first ring. The strain in her voice was obvious to Monica even when she only uttered the simple word "Hello."

"Sophie, this is Dr. Farrell. Is anything wrong?"

"Doctor, I feel like a thief. I don't know what to do."

"Sophie, no matter what you tell me, I am certain that you are not a thief," Monica said firmly. "What's going on?"

"I have another job on Saturday afternoons at Schwab House. After I finished it, I decided to go into Ms. Morrow's apartment and tidy it up. I have a key, of course. I know people will be going through it who will want to buy it, and people will also be there who may want to buy her furniture and so on . . . I didn't want them to see an unmade bed, or a pillowcase with blood on it."

"Sophie, that was very nice of you," Monica assured her. "If you took that pillowcase to wash, no one would ever believe that you wouldn't return it."

"Doctor, that's not what I'm saying. That pillowcase was *missing*. This morning I called Dr. Hadley to see if he had taken it."

Monica felt suddenly chilled. "What did Dr. Hadley say?"

"He got very mad. He said I had no right to be nosing around the apartment. He told me to leave my key at the desk and if I tried to go into Ms. Morrow's apartment again, he'd have me arrested for trespassing."

"Did he tell you that he had taken the pillowcase?" Monica asked, her thoughts filled with the image of Olivia Morrow's face in death and the evidence that she had bitten her lower lip.

"No, that's the problem. If he didn't take it, someone else did, and if anything else is missing, they may blame me, Doctor. I'm so worried. I only went in because I wanted everything to be just so in Ms. Morrow's home. But you see, I *did* take something and I've already turned in the key and I don't know what to do now."

"What did you take, Sophie?"

"I took a pillow that had blood on it, the one that had been covered with the pink pillowcase. I knew Ms. Morrow wouldn't want anyone to see it. Blood always shows on pillow fabric."

"Sophie," Monica asked quickly, "did you throw that pillow out?"

"No, I brought it home, Doctor."

"Sophie, this is very important. Put that pillow in a plastic bag and hide it. Don't tell anyone, especially Dr. Hadley, that you have it. No, better still, give me your address. I'm going to take a cab up to your apartment right now and pick it up."

"Doctor, why would you want a soiled pillow?" Sophie protested.

"Sophie, I honestly can't answer that right now. It's just something I have to work out myself. But please trust me."

"Of course, Doctor. Have you got a pen? I'll give you my address."

An hour and a half later, all thoughts of dinner forgotten, Monica was holding the stained pillow with gloved hands over two pillows piled on her own bed, in the same position as she remembered the ones that had been under Olivia Morrow's head.

Am I going crazy, she asked herself, or is it possible that there is only one way that stain could have gotten on that spot? But why would anyone want to hold a pillow over her face and suffocate a dying woman?

Monica slipped the pillow back into the loose plastic bag. I'll talk to Nan's friend John Hartman, she decided. He's the one who would know what to do. Is it possible that someone in the building got into Olivia Morrow's apartment, maybe to burglarize it, and she woke up? It was pretty generally known that she was dying. But then again, why would Dr. Hadley get so upset with Sophie? Of all people, he should be the one to want to follow up if there's any suggestion of foul play . . .

I'll bring the pillow to the office tomorrow and ask Nan to see if Hartman will come over after office hours and talk to me, she decided.

The decision made, Monica decided not to put off calling Ryan any longer. She dialed his home number and heard his voice. "Sorry to miss your call. Leave a number and I'll get back to you."

I'm not apologizing to an answering machine, she thought. He's probably out to dinner with his girlfriend, so I won't bother him on his cell phone. Oh, well. She went into the kitchen, opened the refrigerator and was disappointed to find that because she had not gotten around to shopping over the weekend, the most she could find was the makings of an omelet.

Then she had a frightening thought. The overhead light in the kitchen was on, which meant that anyone lurking in the back could see her through the panes of glass on the top section of the outside door. I have to get a dark shade for it, she thought, but in the meantime, I'll tack something over it. Feeling under siege, she went into the living room and picked up the afghan from the couch.

As she carried it back to the kitchen, she remembered how tenderly Scott Alterman had tucked it around her after he had rushed to be with her and found her trembling and chilled by her brush with death.

67

On Tuesday morning Tony Garcia, filled with anticipation, was in the waiting room of Dr. Clayton Hadley's office. When I called yesterday, he couldn't have been nicer, Tony thought. I explained that I'd like to buy Ms. Morrow's car and he asked if I realized it was ten years old. Then I offered to pay him the book value in cash and he said that would be fine.

"The doctor will be right with you, sir," the receptionist said, with a friendly smile at the young man in a chauffeur's uniform who was obviously uneasy sitting with a well-dressed couple who were also waiting to see the doctor.

"Thanks very much," Tony said. I still can't believe how lucky I am, he thought. Yesterday, when I asked the doctor if I could possibly get the car right away, even before the ownership transfer papers could be completed, I never thought he'd be so nice. I guess it was because I explained that we could have been killed in an accident when our old car stopped short in traffic. But he did say that it's near the end of the month and there was no use wasting money from the estate paying the garage bill in Ms. Morrow's apartment building.

"You can go in now, Mr. Garcia," the receptionist told him. "The doctor will see you in the second room on the right."

Tony jumped up. "Oh, thank you," he said, as the receptionist assured the couple in the waiting room that the doctor would be with them in a few minutes.

With quick steps, Tony, following instructions, entered the private office of Dr. Clay Hadley. He's pretty fat for a cardiologist, was Tony's first thought, but it passed quickly from his mind. "Dr. Hadley, thanks so much. This means so much to me and my family. I can't tell you how scared I was when all of a sudden my car stopped in traffic. But I won't take your time. I brought the money in cash. My brother-in-law lent it to me. He's a prince."

After the phone call from Sophie Rutkowski the day before, Clay Hadley had been terrified. I panicked, he thought. I should have told her I was having the pillowcase laundered. Did she notice the bloodstain on the pillow itself? I can't ask her that. It will only bring her attention to it.

Take the damn car, he thought, impatiently, as, forcing a smile, he watched Tony offer him six rubber-banded packs of ten one-hundred-dollar bills. "Six thousand dollars in all," Tony said. "Doctor, I can't tell you how much I appreciate your letting me take the car right away. My wife Rosalie's grandmother lives in New Jersey, and she looks forward so much to Rosie visiting her. Without a car it would be impossible."

Clay Hadley raised his hand. "Tony, I have your

phone number. I'll give you a call when we can complete the paperwork. My secretary has called the garage. They're expecting you to pick up the car this morning. They looked through it, but there was nothing personal in it. The insurance card and registration are in the glove compartment. Of course, once we officially transfer ownership to you and give you the title, you get your own registration and insurance. Here is a receipt for the payment now."

"Thank you, Doctor. Thank you so much." Tony started for the door, got as far as the receptionist's desk, then hesitated and turned around. *I wonder if that bag Ms. Morrow asked me to put under the blanket in the trunk is still there?* he thought. *I shoved it pretty far back. The garage attendants may have missed it. Maybe I should tell the doctor about it?*

The receptionist had seen him turn. "Mr. Garcia," she said firmly, "I'm afraid that I can't keep the doctor's patients waiting any longer. I'm sure he's on his way to the examining room now."

Embarrassed, Tony murmured, "Of course. I'm sorry." As he made his way through the reception area, he thought, *if that file is there, I'll just mail it back to Dr. Hadley.*

I should have known better than to try to bother him with it now.

68

On Tuesday morning, Detectives Barry Tucker and Dennis Flynn were sitting in the private office of Department Chief Jack Stanton, sipping coffee and reviewing the case with him. It had been five days since Renée Carter's body had been found.

"Some of this just doesn't add up," Tucker told the chief. "Gannon had the motive, the opportunity, and a very convenient memory blackout. Not to mention the hundred thousand bucks hidden in the drawer in his office."

"What doesn't add up?" Stanton asked.

"We tracked down three of the patrons who were in the bar where Carter and Gannon met. Two of them remembered hearing them arguing but didn't know what it was about. Both of them noticed Carter leaving the bar with Gannon right behind her."

"The third guy we spoke to is the one who's most important," Dennis Flynn said. "He claimed that he had left the bar less than a minute later, and that he saw a man he's pretty sure was Gannon walking down York Avenue alone."

"Which is consistent with what Gannon claimed,"

Tucker said. "This guy swears he didn't see Carter, that she was already gone."

"How reliable is this witness?" Stanton demanded.

"He's an engineer. A one-drink-only regular customer. No connection to anyone involved. No axe to grind. Even though he's not a hundred percent sure it was Gannon that he saw, put him on the witness stand and it's more than enough to give the jury reasonable doubt." Barry Tucker stared into his coffee cup, wishing he had not put so much sugar in it. "If this guy is right, Carter must have gotten into a car," he said. "But what car? Whose car? Peter Gannon's BMW hasn't been out of his garage in a week. We checked the garage records. On top of that, we've gone over the car with a fine-tooth comb. There's no trace of Carter ever having been in it."

"She had that heavy shopping bag," Flynn pointed out to his boss. "Odds are if Gannon *did* walk away from her, she got into a cab or one of those cruising limos. We've checked out all the licensed cabs and none of them picked her up. If she got into one of those gypsy limos, what did the guy who was driving see? A good-looking, well-dressed babe, who according to the babysitter was wearing some decent jewelry. We both know what may have happened next."

"Her jewelry was gone. Her purse was gone. Let's suppose our mystery limo driver killed her," Tucker suggested. "How does he end up going to Gannon's office and hiding all that cash? Why would he put that kind of money back? How would he get into the office in the first place? And where does he stash the body for more than twenty-four hours before he wraps it in a garbage bag and stuffs it under a park bench? None of it makes sense."

Stanton leaned back in his chair. "Let's look at this scenario. Somebody was parked near that bar because he knew Gannon was meeting Carter there. After Gannon stumbled off, that person offered Carter a ride. She wasn't dumb. She probably wouldn't have gotten into a car, other than one of those gypsy limos, with someone she didn't know."

Tucker nodded. "That's where I've been going. And think about this. Peter Gannon's fingerprints were all over the cash and the shopping bag, but there were no fingerprints in the false bottom of the drawer where the money was hidden. Was he smart enough, or drunk enough, to put on gloves to hide the money, but dumb enough to dump the shopping bag into the wastepaper basket where anyone could see it?"

Tucker's phone rang. He glanced at the ID of the caller. "It's the lab," he said, as he answered. "What's up? Oh. Thanks for the rush job." He snapped the phone closed. "The lab has finished going over the clothing that Gannon was wearing that night and the clothing that Renée Carter was found in. There is no trace of Carter's blood or hair or fibers from her clothes on anything he was wearing, and there's nothing on her clothing that came from him."

The chief had been reading the Gannon file before Tucker and Flynn arrived at his office. He turned to a page and reread it. "According to the statement Peter

Gannon gave, he had, only a few days earlier, requested a loan of one million dollars from the Gannon family foundation to pay off Renée Carter, but the most the board members would advance him was one hundred thousand dollars. That means that whoever is on the board knew about Renée and her demands. We both know that some of these family foundations are pretty shaky. I would say your next move is to talk to those people and see what you can find."

Tucker nodded, stood up, and stretched. "I'm beginning to think I should get a job working for the Gannon defense team," he said. "Because that's just about what we may be doing now."

As he and Flynn made their way through the cluttered outer office to their desks, a young detective passed them. "Barry, you looked real good on page three of the *News*," he commented. "My girlfriend says she likes your crooked smile."

"So does my wife," Barry retorted. "But the way this case is going, she's not going to get much chance to enjoy it for a while."

69

Mentally and physically exhausted, Peter Gannon slept soundly Monday night. On Tuesday morning, feeling alert and clearheaded for the first time in days, he showered, shaved, then dressed in khakis and searched in his closet for a long-sleeved sport shirt that he hoped would conceal the electronic bracelet.

Feeling quite hungry, he prepared scrambled eggs, bacon, toast, and coffee. As he was about to sit down, he opened the door to get the newspapers, which were usually delivered by seven A.M. They were not there and he dialed the concierge to have them sent up.

The man was apologetic. "Mr. Gannon, we weren't aware that you were home."

Meaning out of jail, Peter thought.

"We'll send them right up, sir."

I wonder what they'll be writing about me today? Peter asked himself. But when the papers arrived and he opened the *Post*, the entire front page was a picture of a wistful baby girl standing in a crib. PETER GANNON'S ABANDONED LOVE CHILD was the headline.

Peter slumped into a chair and for long minutes stared at the picture. The wide, solemn eyes of his daughter seemed to look accusingly at him. He forced himself to read the story, which reviewed in lurid details the finding of Renée's body, his arrest, the fact that Renée had no known relatives, and that already there had been dozens of calls from people begging to adopt little Sally.

"They're not going to get her," Peter said aloud, slamming down the paper. "Nobody is going to get her." There was only one person he could turn to for help. He dialed Susan's cell phone and reached her at her office. "Susan, have you seen the picture of the baby on the cover of the *Post*?"

"I've done more than that," she said quietly. "I've seen the baby. Peter, I'm going into a meeting. I can run over to your apartment in a couple of hours. I've got to talk to you."

While he waited, Peter resumed the task that had been occupying him when he was arrested on Saturday morning. He replaced the contents of the drawers that had been spilled in the living room, finished putting the paintings back on the wall, straightened out the closets, and put the furniture back where it belonged. When he and Susan divorced, he had lived with Renée in a suite in the Pierre for two years, another wild extravagance. After they split, he had bought this place and left it to a decorator to furnish it.

But I didn't go hog wild, he thought. I gave her a budget. At least in some ways I was starting to get practical.

Get practical. And then I produced two absolutely disastrous musicals, with other people's money.

It was almost noon when he was satisfied that the apartment was orderly again. Too restless to sit, he stood at the window and looked down into the busy intersection below. What do I do now? Do I point the finger at Greg? Do I tell the police that he had a motive to kill Renée Carter? If I say that he may have found out that I told Renée that he was involved in insider trading, I not only put the federal prosecutors on his case, but I make him a suspect in her murder.

Greg would not kill Renée any more than I would. I can't try to save myself by exposing him. My big brother. The guy who wanted me to succeed in the theatre. The guy who said okay whenever I looked to get grants for my theatre projects. There has to be another way for me to prove my innocence without destroying Greg.

I *did* walk back to the office that night, Peter thought. I wanted the fresh air. I knew I was drunk. There was a car across the street from the bar. I can *now* see it clearly in my mind. And I know whose it was: it was Greg's car.

And what do I do about that?

The house bell rang. "Mrs. Gannon is here," the doorman announced.

"Send her right up," Peter said, as he hurried to open the door.

70

Detectives Carl Forrest and Jim Whelan agreed on one of three possibilities. The first scenario was that if Scott Alterman had hired Sammy Barber to kill or injure Dr. Monica Farrell, he had been tipped off by Barber and had fled. The second possibility was that Sammy Barber had gotten one of his fellow goons to get rid of Alterman, to make sure that if Alterman were ever arrested himself, he could never give up Sammy. A third possibility was that having hired Sammy, and in fear of disgrace and imprisonment, Alterman had committed suicide.

On Tuesday morning, Forrest and Whelan went to Scott Alterman's apartment and learned to their chagrin that he had not been seen there since Saturday evening, when, dressed in a business suit and tie, he had walked out of his apartment building.

"He was in a really good mood," the doorman told the detectives. "Not a care in the world, if you know what I mean. I asked if he wanted me to call him a cab, but he said that he wasn't going far, he could walk it."

Their next stop was at his new office in the prestigious law firm of Williams, Armstrong, Fiske, and Conrad. "Mr. Alterman started with us only last week," his secretary said. "On Saturday afternoon, he left a message on my office phone telling me to remind him on Monday that he wanted me to find out anything I could about the background of an Olivia Morrow who died last week."

Forrest made a note of the name. "Have you any idea why he wanted you to do that?"

"Not really," the secretary replied. "But I think it might have had something to do with a Dr. Monica Farrell. You probably heard. She was the young woman who was almost killed by the bus."

"Dr. Monica Farrell." Carl Forrest tried to keep his face impassive and his tone of voice even. "Yes, I know about her. What gives you the idea that Mr. Alterman was connected in some way to this woman Olivia Morrow who died?"

"Last week we were talking in the office about the kind of mentally disturbed people who won't take their medicine and then try to kill innocent people like that young doctor. Mr. Alterman said he knew Dr. Farrell, and of course we asked him more about her."

"What did Mr. Alterman say?" Forrest asked.

"He said that she didn't know she was an heiress to a fortune, but that he was going to prove it."

"He said *what*?" Forrest asked, as Jim Whelan stared at the secretary. "How did you respond to that statement?"

"We really didn't. We thought he was joking. Don't forget, we really don't know Mr. Alterman very well. He just started at the firm a week ago."

"Of course. Please call me immediately if you hear

from him." Forrest and Whelan went down in the elevator together. They were leaving the building when Forrest felt the slight vibration of his cell phone in his breast pocket indicating that a call was coming through. It was from headquarters.

He answered it, listened, then said, "Okay, we'll meet you at the morgue." Then, standing in the inviting sunshine and crisp breeze of the October morning, he told Whelan, "A body has just been fished out of the East River. If the wallet with all the usual identification is accurate, we can stop looking for Scott Alterman."

71

On Tuesday morning at five minutes of eleven, Monica Farrell, accompanied by two members of the board of directors of Greenwich Village Hospital, entered the vast lobby of the Time Warner Center and took the elevator to the floor where the Alexander Gannon Foundation and the Gannon Investment Firm shared connecting offices.

Justin Banks, the chairman of the board, and Robert Goodwin, executive director of development, were men in their sixties. Both of them, like Monica, were passionately dedicated to making Greenwich Village Hospital the finest medical center it could possibly become. Over the years, the hundred-year-old hospital had evolved from a small twenty-bed local clinic to the impressive award-winning facility it now was.

As Justin Banks was fond of saying, "At least half the population of Greenwich Village first saw the light of day in our hospital." Now there was a pressing need for a state-of-the-art pediatric center, toward which Greg and Pamela Gannon had pledged fifteen million dollars with great fanfare at a black-tie dinner a year and a half ago.

When they arrived, a young receptionist invited them to wait in the conference room and offered them coffee. Banks and Goodwin refused, but Monica accepted. "I didn't have my usual second cup this morning," she explained, with a smile. "I had some early patients, and I was rushing."

There was another reason why she had not taken time for a second coffee. Guessing he would be up, she had called Ryan on his cell phone at seven o'clock. He had assured her he was not only up, but about to leave for the hospital. Then she said, "Ryan, I really need to apologize. I was so terribly rude to you."

"You were obviously mad at me," he had said. "But I certainly understand that you don't want to become the subject of gossip."

"Nor do you." She hadn't intended to say that.

"Actually, I wouldn't have minded, but there you are."

And I got mad again, Monica thought, as she thanked the secretary for the coffee. I said that he wasn't being fair to his girlfriend to talk like that.

"My girlfriend!" he had exclaimed. "What are you talking about?"

"When I phoned you last Thursday evening to explain why I didn't get back to my office to give you the file . . ."

"What do you mean you phoned Thursday night?"

"I phoned your apartment. Your significant other, or whoever she is, said you were there but you were changing. I assumed she would give you the message."

"Oh, my God, I might have known. Monica, listen to me."

As Monica heard Ryan's angry but welcome explanation, she had felt as if a weight were lifting off her heart. Ryan was going to meet her at her office tonight. I'll show him the pillow, too, and see what *he* thinks of it. The last words of their conversation puzzled her but he was laughing when he said them: "Okay, Monica, we both have to get moving, and I have one more job to do before I leave this apartment."

I asked him what he meant, Monica thought, and he told me he had to throw out the rest of the lasagna. He said, "I'll explain what I mean when I see you."

She had taken the time to change into a suit because they were going out for dinner.

"Monica," Justin Banks said, "I'm not much for personal compliments but you look absolutely lovely this morning. You should always wear blue."

"Thanks. This outfit represents my fall shopping to date."

Robert Goodwin was looking at his watch. "Ten after eleven. Let's hope these people show up soon and have a check for us. They must have *some* money left. These are pretty fancy offices for a foundation. I happen to know the cost of the rents in this building."

They heard footsteps coming toward them. A moment later three men entered the room. Monica was stunned to see that one of them was Dr. Clay Hadley. She could tell that he was equally shocked to see her. She had been at the dinner announcing the grant and had met Greg Gannon there. The other man now being introduced to them was Dr. Douglas Langdon.

"Dr. Hadley and Dr. Langdon are our board members," Gannon explained. "My wife is not able to be with us today, and I'm sure you're quite aware why my brother is not here. Let's leave it at that."

Gannon then sat at the head of the table, his demeanor solemn and unsmiling. "Let's not waste each other's time," he said. "The fact is that the grant we so willingly pledged last year simply cannot be filled at this time. I don't have to tell you how serious the economic climate has been, and like many other foundations, we were among the victims of a major scam, the Ponzi scheme that has been in the newspapers for months."

"I've followed very carefully the Ponzi scheme I believe you are talking about," Goodwin said, sharply. "The Gannon Foundation has not been listed as being involved."

"Nor do we want it to be," Greg Gannon replied, his tone equally sharp. "The other arm of our business is my investment firm. I don't intend to have my clients worried that their money was lost, because it was not. The Gannon Foundation has given away millions over the years. Our record of generosity is extraordinary, but now it has come to an end. The foundation will be closing. We cannot honor our pledge to you."

"Mr. Gannon," Justin Banks said, speaking slowly for emphasis. "You are a very wealthy man. Would you consider putting some of your *own* money into the hospital's pediatric wing? I assure you the need for it is great."

Greg Gannon sighed. "Mr. Banks, if half the people who are reputed to be very wealthy had to list their assets honestly, you would find that the ten-million-dollar house has a nine-million-dollar mortgage, that the yacht is rented and the cars are leased. I am not saying that is necessarily my case, but I will say that I have already undertaken to personally fund some of our ongoing projects. You have not even put a spade in the ground for your pediatric center. On the other hand, several cardiac research centers and mental health facilities need to be funded until they can be merged with other similar units. I will take care of them, but I cannot do more."

The entire time Greg Gannon was speaking, Monica had been studying Clay Hadley's face. It was glistening with perspiration. There was a nervous tic on the side of his lip that she had not noticed when she met him in Olivia Morrow's apartment. The suspicion that he might have caused Morrow's death was growing into a near certainty. But why?

Douglas Langdon. She wondered what kind of doctor he was. Very, very good-looking. Smooth. The expression on his face was an obviously feigned regret over the situation. He doesn't give a damn, she thought. The guy is a phony through and through.

Where are we going to get the money for the pediatric center now? she asked herself as Greg Gannon got to his feet, signaling that the meeting was over. "Doug,

Clay, wait here," he said. His stern tone indicated that it was an order.

Both men had started to leave, but they sat down immediately. Monica, Banks, and Goodwin followed Greg Gannon to the reception room. It was then that she saw it: the portrait of Dr. Alexander Gannon. Frozen on the spot, she stared at it. *It's Daddy, just the way he looked before he got sick,* she thought incredulously. *He could have posed for it.* The silver hair, the handsome, distinguished features, the blue eyes, were mirror images of the picture she carried in her wallet. Even the expression in Alex Gannon's eyes, wise and kind, was so like the expression she remembered in her father's eyes.

"That was my uncle," Greg Gannon was saying. "As you may know, the orthopedic replacement parts he invented are used internationally. This is the last portrait that was painted of him. We used to keep it in our home in Southampton, but I decided last year that it was more appropriate to hang it here. It's a very fine representation of him."

"It's magnificent," Monica agreed, her lips stiff. She reached into her pocket and stepped away. "Excuse me," she murmured and pulled out her cell phone, as if she had felt it vibrating. As she opened it, she pretended to say a few words into it and took a picture of the portrait.

No wonder Scott kept insisting that Dad had a startling resemblance to Alexander Gannon. I can't wait to compare their pictures.

"It's a great pity that Dr. Gannon's foundation is closing," Justin Banks said. "I am sure that he would never have wanted a pledge such as the one you made to Greenwich Village Hospital to be canceled so abruptly. Good-bye, Mr. Gannon. Please don't bother to see us out."

72

On Tuesday morning Esther Chambers, totally unused to lingering over breakfast, glanced at the clock in her dining area and realized it was time to get herself ready. It was quarter of ten and Thomas Desmond from the Securities and Exchange Commission was coming to her apartment at eleven.

She had phoned him yesterday evening and when he did not answer, too emotionally stressed to go into details, she simply left a message that she had been fired and that she needed to speak to him. Desmond called back an hour later and simply said, "If eleven o'clock tomorrow morning works for you, I will be there."

Nervous at the prospect of having to tell Desmond that she had tried to warn Arthur Saling about investing his money, and that was the reason Greg had fired her, Esther showered and dressed. She chose to wear a cardigan and slacks, not one of her usual subdued business suits. Today is the first day of the rest of my life, whatever that means, she thought.

Desmond was announced from the desk promptly at eleven o'clock. After they exchanged greetings and he refused her offer of coffee, he said, "Ms. Chambers, did anything precipitate Gannon's firing you? Does he suspect that he's under investigation?"

Esther drew a long breath. "You're not going to like this, Mr. Desmond, but here's what happened." In precise detail, she explained why she had decided to warn off Arthur Saling. "It was like watching a lamb being led to the slaughter," she said. "It's no wonder everything had been placed in trust for him. Now, the minute he can get his hands on all that family money, he can't wait to invest it with someone like Greg, who promises he can double or triple it. Mr. Saling has five grown children and eleven grandchildren. I'm sorry, but to know that once his money is in Greg's hands it would just be used to pay other investors whose money Greg has lost in that last hedge fund of his was just too much."

"I understand," Desmond said. "I really do."

"Then to answer your question, when Greg told me he was sure I was the one who had sent that warning to Arthur Saling, he also asked me, as a final test of loyalty, if the SEC was investigating him."

"What did you tell him?" Desmond asked, quickly.

"My answer was to ask him why he would ever think to ask a question like that."

Desmond nodded, approvingly. "Good answer, and please don't be upset about trying to warn Arthur Saling. Who knows? The transfer of his portfolio probably hasn't gone through yet, so he may be lucky. We're arresting Greg Gannon this afternoon. Now that he suspects we're onto him, he'll never communicate with any more insider traders."

"You're arresting Greg today?" Esther asked sadly.

"Yes. Frankly, I should not have told you that, but I wanted you to know that Arthur Saling's money is probably still safe."

"There is no one I would think of telling," Esther said. "It's just that it all seems so impossible. Peter Gannon is accused of murdering his former girlfriend. His baby is in a hospital, unwanted by anyone. His ex-wife, Susan, was and is a gem. Greg Gannon had the most wonderful wife and two fine sons, and he left them for a gold digger like Pamela. Now, from what went on yesterday afternoon at the office, he's caught on to the fact that she's involved with someone else. Do you think Pamela will stay by his side when he's arrested? Not on your life!"

Desmond got up to go. "Unfortunately, we see this kind of thing all the time in our business. We'll be in touch with you again, Ms. Chambers. But, a friendly word of caution: don't be too sorry for the Gannons. They're the architects of their own misery. And they have caused a lot of misery to others."

It was only after Desmond left that Esther realized Diana Blauvelt, the decorator whom she had left a message for in Paris, might very well have returned her call. She dialed her phone at her desk in the office, hoping that no one else had picked up her voice mail. But if Blauvelt had left the message, it had been erased.

I have to know, Esther thought. Peter's lawyer said it was so important. She had written Diana Blauvelt's Paris phone number in her daily reminder book. It's five thirty in the afternoon in Paris, she thought. I hope I get her in.

A sleepy "Allo" told her that she had reached Blauvelt. Oh, for God's sake, Esther thought, don't practice your French on me. "Diana," she said, apologetically, "you sound as though you might have been napping, but it's important that I talk to you. Did you get my message and do you remember anything about that desk with the false bottom in it?"

"Oh, it's you, Esther. Don't worry about waking me up. I'm going out to dinner later and I just thought I'd rest for half an hour. Of course I remember about the desk. As I told Greg Gannon, when I called back after you'd left your office yesterday, I bought two of those desks."

"*Two* of them?" Esther exclaimed.

"Yes, one for Peter, and one for Dr. Langdon. I never did see Peter to show him the false bottom in the big drawer, but I did show Dr. Langdon. He had his desk sent to his office where he sees his psychiatric patients, not to his office at the foundation."

"You're sure of this, Diana?"

"Absolutely. And I told Greg Gannon that his wife can back me up. Pamela was there when I showed Dr. Langdon the hiding place in the desk."

Stunned, Esther realized the possible ramifications of what she had just heard. Then Diana, after a moment's hesitation, added, "Esther, I understand from Greg that you're retired now. I've got to ask you. Don't you think that Pamela Gannon and Dr. Langdon have been pulling the wool over Greg Gannon's eyes for years?"

73

Susan had never been in Peter's apartment. Now she looked around intently as she walked into the living room. Then, with a fleeting smile, she said, "I like what you've done here. You always had good taste."

"Whatever good taste I have as far as home furnishings go, or anything else, for that matter, came from the women in my life, my mother and you." He took a deep breath, and told her what had been weighing on his mind since the moment he saw Sally's picture. "Susan, I know what you think of me as a father, but now I beg you to help me as my attorney. I want my daughter. Granted, I have never seen her, but when her mother and I broke up, I gave Renée two million dollars so that she would be able to have the best possible medical care while she was pregnant, and then never contact me again. I was told that Sally was going to be adopted by responsible people, and at the time it seemed like a good idea."

Why did I have the nerve to think that Susan would help me with this situation? Peter asked himself as he tried to justify his neglect of his child. Nevertheless, he persisted. "I would have continued to support my daughter. You know my quarrel with Renée wasn't about that. It was about Renée's ability to hurt Greg with what she knew."

Susan looked at her ex-husband, her expression calm. "What are you trying to say, Peter?"

"I want Sally. I did not kill her mother. I cannot bear the thought of her being placed in a foster home. I have been accused of a crime, but not convicted of it. What right has anyone to say that I cannot visit her?"

"Peter, are you being serious? Are you telling me that you not only want to *see* Sally, but you want custody of her?"

"Yes, I do."

"Peter, you are going on trial for murder. No judge will grant you custody now. And I very much doubt that you would be allowed even supervised visitation, since you have never even seen the child."

"I do not want my daughter in a foster home. Susan, there's got to be a way to stop that. Look at her picture. My God, she looks so forlorn." Peter realized there were tears in his eyes. "I'll find a good nanny and beg the judge to let me have her. I may not go on trial for a year or more. You know how slow the court system is. I have never, ever been in trouble, not even any kid stuff while I was growing up. Susan . . ."

"Hold on, hold on," she said, softly. "Peter, there is another solution, and one that I'm pretty sure the judge will accept. I want to request custody of Sally."

Peter stared at Susan. "*You* want Sally!"

"Yes, I do. She is the sweetest little girl and it is pathetic to see how starved she is for affection. And, Peter, she is so smart. I guess her babysitters at least must have read to her, because she was picking out words in some of the books I brought."

"How many times have you seen her, Susan?"

"Twice. The nurses let me take her out of the crib and hold her. The newspaper picture doesn't do her justice. She's a beautiful baby. She's the image of you."

"You would want my child?"

"Peter, you seem to forget that for the twenty years we were married I wanted a child more than anything else. I still do. Kristina Johnson, the young nanny who probably saved Sally's life by rushing her to the hospital, came in to visit her while I was there. It's obvious that Sally is attached to Kristina. She had such a big smile for her. Kristina would be glad to take care of Sally again while I'm at work. And there's no problem about room. As you're well aware, there are three bedrooms in the apartment."

We bought that apartment when we'd only been married a couple of years, Peter thought. Susan was pregnant, and we felt that we needed a bigger place. Then she miscarried three times. It broke her heart, but she said we still had each other. So we stayed in that apartment.

And then I left her.

"You think you can get custody immediately, that she won't have to go to a foster home?" he asked, his voice shaking.

"I will file for an emergent hearing before Sally is released from the hospital. Why would a judge turn me down? Forty-six isn't too old. My reputation is spotless. I have the room. As your ex-wife, I classify as a concerned relative. And I want her. The minute I saw her, I knew she would make up for all the heartbreak of losing the others."

Her eyes suddenly moist, Susan looked at Peter. "You are her father, of course. The judge will probably give you some input in this. Will you let me have Sally?"

"Are you talking adoption or custody while my case is pending?"

"Both. If I take her, I can't lose her."

"Susan, you can keep Sally, but only if I can visit her and can really have a part in my daughter's life. I can't lose her, either."

They were clasping each other's hands. Without letting go of Susan's entwined fingers, Peter said, "I have started to get flashes of memory of that night. I wasn't going to tell anyone, because I didn't want to give Greg up, but I'm not sure I'm strong enough to spend the rest of my life in prison, even for my brother."

"Peter, what are you talking about?"

"Greg's car was parked across the street from that bar. Renée knew him when we were seeing each other. If he offered her a ride, she'd take it."

"Greg knew that she was extorting money from you, didn't he?"

"Sure. He was at the foundation meeting when I asked for the million-dollar loan, but he thought it was because she was going to reveal to the gossip columnists that I was Sally's father. That didn't upset him at all. His attitude was, 'So what?' I didn't tell him at the time that there was a lot more to it."

"Then why would he have been waiting outside the bar?" Susan asked.

"I was desperate to get that money. After he turned me down, I called Pamela and told her that Renée was going to blow the whistle on Greg's insider trading. I knew Pamela could give me the money. Greg has put plenty in her name. She must have told him, and maybe it drove him over the edge." He paused. "Susan, I think my brother killed Renée."

Peter shook his head. "How can I give him up?" he asked, his voice anguished. "How can I?"

"How can you not?" Susan demanded. "But it's your decision to make and live with, Peter. I have to get back to the office. I'll see you later."

74

At two thirty on Tuesday, Barry Tucker went directly from the morgue, where he and Detective Flynn had viewed Scott Alterman's body, to headquarters to report to Chief Stanton. Flynn went from the morgue back to Alterman's apartment building to question the staff there.

"Dennis is trying to get a handle on Alterman's activities, from the time he visited Monica Farrell on Thursday evening until he left his apartment late Saturday," Tucker told the chief.

"Carl, do you think this looks like Scott Alterman was behind the attempt on Dr. Farrell's life?" Stanton asked. "Does the medical examiner think he's dealing with a suicide?"

"Too soon to tell. No marks on his body. We've contacted Alterman's parents and siblings. They haven't talked to him since last week. The ME thinks he may have been drugged before he fell into the river. Or was pushed. We won't have the drug tests from the lab for at least a week. If he did order the hit on the doctor, he may have panicked, and overdosed himself. On the other hand," Forrest speculated, "according to the doorman, when Alterman left his apartment building on Saturday night, he was in good spirits."

"Which tells us nothing," Stanton observed. "Sometimes when people decide to let go, they get a sudden sense of peace."

"I'm wondering if Alterman wasn't a little wacky," Forrest said. "On Friday, in his office, his secretary and some of the other staff were talking about Monica Farrell almost being killed by the bus. Alterman told them he knew her and was going to prove that she was the heiress to a vast fortune."

"That does sound wacky," Stanton agreed. "I really do think that he was the guy who hired Sammy Barber. I just wish we could nail that lowlife, too."

"So do I, but . . ." Carl Forrest stopped in midsentence and pulled out his cell phone. "It's Flynn," he said, then answered it. "What's up?"

Jack Stanton watched as a look of astonishment came over Forrest's face.

"You mean that Alterman rented a car and driver and went to a cemetery in Southampton, then to Greg Gannon's house on Saturday?" Forrest asked, incredulously.

"I spoke to the driver," Flynn reported. "Alterman had found out that an old lady, Olivia Morrow, who died last Tuesday night, had gone there last Tuesday afternoon. He got in touch with the driver and hired him for the same drive as the Morrow woman. She told the driver she had grown up in a cottage on the Gannon property. The house still belongs to Greg

Gannon, Peter Gannon's brother. The driver told Scott that Olivia Morrow didn't go into the house, but Scott Alterman did on Saturday afternoon, and stayed for about an hour."

Forrest went back to the call with Flynn. "Okay, Dennis. Thanks. Has the driver agreed to come in and make a statement?"

Forrest snapped the phone shut. "The driver can't wait to give us the details. Flynn said he's a real talker and is enjoying the situation."

"I wish there were more like him," Stanton observed. "This woman Olivia Morrow who died last week? See what you can find out about her."

Fifteen minutes later, Forrest burst back into Stanton's office without knocking. "Chief, you won't believe this. The person who found Morrow dead was Dr. Monica Farrell. She told the medical team that responded to the emergency call at the apartment that she had had an appointment with Olivia Morrow that evening. She told them that Morrow was going to reveal some important information to her about her grandparents. It seems Farrell's father was adopted, and had no idea of his background."

The two detectives looked at each other. "Maybe Scott Alterman wasn't wacky, after all," Stanton said. "Maybe he had become dangerous to someone. And let's take a good look at Olivia Morrow's death. Find out who signed her death certificate."

75

Harvey Roth's normally calm voice was crackling with excitement when he phoned Peter Gannon. "Peter, we have two big breaks. A credible witness is prepared to say he saw you walking down York Avenue alone just after you and Renée left the bar. He said Renée was already gone. Our guys found him this morning and he made a statement to the cops."

"Is that enough for reasonable doubt?" Peter asked.

"It's a big help, let me tell you. That, and the fact that your clothes and car show no traces of Renée's presence."

"Thanks, Harvey. It's going to take some time to digest this."

"I can understand that. Peter, we're a long way from being sure of an acquittal when you come to trial. We still can't explain the money hidden in your desk and the shopping bag. But we *are* getting some breaks."

Fifteen minutes later, Harvey Roth called back. "Peter, I just spoke to Esther Chambers. She traced that decorator who ordered the desk with the false bottom in the drawer. The fact is that she ordered *two* of them. One was for you, the other for Dr. Langdon. The decorator says she absolutely did not discuss the secret compartment in the desk with you, but distinctly remembers telling Langdon and your sister-in-law, Pamela, about it. Very interestingly, the decorator also said she believed there was something going on between them."

Pam and Doug Langdon, Peter thought, his heart pounding. Of course it was possible that they were involved with each other! Would they have tried to stop Renée from exposing Greg's insider trading? It's possible. Of course it is. It makes sense. If the SEC ever goes after Greg, they'll grab all his assets to pay off all the investors who lost money because of him, and that would include all the money and property and jewelry he's given Pamela over the years.

A huge sense of relief was running through him. I might easily have left a set of keys to my office at the foundation, he thought. Doug and Pam have both been there, and know the layout. I never saw who was driving Greg's car. It might have been Doug. My brother may be a thief, but I don't believe he's a killer.

"Peter, are you still there?" Harvey Roth asked, his voice now anxious.

"You bet I am," Peter said. "You bet I am."

76

At three thirty P.M., the moment Greg Gannon had been dreading for a long time arrived. Two federal officers, their manner brusque, walked past the secretary who was sitting at Esther's desk and opened the door of his private office. "Mr. Gannon, stand up, and put your hands behind you. We have a warrant for your arrest," one of them said.

Suddenly infinitely weary, Greg obeyed. As he listened to his rights being read, he looked down at the wastebasket. He had shredded the papers Arthur Saling had signed that had given him control over his portfolio. One last small decent thing to do, he thought grimly.

Everything is going to blow up now. They'll look into the foundation, too. We've all been treating it like a piggy bank. We could all face charges on that. I know I'm going down, but I'm also going to hang Pam and Doug out to dry. I'm glad I finally found out about their little love nest on Twelfth Avenue. She probably has more jewelry stashed there. I don't want either one of them left with so much as a penny.

Another thought crossed his mind as he was led out of his office for the last time. My brother's a murderer. I'm a thief. One of my sons is a public defender.

I wonder if he'd care to represent either one of us.

He doubted it.

77

At six thirty the last of her small patients was gone. Monica went into her private office, where Detectives Forrest and Whelan and John Hartman had been patiently waiting. "Why don't we go into the reception area?" she asked. "You have to be careful not to trip over toys, but we'll have more room there."

When she had returned from the meeting at the Gannon Foundation, she had asked Nan to call John Hartman and ask him to stop at the office at around six. Then, halfway through the afternoon, Nan reported that Detectives Forrest and Whelan wanted to have another meeting with her.

"I told them, they'd just have to wait until six o'clock," Nan had reported. "They were nice about it."

"Dr. Jenner will be coming over, too," Monica had told Nan.

Nan's delighted smile telegraphed to Monica that she, too, was aware of the gossip about Ryan and herself.

Nan had tidied up the reception room. Without being asked, Forrest adjusted one of the couches so that they all sat facing each other. "Dr. Farrell . . ." he began.

The phone rang. Nan hurried to answer it. "It's Dr. Jenner," she said.

Monica got up and walked quickly to take the receiver from Nan's hand.

"Monica," Ryan said, "there's been a nasty accident on the West Side Highway. Some head injuries. I'm waiting to see if I'm needed for surgery."

"Of course."

"I'll call you back when I know how long I'll be here." He hesitated. "Unless it gets too late."

"Call me back. I don't care what time it is," Monica said, then added, "I'm dying of curiosity about the lasagna."

"I may never eat it again. I'll get back to you."

Monica replaced the phone on the cradle then went back to the reception room. John Hartman held a chair for her. As she sat down, she said to the detectives, "I'm glad you're here. There *is* something that I was going to give to John, and I think it's just as well that I'm able to talk to all of you about it."

Carl Forrest said, "Before we discuss that, Dr. Farrell, I am very sorry to have to tell you that the body of Scott Alterman was found in the East River this morning. It may or may not be a suicide, but we are beginning to believe his death may have had something to do with his belief that you are connected to the Gannon family."

"Scott is dead?" Monica repeated. "Dear God! But only yesterday at this very time you were suggesting that he might have been behind the attempt to kill me."

Forrest nodded. "Dr. Farrell, you told us yourself

that he had been obsessed with you. You told us that he called you shortly after you reached home, when you were pushed in front of a bus. What you did *not* tell us is that he believed you might be the granddaughter of Dr. Alexander Gannon—which, of course, would put you in line to inherit much of the Gannon fortune."

For a long minute, Monica could not speak. In a whirlwind of memory, she thought of being her best friend Joy's maid of honor at her wedding to Scott. She thought of how close she had been to both of them until after her father's death, when Scott started to bombard her with phone calls and passionate e-mails.

"Scott was my father's attorney," Monica said, trying to choose her words carefully. "When my father became terminally ill and finally had to be placed in a nursing home, Scott handled all his affairs. My father was adopted, and was always seeking to learn his background, to find his birth family. He was a researcher, who late in life was a consultant in one of the labs in Boston founded by Dr. Alexander Gannon. The few years my father worked there, I was in medical school in Georgetown."

She stopped as memories of trying to get back to Boston whenever she could possibly squeeze in a day or two, and her comfort in the fact that Joy and Scott had visited her father so frequently, raced through her mind.

"As long as I can remember, my father would cut out pictures of people whom he thought he resembled and wonder if he was related to them," she said, sadly. "It became a desperate need for him to discover his roots. I used to tease him about it. Shortly before he died, he became fixated on the notion that he bore a striking resemblance to pictures he had seen of Alexander Gannon. Scott took him seriously. I never did, until today."

Trying to keep her voice steady, Monica asked, "Nan, would you please print out the picture I took this morning on my cell phone?" She got up. "I have my father's picture in my wallet but I have a larger one on my desk. Let me get that one and I'll show you exactly what I saw this morning."

She walked into her private office and for a minute stood there, hugging herself tightly to stop trembling. Scott, she thought. Poor Scott. If someone killed him, it was because he was trying to help me, because he thought I would come into a fortune.

She picked up her father's framed picture and carried it back to the reception room. Nan had already printed out the one she had taken of the portrait of Alexander Gannon. Monica laid them side by side on the table. As the detectives leaned over to study them, she said, "As you can see, the pictures are virtually interchangeable."

Without taking her eyes off the pictures, she said, "I think Scott Alterman lost his life trying to prove there was a blood relationship between Alexander Gannon and my father. And I also think that it doesn't stop there. I believe that Olivia Morrow, the woman who was about to reveal the names of my grandparents, may have died last Tuesday night because she confided to someone else that I was coming to visit her on Wednesday evening."

"Who is that person?" Forrest asked sharply.

Monica raised her head and looked directly across the table at him. "I believe Olivia Morrow told her cardiologist, Dr. Clayton Hadley, that she was going to give me proof that I am a Gannon descendant. Dr. Hadley is not only on the board of the Gannon Foundation, but he also visited Ms. Morrow late Tuesday evening. The next evening when I arrived at her apartment, she was dead."

Monica turned to John Hartman. "I asked you to come here for a specific reason and it ties into all of this."

Once again, Monica went into her private office and this time when she returned, she was carrying the plastic bag containing the pillow with the smear of blood that Sophie had taken from Olivia Morrow's apartment. She explained to them why Sophie had taken it, and described Hadley's response to Sophie about the missing pillowcase.

Forrest took the bag from her. "You have the makings of a good detective, Dr. Farrell. You can be sure we'll take this to the lab right away."

A few minutes later, they all left together. Declining John and Nan's invitation to have dinner, Monica got in a cab and went home. Thoroughly exhausted from the events of the day, she double-locked the door, walked back into the kitchen, and looked at the afghan that was still draped over the glass half of the kitchen door.

When I put that up last night, it was because I was worried that Scott might harm me, she remembered. *And now he's dead because of me.*

As a sort of unconscious tribute to him, she took it down, carried it back into the living room, curled up on the couch, and pulled it over her. Ryan may call anytime, she thought. I'll keep both phones right next to me and close my eyes. I don't think I'll fall asleep, but if I do I just can't miss his call. I need him.

She glanced at her watch. It was quarter of eight. Plenty of time to still have dinner, if he can get away, she thought.

At nine o'clock, she awoke with a start. The buzzer to her apartment from the front door was being pushed repeatedly. The sharp, urgent jabs were terrifying to hear. Was the building on fire? She jumped up and ran to the intercom. "Who is this? What's the matter?" she demanded.

"Dr. Farrell, this is Detective Parks. Detective Forrest has sent me to protect you. You must leave your apartment immediately. Sammy Barber, the man who tried to push you under the bus, was spotted in the alleyway behind your house. We know he has a gun and is determined to kill you. Get out of there now."

Sammy Barber. In a moment of sheer panic, Monica thought of the bus bearing down on her. She ran to the table and grabbed her cell phone. Not bothering to look for the shoes she had kicked off when she lay down on the couch, she ran from the apartment, down the corridor, and flung open the outer door.

A man in plainclothes was waiting there. "Hurry, hurry," he said urgently. He put his arm around her and began to rush her down the steps to a waiting car. There was a driver at the wheel, the engine was running, and the back door was open.

Suddenly alarmed, Monica struggled to pull away from his iron grip and began to scream for help. He clasped a rough hand over her mouth and with violent force tried to shove her into the car. Dragging her legs and butting her head back against his chest, she frantically tried to break away.

I'm going to die, she thought. I'm going to die.

It was at that moment from somewhere nearby, she heard a command shouted through a bullhorn. "Let go of her now. Get your hands up. You're surrounded."

Monica felt herself being released but was unable to keep her balance, and fell backward on the sidewalk. As her would-be assailant and the driver were grabbed by a swarm of undercover officers, the cell phone she was still clutching rang. Too stunned to react except in a robotlike manner, she answered it.

"Monica, are you all right? It's Ryan. The accidents weren't that bad. I'm leaving the hospital. Where shall I meet you?"

"Home," Monica said, her voice breaking as strong arms lifted her to her feet. "Come over now, Ryan. I need you. Come over right now."

78

It was Thursday morning, two days after Monica had been assaulted at her apartment. "Looks as though we've got the whole rotten bunch of them," Detective Barry Tucker commented with satisfaction. He and his partner, Dennis Flynn, along with Detectives Carl Forrest and Jim Whelan, were at headquarters, in the office of Chief Jack Stanton. They were rehashing the series of events since Tuesday night.

"When Dr. Hadley broke down and confessed the minute we walked into his office to question him, he told us that he knew we would be coming. He admitted he suffocated that poor old woman. He even handed over the bloody pillowcase before we asked for it," Flynn said.

"Langdon isn't talking, but his girlfriend, Pamela, can't *stop* talking," Carl Forrest said, his voice scornful. "She knows she has no way out of this. Greg Gannon got suspicious of her and found out about the apartment she was keeping with Langdon. Renée Carter's purse and a card with that address written in Scott Alterman's handwriting were both there. Pamela admits that Carter got into the car with her and Langdon. They promised to pay her the other nine hundred thousand that Carter was demanding, and she fell for it. She went back to the apartment with them. They gave her a drink with knock-out drops and then he strangled her. They kept her body there until they could safely dump it."

Forrest picked up a glass of water, and swallowed. "Pamela Gannon is one cold fish. She admits she gave Hadley and Langdon the orders to get rid of Olivia Morrow and Dr. Farrell. She also told us that Langdon had hired Sammy Barber to kill Monica Farrell. We got a search warrant for Barber's apartment and found a tape of him and Langdon talking about getting rid of Dr. Farrell. So they're both cooked. Not to mention Larry Walker, who tried to abduct Farrell outside her apartment. He said that Barber had hired him to kill her since there was too much heat on him. Sammy has taken off, but there's a warrant out for him. We'll find him."

"Why was Scott Alterman ever fool enough to go to that apartment?" Stanton asked.

"Pamela was in the Southampton House when he got there. She told him she was divorcing Greg, that he had been miserable to live with, and she had found proof that his uncle had an heir. Alterman walked into her trap that night. When he went to the apartment, she put just enough knockout drops in his drink to make him look drunk, and then Langdon hustled him down to the river. The poor guy never had a chance," Forrest answered.

"Langdon planted the money and the shopping bag

in Peter's office to set him up," he continued. "He went directly to Peter's private office after he killed Renée Carter. He never realized that Peter was sleeping it off in the next room. It's a good thing that Langdon didn't see him there or I don't think he'd still be alive.

"Now the way it looks, Greg Gannon will spend the next twenty years or so in prison. Everything he owns will be sold to pay back the investors he defrauded. Everything Pamela Gannon has will be taken from her, not that she'll have any use for any of it. She's looking at several life sentences."

"I'll take it from here, Jack," Barry Tucker said, briskly. "The DA is going to dismiss the charges against Peter Gannon." He dropped his notebook in his pocket. "And we'll all get a few days off."

"Oh, I forgot. Your wife likes your crooked smile," Forrest said. "Isn't that what you told somebody the other day?"

"It seems more like a year ago. The pity is that even if she could manage to prove she's Alexander Gannon's granddaughter, Dr. Farrell probably will never see a nickel of the Gannon money. Langdon, Hadley, and Pamela Gannon have been hemorrhaging it into their own pockets. The foundation money that went into some of Peter Gannon's theatre projects may cause him trouble with the IRS."

Jack Stanton stood up. "Good job, all of you," he said. "Hopefully at least some of the money that Langdon and Hadley stole from the foundation will be recovered when they seize their assets. That means if Monica

Farrell could actually prove she was the granddaughter, other properties like Alexander Gannon's home in Southampton may be hers. But I gather at this point she can't prove anything. Look-alike pictures don't cut the mustard in court."

"Carl, does anyone know who Dr. Farrell's grandmother actually was?" Dennis Flynn asked.

"Dr. Hadley told us that she was Olivia Morrow's older cousin, a young woman who later became a nun and is presently being considered for beatification by the Catholic Church. He thinks that the file with the proof of her relationship with Gannon was destroyed by Morrow before she died."

Stanton looked from one to the other of his detectives. "Obviously all of this has to be included in the detectives' reports. Can you imagine the gossip Dr. Farrell will have to deal with when it comes out? As it is, she's already survived two attempts on her life. If our guys hadn't been covering her outside her apartment Tuesday night, she'd be in the river just like Scott Alterman."

Stanton took a long breath. "Okay, guys, now it's time to do the paperwork and wrap this up."

79

On Thursday afternoon, with enormous pride, Tony Garcia washed and polished his newly acquired Cadillac. With loving hands, he vacuumed the interior and wiped the dashboard and door handles with a damp cloth. Finally, he opened the trunk and it was then that he remembered that he had not yet looked to see if the file that Olivia Morrow had asked him to place in it was still there.

With absolute shock, he had read that Dr. Hadley had admitted killing Ms. Morrow. The nicest lady you'd ever want to know, he thought. Fearful that he might lose out on the car, he'd phoned his brother-in-law and been reassured that as long as he kept the receipt for the cash he had handed Hadley, there shouldn't be any problem getting the car transferred to his name.

The trunk was deep and the lap robe that had been covering the manila file was almost as dark as the black interior. I wonder if that file is still there, Tony thought, as he bent down and leaned into the trunk. Dr. Hadley had said that the garage attendants took out any personal stuff that Ms. Morrow had in the car. But maybe they didn't bother looking under the blanket.

He lifted it up and it was there. The manila file. He pulled it out and held it in his hand, wondering what he should do with it. Maybe he should turn it over to the cops.

He walked up the three flights to their apartment. Rosalie was out in the park with the baby. Tony left the file on the table, changed, went back downstairs, drove the car to the service station where his buddy let him park it cheap, then headed for the Waldorf where he was working at one of the black-tie affairs.

When he got back home at one in the morning, Rosalie was sitting at the table, reading. Her face transfixed, she said, "Tony, this file belongs to Dr. Monica. It has so many letters from her grandmother to Ms. Morrow's mother and proof of Dr. Monica's grandparents. Dr. Monica's grandmother was a nun. When you read the letters she wrote about giving up her own child and spending her life taking care of other children, you'll want to cry." She wiped her eyes. "Tony, these letters were written by a saint."

80

On Friday afternoon, Monica and Ryan drove to Metuchen to give testimony in the cause of the beatification of Sister Catherine Mary Kurner. Monica had taken the day off and had hoped to simply have a quiet morning before Ryan picked her up.

But when Tony Garcia learned from Nan that Monica would not be in the office, he rushed to her apartment. Still in her robe, she answered the door.

"I won't come in, Dr. Monica," Tony said, "but I couldn't wait another second to get this file to you. In fact, Rosie thought that I should bring it up to you at one o'clock this morning, if you can believe it."

"Nothing can be that urgent." Monica smiled, as she took the file from him.

"Dr. Monica, believe you me, it *is* urgent," Tony said, simply. "You'll understand when you read it." With a quick smile, he was gone.

Puzzled, Monica sat down at the table, poured a cup of coffee, and opened the file. She could see that it was composed mostly of letters, and a quick glance told her that the early ones had been written in the 1930s.

Puzzled by why Tony had felt it was so important

for her to read the file right away, she decided to start with the earliest letter. Then she saw the name on the letterhead: Alexander Gannon. The date was March 2, 1934.

My darling Catherine,

How can I possibly find the words to beg your forgiveness? There are none. The thought that you were leaving in the morning to enter the convent, the knowledge that all hope that you would change your mind had ended overwhelmed me with my need for you. I am so ashamed. That night I could not sleep knowing that I was losing you. Finally I got up and walked from the house to the cottage. I knew that the door was never locked and that Regina and Olivia would be asleep upstairs. I had no intention of coming in. I swear it. Then I simply wanted to be near you one more time and so I came into your room. You in your sweet innocence were sleeping. Oh, Catherine, forgive me. Forgive me. There will never be anyone in my life except you. Examining my conscience and my soul, I believe that it was my hope that if you were to become with child, you would be forced to marry me. Oh, Catherine, I beg your forgiveness. If that were to happen, I implore you to become my wife.

Alex

The next letter was from the Mother Superior of Catherine's convent.

Dear Regina,

I am returning the letter Alexander Gannon gave you to send to Catherine. She does not wish to read it, but I did tell her it contained his profound apology. Please instruct him never again to contact Catherine.

Eight months later there was another letter from the Mother Superior.

Dear Regina,

This morning, in Dublin, at five a.m., your cousin Catherine gave birth to her son. The baby was immediately registered in the name of my nephew and his wife, Matthew and Anne Farrell. They have already sailed from Ireland with the infant. It took great courage for Catherine to give up her baby, but she has steadfastly maintained that she must follow the calling that she has always known was hers. She does not want Alexander Gannon to ever learn about the child because she fears he would want to raise him on his own. It was a difficult and long labor and it became necessary for the doctor to perform caesarean surgery. When she recovers her health, Catherine will return to the novitiate in Connecticut and resume her role as a postulant.

Sister Catherine is my grandmother, Monica thought, stunned. Alexander Gannon is my grandfather. For the next two hours, she read and reread the letters. Most of them were from Catherine to Olivia's mother, Regina. Some of them referred to her child.

. . . Regina, there are times when my arms ache for the baby I gave up. And yet when I reach into a crib and pick up an abandoned little one, a child damaged in body or mind, I fill that need. Mother Superior placed my baby with a fine family. I know that. I can't know any more than that. He belongs to the people who are now his parents and I am living the life that God intended for me.

. . . I tell my young sisters that they must realize that when they enter the convent they do not surrender their human emotions, which I suspect countless people believe is the case. I tell them there will be times when they see the joy of a mother with a child that they may wish with all their hearts that they could know that joy. I tell them that there are times of loneliness when they may see a husband and wife, obviously content in their marriage, and know that they might have chosen that life. And then I remind them that there is no joy so deep as that of surrendering all human emotions to the God who granted them to us . . .

All of Catherine's letters were similar. Her eyes glistening with tears, Monica realized the struggles of the nun who had been her grandmother to open yet another hospital, to beg funds for urgently needed medical equipment.

Dear Regina,

Polio is rampant. It breaks the heart to see little ones in iron lungs, unable to breathe on their own, their limbs wasted.

It was the call from Ryan that startled Monica into awareness of the time. "I'll be about ten minutes late, love, there's a lot of traffic," he said.

It was eleven fifteen. They were due to be in Metuchen at one o'clock to testify at the beatification hearing. Monica rushed to shower and dress but took the time to scan the letter from Alex Gannon to Catherine and the letter from the Mother Superior to Regina Morrow so she could keep electronic copies.

When Ryan called again to say that he was waiting outside in the car, she said, "Ryan, let me drive. There's something I want you to read."

Monsignors Kelly and Fell and Laura Shearing were waiting for them when they arrived, barely on time. Monica introduced them to Ryan, then said, "I have something very important to show you, but if you don't mind I'd prefer to do it after we give our testimony."

"Of course," Monsignor Kelly said.

His voice firm and sure, under sacred oath, with quiet

intensity Ryan testified that as a neurosurgeon he could find no medical explanation for Michael O'Keefe's cancerous brain tumor to have disappeared. "Nor will anyone else find an explanation," he said. "I only wish that there were more miracles granted to the agonized parents who are losing their children to cancer."

When Monica testified, she said, "I cannot understand why I was so resistant to the idea that the power of prayer was the cause of Michael's return to health. I was a witness to the absolute act of faith of his mother when I told her he was terminally ill. It was arrogant of me to be so dismissive of her faith, especially since the proof of it is her eight-year-old healthy little boy."

It was only after she had completed answering their questions and Monsignor Kelly had thanked them for coming, that Monica laid the file marked CATHERINE on his desk. "I think I would prefer that you read this after I leave," she said. "Then, if you wish, we can talk again. But if it is determined that Sister Catherine is proposed for beatification, I would like to be invited to the ceremony."

"Of course." Monsignor Kelly stood up. "Dr. Jenner, perhaps you'd like to see a picture of Sister Catherine."

"Yes, I would."

"Dr. Farrell, I don't think you saw this picture when you were here. It was taken when she was quite young, in her early thirties, I believe." Monsignor Kelly reached into his desk and took out the photograph of a nun in traditional habit, smiling as she held two babies in her arms.

Ryan looked from the picture to Monica. "Sister Catherine was a beautiful woman," he said, as he handed it back.

He and Monica did not speak until they were in the car. "After they read the file, they'll take that picture out and look at it again," he said. "Your resemblance to her is unmistakable, especially the smile."

Before he turned on the ignition, he said, "Alexander Gannon loved Catherine so much that he never looked at another woman. I understand how he felt. That is how much I love you."

81

One week later

It feels a lot different than the last time I discharged Sally from the hospital, Monica thought, remembering Renée Carter's impatient order to Kristina Johnson to hurry up and dress the baby because she was late for lunch.

Today, she was releasing her into the welcoming arms of Susan Gannon, who had come to the hospital alone. "Peter is waiting for us at my apartment," she explained. "He said he was afraid that if he met her for the first time here, he'd break down and cry." As she nuzzled Sally's cheek, Susan smiled and added, "Which is exactly what I expect him to do when I get this little girl home. He's frantic to meet her. Kristina will start to work for me tomorrow morning. Peter and I both wanted Sally to ourselves today."

"I know what Peter has been through," Monica said. "I hope everything goes well for him from now on."

"He's going to have to face some tax issues but no criminal charges," Susan said frankly. "He'll weather them. It's a big relief for all of us that Greg and the others may plead guilty. I'll be very grateful if we don't have to go through so many criminal trials."

"So will I," Monica agreed fervently. "The last thing I want to do is to have to testify in court. It would especially sicken me to have to look at Dr. Hadley."

Susan hesitated, then said, "Monica, now that you have the proof that you are Alexander Gannon's granddaughter, I hope they'll be able to recover for you some of the money that is rightfully yours."

"We'll see what happens," Monica said quietly. "If they do, most of it will go toward the pediatric center we need here. I am thrilled to know my background, and it is a joy to discover that Sally is my second cousin. No wonder she's always been so special to me. The great sadness is that three people died because of that money."

"You are going to come and see her?" Susan asked. "And I mean regularly, as family. I promise you'll like Peter. He's going to be around a lot, and remember he's your cousin, too."

Monica reached out and took Sally from Susan's arms. They walked down the corridor, then, with a final hug, she handed the baby back to Susan.

"Bye-bye, Monny," Sally called, as they got into the elevator, and the door closed behind them.

She felt a hand on her arm. It was Ryan. "Don't feel too bad. One of these days you'll have your own," he said.

Her smile radiant, Monica looked up at him.

"I know," she said. "I know."

1

It was the persistent sense of impending doom, not the nor'easter, that made Natalie flee from Cape Cod back to New Jersey in the predawn hours of Monday morning. She had expected to find sanctuary in the cozy Cape house that had once been her grandmother's and now was hers, but the icy sleet beating against the windows only increased the terror she was experiencing. Then, when a power failure plunged the house into darkness, she lay awake, sure that every sound was caused by an intruder.

After fifteen years, she was certain that she had accidentally stumbled upon the knowledge of who had strangled her roommate, Jamie, when they were both struggling young actresses. And he *knows* that I know, she thought—I could see it in his eyes.

On Friday night, he had come with a group to the closing night of *A Streetcar Named Desire* at the Omega Playhouse. She had played Blanche DuBois, the most demanding and satisfying role of her career to date. Her reviews had been wonderful, but the role had taken its emotional toll on her. That was why, after the performance, when someone knocked on the door of her dressing room, she had been tempted not to answer. But she had, and they all crowded in to congratulate her, and out of nowhere she recognized him. In his late forties now, his face had filled out, but he was undoubtedly the person whose picture was missing from Jamie's wallet after her body was found. Jamie had been so secretive about him, only referring to him as Jess, "my pet name for him," as she put it.

I was so shocked that when we were introduced, I called him "Jess," Natalie thought. Everyone was talking so much that I am sure no one else noticed. But *he* heard me say his name.

Who do I tell? Who would *believe* me? My word against his? My memory of a small picture that Jamie had hidden in her wallet? I only found it because I had lent her my Visa card and I needed it back. She was in the shower and called to me to get it out of her wallet. That was when I saw the picture, tucked in one of the compartments, behind a couple of business cards.

All Jamie ever told me about him was that he'd tried his hand at acting and wasn't good enough, and that he was in the middle of a divorce. I tried to tell her that was the oldest story in the world, Natalie thought, but she wouldn't listen. She and Jamie had been sharing an apartment on the West Side until that terrible morning when Jamie was strangled while jogging early in Central Park. Her wallet was on the ground, her money and watch were missing. And so was the picture of "Jess." I told the cops that, she thought, but they didn't take it seriously. There had been a number of early-morning muggings in the park and they were sure Jamie just happened to be one of the victims, the only fatal victim, as it turned out.

It had been pouring through Rhode Island and Connecticut, but as Natalie drove down the Palisades Parkway the rain steadily lessened. As she drove farther down, she could see that the roads were already drying.

Would she feel safe at home? She wasn't sure. Twenty years ago, after being widowed, her mother, born and raised in Manhattan, had been happy to sell the house and buy a small apartment near Lincoln Center. Last year, when Natalie and Gregg separated, she heard that the modest house in northern New Jersey where she'd been raised was for sale again.

"Natalie," her mother warned, "you're making a terrible mistake. I think you're crazy not to try to make a go of your marriage. Running back home is never the answer for anyone. You can't re-create the past."

Natalie knew it was impossible to make her mother understand that the kind of wife Gregg wanted and needed was not the person she could ever be for him. "I was unfair to Gregg when I married him," she said. "He needed a wife who would be a real mother to Katie. I can't be. Last year I was away a total of six months in all. It just isn't working. I honestly think that when I move out of Manhattan, he'll understand that the marriage is really over."

"You're still in love with him," her mother insisted. "And he is with you."

"That doesn't mean we're good for each other."

I'm right about that, Natalie thought, as she swallowed the lump in her throat that was always there when she allowed herself to think about Gregg. She wished she could talk to him about what had happened Friday evening. What would she say? "Gregg, what do I do about having the certain knowledge that I know who killed my friend Jamie, without a shred of proof to back me up?" But she couldn't ask him. There was too much of a chance that she'd be unable to resist his begging her to try again. Even though she'd lied and told him she was interested in someone else, it hadn't stopped Gregg's phone calls.

As she turned off the parkway onto Walnut Street, Natalie realized she was longing for a cup of coffee. She had driven straight through and it was quarter of eight. By this time, on a normal day, she would already have had at least two cups.

Most of the houses on Walnut Street in Closter had been torn down to make way for new luxury homes. It was her joke that now she had seven-foot hedges on either side of her house, giving her complete privacy from either neighbor. Years ago, the Keenes had been on one side and the Foleys on the other. Today, she hardly knew who her neighbors were.

The sense of something hostile hit her as she turned in to her driveway and pushed the clicker to open the garage door. As the door began to rise, she shook her head. Gregg had been right when he said that she became every character she played. Even before the stress of meeting Jess, her nerves had been unraveling, like those of Blanche DuBois.

She drove into the garage, stopped, but for some reason did not immediately push the clicker to close the garage door behind her. Instead, she opened the driver's door of the car, pushed open the kitchen door, and stepped inside.

She felt gloved hands dragging her in, twirling her around, and throwing her down. The crack of her head on the hardwood floor sent waves of pain radiating through her skull, but she could still see that he was wearing a plastic raincoat and plastic over his shoes.

"Please," she said, "*please.*" She held up her hands to protect herself from the pistol he was pointing at her chest.

The click as he pushed down the safety catch was his answer to her plea.

2

At ten minutes of eight, punctual as always, Suzie Walsh turned off Route 9W and drove to the home of her longtime employer, Catherine Banks. She had been the seventy-five-year-old widow's housekeeper for thirty years, arriving at eight A.M. and leaving after lunch at one P.M. every weekday.

A passionate theatre buff, Suzie loved the fact that the famous actress Natalie Raines had bought the house next to Mrs. Banks last year. Natalie was Suzie's absolutely favorite actress. Only two weeks ago, she had seen her in the limited run of *A Streetcar Named Desire* and decided no one could ever have played the fragile heroine Blanche DuBois better, not even Vivien Leigh in the movie. With her delicate features, slender body, and cascade of pale blond hair, she was the living embodiment of Blanche.

So far Suzie had not met facc-to-face with Raines. She always hoped that she'd run into her someday in the supermarket, but that hadn't happened yet. Whenever she was coming to work in the morning, or driving home in the afternoon, Suzie always made it her business to drive past Raines's house slowly, even though in the afternoon, it meant driving around the block to get to the highway.

This Monday morning, Suzie almost realized her ambition of seeing Natalie Raines close-up. As she drove past her house, Raines was just stepping out of her car. Suzie sighed. Just that much of a glimpse of her idol was like a bit of magic in her day.

At one o'clock that afternoon, after a cheerful good-bye to Mrs. Banks and armed with a shopping list for the morning, Suzie got into her car and backed out of the driveway. For a moment she hesitated. There wasn't a million to one chance that she would see Natalie Raines twice in one day, and anyway she was tired. But habit prevailed, and she turned the car left, driving slowly as she passed the house next door.

Then she stopped the car abruptly. The door to Raines's garage was open and so was the driver's door of her car, exactly as it had been this morning. She *never* left the garage door open and certainly wouldn't be the kind to leave a car door open all day. Maybe I should mind my own business, Suzie thought, but I can't.

She turned into the driveway, stopped, and got out of her car. Uncertainly, she walked into the garage. It was small and she had to partially close the door of Raines's car to reach the kitchen door. By now she was sure something was wrong. A glance into the car had revealed a pocketbook on the front passenger seat and a suitcase on the floor in the back.

When there was no response to her knock on the kitchen door, she waited, then, unable to go away unsatisfied, turned the knob. The door was unlocked. Worried that she could end up being arrested for trespassing, something still made Suzie open the door and step into the kitchen.

Then she began to scream.

Natalie Raines was crumpled on the kitchen floor, her white cable-knit sweater matted with blood. Her eyes were closed but a soft, hurt cry was coming from her lips.

Suzie knelt beside her as she grabbed the cell phone from her pocket and dialed 911. "80 Walnut Street, Closter," she screamed to the operator. "Natalie Raines. I think she's been shot. Hurry. Hurry. She's dying."

She dropped the phone. Stroking Natalie's head, she said soothingly, "Ms. Raines, you'll be all right. They'll send an ambulance. It will be here any minute, I promise."

The sound from Natalie's lips ended. An instant later her heart stopped.

Her last thought was the sentence Blanche DuBois utters at the end of the play: "I have always depended on the kindness of strangers."

3

She had dreamt of Mark last night, one of those vague, unsatisfying dreams, in which she could hear his voice and was wandering through a dark, cavernous house looking for him. Emily Kelly Wallace woke up with the familiar weight on her mind that often settled in after that kind of dream, but determined that she wouldn't let it grab hold of her today.

She glanced over at Bess, the nine-pound Maltese her brother, Jack, had given her for Christmas. Bess was fast asleep on the other pillow, and the sight of the dog brought immediate comfort. Emily slid out of bed, grabbed the warm robe that was always close at hand in the cold bedroom, picked up a reluctantly awakening Bess, and headed down the stairs of the home in Glen Rock, New Jersey, that she had lived in for most of her thirty-two years.

After a roadside bomb in Iraq had taken Mark's life three years ago, she decided she didn't want to stay in their apartment. About a year later, when she was recovering from her operation, her father, Sean Kelly, had signed over this modest, colonial-style house to her. Long a widower, he was remarrying and moving to

Florida. "Em, it makes sense," he had said. "No mortgage. Taxes not too bad. You know most of the neighbors. Give it a try. Then if you'd rather do something else, sell it and you'll have a down payment."

But it *has* worked, Emily thought, as she hurried into the kitchen with Bess under her arm. I love living here. The coffeepot set to a seven A.M. timer was squeaking its announcement that the coffee was ready to pour. Her breakfast consisted of fresh-squeezed orange juice, a toasted English muffin, and two cups of coffee. Carrying the second one, Emily hurried back upstairs to shower and change.

A new bright red turtleneck added a cheery note to last year's charcoal gray pants suit. Suitable for court, she decided, as well as an antidote for this overcast March morning and the dream of Mark. She took a moment to debate about leaving her straight brown hair loose on her shoulders, then decided to pin it up. A quick dash of mascara and lip liner followed. As she snapped on small silver earrings the thought crossed her mind that she never bothered to wear blush anymore. When she had been sick she'd never gone without it.

Downstairs again, she let Bess out in the backyard one more time, then, after an affectionate squeeze, locked her in her crate.

Twenty minutes later she was driving into the parking lot of the Bergen County Courthouse. Although it was only eight fifteen, as usual the lot was almost half full. An assistant prosecutor for the last six years, Emily never felt more at home than when she got out of her car and crossed the tarmac to the courthouse. A tall, slender figure, she was unaware of how many admiring eyes followed her as she moved swiftly past the arriving cars. Her mind was already focused on the decision that should be coming from the grand jury.

For the past several days, the grand jury had been hearing testimony in the case involving the murder of Natalie Raines, the Broadway actress who had been fatally shot in her home nearly two years ago. Although he had always been a suspect, her estranged husband, Gregg Aldrich, had only been formally arrested three weeks ago, when a would-be accomplice had come forward. The grand jury was expected to issue an indictment shortly.

He did it, Emily told herself emphatically as she entered the courthouse, walked through the high-ceilinged lobby, and, scorning the elevator, climbed the steps to the second floor. I'd give my eyeteeth to try that case, she thought.

The Prosecutor's section, in the west wing of the courthouse, was home to forty assistant prosecutors, seventy investigators, and twenty-five secretaries. She punched in the code of the security door with one hand, pushed it open, waved to the switchboard operator, then slipped out of her coat before she reached the tiny windowless cubicle that was her office. A coatrack, two gray steel filing cabinets, two mismatched chairs for witness interviews, a fifty-year-old desk, and her own swivel chair comprised the furnishings. Plants on top of the files and on the corner of her desk were, as Emily put it, her attempt to green America.

She tossed her coat on the unsteady coatrack, settled in her chair, and reached for the file that she had been studying the night before. The Lopez case, a domestic dispute that had escalated into homicide. Two young children, now motherless, and a father in the county jail. And my job is to put him in prison, Emily thought, as she opened the file. The trial was scheduled to begin next week.

At eleven fifteen her phone rang. It was Ted Wesley, the prosecutor. "Emily, can I see you for a minute?" he asked. He hung up without waiting for an answer.

Fifty-year-old Edward "Ted" Scott Wesley, the Bergen County Prosecutor, was by any standards a handsome man. Six feet two, he had impeccable carriage that not only made him seem taller but gave him an air of authority that, as a reporter once wrote, "was comforting to the good guys and disconcerting to anyone who had reason not to sleep at night." His midnight blue eyes and full head of dark hair, now showing light traces of gray, completed the image of an imposing leader.

To Emily's surprise, after knocking on the partially open door and stepping inside his office, she realized her boss was scrutinizing her carefully.

Finally he said, crisply, "Hi, Emily, you look great. Feeling good?"

It was not a casual question. "Never better." She tried to sound offhand, even dismissive, as though she was wondering why he had bothered to ask.

"It's important that you feel good. The grand jury indicted Gregg Aldrich."

"They *did*!" She felt a shot of adrenaline. Even though she had been sure it would happen, Emily also knew that the case was largely based on circumstantial evidence and would certainly not be a slam dunk at trial. "It's been driving me crazy to see that creep plastered all over the gossip columns, running around with the flavor of the month when you know he left his wife bleeding to death. Natalie Raines was such a great actress. God, when she walked onstage, it was magic."

"Don't let Aldrich's social life drive you crazy," Wesley said mildly. "Just put him away for good. It's your case."

It was what she had been hoping to hear. Even so, it took a long moment to sink in. This was the kind of trial a prosecutor like Ted Wesley reserved for himself. It was sure to stay in the headlines, and Ted Wesley loved headlines.

He smiled at her astonishment. "Emily, strictly and totally between us, I'm getting feelers about a high-level job that's coming up in the fall with the new administration. I'd be interested, and Nan would love to live in Washington. As you know, she was raised there. I wouldn't want to be in the middle of a trial if that situation does work out. So Aldrich is yours."

Aldrich is mine. Aldrich is mine. It was the gut-level-satisfying case that she'd been waiting for before she was derailed two years ago. Back in her office, Emily debated calling her father, then vetoed that idea. He'd only caution her not to work too hard. And that's exactly what her brother, Jack, a computer designer who worked in Silicon Valley, would say, she thought, and anyhow, Jack's probably on his way to work. It's only eight thirty in California.

Mark, Mark, I know you'd be so proud of me . . .

She closed her eyes for a moment, a tidal wave of pure longing washing through her, then shook her head and reached for the Lopez file. Once again, she read every line of it. Both of them twenty-four years old; two kids; separated; he went back pleading for a reunion; she stormed out of the apartment, then tried to pass him on the worn marble staircase of the old apartment building. He claimed she fell. The babysitter who had followed them from the apartment swore that he'd pushed her. But her view was obstructed, Emily thought, as she studied the pictures of the stairway.

The phone rang. It was Joe Lyons, the public defender assigned to Lopez. "Emily, I want to come over and talk about the Lopez case. Your office has it all wrong. He didn't push her. She tripped. This was an accident."

"Well, not according to the babysitter," Emily replied. "But let's talk. Three o'clock would be good."

As she hung up, Emily looked at the file picture of the weeping defendant at his arraignment. An unwelcome feeling of uncertainty nagged at her. She admitted to herself that she had doubts about this one. Maybe his wife really did fall. Maybe it *was* an accident.

I used to be so tough, she sighed.

I'm beginning to think that maybe I should have been a defense attorney.

4

Earlier that morning, through the tilted slats of the old-fashioned blinds in the kitchen of his house, Zachary Lanning had watched Emily having her quick breakfast in her kitchen. The microphone he had managed to secretly install in the cabinet over the refrigerator when her contractor left the door unlocked had picked up her random comments to her puppy, who sat on her lap while she was eating.

It's as though she was talking to me, Zach thought happily, as he stacked boxes in the warehouse where he worked on Route 46. It was only a twenty-minute drive from the rented house where he had been living under a new identity since he fled from Iowa. His hours were eight thirty to five thirty, a shift that was perfect for his needs. He could watch Emily early in the morning, then go to work. When she came home in the evening, as she prepared dinner, he could visit with her again. Sometimes she had company, and that would make him angry. She belonged to *him*.

He was sure of one thing: There was no special man in her life. He knew she was a widow. If they happened to see each other outside, she was pleasant but distant.

He had told her he was very handy if ever she needed any quick repairs, but he had been able to tell right away that she would never call him. Like all the others during his whole life, she just dismissed him with a glance. She simply didn't understand that he was watching her, *protecting* her. She simply didn't understand that they were meant to be together.

But that would change.

With his slight build, average height, thinning, sandy hair and small brown eyes, in his late-forties, Zach was the kind of nondescript person whom most people would never remember having met.

Certainly most people would never imagine that he was the target of a nationwide manhunt after coldly murdering his wife, her children, and her mother a year and a half ago in Iowa.